Acclaim for David Treuer's

The Translation of Dr Apelles

"Deeply considered and intrepid....A spellbinding tale of innocence, nature's fecundity, human greed, divine intervention and love. Rendered in sensuous detail....So transfixing are the lavish descriptions, so supple the narrative, so involving the characters, that the reader readily accepts fantastic occurrences and the other tricks Treuer is up to."   *--Los Angeles Times*

"A myriad of false documents, questionable authorships, stalled sexual encounters, and narrative disjunctions.... Treuer pushes the metatextual games of writers like J. M. Coetzee and A. S. Byatt past the point of parody."
                                                    —The Village Voice

"This book describes itself as 'a love story,' and it is certainly that, but its ambitions are larger than usual: as a novel, it has elements of satire (of Hemingway, among others), metaphysical whodunit, and urban legend. The miracle of this book is that it makes two seemingly incompatible stories into a hybrid, a story about stories of death and rebirth. Formally daring, *The Translation of Dr Apelles* may be David Treuer's best book; it is certainly his most courageous."   —Charles Baxter

"Treuer's double narrative works like a pond in which two stones have been dropped; the two circles of expanding ripples meet, overlap and flow on. Calvino comes to mind....Tender and lovely."
                                                    —The Washington Post

"If widening the possibilities for Native American literature...is what Treuer has in mind, then *The Translation of Dr Apelles: A Love Story* might do just that."

—*The Literary Review*

"Love of language and literature suffuses David Treuer's novel.... The love story alone would appeal to anyone, even the most cynical....Playfully engages in some metafictional hijinks, placing books within books, sometimes literally."

—*Minneapolis Star Tribune*

"This is a novel that juxtaposes the bucolic life of a young, beautiful Native American couple against the lonely existence of a translator and researcher. Both are stories about Indians and both are about the torment and bliss of love. But the alienation of Dr Apelles the translator has a post-Edenic starkness when contrasted with the prelapsarian paradise of the story he is translating. Imagine Longfellow's *The Song of Hiawatha* written by Nabokov and you will get some idea of the linguistic fireworks and the suavity of the prose in this extraordinary book."

—Edmund White

DAVID TREUER

The Translation of Dr Apelles

David Treuer is Ojibwe from the Leech Lake Reservation in northern Minnesota. He is the author of two previous novels, Little and The Hiawatha. He teaches literature and creative writing at the University of Minnesota and is the recipient of a Guggenheim Fellowship.

~ The Translation of Dr Apelles ~

The Translation of Dr Apelles

A Love Story

DAVID TREUER

VINTAGE CONTEMPORARIES
Vintage Books
A Division of Random House, Inc.
New York

FIRST VINTAGE CONTEMPORARIES EDITION, FEBRUARY 2008

Copyright © 2006 by David Treuer

All rights reserved. Published in the United States by Vintage Books,
a division of Random House, Inc., New York, and in Canada by Random House
of Canada Limited, Toronto. Originally published in hardcover in the United States
by Graywolf Press, Saint Paul, Minnesota, in 2006.

Vintage and colophon are registered trademarks and Vintage Contemporaries
is a trademark of Random House, Inc.

The Library of Congress Cataloging-in-Publication Data
Treuer, David.
The translation of Dr Apelles : a novel / David Treuer.—
1st Vintage Contemporaries ed.
p. cm.
1. Translators—Fiction. 2. Indians of North America—Fiction.
PS3570.R435 T73 2008
813'.54—dc22
2007027351

Vintage ISBN: 978-0-307-38662-5

Book design by Wendy Holdman

www.vintagebooks.com

Printed in the United States of America
10   9   8   7   6   5   4

— for gretchen —

There is only one event in life which really astonishes a man and startles him out of his prepared opinions. Everything else befalls him very much as he expected.

– Robert Louis Stevenson, "On Falling in Love"

"Read it aloud, your grace," said Sancho. "I really like things that have to do with love."

– Cervantes, Don Quixote

Apelles' Song

CUPID and my Campaspe played
At cards for kisses,—Cupid paid;
He stakes his quiver, bow and arrows,
His mother's doves, and team of sparrows:
Loses them too; then down he throws
The coral of his lip, the rose
Growing on's cheek (but none knows how);
With these the crystal of his brow,
And then the dimple of his chin:
All these did my Campaspe win.
At last he set her both his eyes;
She won, and Cupid blind did rise.
O Love, has she done this to thee?
What shall, alas! become of me?

– John Lyly,
Alexander and Campaspe, 1584

Translator's Introduction

I was looking for a book.

A very particular book in a vast and wonderful library. I found what I was looking for. It hadn't been opened for quite a long time judging by the dust that coated the upper edge and by the way the paper had yellowed on all the sides creeping toward the gutter. When I opened it, some loose pages different from those of the book fell onto the floor. I picked them up and noticed that they were covered with text in a language I did not understand.

After much searching I found someone who could make sense of those words for me. I listened as he spoke the story out loud. What I heard was the most amazing tale I've ever heard—full of Indians beautiful to look at and also Indians who were treacherous, full also of hunting episodes, of capture and recapture. The tale was about foundlings (who are only called that because once they were lost) and about animals, too, and kidnappers and prostitutes. In this story there is war and reconciliation, a marriage, and the death of a boy. Ultimately, what I heard was a story about the quest for beauty. It is sometimes surprising where you find it.

I was moved. What I heard was profound. And I decided to try and render that story into English and into a language, an idiom that, God willing, can be translated into other languages as easily as we shed one set of clothes only to don another. I have also tried to paint a portrait of the body underneath those clothes that is beautiful even in its smallest part and that will be beautiful no matter what language it wears. Because, above all, I have written this down as an offering, as an offering to the world, an offering of beauty and of _____. But I cannot write that because that word has lost its meaning. So. An offering of beauty because beauty endures no matter what and no one is immune to it, no one has escaped from it, and no one ever will so long as there are eyes to see, ears to hear, and ink with which we can preserve it forever.

I hope you accept this offering, this book, this gift of beauty, and that you read it to the end. And then, turn back here and read it again.

In the meantime, the task is before me. I only hope that I can hear what few have heard, see what few have seen, and emerge full, whole, healed, on the other side. I hope I can relate the lives and feelings of others, the beauty of it all, without losing my mind. But as with many beautiful things, this story was born out of conflict. They were difficult times. It was a time of

~ Prologue ~

war.

1. Not between the people and their enemies across the river, or those farther up near its source—they were enemies still. All were hungry for the rice beds and trapping grounds, and for the protection of the village with its store of guns, axes, traps, skinning knives, and sacks of flour and oats stacked high in the storeroom. But the village (known as Agencytown because the Agency along with a church and a lumbermill was located there) with all its riches, with all its advantages, was more of an illusion than a real prize. The white people might be able to grant favors—trade, protection, and loans. But neither the rich nor the poor, the powerful or the weak, Indian or white, could grant mercy. And this was what the people of the small band camped near the source of the river needed most. Mercy to spare them from the winter.

First it snowed. It snowed without stop. The ground was covered, hollows in the land were drifted over. Low bushes, ground hemlock, and juniper wore a heavy coat of snow. The lace of rabbit snares disappeared overnight. It kept snowing all the next day and through the following night. Fox snares set out on game trails and the box traps for lynx and bobcat were nowhere to be found—they, too, disappeared underneath the snow. It continued to snow and with it came a great wind. It blew over the gullies and sloughs. The pits at the portages filled with squash, corn, and rice were lost. The blowing snow leveled off the creek beds, covered the beaver houses and the moving water at beaver dams and springs.

The flakes were too small, too icy and fine to catch on the branches, and so they sifted through and continued down. It was a terrible dry, white blanket that was pulled over the land. Those at trapping camps struggled back to the village, but after they returned, no one could break out. The snow was too dry to support snowshoes.

The people cowered in their lodges and rolled together in their furs and the few trade blankets they possessed. The snow stopped after four days, but the damage had been done. They were trapped. It grew colder. Those who stirred outside and tried to break trails to fetch wood and water or to access the caches of meat built on platforms were burned by the cold. Their lips were seared, their noses and ears singed. And though they walked out of their lodges to lift the siege of winter, they crawled back spitting blood into their blankets.

Soon there was no food, water, or wood in camp. The lodges were cold. Body warmth was the only relief, but not for long; it was stolen first from the strong, and then from whoever was careless or compassionate enough to give it, and always the wind and cold took their share. One by one the people died. And with them died history, knowledge, memory, experience, and desire. They died quietly. It was a bloodless massacre.

The children died first and with them gone, what is the use of tears? Why else wail and cry and scream and beat at the snow if not for them? And so the people passed silently, and not even into memory (which is a form of life after all) because there was no one left to remember them. They all died, save one, who was too young to remember anything.

In one lodge there had been one who still lived: a boy who had just seen his fourth birthday. His three brothers and two sisters were dead. The boy's mother had made sure he would live. The father, struggling away through the snow in search of food, had left them. He had not come back

On the seventh day of the siege all the children were still alive. They were arranged around the ashy firepit, each in a blanket with a hot rock held to their stomachs to keep them warm. The boy was awake—and he was too young to be afraid of death. He watched his mother. She had got up out of her blankets and looked at her children one by one. The youngest boy was still of nursing age, the next was a toddler, the twin girls were two, the next boy just over three, and he was the oldest. His mother had been pregnant every year since he had been born. When she watched her children she saw the very contours of her life.

He saw that she had been looking at him for some time but in a way she never had before: not as a whole, but piece by piece—first at his legs, hidden under his blanket, then, after a time, at his torso, then at his arms, his hands, and lastly, his face. She smiled. And, across the sleeping bodies of her five other children she said calmly, as though mentally dressing him in fine clothes, *You, my son, will live. You alone.* He fell asleep.

When he awoke the next day the toddler boy was dead. He lay outside the lodge wrapped in a fawnskin, and the boy's mother handed him his dead brother's woven rabbitskin blanket that she had resewn into trousers. *Put these on,* she said. He said nothing and did as he was told. On the next day the twin girls, just two years old, lay beside his brother outside the lodge, resting now, in a bed of snow, wrapped in flour sacking. The air in the lodge was cold—crystals coated the elm-bark roof. *Put this on,* his mother said, holding up his sisters' rabbit blanket, transformed overnight into a long tunic. His mother took what toys and objects they had—a small bow, a doll, the infant's cradleboard—and with a precious match, turned them into a small fire. *Warm yourself,* she said. On the third day his brother, just a year younger than he, was dead and slept in the snow alongside the other three, and his blanket—which he no longer needed—was no longer a blanket. His mother handed him a pair of rabbit-fur gloves and a hat. *Put these on so you will live,* she said. He said nothing and did as he was told.

The next day was a long one—he did not even so much as look outside. He did not want to see his sisters and his brothers sleeping in their cold beds. Four sleeping outside, and three not sleeping inside—him, his mother, and the infant, who, ignoring the rules of silence, began to cry. He cried for food, for warmth, and perhaps, with the knowledge of what was to happen next.

His mother did not nurse him. He continued to cry—sometimes loudly and at other times in an insistent whine that filled the lodge. The boy had nothing to do and nowhere to go, and so he had to listen all day and into the cold, cold night, to his brother's cry, his desperate clamor for mother's milk. Sometime during the night the crying stopped. The boy heard his mother move quietly about the lodge and then, with his eyes shut and his body buried in all the remaining blankets, he felt a slap of cold air against his body as his mother opened the flap to put the baby to bed next to his brothers and sisters.

It was still night, all was quiet. The village dogs had been eaten before, and so there was no one left to comment on the misery of the people. Usually the dogs, the ones without language, cry for the people, and such an arrangement brings comfort. But the dogs were gone, and more terrible than their absence, was what the boy heard—the very close, small sound of his mother's grief.

When the morning was light, he opened his eyes, afraid of what would greet him. He saw his mother sitting with her back to the firepit, a halo of light from the smokehole over her head. He crawled to her and she opened her arms, and he did not know what to expect to find there. But he had nothing to fear. When he reached her lap, she lifted her shirt and exposed her breasts and guided his head where it was needed and nursed him. She stroked his hair as he nursed and called him by his name. And as he continued to nurse she called him, repeatedly, and in the order of their birth, the names of his martyred brothers and sisters. And so, just as he had taken their clothes and their furs and their food, he took their names as well.

He fell asleep, full for the first time in days. He woke to nurse the other breast and slept again. This continued throughout the day and into the next. Each time he woke she was ready to give him more milk, though each time she grew weaker, and there was less and less milk to give. It was as though he were pulling the single thread of her life out of her body through her nipples. The next morning he woke out of habit. In the past, morning had meant getting kindling for the fire, hitting his moccasins against the rocks that surrounded the firepit to soften them; it meant waking his siblings. It had meant checking his snares and fetching water, hearing his father leave to go hunting. It had meant walking to the meat cache to chop off scallops of icy flesh to boil into soup, and hearing his mother sing as she roused her family to life. Now "morning" meant only that the sun had risen on a cold world in which, other than the motion of the planets, his body was the only thing that moved.

He peered around the lodge, and when he did not see his mother, he did not need to look outside to know that she was dead and that she had joined his brothers and sisters for one last sleep. He stayed where he was for two more days. He heard no voices, no dogs, no sounds of activity; he smelled no wood smoke, or roasting meat. He lived in a world that had stilled itself. He lay clothed in his suit of rabbit fur and under the other skins left by his family, buried and left to wait for warmer temperatures like a seed thrown into the brush. He did not melt snow for water, he had no method to do so. He did not eat snow either because he knew that to do so would invite the cold to enter his body through the door of his mouth and that he would end up as cold and as dead as the rest of his family.

After two days of this he was faint. The food on which he had lived—his mother's milk—was gone. The memory of her savage sacrifice, the only thing that kept him alive, had thinned into the thinnest of broths. It alone had sustained him. The weather had broken. It was clear, the snow had stopped. But the cold was vicious.

And then he heard something like a footfall. The sound was loud in his ears—amplified by the silence and by the bark covering of the lodge as though the walls were a membrane that transmitted the smallest sound. Whoever it was walked heavily toward the lodge. Slowly. Stopping every now and then. Soon the noise came from immediately outside the doorflap and changed—along with footsteps came the sound of scraping. The snow was being removed from the edge of the doorflap. He waited for the flap to be raised, for light to flood the interior, for the warm hands of his savior, whoever he might be, to pluck him out. But no one tried to open the flap. The boy tried to call out, but his throat was too dry.

Afraid the people he imagined searching the snow might leave, the boy sat up. He was dizzy and almost fell back down, but he crawled on his hands and knees from under the pile of furs and blankets toward the door. He reached the skin but he could not lift it. He tried to stand but could not. The bottom edge of the doorflap had been iced fast to the lodge poles and to the ground. He was too weak to break the grip the winter-maker had laid on his lodge. He curled up on the ground and kicked at the bottom of the doorflap with what energy he had. At least the one outside might hear him. Little by little the bottom began to move. Snow sifted in. He kicked and pushed some more and soon more snow slid in along the bottom.

In desperation he knelt in front of the doorflap and pulled and tugged and succeeded in opening a space big enough to crawl through, though the door was banked with snow on the other side. He pulled on his moccasins, his rabbitskin gloves, and rabbitskin hat, and looked around the lodge to see if there was anything else he could use. There was nothing, only his father's pipebag. He felt through the skin and the pipebowl was still there. The stem had been used for firewood. He tucked the bag inside his pants and, drawing breath as though diving underwater, he pushed under the flap with his hands, and with his eyes squeezed shut, he wriggled his small body headfirst into the snow and began to worm his way out.

It was cold. His face was scraped and bruised and shaved by the snow. It clung to his lips and his purled lashes and was shoved up his nose. As much as he pushed against the snow it pushed back into his clothing—in his moccasins, under his shirt, down his back, inside his gloves. He wriggled and squirmed and when the edge of the lodge was even with his thighs he brought up first one leg then the other and pushed against the frame until his whole body was through. He had used all his energy, but he knew if he could not sit up no one would see him and he would surely die, not more than arm's reach from the bodies of his family. He tucked his knees and hands under his body and pushed up until he knelt like a dog and thrust up his neck and then his head broke the surface of the snow. He gasped and tried to open his eyes. He shut them tight again—the sun was too bright. It had been eight long days since he had seen the sun. He flipped over on his back and shook off his gloves and wiped at his eyes, trying to clear away the crust of snow and ice from his face.

He heard no voices, no shouts of surprise, no murmurs of those witness to the spectacle of his birth from the snow. He wondered, helpless, blind, if he was surrounded by a silent enemy, warriors from across the river laughing at him. He vowed he would kill them if he could.

He rubbed his eyes some more and they fluttered against the light. The light was too strong, his eyes were too weak. The melting snow was freezing against his skin. His clothes were becoming stiff with ice. He resisted the urge to lie back down in the snow and go to sleep. He turned his head to the left and to the right and caught again, this time very close, the sound of footsteps, crunching through the deep snow. They came from the left, and he turned once again in that direction. He still couldn't see, but he relaxed his eyes and opened them, shut them quickly and opened them again to become accustomed to the light. The footsteps drew nearer—advancing slowly, unhurriedly.

Finally they drew even with him and stopped next to the lodge. Whoever it was pushed against the doorflap and scraped the bark covering. The boy was afraid to reach out and touch his companion. His tongue clacked against the roof of his mouth.

The footsteps continued, so close the boy could hear his breath: great furls of air, great labor of life. And then, mercifully, whoever it was took another step, and the sun was blocked out by his body. A gentle dusk descended on the boy's face, a blanket for his eyes. He opened them—still squinting and blinking—and he could see.

It was as though he had stepped into a cave. He was surrounded by trees, their black trunks growing up to meet the low ceiling of this movable night that hovered above him. His eyesight improved as he continued to look up at what he thought was a shadow, but proved to be not at a shadow at all but the distended belly of a cow moose. Her underside was covered in coarse, nearly black hair, and heaved in and out with each breath. Snow clung to the hair in places, mostly over her rib cage, which swung close to the deep snow. She was not concerned about the boy, if she even noticed him. Whether because of her own distracted hunger, poor vision, or his rabbitskin camouflage—he was invisible. Again and again she thrust her nose against the lodge where the snow was less deep, and by blowing and shoveling the snow out of the way, she tried to find the remnants of summer grass growing there.

The boy looked at the cow moose's belly, and with growing clarity, saw her low-hanging teats sagging away from her body and noticed a rind of dried milk around her nipples. He thought of his own mother's milk—the last meal she had given him.

Dazed, starving, and desperate, he rocked forward on his knees and sat up. Ready to receive a new mother, to receive a new life. He took one flattened teat in his hands, and when she did not run or step or kick, he grasped it more firmly and took the cold spout between his cracked lips and began to suck.

2. A hunting party from Agencytown had been in the area. They had been careful to hunt on their lands and not to cross over into the enemy territory. But when the snow began and the hunters became stuck, they had no choice but to try and seek shelter at the enemy village near the river's source. They had toiled against the storm for four days, fighting the drifts. Their legs ached, and the only reason they survived was that they had carried a heavy store of meat with them.

Finally, they rounded the bend and saw the enemy village. There were no tracks, no sounds of village life, and they smelled no wood smoke. It was ghostly quiet and despite their history of conflict, the cold and snow were enemy to all and so they were very concerned. They all imagined the worst and were soon greeted by it. The human enemy was dead.

The hunting party spread out and searched all the lodges for survivors. They found none. In lodge after lodge they didn't disturb anything except ragged piles of rags and hides under which the enemy had burrowed only to die. But it was with surprise that a man named Jiigibiig—still searching, still hoping—rounded the last lodge on the far side of the village and saw the cow moose.

He looked closely and saw something underneath. A boy? A rabbit? Was that what he saw? He couldn't be sure. Really it looked like a large rabbit was nursing on the moose's teats. Meat was scarce, they had eaten their whole supply, and so Jiigibiig acted quickly. He raised his gun and shot for the moose's heart. At such close range he couldn't miss. The moose toppled over where it stood. And directly beneath it—blinking confusedly in the sudden light and stunned by the report of the rifle—was a young boy in rabbit-fur clothing.

The boy was no older than four years old, and he covered his ears and blinked and twisted his head, confused by the sound rushing in his ears. Jiigibiig leaned his gun against the lodge and approached the boy with his arms empty and outstretched. He called to him softly. The boy didn't try to run and didn't scream or cower. Jiigibiig drew near and nearer still, and when he was close enough, he reached out and picked the boy up. Jiigibiig was old—perhaps forty—and he had no children of his own so he hardly knew what to do, much less what to expect. But the boy knew—he wrapped his arms around Jiigibiig's shoulders and his legs around his waist and burrowed his face into the human warmth that had been lost to him for so many days.

The men in the hunting party camped in the enemy village for the next few days during which they constructed sleds to carry back the moose meat. Jiigibiig searched the lodge near where he found the boy, but most everything inside had been burnt. Just outside the doorflap lay the frozen bodies of a woman and five children.

They waited patiently for survivors to straggle into the village but none came. So the men burned the bodies and put the bones in a scaffold so the animals of the forest would not eat them. They fed the boy boiled pemmican and made sure he was warm. They tried to talk to him in all the languages they knew, but the boy would not respond and it was clear he did not want to speak. He had been given a new life, and he came to it fresh.

Finally, when they were ready, the men loaded the sleds and Jiigibiig pulled the biggest one loaded with meat and with the boy. It took them four days to reach Agencytown and when Jiigibiig opened the door to the shack he shared with his wife Zhookaa-giizhigookwe, she was very surprised to see he carried a boy in his arms.

Since they had no children they decided immediately to raise the boy as their own. Zhookaagiizhigookwe stripped him down and dressed him in regular clothes. She carefully rolled his rabbit-skin outfit together with the pipebag and bowl and put them in a flour sack filled with crushed cedar and stowed them in the rafters of the small shack. After years of wishing and hoping they now had a boy of their own, whom they named Bimaadiz, because he was alive, against all odds, and their hope for a family had been rekindled, too.

3. The next year was just as disastrous for other Indians in the area, but this time hardship came to a village on the big lake not far from Agencytown. The people had been threatened with famine for some time. The stores of food procured in the summer were running low and winter had set in. And then came a devastating plague. Many died and were buried, blanketed by piles of rocks to wait until spring when the survivors could dig proper graves. A small band, the last of their tribe and consisting mostly of one large family, left the village site to camp on an island in the big lake two miles from the mainland, near the fall fishing grounds.

Their nets were hung over deep water with the hopes of catch-ing trout as they followed the cold water to the surface. More nets were set in the branches of the trees for partridge and spruce grouse. All the people had to do was wait for those that swim and those that fly—the golden apples of the sun and the silver apples of the moon—to be plucked. The people waited for the fish and the fowl, waited to be nourished by these generous animals.

But it was not to be. The winter-maker—that great mason of the North—held back the snow and sent a slurry of ice over the land. The temperature dropped, but still no snow. Ice covered the lake.

The fowl did not fly into the nets. The fish nets waited below the surface for the people to pull them up, but the ice was too thin to support human weight and too thick to be chopped away. No one was alarmed—winter sometimes came on this way—persistent but shy. Soon the cold would come in earnest, freeze the lake solid, and they could walk out and check their catch. But the ice did not thicken. The weather turned neither warmer nor colder.

The ice would not thicken or thaw. The birds did not fly toward the nets. There was no snow by which to set snares. It was a hard and empty world, and there was nothing to do. A few of the smaller men volunteered to crawl out on the ice with axes. They slipped and slid on their hands and knees, dragging a canoe after them, but it was of no use. One by one they drowned as those in camp watched.

Still the brave among them tried to reach the nets even though death seemed certain. And so, afraid they would die and sink in the lake and leave nothing for their families to bury, they each left something of themselves in the village. Solemnly, one man cut off his finger and gave it to his mother to hold, and then he crawled out on the ice only to disappear below. The next, seeing the wisdom of the man who had just drowned, the man who was also his brother, handed his father a toe. The next parted with his ear, another with a patch of skin from his thigh. Altogether, those remaining onshore were almost able to assemble a whole man out of the parts left behind.

Their families cried over these relics—over the finger that had rung the edges of the sugar kettle, for the ear that had drunk in song so happily, the skin that had covered such a swift leg. Each time a man died they spoke for him and buried what he had left behind. Soon there were clusters of rocks standing alongshore where so recently there had stood clusters of men. The winter-maker's message was clear: the people were to be turned to stone.

It was with wailing and crying, with the soughing of human anguish, that these brave men tried to feed their people, but they only succeeded in feeding the lake. And the memories of their men weighed on the living as much as the stones that covered their bodies. Perhaps it is merciful for us that we have only their names, which for us are mere markers of stone: Beaver Hat, Skinny Sticks, Moose Dung, Sleeping Sky, and Redgut.

Soon, there were none left who could or who would crawl out on the ice. Until one day, the people living lower in their stomachs, everyone near the end, the sun appeared and leads opened up between great sheets of ice. It so happened that a mother and a father of a newborn girl, being the fittest, were able to paddle out to the nets.

What heartbreak! The nets were empty save for a single pike—all teeth and head and little flesh—which resembled the people themselves. The men had died for nothing—the nets had been empty after all. No gold-sided walleye, or silver-mailed tulibee, or pouting sturgeon, or wise bullheads, or laughing bass had conde-scended to be caught.

Being the healthiest yet in camp the mother and father left their little girl with her grandmother and paddled on through the shifting ice toward the portage where they had stored some caches of rice and squash. They were to paddle out, cross the portage, dig up the food, and bring it back. They were not seen again. Soon after they left, with the ragged remnants of the band watching their birch-bark canoe zigzag slowly across the lake, the weather reverted to its previous aspect; the leads froze over and yet, as before, the ice refused to thicken, and the people were stranded once more.

The people had lost their chance with the disappearance of

the girl's parents. She continued to gurgle and babble from her cradleboard, nourished by her mother's milk still flowing through her body and by the hank of deerfat—the only food in camp—that her parents had given her.

Now, except for the sounds of the little girl's contentment, the camp—unlike the wailing and crying that had marked the hours when the men crawled on the ice only to drown—was quiet. No one spoke. No one cried. No sounds were heard as the people, one by one, began to die. The living were too weak to bury the dead. And even so, they saved what energy they had to buy themselves a view of the lake, of the treacherous ice, of the gray seam of the far shore. They propped themselves in the doorways of their lodges and fixed their eyes on the lake in hope that they would see—before they drifted off—the canoe coming back, riding low in the water, loaded to the gunwales with rice and squash. Only the little girl, swaddled and nestled into her cradleboard, remained as she was before the flight of her family to the island. She contentedly chewed the strap of jerky she had been given and let herself be mesmerized by the clicking of the bare branches and the occasional cursive swoop of a woodpecker as it wrote its way through the treetops. She laughed and gurgled.

The people who looked toward the lake began to see things. Far out on the ice they thought they saw movement—dark shapes running back and forth. They couldn't be sure, it could be simply the swirling of mist. Or their eyes, straining toward the distance, could be making the trees jump and change position with every watery blink. But still, everyone saw the shapes, and it gave them hope. Only to have it taken away when the black shapes did not draw any nearer. They watched night fall and hoped that what they had seen was a group of people trying to get across and bringing with them food and comfort.

The next day the distant activity was renewed. They were certain they saw something—movement, something or someone running or skating on the ice. Closer this time. It was only a matter of hours before whoever it was would draw nearer.

Each day the shapes in the distance appeared closer and suggested frantic activity. It further exhausted the people to watch this motion—hope exhausted them. Each day in the stilled village the people woke to the sight of these shapes slowly drawing near. Each night they prayed they would last through till dawn, possibly, the dawn of their delivery.

And then, one morning, through the pearly mist—a lighter shade of gray over the gray ice—they saw the result of their vigil. They would not be saved. Out of the mist, nearer, but not close, not yet, they saw the shapes emerge and they were not people, not other Indians, not the deliverance for which they had longed.

A lean pack of timber wolves had caught their scent and, over the days, had circled closer and closer, orbiting the island on which the band was camped. They circled, crossed, and cantered, testing the air at regular intervals for the change that would tell them that the people had all died. They would not attack the band, would not come tearing through the camp. The wolves were content to wait—benevolently vicious—until the people died and to only enter the camp at that time for their feast. Until then, they circled in wild dressage—never running full-out, rarely stopping, and in complete silence. There was no need for encouragement or communication; they continued to orbit and sample the wind as though checking a clock for the appointed hour.

The people were broken. What the hunger had started, the sight of the wolves finished. They began to die quickly. And not one by one, but rather in groups, lodge by lodge, as nighttime clouds darken whole sections of the starred sky. And there was great relief in such death. Without hope it was easy to die.

Within two days of seeing the wolves, everyone was dead, save one.

The little infant girl in her cradleboard was still alive, sustained by the scrap of smoked beaver she had managed to gnaw on. She laughed occasionally, and since she was bound to the cradleboard, her eyes played with the view and she was content, except for her swaddling of moss, which was soaked with urine and caked with shit. This made her uncomfortable—and it is only discomfort, the wants of life, that occupy the minds of babies. That was all—dirty diapers—that concerned her, and since she was barely three months old, everything was new to her. She had not yet learned of the terrible promise of life's comfort, had not learned to expect comfort at all, not learned that she could expect to be delivered from hunger or dirty swaddling, to be cleaned with an infusion of boiled willow bark, caressed with the ears of mullion. She was like a wild animal, because they, even when mortally wounded, will not make a sound. The sounds we make are for the ears of those that can help us. She did not cry.

The camp was silent, and the wolves—so careful, so concerned with their own safety—after almost endless circling, disembarked from their ship of ice onto the human shores of the island. One after another, in the tracks made by the first, they entered the defeated city through a gate of smell and sight. Once ashore, in keeping with their roles as victors, they did not at once rush to the village center and rip into the bodies. They were secure in their victory, and they could wait. Instead, crossing one another's tracks, they wove a road around the camp, circled the island, demarcating a domain that was once someone else's, but was now theirs. Satisfied, they stopped and howled, exultant, and headed with their noses to the ground into the center of the camp.

If there had been anyone to see it, what happened next would have looked like the most awful of massacres, but since the people were already dead, killed by a much greater force, it was not a massacre, except perhaps a massacre of memory. If seen by someone else—one wolf standing on the chest of a dead woman while his partner twisted on her ankle until the foot came off; another wolf, working alone, grabbing up a jawful of a boy's clothed chest and jerked, shoulders hunched, until the skin and the breast came away along the zipper of the boy's ribs—it would have seemed a brutal meal. But no one did see it, and as such feasts go, this one was a delicate and respectful satiation. The wolves did not fight each other for the meat. When full, they did not, as they often do, regurgitate their meal into a pile of bones, scraps of clothing and hair, only to swallow it down again. Rather, they slept next to the corpses, the ground serving as both bed and plate. And so with wild patience, the villagers disappeared. Except in a quiet corner of the village something else entirely was taking place.

The girl, quiet, content to wonder at the branches pleached overhead, and lulled by the sound of eating and of movement around her, was resting in her cradleboard. And she was discovered there by a lone she-wolf.

The wolf approached her cautiously. The cradleboard and its contents still exuded live human scent, but of a different quality than usual, for this human had not eaten much meat and so it did not smell the same as other humans. Honoring an old agreement between wolves and people, she was loath to go near if the morsel of life there was indeed human. Yet other scents mingled with the human scent to lure the wolf closer: the smell of beaver fat, of freshly cased martin, of shit and urine, and something else, mother's milk. Mother's milk is just that and is attractive to all creatures. The she-wolf had weaned her pups earlier that fall, had chased them from the hearth of her belly, and yet her milk had not stopped pooling in her teats. And since the milk still flowed, the desire to put it to use did too. So she came near—slowly, each step a motion forward but loaded with tension. She was ready to spring away, sensitive to any trick or trap. All the while the she-wolf alternately stood erect and sniffed the air or crouched to test the trampled leaves and ground currents for the taste of danger. She finally arrived nose to nose with the little girl, and as a last test, pressed the great wet world of her nose against the girl's cheek.

The wolf's nose was as big as the girl's cheek, and the wolf had to flatten her neck in order to get down to the girl's level. And what a sight it must have been for the little girl. The wet hot breath blowing in her face; breath so thick and sweet it made the girl blink. It was the only movement the girl could make—her arms and feet were bound in her otterskin robe and her head was wrapped close around the neck so it would not flop forward.

The she-wolf was undecided about what to do with this thing—this creature with the body of an otter and the head of a human; this thing that made no sound and that was pungent with the scent of milk.

Two young wolves in search of more food trotted up behind the she-wolf. Instinctively, the she-wolf wheeled to face them, to claim the girl as hers. As she did so—her back legs swinging round, her shoulders hunched—the cradleboard, reclining on its stand, was suddenly positioned right below her belly. Her nipples slapped the girl's face. The girl's nose, being weaker than the wolf's, only then scented milk. With the rough nipple in front of her face, she latched on and began sucking. The she-wolf flinched, surprised, but did not move—such was her pleasure, such was her relief.

The young wolves turned and vanished; only their breath was left hanging in the air where they had been standing.

4. A party of timber cruisers had come to the lake that day. They were from Agencytown—four days' paddle from the dead village camped on the island. The timberjacks and sawyers were done with milling the previous year's lumber and were out scouting locations for the mill's winter camp.

They carried their bedrolls and camp gear on their backs and were armed with a transit and a rifle. In addition, more out of hope than necessity, they had packed blades to attach to their boots, on the chance that instead of walking the shoreline of the big lake, they could skate.

They were a rough, merry bunch. Hardworking and wild, they grasped at every opportunity to stretch the fabric of their lives to make a garment big enough to contain work and pleasure. Their existence in the lumber camp was little better than that of convicts: a strict schedule, bad meals, hard work. They drank, whored when possible, stole, trapped or shot anything of value they happened upon. As it was, they had spied the thickly timbered island from shore, and since it looked like a good place for winter camp they strapped their skates to their boots and set out across the ice.

They skated toward the island in single file. It was the first chance they had to break the slow rhythm of their lives—the agonizing repetition of pushing each log free with peaveys, of gaffing them with picaroons onto the chute, of feeding them into the blade, of quarter-sawing again and again the reluctant pine, of stacking the lumber and burning the slab, of hauling water to the barrels that were balanced on the roof-ridge in case of fire below. They flew across the ice in silence and did not, as they later would, shout and race one another, did not pull on the leader's coattails to slow him down. They stayed in line—conscious only of how fast they were going, of the rasp of their blades on the ice, and of the shores of the island drawing nearer and nearer. They reached the island more quickly than they thought possible, and since the pleasure of speed was, after long interruption, so new again, they did not stop and instead circled the small nipple of land. Without knowing it they were doing what the wolves had done before them. Their breath blew out behind them, wreathing the island. When they had circled twice, the leader who carried the gun slowed and stopped. It was getting late—they had work to do after all. No sooner had he stopped than he looked inland among the trees and saw the dark lodges of the village and, standing stock-still, its head turned away, was an enormous gray wolf.

Here was a gift! he thought and without waiting he set the hammer, shouldered the rifle, and fired.

The wolf toppled and so did Aantti Home; the wolf fell because a .30-.30 bullet hit a rib, flattened out, and pushed its way through the animal's heart. Home fell because he was still on his skates and the recoil slammed him over flat on his back. He hit his head on the ice and lay still.

The other men divided into two groups. Some stayed with Home to see how badly he was hurt, and the others unlaced their blades and rushed up to see what had happened to the wolf. They found the animal tipped over on its side. Where the she-wolf had been standing, they found the cradlebord with the little girl blinking into the newly emerged cathedral ceiling of the canopy. She began to cry; her milk had been so abruptly taken away.

The men spread out to see what other surprises the island held, but there were no surprises, only death, which, among those people, was not surprising. They found no more wolves. The others had funneled off into the approaching night after the rifle shot. All that remained were the half-eaten corpses of the villagers. The bodies were badly damaged along with all the tunics and moccasins and gloves they wore. So, after collecting as many bandolier bags, pipes, and drums—which they would sell—they picked up the girl in her cradleboard and dragged the wolf by its front paws and convened on the shore around the unconscious body of Aantti Home.

Home had not awakened, but since it was his kill, the others did not dress out the wolf. No one wanted to stay on the island at night. Quickly, they built a sled for Home out of balsam poles and set off the way they had come.

It was almost night, and in profile their party made for a strange sight, seen only by the hidden eyes of the wolves who had retreated into the bush: the foremost man carried the baby in its cradleboard, followed by the four others. The second-to-last man dragged Home on the sled. He was followed by one more man who dragged the dead wolf by a rope attached around its neck. It was too dark for even the wolves to see the details, light enough only to see the shapes: a line of men—the first without arms that were held close to his body in order to hold the cradleboard, four more swinging their arms and singing in time with the rhythm of their skates, the fifth pulling a man who faced back toward the deadly little island, and all of them chased by a wolf that decided to slide over the ice instead of run, and who made no sound at all.

5. By the time the sawyers reached Agencytown, Aantti Home had recovered from his fall on the ice, and he opened the door to his house with a large lump on his head, and bearing the little girl still strapped in her cradleboard. The wolf he had killed he set in the woodshed next to the house so as not to frighten the dogs. Aantti's wife, Mary, was an Indian from Agencytown. In addition to being a practical woman, she had been longing for a child of her own—all of their pleasurable efforts had so far been to no avail. So, as Aantti lit his small clay pipe with a sliver of wood held under the grate of the cast-iron stove, Mary got busy. She unswaddled the girl and cleaned her with her softest rags and made her an Indian swing out of a blanket and some rope. After that was done and the girl was asleep in her swing, she put on her husband's wool coat and went outside to hang the wolf in the woodshed. By lantern light she skinned the beast, pulling down the hide, separating the skin from muscle with careful quick strokes of her skinning knife.

She was done in a matter of hours and brought the hide into their cabin so it would not freeze—she would stretch it the next day. Back inside she found her husband asleep in the chair and the little girl alert but silent in her swing. Mary carefully cleaned and dried the otterskin blanket and the cradleboard and under the watchful eyes of the girl, she stored them high up under the eaves. These items could be used to identify the girl should her parents ever come to Agencytown to claim her. Mary hoped they would never come. They named the girl Eta because she was the only one from the island village to survive. They raised her as their own.

Dr Apelles looks up from the manuscript in front of him on the library table, he has just finished the first part of his translation.

He has an hour before the archive closes.

He has discovered a document that only he can translate. And it has occurred to him that he has never been in love. Or, rather, finding the document *makes* him realize that he has never been in love. Suffice it to say, when he first found the document, his world, as it was, collapsed. And he relives, each and every day, the feeling of that discovery.

He puts his hand to the left side of his chest, and there, under the fat and muscle and bone, he feels his heart beating. He is a doctor of philosophy, not of medicine, so he has no language with which to envision it accurately, but he imagines his heart pushing blood through his arteries and sucking it back again along his veins endlessly. Endlessly for now because some day his heart will stop. But his heart has not been put to use for years except to send his blood along its appointed rounds. His heart has never beat in the service of love.

He feels faint, dizzy. It is the same feeling he had when he boarded the plane to fly away to college all those years ago. He had never been on a plane before and had rarely been off the reservation. And of a sudden there he was, leaving. As the plane picked up speed he could not fathom how it could leave the ground. It felt heavy, awkward—rooted to the place like he was. But then seconds later the ground was receding and he, inexplicably, began to cry. Not because he was scared or because he was sad about leaving the reservation, but because that awkward heavy connection, that love of place and the sense of self it can bring, can be severed so easily.

Dr Apelles has found a document for which he himself is the only remaining key, and because of it he knows that he has never been in love. The reasons for his strange predicament are nowise clear to him, but he can sense there is a connection between the translation and love. But the question of love itself will have to wait. After all, the never-asked question of its absence has been waiting for forty-three years. A few more minutes, a couple of hours, even a day or two will make no difference. He has never loved, and now he knows this.

What he has just read demands his attention. That which comes from outside of us, that presents itself at a certain moment, or on a certain day, can be so easily lost. As lost as the years. Already the words on the ancient manuscript page, that shy paper, are beginning to swirl, mix, and change. The words don't fade in his mind as dreams do. Rather, they break through the cover of obscurity that has hidden them for so long and hide in the lush foliage of what he already knows—other languages, other landscapes, other stories. But it isn't really the manuscript or the words written there that are moving. They are, physically at least, resolute, still. It is what is within him that is moving. The treasures of his mind are being rearranged and reordered, as well as the habits of his heart.

He looks down at the document. It is still there. The words are still there. And they still mean something. But only to him. Only he can translate it. Any story, all stories, suppose a reader. Stories are meant to be heard and are meant to be read. And translations, no matter what the subject, are like stories in that regard, only more so. Twice the effort has been put into a translated document than has been put into the original: it has to be created in the first place and then it has to be recreated.

There are no readers for this translation, and if he wanted to he could make it up; he could, he sees, make that poor document say anything at all and no one would be the wiser. This feeling, the singular feeling that no one is watching us, the feeling that no one is looking over our shoulder, is something all of us have felt, that everyone feels at one time or another. And this feeling, the abyss of unknowing, comes on cat's feet, surprises us. We shudder. We could do something or not do something and it wouldn't matter because it would have no perceptible effect on the world. What we feel is freedom. And what we feel is also oblivion. But the feeling passes. It has lasted but a moment. Life's sound track resumes, the world—suspended while we consider the abyss—once again begins turning.

But the world does not begin turning right away for Dr Apelles. His moment does not pass because no one is looking over his shoulder. No one is looking at him at all. And no one has looked at him for years. If he ceased to exist no one would notice. These two concerns, one about the manuscript and one about his heart, are linked. This is why Dr Apelles is so shaken, why his world, as he has known it, has come to an end. He has no reader for his heart. And he never has.

Most people begin practicing love when they are young, and through the years they hone, mistake by mistake, the satisfying sorrow love brings. But Dr Apelles had only a childish infatuation as an adolescent and a banal affair when he was in college, and that was not enough. He has found, over the years, too much satisfaction in his own mind, too much comfort in the bouquet of languages he holds so dear. But, as air bubbles travel from the ocean floor to burst on the water's surface, his need for love has been traveling toward the surface of his life for some time and has suddenly burst open. And perhaps, too, the translation and the question of love are linked for no other reason than they both occur inside him—they are both near neighbors in his mind and you can only jump from one to the other for so long without mixing the two together.

Like everyone else, he thinks about love. And like all readers, he has read his fair share of love stories. But as a translator he had begun to see himself as standing outside *all* stories, written and lived. It was his job to move them from one place to another, from one language to another, and it mattered little that a particular story was about love or about war or about anything at all. Dr Apelles has grown accustomed to the idea that stories happened to other people, not to him.

Now, even that rare document he has found seems better off than he: at least it has one person that can understand it. As for him, he now sees he is alone. He feels, again, the terror of the plane lifting off the ground, the painfully painless separation, the great distance between things. But after the plane had crept into the sky—his sky, which domed his little world—and he had quit crying just as the fine rain had been wiped off the windows by the speed of their departure, he looked down on the land that had so recently been his. And he was terrified all over again because he saw, here and there, cupped in the reach of the trees, small swamps and marshy little ponds, and there were so many more than he had ever thought there were. Here and there he could see a beaver lodge poised on the edge of the round pond like an off-side nipple. And he remembered the days of his youth when he would walk the hills and creep to the potholes and sloughs to jump mallards and wood ducks that he would bring home to his mother to make into soup and where he first experienced a sense of completeness—each muddy swamp, ringed with dead ash and elm and studded with clumps of cattails, marsh grass, and wiike, was a world unto itself: finite and complete and endless. But he was in the grip of the plane now and he fell away, up, higher, from those small anonymous and communal worlds he knew so well, and he had felt, acutely, that he was leaving himself behind.

And that is why the document he found, quite by accident, has unsettled him so, and given him that sickening sense of vertigo. It is with terrifying certainty that he realizes now that he has been falling away, away, forever.

This is why when he looks at the document he feels dizzy and needs to hold onto something more solid than the table edge, or his pencil, or his past. The document has languished—unknown and untranslated in a language no one save him speaks. It is one thing to translate a thing, and something else completely to have that thing read. It is one thing to love someone, and something else entirely to be loved in return. When he reads the document, and contemplates translating it, he looks up wildly around the archive at the other researchers and is suddenly tempted to try and anchor himself to them. He has the urge to stand up, walk to the next table, and hug the man over there. Or to approach the reading-room librarian and tell her that he loves her. To love someone. To have that person love him—this might just keep him from the deadly atmosphere high above the earth toward which he is falling at incredible speed. But that is impossible. It is impossible. He cannot suddenly cling to just anyone simply because he is lonely and alone. And what would that person do? Would she love him back? No. The answer is no.

He, once again, looks back down at the document. Still there. He can't seem to keep his eyes on it. Every time he focuses on it his mind is sent spinning in another direction. And he, once again, feels like he is falling and thinks, again, perhaps he has always been falling. And suddenly, he can't help it—the document, and the feelings it stirs, throw him back to his childhood. In and of itself it was nothing special, merely *his* childhood. Everyone's got one. Everyone's had one, some people more so. But all the same . . .

As his fingers stroke the smooth plastic film of the document cover he is reminded, because the surface is so smooth and cool, of the sensation of rubbing his cheek against a wool blanket. And before he can help it, do anything, he is beating back against the tide of memory and suddenly there he is—his cheek resting uncomfortably on his father's prized Hudson Bay blanket, his feet cupping each other for warmth, the tip of his nose so cold it is without sensation—lost in the shadow of his parents' small cabin. He is six years old, winter is full on, his parents are sitting at the small table, and Apelles is trying to make himself cry because his baby sister has just died. If he lifts his head a little he can see the small cola crate in which she rests wrapped in calico on the table between his parents. They lean over the box and fuss with the wrappings. They are lit by the kerosene lamp overhead and, if you didn't know that they were contemplating the corpse of their youngest, they would look as though they are carving a cold roast. Theirs is a feast of grief.

Later he will think of his sister only on crisp winter mornings. Four days after her death, when the sun was just over the trees, Apelles woke to hear his father splitting cedar shakes for her gravehouse with a hatchet and froe. The sound was clear and singular and rang out through the yard all the day; his father was making scales to cover her gravehouse: her ark that would bob the slow swell of earth where she was buried. The dot dash of his father's activity—the ping of the hatchet hitting the froe and then the ripping sound of the shake being levered from the round—was all Apelles heard. Over and over. Blow after blow. The sound carried on the morning air, and so it is always that on the first days of autumn he can't help it, he thinks of her. Just as for most of his life he won't be able to bear the sight of women's makeup because, before she was buried, when the house was still full of people, the boss ladies from the big drum painted his sister's cheeks with lipstick to make her look happy in the afterlife. But that first night he can't think of her, and so he tries instead to make himself cry, to think of his own tears instead, but can't because the wool blanket irritates his skin.

Now, he realizes, he couldn't cry then because he had no language for his grief. And no way to translate his sorrow, his private, pitiful, meager sorrow into something more lasting, more noble.

She died suddenly, with little warning, of the flu. His parents were stunned. At first, when she fell sick, when she stopped eating and her fever rose, there was a lot of activity in their small cabin. Baths were made, medicines were picked, and as a last resort she was driven to the clinic off the reservation. But when it was clear that she was dying and there was nothing else to be done, they came back home and waited and waited for her to die. Once she did die, his parents had nothing to say and nothing to do but prepare her and the ground for her funeral, which was presided over by Apelles' uncle. As for Apelles—his life, what there was of it, stopped. He hadn't realized how much his life of life had been spent as a brother. Between meals and during chores or on their way to ceremony or in the fields he had fed her and poked her drum-like belly and had balanced her on his hip while she grabbed onto his overall straps. When she rode on his back, she had gripped him under his collarbone. He had made her necklaces out of lilyroot and chains of pine needles. He had done all these things but would no more and what was left was an awful silence. He was not encouraged to speak about his feelings. His sorrow was held in check because it was of no use to her at all and would only make her trip on death's road more difficult—sorrow itself was an impediment, like deep and shifting sand. His grief took the form of an unbearably quiet kind of boredom and acute physical discomfort upon going to bed with the wool blanket itching his face. Apelles couldn't sleep that night. His face felt hot and flushed against the wool. And it was all made worse because he had thrashed and coughed, at which point his father had unhooked the lantern from over the table and brought it near Apelles' face. He had reached out with his rough wide hand and felt Apelles' forehead and then his chest. There was no expression on his face. After a moment he said—"Gego babaamamaazikaaken. Bizaan dana gosha"—and retreated to the table, the lamp once again swinging on its hook. Apelles tried to obey, and he shuddered with the effort.

And so it was for a long time that he could not abide the feel of wool against his cheek because the sensation, the very feeling, was, for him, the raw, blank, depthless, unending sensation of sadness. He must have carried much of his sorrow with him all these years, making of him a serious boy and a serious man and causing sadness to range wide and cover much of life's retrospect.

These are the kinds of scenes and memories, so long buried, that have moved to the surface. He feels faint. Dizzy. He closes his eyes and opens them, double-checking the solidity of the room. Sure enough, the green-shaded table lamp is still solidly affixed to the wide oak table and still casts its light in a gentle yet focused beam on his manuscript and his yellow legal pad and his hands, in their ghostly latex, and his squad of green pencils lined up to the side of the notepad. To his side the "Doc. File #492" is filled with yellowed pages neatly arranged by date and encased in tinted plastic folders. The reading room is solid and unchanged. His table is one of six, all identical, arranged in two rows of three. All have three green-shaded reading lamps fixed in their centers and their wooden surfaces are use worn but well taken care of. The green carpet has not changed. The oak bookshelves along the two far walls hold their accumulation of indexes and reference books. In front, the raised reference desk, much like a judge's bench, where the reading-room librarian holds court over the researchers, is still there. Above, the plaster ceiling, twenty-feet high, and approximately white as though to suggest the purity of archival research, though in the dim wintry light it could be gray or blue, still vaults the darkness that must surely have fallen on the world outside. All is where it should be. The whole room is designed to suggest the patient eternity of information. Information that exists whether there is anyone interested or able to interpret it or not.

The turmoil, in the form of two realizations—one about a translation and the other about love—has not yet subsided and Dr Apelles glumly thinks that this is the very price we pay for transforming our knowledge into wonder. He is paying with his peace of mind. And as with all forms of tranquility, it is not easily won nor is it long lasting; there are always skirmishes at the frontier of the soul.

It is strange for him to think of himself as having a soul. He would like someone to help him chart its dimensions. He touches his chest with his fingertips and thinks: there is something inside. Past my shirt, and past this old skin, and deeper still, there is something inside of me. I can sense it yet, even if I cannot see it. Just as I cannot see, not fully, the scenes of my past: my sorrows and my joys. And my tribe, which in itself is strange to say. I have been studying the languages of others for so long I have not thought of myself as having a tribe or a reservation any longer. But those things are inside me, too. I remember once, talking to the old man, the ceremony man, and he told me just before I left that we have two souls, not one. We hide one in our heart and the other hides someplace on our body only we know where—in our left hip, perhaps, or in the shoulder blade, or the kneecap, and this soul is the soul that roams. It is roaming now.

He touches the parchment. Because of the latex gloves and the plastic cover, it feels distant. He strokes the surface of the document. How rare, and how sad. What has existed has existed, and what has been destroyed has been destroyed. What can he do to undo all of that? He is only a middle-aged bachelor. A mere translator (not even a professional translator) of languages that have ceased to matter to most people. He cannot create anything. God creates. God is the utterance and he is merely the air of language that can transmit the sound. Sad, too, to think that the page, in and of itself, has no meaning without him. He is the only one who can make sense of the thing, or who can give it sense, give it life. Maybe he is a god after all—one who rules the smallest of worlds.

All he might be able to do is breathe onto the page as onto a stunned bird he once held as a child. It had flown into a window and he picked it up. It was lifeless, still. His father, unconcerned, said, "Blow on it. Like you're warming your hands." He did, cupping the finch and blowing, slowly, with all his hope and hot breath. The finch revived, sat in the nest of his hands for a second, and suddenly flew into the trees. For the document, though, there is no sky into which it can climb. Because, for stories, the sky is made of the endless dome of readers and freckled with constellations of the kindly and curious.

He looks up from the document. The hours have passed quickly. He places the precious pages back in the box and carefully puts his pencils in the breast pocket of his shirt and stands. His back is stiff from hunching. He is hungry. He is surprised to remember that he has a body of his own. He picks up the box and brings it to the cart set to the side of the reading-room librarian's desk. He then confronts the logbook and prepares to sign out. The librarian looks up from her work, and asks, as she usually does,

Did you find everything you needed?
Yes. I found everything.
Was it to your satisfaction?
No, it was not.
Why not?
I am afraid I have made a discovery.
Discoveries are what bring scholars and translators here. You are
    here to make them.
But I do not come here to make discoveries. I come here to con-
    firm what I already know.
Aren't you here for knowledge?
No. I and everyone else come for evidence.
For evidence?
What about knowledge?
Knowledge is not found here.
Where then?
It is not to be found at all. It is created.
Out of what?
Out of our desire for it.
Well, where does that desire come from?

He falters. This when he pauses, already surprised at the nature of the exchange.

I don't know. That's what I don't know.

His heart is beating wildly and without any kind of rhythm he can detect. Instead of saying Good night, See you tomorrow, Until next time, he nods curtly and turns and leaves the room. After collecting his coat and briefcase from his locker, he finds himself on the front steps of the archive.

He breathes deeply. His heart is slowing down, and his chest doesn't feel as tight. He is conscious of the cool air. It restores him. The oxygen helps his troubled head, but more than that, he is cheered, thrilled, to remember there exists a world in which he actually lives. A world he shares with other people. There is a place that continues, that has not gone the way of dust and death, that is represented by more than a few words on a page. He looks up at the sky. It is gray and low, and soon it will be night. For some reason this sky reminds him of his childhood and of his reservation with its thin trees and ever-stretching swamps. And of his people. They are waking up in his mind, stirring, as though to start a new day in which they are remembered again. That is their job now. To be remembered.

He has not moved yet, and the few researchers, librarians, and guards who are leaving, must do their 180-degree turn in the revolving door and then step around him to continue down the steps. He surveys the city in front of him—his gaze trips down the wide granite steps, across the small park where they have jazz concerts in the summer, and then, since the eye muscle moves so quickly, his gaze splits left and right down the broad busy avenue filled with people and cars and buses. Everyone is going home for the evening, and just as the horizon has shut the door on the sun, they have shut the door on the day's work.

He is afraid to step into the stream of people. The archive with its milky marble walls and stout Doric columns feels like the only still point in this world, the only possible refuge. The life outside the archive, outside his translation, seems anonymous and barren, unknowable and without safe harbor. He longs to duck back into the forest of texts behind him. It is not for no reason that songbirds sing from the safety of the trees.

But he is in the way. People, anonymous or not, need to get out of the building and he is in the way. The security guard at the front desk in the foyer has seen him and has been watching him for a while. But it is dark and he mistakes Dr Apelles for a home-less man many of whom often seek shelter under the portico of the archive. He gets up from his seat and takes his turn in the revolving door. He stands to the side and says,

You can't stay here. You have to find someplace else to sleep.
I suppose I will. Humans don't sleep standing up.
Oh. Dr Apelles. My mistake.
Yes, me.
I thought you were a bum.
They are called the homeless now.
Maybe. But my dad called them bums.
My father did, too. But times have changed.
A bum's a bum, isn't he?
Yes. But the difference is important. Bum suggests action—to bum, to beg. Homeless is an adjective, it describes a condition.
I never thought of it that way.
Neither had I. I'm sorry. I'll move. I should have known I was in the way.
No problem. Good night, Dr Apelles.
Good night.

But is it a good night? He is not sure. It is unusual, though. He blinks, trying to clear his vision. Maybe I'm sick, after all. Maybe I'm having a stroke, he thinks. He blinks and slides his hand be-hind his glasses to rub his eyes. There has been no day like this that he can remember. He feels sick in a way that would not be noticeable to a specialist. But he has no one to turn to, no one to ask. No one whom he could ask, *Am I sick? Do I have a fever? Here, feel my forehead.* Dr Apelles remembers his mother's words when he was a child. Don't get sick. Don't ever get sick. Sick Indians die. The ghost of his sister coming between them.

With a sigh he shoulders his bag and takes the first step and the second, and next the third. Before he knows it he is in mo-tion. He finishes the steps and walks forward and onto the sidewalk and turns left and he is within the flow of people, ordinary people after all, on their way home.

He has not decided yet about dinner, which he usually takes alone at a small restaurant near his apartment. Decisions about dinner can wait. Instead of looking down at his feet as he usually does when he is thinking hard, he looks up at the people around him.

Some are traveling the same direction he is. Others come from the opposite way. It makes little difference which way they are headed—all use the same physical grammar. There is no argument about how they use the sidewalk. Some walk faster than others, weaving between the young and elderly. Others, burdened with bags or packages, or with infirmities, or thoughts, move much more slowly. What is remarkable is that the crowdedness of the city that he first noticed when he moved there as a younger man and quickly learned not to notice has been replaced with a sense of vacancy: everyone feels miles away from him. What he doesn't know is whether it is always like this, and he hasn't noticed because he so rarely looks up into the faces and lives around him, or if it is solely a result of his recent research. Usually, except for the two Fridays a month when he is a translator of Native American languages instead of a librarian of sorts, he pushes his languages to what he actually envisions as the back of his mind, in the bowl of bone atop his neck. There is no point in keeping languages he cannot use—with the waiters at the restaurant, at the dry-cleaners, with the librarians or floor workers he works with—ready, on the tip of his tongue. It is better to keep the whole cushion of his brain between them and his everyday language. But when he occasionally meets with Indians from his tribe, or other tribes, he can bring those beautiful languages to the front of his mind. So special are they to him that he produces them with the clumsy flourish of a teenager presenting a bouquet of flowers to a date. And he is a different person when he speaks those languages. He is sly and can tell a good joke. The puns and play come naturally. He can flirt in those languages. And they lend themselves to memory. Or perhaps his memory borrows against his English because he can think about things like Victor's death and Annette's betrayal and the other scenes of his youth, both happy and sad, in those languages, but his English has no credit, can make no purchase on them. Dr Apelles' languages all have different values and those values change according to what he is doing or what he is thinking about, and when he bothers to think about his feelings, there is a kind of linguistic arbitrage that takes place wherein English loses all its value.

He hasn't had time to bury the day's discovery back where it belongs. So it must be that the distance he feels, the darkness, the dizziness, arises from what he has read in the archive and not from the people or the place. People look at one another all the time. Looking at other people can't cause sickness, anxiety, or light-headedness.

He has arrived at the restaurant. To eat there tonight does not seem possible. He usually sits at the bar, never crowded during the early dinner hours, and has his meal and a beer (no more than one), while he reads. It is a comforting kind of public seclusion—the way he imagines city statues must feel after dark; still a part of the city, still able to hear and see the thrum of life, but unnoticed and unremarked upon. Consciousness, the pesky reality in which he and everyone else is enmeshed, does sometimes intrude on his solitary dinners, usually in the form of fantasies about the hostess and the bartendrix, Zola and Elizabeth. It is a comfort to dine alone, he reminds himself, not the sad necessity of a lonely but, as of today, hopeful bachelor. It is a pleasure to dine alone with only a beer and a book for company. A pleasure, he thinks as he looks in the restaurant window, most people don't know how to enjoy. Such a time—after work and before going home—is the temporal crossroads of his day: a breezeway connecting the separate buildings of labor and domestic life. His time in the restaurant is a chance for the emissaries from the different kingdoms of his life—scholarly, domestic, and gustatory—to meet on neutral ground.

But he knows he will not be able stop the whisperings coming from within his own mind, and so he will, tonight, exile himself and eat at home.

The waitresses are visible through the glass that, as it gets darker, shows them in increasingly greater relief. He knows them all by name but is not chummy with any of them—and tonight they seem both too familiar and too distant to speak to them safely. They are a part of his life enough so that it would be strange, it would *feel* strange, not to tell them about the drastic changes that have occurred inside him, yet they are too distant from him to really share anything meaningful. "Elizabeth," he might say, "I found something in the archives this afternoon. It might change my life." And she would respond by saying, "Wow. That's really something. What does it say?" And he would respond, after taking a sip of his beer, "Well, it's about the most amazing thing of all . . ."

He turns from the window. It is not far to his apartment. Night has truly fallen. The hint of light in the sky before—uniformly blue, all the more deep and blue because of the blackness of the buildings, all the more blue because it has been cut into strips and framed by the buildings, like the streets directly below the sky, like canals, rivers of night—is all gone. The streetlights illuminate the sidewalks, but barely. They are still crowded with people, and more light comes from the lighted windows of shops and apartments and offices.

He hurries. He reaches his building, nods to the doorman, and takes a right past the front desk. It is a small affair; after all, what need does a doorman have for a big desk? It is the safety projected by his presence and his demeanor and the power of his memory for the residents of the building that are his tools.

Dr Apelles takes three steps to the bank of mailboxes. He opens his with its special brass key, but there is nothing inside except a single medium-sized envelope from an obscure academic journal that contains the page proofs of a short, overcautious article about the use of obviation in Algonquian languages. He closes his mailbox and goes back down the three steps and turns left and punches the elevator call button and waits and when the door opens he steps in, pushes the button for the eleventh floor and the door closes, the elevator starts.

His thoughts climb through the various levels of his life as the elevator heads steadily toward his floor.

His parents are dead. He has no children. He had crushes in high school and a brief painful affair in college. But nothing for a long time. And he has not missed the absence of obligation. He has been content with the shape of his life.

He does not own his apartment. He has no need of a car. Mortgage statements, insurance, and assessments will find their way to other mailboxes. He does not carry a credit card, and so he does not receive mailers, promotions, or solicitations. This has been, until today, a source of pride for him. He is, so he has thought, an unencumbered man, obligated only to his job—he does have a job after all—and to the dead languages that keep him company.

The elevator stops. He turns right and walks the hall to his door, which he opens deftly. After he sets down his satchel and hangs up his jacket and takes off his blazer, he grills himself a cheese sandwich and opens a beer. Home at last.

What then?

What is there that can satisfy him? Nothing it seems. He is restless. He lost his usual poise somewhere between opening the manuscript that morning and sipping the last of his beer in the evening. The journals and magazines—dry speculations on translations, on narrative and discourse—that he usually nods off to at day's end will not suffice. He is too agitated to let himself be lulled by the intellect. And masturbation seems just as unsatisfactory. He already feels emptied out and does not have the energy to call forth his own orgasm because the expense would exceed the payment of pleasure. Mai's Massage Parlour is probably still open, and he could go there, to his usual place, and have someone else lend him a hand. But it is not his usual night to go there and the distance feels too great and the degree of need too extreme, too pathetic. He almost picks up the phone—what lonely people do in movies, what agitated people do in movies. He doesn't have anyone to call. Neither his brothers, or his sister, or the few friends he has, are the kind of people with whom he could discuss, truly, what is bothering him.

He feels hot, stifled, and actually moves his hand to his throat to loosen his tie—another cinematic gesture—which he is not wearing. He stands and walks to the window. The sounds of traffic instantly greet his ears—horns, sirens in the distance, someone far below whistles for a cab in the reverse of birdsong, which usually comes from above. All of it movie-set noise, separated from him, surrounding him. The lighted windows in the buildings across the way seem to promise something, but he does not know what. But what?

He looks out the window at the scatter of light from thousands of other windows just like his, opening into apartments just like his, with people looking out into the terrible and wonderful night, people who are not at all like him. Feeling as he does and thinking what he thinks and knowing what he knows, he knows he is alone.

And the freedom he usually associates with singularity feels like freedom no more. He is a ghost. No one has claim, or investment, or stake in him. He is not needed by life, and this is result of his past choices as much as a result of what he has learned today.

I want to love somebody but I don't know whom. And I don't know how.

He is standing by the window, his arms braced on either side.

I've translated more difficult things. I have translated the ravel of more complicated thought, like rivers through strange lands. I should therefore be able to make love happen. I should be able to make love. I should be able to translate it into a language that someone, somewhere, will want to read. And he knows, surely, that the answer to both the translation and to love will be the same.

He can see, from his vantage by the window, the city below. But he can also see—reflected in the glass, himself, a pale reflection of himself, and he can also catch glimpses of his life in review—the days of his childhood, and then school, and college, his affair with Annette, and his more lasting affair with the wonder of language, his walks from the archive and his little restaurant with Zola and Elizabeth, and his job at RECAP and the people there, Ms Manger, and Campaspe, in particular, and his time alone and his time spent with people. The whole of it running breathlessly to this point—the full stop of his existence. And he sees, for some reason, the figure of his coworker, Campaspe, as she goes about her work. Maybe her? he wonders. Maybe I can love her.

He is ready. He looks to each side—and though he is alone in his apartment, he feels as though someone is watching him. He clears his throat, a small frail sound itself swallowed by the larger mouth of the night. The city noise is hushed. The night has become quiet, a silent theater for the drama of his heart, a silent audience for the play of his tongue.

He says something as he faces the window.

And it is free. It has been released from his mouth, too early perhaps, because the words seem to fall through the air, unable to support themselves. But then, they recover their balance, put out their wings and fly, and who knows where? He is satisfied. It is perfect. He looks up from the manuscript in front of him on the library table, he has just finished the first part of his translation.

~ **Book I** ~

1. From an early age, from the time Bimaadiz was five or six, upon watching the men prepare to hunt, he would set up a piteous wail until Jiigibiig—not without some embarrassment—fitted him with his own set of snowshoes made just for him and told him to follow along. Once in the bush he quieted down and never once scared the game by making noise and never once ruined the hunt by urinating when the wind might blow the scent toward the game. He was happy only when he was in the woods—and so, since Jiigibiig and Zhookaagiizhigookwe only wanted Bimaadiz to be happy, they let him go hunting at his pleasure. By the time he turned sixteen (and the time at which our story really begins), he was such an accomplished hunter he single-handedly supplied the village with most of the meat it needed. Such was his skill and care that Jiigibiig let the youngster use the Winchester repeating rifle. Bimaadiz didn't need more than one shot, unless there was more than one deer or moose, but it was an honor to carry it. Jiigibiig and Zhookaagiizhigookwe, and those who remembered how he was found, suspected his power was the result of his contact with the cow moose during his infancy. Once, after hearing Bimaadiz shoot, Jiigibiig walked back into the woods with a sled to help him haul out his catch (for he was sure to have killed something, no doubt there was meat cooling on the ground), and he saw Bimaadiz kneeling over a dead moose, singing gently to the animal as he skinned it. It sounded like a lullaby, not a victory song, and the way Bimaadiz skinned the animal made the scene seem more like a birth than butchery. Because of the nimbus of affection surrounding him and because of the gifts given to him by his first mother and the milk he received from his second mother, the moose, Bimaadiz grew into a singular young man. He was tall and strong but not thick; his body was supple and slender, with wide shoulders and very long fingers. His waist was narrow, but like a coiled spring—full of potential strength. His black hair was thick and smooth and he kept it cut short and parted in the middle, slicked down with hair oil. All the girls, even the older women, gasped when he walked by. It was a good life at Agencytown in those years; meat was never so plentiful and everyone loved the quiet hunter who provided for them so well.

2. Eta had grown up, too. She alone, perhaps, possessed more beauty than Bimaadiz did. She was tall for her age, and though not fine boned, she was lean and strong. Yet she had delicate fingers, and straight black hair that was always in two braids that hung down to her lower back. Her waist was narrow and her breasts, in advance of her years, were round and firm. All the boys and all the men sighed when she walked past. Her skin was smooth, clear, coppery, and healthy year round, except on her left cheek there was a dark round mark, very faint, that looked as though it had been left there when the wolf who had suckled her had kissed her cheek with her nose. It was really only a birthmark, it had been there before the she-wolf nosed the infant, but Aantti and Mary liked to think the wolf had left its mark.

It seemed to the villagers that Eta had acquired some of the wolf's characteristics: she was incredibly intelligent, patient, concerned for others, and serious when anyone was looking, but silly and girl-like when she thought she was unobserved. Aantti and Mary were overjoyed at the unexpected gift of a daughter, especially since they thought they would never have one of their own. And so, being the object of so much happiness, Eta grew up receiving happiness. Her parents doted on her and gave her whatever it was that she wanted. They didn't have much to give—a poor sawyer and his Indian wife. Buttons, a bit of cloth, these were her toys. But all the same, the girl didn't want much. And she worked hard. Once her mother saw her hanging off the pump handle, her feet off the ground, as she tried to fill the water bucket. She helped her mother in all things—fetching water, wrapping big blue stem with wiigoob to make brooms and whisks. The thing she really wanted was to accompany her mother on the trapline, and this from even before she could walk properly. Mary bundled her in furs and placed her in the toboggan along with the snares and mink bait and set off for the string of lean-tos and temporary shelters along their trapping grounds.

Mary never had to worry that Eta would struggle out of her wrappings or cry with impatience or trample the clean trails where she set the snares for rabbit and fox. Eta stayed in the toboggan, and as long as she could see above the tumble of tools and furs and watch Mary's hands at work, she was happy. Even when she was teething, all her mother had to do, upon finding a rabbit in a snare, was cut off the lower leg and hand it to Eta for her to chew on—the flesh was so tough and cold, so laced with tendons that the rubbery texture soothed Eta's gums and she did not cry and sat quietly and observed Mary's broad back in front of the heavily loaded toboggan. As soon as she could walk, Eta followed behind the toboggan. Sometimes Mary pulled out of sight because Eta was still a small child and could not keep up, but all she had to do was follow the marks left by the toboggan and she would catch up eventually. By the time she was six years old she was setting all the rabbit snares herself. They never ate so many rabbits as when Eta set her snares. She secured them at just the right height and was so adept at matching the color of the snare to its surroundings that even a creature as suspicious as a rabbit could not see it.

Mary said nothing about why she thought Eta was such a good trapper, but she suspected it was a result of her contact with the she-wolf, a benefit of the wolf's milk. By the time Eta was twelve years old (and the point at which our story starts), she had taken over all the trapping. Mary could stay in the village and found much relief in her daughter's abilities; Mary was getting old and trapping had become difficult.

For Eta trapping was as easy as breathing. She loaded the sled herself and, sometimes with a team of dogs pulling the sled, sometimes pulling it herself, set off for weeks at a time. When she came back the sled would always be full of fur—beaver, mink, martin, fisher, weasel, bobcat, lynx—and loaded with meat too because sometimes she did some hunting on the side. Aantti was so pleased he gave her his puukko, the only possession that remained with him that he had taken from Finland. It had been his father's and the curved steel blade was perfect for skinning. Eta kept it sharp and made sure it never rusted. Who could hope for a better child? Skilled, earnest, respectful, concerned only for her parents and the animals she trapped. Her parents' only worry was about her beauty. She was so beautiful she caused everyone near her to shudder with longing, to stand up straight, to talk loudly in voices meant for her to hear. Some of them bragged about what they'd caught in their traps. But this only made her ignore them all the more. Eta loved the animals she trapped and took care to put their carcasses where the dogs would not ravage them. She brushed their fur before she sold them, conscious always of the life the animals were bestowing on her family. To brag about killing them was beneath her contempt. So, for the time being, Aantti and Mary put their worries aside. Eta seemed to be safe from the dangers of desire.

3. Bimaadiz had one other interest other than hunting and that was Eta. As for the beautiful girl, Bimaadiz was as precious to her as the animals she trapped. From an early age Bimaadiz's hunting and Eta's trapping had brought them together since his hunting grounds and her trapline overlapped. Bimaadiz, drawing out the first syllable of her name, would say "Eh-taa"—and shyly, in response, she would elongate the second syllable of his name, saying Bi-maaa-diz"—and so they had a special of addressing each other and took the greatest pleasure in each other's company.

Bimaadiz would tell Eta where he had seen some rich fox runs and so, on his advice, Eta would hang her snares there to catch them. For her part, upon seeing moose tracks around an isolated slough, she would inform Bimaadiz and, sure enough, a few days later he would have killed a fat cow and a tender calf, enough to feed to the whole village for a week. They were such good friends that he would save the tongue for her and her parents. And having caught a fawn in one her snares, she tanned the hide and sewed it into a bandolier bag for Bimaadiz to keep his shells and food in. When she was sick, he would check her traps for her, and she would kill some game for him when he had other chores to do around Agencytown and could not get out into the woods.

But they were children after all, and so their activities weren't always so serious. As a joke she made a doll out of marsh grass (having no cornhusks at that season to make a proper doll). She used the guard hairs from a fisher for the doll's braids, and the broken trigger from a steel trap was used to represent his gun. All in all it was a good likeness of Bimaadiz. Seeing some deer tracks she set the doll on the trail where she knew Bimaadiz would find it. Bimaadiz also made trinkets for his friend—toy snares only big enough for mice and hoops made from willow twigs for stretching them. This continued—their ideal friendship, their ideal life, until the spirits conspired to make things more difficult for the two.

Dr Apelles looks back down at the manuscript.

The bell will sound at any moment now. His translation has lodged itself deep in his consciousness. It, and another significant question, continue to plague him. But now, it is no accident, his thoughts turn to the library—not this one, not the archive—in which he works.

It is universally acknowledged that—in addition to the history of Charlemagne and of the printing press and also in addition to narratives told to us by a friend detailing the dreams of other friends of his whom we do not know—the description of a person's typical day at work is among the most boring kind of story in existence. However, since Dr Apelles' vacation in the country of his imagination, governed in part by the itinerary of the manuscript, which, it must be said, is also impossibly linked to his daily work, we must follow him to work and hear out the story of his days.

The bell will ring soon.

It should be said that the archive to which he goes every other Friday is, strictly speaking, not a library, and neither is the building in which he works the other nine days out of the fortnight. Those days, the nine days (not counting holidays and weekends) out of fourteen that form the architecture of his life if not the action (though this will change), are spent at RECAP, which, as we have said, is a library but also is not a library. Since, if it isn't apparent yet, RECAP is a place where books are captured, tagged, and then withheld from—not released into—the general population of other books; where, to put it another way, books are forced into a system designed to keep track of how they are forgotten; that is, designed to give structure and meaning to ignorance and anonymity; to create a special place for books that haven't been read or if they have, not often enough; all of this is to say that, contrary to what we have come to expect from stories such as this—the forgotten or unknown or undervalued or obsolete significance of Dr Apelles' works and days—the dusty corners of his life, if his life were a house (and if it were we would expect to find it represented by, signified by, a single dusty houseplant, an umbrella, or a shoe tree at best, and an empty flower pot, a persistent water ring on the floor, and a broken bit of string, at worst), is where we should begin looking at the no longer dreary dream of Dr Apelles' days.

He had long been settled in apartment 33J. Long enough to have begun to feel as though he owned the place. He was well thought of in the neighborhood of the other apartments. Having lived there for so long, he possessed a remarkable amount of information about his neighbors: their ages and ailments, the progressive ages of their children, their various and varied occupations and so on. Most of all, he was quite good at remembering names. And so, when in conversation with his neighbors they always felt, given Dr Apelles' polite and thoroughly informed interest, that his portraits of them, of their public and semi-public virtues, were such accurate and pleasing likenesses that he was, as far as they were concerned, the perfect neighbor. In short, he flattered them, but not intentionally.

Not forgetting for a moment that it is Dr Apelles' working life we are here interested in exploring, we will, in any event, step into his apartment. First, because his domestic life is the anchor point for his working life and informs his work in ways that, since he is almost a third of the way done with the translation, will become important soon, and, second, as he thinks, his thoughts turn to the very shape of his own life, his own self-portrait as it were, and that portrait, while primarily colored from the palette of his working time, is also shaded and filled in by the tints of his time at home. So the picture of his life could be seen as part craft and part found art—the kind of art that includes cups, teaspoons, cedar hangers, and most of all, his bed—which cannot go unmentioned in relation to a man who has so recently discovered that he has never been in love. For instance, just as Dr Apelles' job at RECAP requires an artistically exact bureaucratic technique, and also, since his translations of Native American texts require him to be more faithful to the language he is translating than to the moment of its expression (and this is the principal difference between translating Native American languages and translating all others; more care is usually given to the fragile vessel than to its contents), structure more important than style, form more precious than content, rules more actual than the behaviors either allowed or prohibited, we should therefore not be surprised that the organization and sensibilities that govern Dr Apelles' domestic life are quite well thought out. What is surprising, but shouldn't be, is that for a single man to have one queen-sized bed, two cups and saucers, two mugs, two plates, two knives and forks and spoons, two towels, two washcloths, and so on begs the question of who the user of each of the doubles will be. The surprise should be that it took a translation to make Dr Apelles realize he had never been in love when his domestic prerogatives suggest a man who desperately wants to be in love; a man, in fact, who is ready for it.

Ready or not, aware of his own habits or not, Dr Apelles had, as usual, woken up at six-thirty in his queen-sized bed and sighed. He sighed and straightened his legs and slid his hands under his head, but did not leave his bed quite yet. This was his usual ceremony. He sighed for two reasons—because it felt good to wake up and to gaze at the approaching day from atop such a comfortable mattress and because he always sighed upon waking—and since he was the kind of man who appreciated the ceremony of his own habits it would have been odd not to sigh. As usual, he kicked off the blankets and looked down at his toes and noticed that his brown skin was its usual smooth, hairless self, and that it was getting harder to see over his stomach. Not that Dr Apelles was fat or would ever be fat. His stomach was not round or rounded. Rather, as valleys are, over the years, filled in with dead organic matter and so lose their depth, so too did his torso; his ribs were less pronounced, his hip bones were barely noticeable, his stomach as soft-looking as a baby's. "And so time does pass after all," he said to himself. After which he got up, put on the coffee, filled a mug halfway with milk, and abandoned the kitchen for the bathroom where he showered (hair body face) and put his robe on and strode back out into the kitchen to catch the coffee gurgling its way to completion. He filled his mug the rest of the way up with coffee, added one level teaspoon of sugar, and stood by the window and drank it down. When he finished he went back to the bedroom and opened the wardrobe in which hung eight shirts, four pairs of slacks, four pairs of chinos, four sweaters, and four vests. Folded in a drawer below were eight pairs of socks, eight pairs of underwear, and eight handkerchiefs. On the shoe rack below this were four pairs of shoes—two black and one brown and one pair of once-white sneakers. This inventory should not lead us to believe that Dr Apelles is either quaint or neurotic. He simply made sure he always had what he would need for one week plus one day extra. That way, if there was some interruption in his schedule—a doctor's appointment, a holiday—he would not be caught short, and this proves he was not neurotic after all since what it shows is good sense, not sense gone bad. After he dressed he went back to the kitchen and made toast and packed his briefcase while the bread was browning. It popped up. He buttered it and chose a spread from an assortment of different jams and jellies, applied that, ate the toast, wiped his mouth, swept the crumbs off the table into his cupped hand, carried them to the trash can, put the plate in the sink, and left his apartment.

It is important to know all of this. It truly is, for reasons that are not at all obvious yet. It is important to know this because it demonstrates the qualities of Dr Apelles' mind—it is a "speech moment" in which the structure of thought is revealed. Dr Apelles has created a very well-regulated order to his life because, by doing so, the inevitable and pleasurable deviations from that order are thereby revealed and can be seen more clearly and enjoyed more thoroughly. This way, a surprise stain on his shirt or toast that is a little too thick and must be evacuated from the toaster with a butter knife become not exactly exciting moments but unique expressions of life—not at all unlike the surprises that language holds hidden in the palms of its rules. So, it matters little that on this day, a Friday and an archive day, he wears a white shirt with brown and yellow pinstripes or that his coffee mug is green or that he likes seven-grain bread. Also, the importance of the order of Dr Apelles' day will become clear when certain things happen to him later on.

To jump back in time a little, when he opened the manuscript so important to this story and realized that he had found a truly unique document and that he had never been in love, the second realization was not as transparent as the first. "Ah love! That's what's been missing from my life!" was not what Dr Apelles thought or said. He was not capable of saying such a thing, much less thinking it, any more than after spending a week in Paris a traveler can read Proust in the original. Rather, he realized that if he were to die that instant, if a great piece of plaster fell from the painted ceiling of the archive, he would die without being known at all, even by those with whom he was acquainted. If he died then and there (by the release of poison gas in the archive's ventilation system), no one would understand his shirts and his four slacks, the importance of his toaster or the wonderful comfort of his bed; no one would hear or understand, much less cherish, his singular and heretofore solitary morning sigh. If he were to die (a heart attack was not out of the question), he would die as languages do: with no one left in this world to speak him. These were the thoughts that occupied him when he found the document and caused him to labor so much over the translation and why he was still tentative about the ending.

The bell sounded.

He packed away his things, put the manuscript back in its file, and handed it to Ms Fabian, the reading-room librarian.

"Did you find everything you needed? I trust the translations are going smoothly," she asked, sweetly. These people seem to have so much trust, but in what, even they could not possibly say.

"Yes, Ms Fabian. Yes, I think I found everything I could possibly have hoped for," responded Dr Apelles.

"So I assume, since you seem so pleased, that everything was to your satisfaction?" Ms Fabian removed her glasses as she said this.

"Satisfaction. Yes, well, I suppose I was satisfied, though I think I am well beyond 'satisfaction' as you call it. I am somewhat afraid I have made a discovery," confessed Dr Apelles.

"But," protested Ms Fabian, "discovery is, as you must surely agree, what brings scholars such as yourself here, within the walls of the archive."

"Of course, of course,"—exclaimed he hastily—"that is one reason to come here, but it is a false reason, or, to put it another way, it only seems as though we come here to make discoveries when we don't come here for that purpose at all."

"Now really, Dr Apelles," interjected she, "knowledge, you must admit, is the reason these archives exist. You simply must come here for knowledge, my poor Doctor, it's certainly not for the air, which is bad. It's not healthy, it can't be!"

"No, no, no," said Dr Apelles, rocking back on his heels and heaving his shoulders with mirth, "I do not come here for the air. But, my dear Ms Fabian, knowledge is not to be found here. It can't be. Knowledge is never found, of course, it is created."

"I submit," said she, "it is created, of course, how could it be otherwise? But, dear sir, out of what is it created?"

"That is what I do not know. That is the problem after all. But, in the end, it is my problem, so I bid you good night."

"And to you as well," she returned cheerfully, "and I look forward to seeing you in two weeks' time."

He, bowing slightly, turned and made his way, to his locker

where he recovered his coat, scarf, and briefcase, and, after passing through the security gate, made a half turn through the revolving door and stood for a moment on the granite steps of the archive, and, to his surprise, he sighed as he usually did in the morning when he woke up in his very comfortable bed. It wasn't a sad sigh or one filled with resignation. It would be, if we were pressed to do it, hard to classify—but if we were to hazard a guess or a simile, we could say that the sigh was like a full stop in the run-on sentence of his life or like a page break inserted before a new

Eventually, after a short conversation with Mr Blackwood, one of the security guards at the door, he moved on down the steps and onto the sidewalk, leaving the neoclassical façade of the archives behind him. The sidewalks and avenues were, as usual at the hour, crowded with foot traffic and motor traffic respectively. It was winter, though temperate for the depth of the season, with enough of a chill to hasten the city's workers homeward, but with, nonetheless, a crisp bite too that made many, Dr Apelles among them, think of autumn apples, the frost of windowpanes, and a matter of leaves on a forest trail. It was his habit to walk the ten blocks from the archive to his apartment—a constitutional from institution to institution—and as he strolled, more slowly than the other people around him, he once again began mulling over the translation.

This was, as we have mentioned, a Friday at the archives, and as such, it was a twice-monthly exception to his usual routine, though it was, by its sanctified regularity, both routine and regular. Dr Apelles, lost in thought, quickly reached the restaurant where he usually took his evening meal, and after a cursory glance inside, he decided, once again, not to eat there. He continued on to the end of the block where he crossed the avenue and walked toward his own domicile on the smaller side street. It is here, at the intersection of the avenue and the side street that the two programs, the two very different schedules—research at the archives and work at RECAP—are reconciled. Let us examine. If, instead of going to the archive, if instead of it being the third Friday of the third month of the year, it is a workday, say, a Tuesday, Dr Apelles would have arrived at this street corner down from the opposite direction; that is, he would have arrived at the same point, from the other way and at a slightly later time. A workday began and ended exactly the same way as an archive day. Dr Apelles woke, sighed, got up, made coffee, showered, toweled, drank his coffee by the window, ate his toast, got dressed, and packed his briefcase, and left—all of this comprised the gate through which he passed from the confines of his solitude into the activity of his day. On a workday he reached the corner and instead of turning left toward the archive he turned right. There was a slight rise—the remnants of a hill, a natural feature that the city had not been able to completely obliterate—that added some variety to his stroll and provided him with a little more exercise. And in addition to this geographical feature, barely perceptible, the origins of his neighborhood, the historical remnants of its birth as the mercantile district, were also present. As a port city all kinds of goods were unloaded there, from pigs to pig iron and Dr Apelles' neighborhood had been the center of trade for manufactured goods for many a year. Barrels and window sashes and all kinds of other wood products had been sold there. Linen and broadcloth, rope and tack, and more exquisite material as well—liquor, tobacco, china, umbrellas, footstools, pens, paper, and books. These things no longer arrived by ship, of course, and their consumption and sale was spread out through the city entire. Nonetheless, some shops remained from this era—a cigar store, a shop that specialized in fountain pens, three small hardware stores, numerous small groceries, boutiques, really, in which one could find Greek, French, and English specialties. From the corner at which Dr Apelles turned it was ten blocks to the train station, the same distance, more or less, as it was to the archives, and it was, all told, a pleasant walk. Though in the eleven years Dr Apelles had been walking it, the amount of traffic had increased so much that exhaust and noise would have been, for a man less skilled at staying in his own mind, distracting. Once at the train station it was only a matter of flashing his very modern commuter pass in front of the sensor that activated the turnstile, and he was granted access to the platform, and then, with an efficient amount of screeching and wheezing, the train arrived, Dr Apelles boarded, and he was quickly whisked out of the city and into the country. The tag-lined tunnel soon gave way to the backsides of soot-stained buildings, the tracks rose and the train crossed the river, and the gray gave way to tan, and then to green—the fields crowded the highways, trees crowding the lanes, and sub-divisions crowding the hills like Norman towns—and the city was far far behind. Dr Apelles was now in the country. A fine country it was—though like many American landscapes it was good for walking no longer, cut and transected by rail lines, roads, fenced car parks, freeways, and the like. All said, it did not excite Dr Apelles' curiosity in the least and morewith—RECAP itself, a short walk from the train station, did not encourage, and in fact, demanded the suppression of curiosity. RECAP was situated, to fine advantage, in an old compound originally given to nuclear research during the 1950s and '60s and comprised a sprawling collection of small brick cottages connected by gravel paths all fronted by quiet plantings of boxwood and shaded by sycamores and beech, all leading or existing in relation to the central research and storage laboratory that had been torn down and replaced with the RECAP building—a fortress of a place.

In many ways the library resembled a prison, and in many ways, it was. RECAP stood for Research Collections and Preservation (Consortium) and it was a prison for books. Like a prison, RECAP was the response to many a social predicament. The most basic and disgusting fact that gave rise to RECAP was that there was a surplus of books in the world—more than the people needed and certainly more than they read. Thousands and thousands of books were written every year and added to those written the years before, and these books must be multiplied by all the different languages in the world. The result? The number of books, prints, maps, catalogs, pamphlets, indexes, compendiums, leaflets, fliers, and so on is difficult to imagine and even more difficult to contain. Six of the usual kind of library—the kind created to facilitate the meeting between books and people—could no longer hold all the texts in their collections. And the terrible question became this: what to do with the books one likes or that one recognizes as important or as potentially important but for which one has no use or that has not been read and never will be read? They can't be destroyed because the nagging question is this: what if this or that text will be important, indeed, invaluable, someday? So, wrestling with these questions, the six greatest university and public libraries in the world convened and, together, cabalistically one might be tempted to say, they dreamt up RECAP. It would hold the books until some future researcher needed them, until time itself swung around and made the books relevant again, or for the first time. RECAP was, therefore, like a prison for memories that a person had not yet had, or, if already experienced, weren't sure they'd ever need again—however, unlike human memories, the ones contained in RECAP were organized by a system of perfect recall. In theory, any text could be found and recalled at a moment's notice. The location of everything was known, but recall was only a theory because of the millions of texts already stored in RECAP, of the hundreds of millions of sentences, of the billions of words, not one had ever been read since they passed through the gates, and so far—in the fifteen years since RECAP's inception—not one had been released back out into the world. It was a heavy sentence. Only an artist, a madman, or a scientist could have imagined and created such a perfect system for organizing and storing the unknown and unbeloved so lovingly. Obsolescence had never before been given so much care and attention.

Having disembarked from the train and wound his way past the cottages and the sycamores and the beech and boxwood, Dr Apelles approached the fortress. The whole structure was, interestingly, designed to look like a giant, rectangular cardboard box, a banker's file box. The building was three hundred meters wide and six hundred meters long, and though one could not tell from the outside, it was divided into three discrete sections—the Operations Center, the Sorting Area, and the Stacks. There were only two entrances, one on the end of the long side of the box designed for people, and another halfway down the middle of the opposite side—a bay large enough for three semi-trailer trucks to idle side by side. This entrance was for books. There were no exits as such, although, again, theoretically, both books and people were allowed to leave. Dr Apelles waved his pass in front of the sensor mounted to the right of the human door. He heard the lock click, and he swung the door open and stepped into the entryway. Once inside he nodded to the two guards, a Mr Florsheim and a Mr Bass, and took off his jacket and placed it, along with his briefcase, on the X-ray machine where they were scanned to make sure they did not contain—in addition to the usual contraband such as box cutters, scissors, explosives, or acid—any printed material such as books, magazines, or newspapers. The Designer had realized that workers shouldn't be allowed to introduce any of their own reading materials into RECAP through the human entrance. It wouldn't exactly hurt to lose a book into RECAP, to have a surplus book or two mixed in—the only one who could possibly object would be the owner of the lost item—but to do so would violate the principle of RECAP as a sacred location where every book had its place.

Once Dr Apelles was cleared into the building he stowed his jacket and briefcase in his locker outside the break room, or Reading Room, as it was officially known. The Reading Room, like every other space in RECAP, had an overseer, a person whose job it was to make sure that no books were unofficially introduced into the building or illegally removed from it. The Reading Room was governed by Mrs Millefeuille. She sat at a desk, open at the bottom and sides so that nothing could be hidden inside or underneath it, and monitored the workers who came to the Reading Room to eat and relax during their two fifteen-minute breaks and their half-hour lunch break. The Designer recognized that it would be cruel to simultaneously surround the workers with books and not allow them to read. So, in addition to monitoring the workers, Mrs Millefeuille was responsible for stocking the Reading Room with newspapers. Every morning, before the rest of the workers arrived, she secured the newspapers on wooden dowels and removed the advertising inserts and coupons, she then counted all the pages in all the newspapers and wrote the number on a ledger open on her desk. During the day, when the workers came in to eat and to read the papers she wrote down who read which paper, and at the end of each break—at 10:45, after the lunch break at 1:00, and again at 3:30—she recounted all the papers and submitted them to the used-paper department situated in the rearmost office that vetted every sheet of paper used in the offices during the day to make sure they were indeed useless scraps and not pages or fragments of books, and these were recycled. Who can say if they ended up being paper on which was printed a book that ended up back in RECAP? It was rumored that Mrs Millefeuille had developed very specialized hearing—akin to the truffle-smelling ability of specially trained pigs—that could detect the faintest sound of ripping paper.

There were three sets of offices past Mrs Millefeuille's Reading Room, and the activities that took place in each were not terribly interesting, but suffice it to say that they were organized along hierarchical principles. First was the Operations Center where the computers were kept that tracked the books that came into RECAP—how many arrived each day, where they were from, and for whom they would be stored. The O.C. also, with the aid of powerful computers, monitored the movements of the workers, created the proper balance of heat and humidity—the place must always remain at 64 degrees Fahrenheit with 54 percent humidity in order to ensure the books would never decay—and ran the security system comprised of motion detectors, video monitors, X-ray machines, and such. The next office was, again, a mixture of man and machine—and here the staff dealt with the six libraries that belonged to the consortium and coordinated with them so that the flow of books into RECAP was steady and regular. If twenty shipments of books arrived on one day and one shipment the next, mayhem would undoubtedly ensue. Also, and of equal importance, this office coordinated the schedules, sick leave, payroll, retirement programs, hiring and firing of the personnel. So, in short and in brief, this office dealt with both human and paper traffic. The last office, and the only one with a view (a terrible view of a green lawn, a short hedge of burning bush, and beyond that the backside of a shopping mall), housed the director of RECAP, one Ms Manger. She had an important role, of course. She was in charge. It was inspiring for her to see the trucks sidle past her window on their way to the bays loaded with books ready to be eaten by RECAP. She was a delightful woman, really. Since Ms Manger was in charge she had access to all the data in the O.C. and could view all the cameras located in the S.A. and monitor the atmosphere and activity in the Stacks.

Dr Apelles did not enter any of these offices. Though he did muse, as he closed his locker and strode down the hall toward the entrance to the Sorting Area, that Ms Manger was, if not fond of him, then at least unusually aware of his presence, if only because, as a trained bibliographer and a librarian, she had seen and snacked on two of his translations that had appeared in small journals. One was a translation of a Mesquakie "Thunderbeing" story, the other a treatise on the relation between song and vocables in Ojibway as evidenced in Schoolcraft's transcription of "Chant to the Fire-fly." Ms Manger was a translator, too (of sixteenth-century French chansons), and since she was terribly uncomfortable around most people most of the time, any possible connection with any of her workers was seized the way a hungry stranger at a stuffy reception grabs for a table cracker before dinner is announced. Another reason for her vicious timidity was that she suspected that the workers thought she only brought up things like translations or recipes submitted to local cooking contests because she was suspicious about print. Books were seductive, and if one of her workers was a writer, he or she could very possibly get into serious trouble being surrounded by all the books in RECAP. This was partly true insofar as she kept track of both print and her workers' relationship with printed material, but she was also genuinely interested in her workers and really did like translations and cooking contests.

She was aware, therefore, that Dr Apelles had his PhD in linguistics and philology—and this made her interested in him since he was only a floor worker, a cataloger of books along with the others, none of whom held advanced degrees. Ms Manger was the first person he met at RECAP when he arrived for his interview. She had met him in the Reading Room. He was nervous. He had held various teaching positions and research posts as a graduate student and as a post-doc, but he had never liked the work. People made him feel jittery and insecure. RECAP looked like a perfect place—a place of books but with very few people to go with them.

He had stood nervously, eyeing the newspapers while Mrs Mille-feuille eyed him. After a few minutes Ms Manger had breezed in and shook his hand.

"Dr Apelles?" She seemed nervous, too.

"Yes."

"It would be a great asset for us if you were to work here. It would lend a certain prestige to RECAP to have a PhD on the floor." She was all business, but she had a thin, sunny air about her.

He was hired after his tour of the facility and another short meeting in her office. But how quickly our first impressions give way to new impressions! After he signed his contract, then and there, something changed. There was a deeper glint in Ms Manger's eye.

"I hope you stay with us for a long time," she said, a little breathlessly.

"I hope so, too."

"I must say, I looked at your curriculum vitae and have acquired some of your translations for RECAP. They are most impressive."

"Modest, Ms Manger. Modest. They are really nothing."

This gave her the opening she needed.

"More than that! And you are more than that, too, I suspect." And the way she said it made him feel as though she had been, in some way, if only by reading his work, stalking him.

That was eight years ago and still she seemed to have some secret agenda, some secret surplus of feeling that did not set Dr Apelles at ease.

A final word about Ms Manger: in order to imagine her completely and without a excess of thought or description; imagine a teenage girl in 1952 in thick cat's-eye glasses, a yellow pleated pina-fore, and a pink blouse waving excitedly from shore at a tanned white-toothed college boy piloting his sailboat out of the resort harbor in the company of a much prettier blond girl, completely oblivious to Ms Manger's adieu and even of her entire existence—and you will have a portrait of Ms Manger's personality and position even though she was raised in Lawrence, Kansas, and had never been on a boat and we are in the year 2002.

Anyway, as we said, Dr Apelles did not see her this day. He turned left and flashed his pass again, this time to enter the Sorting Area where he did his actual work. The Sorting Area (S.A.) was vast, three hundred meters squared, and was divided into three sections. The books arrived in the semi-trailer trucks and were unloaded in the Receiving Area (R.A.). RECAP usually received 6 truckloads a day, and the total number of volumes ranged from between 300,000 and 750,000, depending on the size of the books. These books were unloaded by the modern equivalent of longshoremen onto metal carts. Once a load, or a fraction of a load, of books was moved onto a cart, the workers scanned the cart with hand-held scanners that transmitted information simultaneously to the O.C. and to the S.A. Once scanned, the carts were physically moved into a long queue that officially separated the R.A. from the S.A. The S.A. consisted of eleven stations, each station manned by one sorter, who took the books from the cart in front of their station, one by one. By now Dr Apelles had donned an apron (blue) and latex gloves (cream-colored—just like the ones he wore at the archive), scanned his pass into the computer at his workstation and was ready to begin his actual work. He removed all the books from the top rack of the cart and, one by one, he turned each book face-front, back-front, spine-side and page-side, top-edge, and bottom-edge and then held the volume by its cover and fanned it to make sure the book was fit to be stored in RECAP. Torn, mildewed, or otherwise damaged books were not allowed. If such books were discovered by the sorters, they, along with the entire lot, were sent back to their home library to be rebound or disinfected. He then took each book and laid it on the corner of his workstation countertop where an x/y axis ruler was inlaid on the surface. Once the book was sized he affixed a barcode sticker inside the cover and put another one on the spine, and then placed the book into the appropriately sized black, acid-free, pasteboard box. Once the box was full, he stuck the master label that designated the lot, the collection, and the home library from which the books had come on the upper left-hand corner of the box. The whole box was then loaded on an empty cart on the other side of his station. Each of these carts was filled only with boxes headed to the same area of the Stacks, otherwise it would mean a lot of trouble for the shelvers and could result in confusion or misplacement. Dr Apelles usually did this all day long. He did not take fifteen-minute breaks or break for lunch because he saved up his break time, so after nine days of work he had earned the nine hours he used to take off every other Friday to work on translations in the archives.

The workers on either side of his station, at stations number six and eight, were, like the others, more "typical" workers. That is, they enjoyed their breaks and lived them till the last possible moment. These two, Jesus Knoepfler—a big, jolly Puerto Rican fellow—and Campaspe Bello, either Greek or Italian or both, judging from her name, were very typical workers indeed, which is not to say that they weren't intelligent or interesting or unique. Rather, they watched the clock and talked to each other over and past Dr Apelles' station and mimed fatigue and annoyance and indulged in silent laughter with their heads thrown back, which then sunk back down toward their workstations as their shoulders lifted and jerked, carrying the weight—not of the world because that is Atlas' job after all—of their mock mirth, which can be a heavy weight because as workers in that kind of repetitive and relatively unrewarding mode of employ, life can feel quite heavy. They were friends and they were friendly. And to the casual observer it might even seem as though they flirted and were perhaps involved with each other, if not for a certain sensitivity on Campaspe's part to Dr Apelles' presence.

This sensitivity had been present since she was first hired five years after Apelles began working at RECAP. Apelles had been working at his station, dutifully doing his work. And though he knew that there would soon be a new worker at the station to his right, he hadn't paid much attention to when that might occur. Suddenly, he heard Ms Manger's voice. Since she always made him a little nervous, put him a little on edge, he had looked up, only to better gauge whether or not she would be interacting with him, and saw Campaspe.

She was very beautiful, rosy and golden. And very young, at least half his age. As Ms Manger went over her duties, Campaspe nodded eagerly and smiled at the conclusion of each instruction, which made her seem all the younger. And then Ms Manger introduced Apelles.

"Everything you need to know you can learn from him," she had said cheerfully.

"I doubt that," he said wryly. He couldn't think of anything he knew that would be of any use to anyone else.

"Oh no! It's true! He is amazingly good at his job." As always, there was something hungry and brittle behind her praise.

"Then I am in the perfect spot. I like to learn," said Campaspe. And there was something sexual behind what she said. Or so it seemed to Apelles.

They each strode around their respective stations and shook hands, and that was the only time they had touched.

And Apelles stopped, at that moment, thinking about her. Not because she wasn't attractive—she was beautiful. And not because she wasn't nice—she absolutely was. Rather, he stopped thinking about her because she was beautiful and nice and in being so, not worth thinking about because she would never, ever, want anything from him except work advice and dull daily conversation. Or so he thought. He didn't even allow himself to think about her while he masturbated even though his mind's eye usually wandered far and wide during those moments. Because in order to fantasize about her he needed to feel, even just a little bit, that she was attainable. And he couldn't imagine that she would ever be. All in all, their first meeting didn't leave much of an impression at all.

As for Campaspe, she didn't talk to him beyond saying "Hello" in the morning and "Good-bye" in the afternoon and not, we can be certain, because she wasn't talkative; rather, she took her cues from Dr Apelles, who did not say much to anyone and who, it must be said, seemed, to his coworkers at least, the kind of quiet, hardworking fellow who was sustained in private, always in private, by some obsessive and unique mania for model trains, or stamps, or the history of arctic exploration, or medieval fortress towns of the Loire—none of which, in fact, he was interested in. Dr Apelles' life had grown so quiet and his translations had grown so loud as to effectively drown out any human noise around him. And yet in the silence that followed the thunder peal of this last translation, he began to hear those around him again.

But his coworkers did not know this nor did they yet notice the change. And so, no one, including the pretty Campaspe Bello, talked to Dr Apelles this morning. But she was, now, tuned to him. Today, for example, when he dropped a book and bent down to retrieve it, she had looked in his direction, that is, to her left, until he reappeared, at which time she looked instantly away. Later, when he passed her to check on or double-check on a cart and its number, her eyes followed him. Without really looking at him or engaging him, she kept track of where he was and what he was doing, and, in general, as much as she joked with Jesus, her thoughts were directed at the nearer target of Dr Apelles. She often wondered what lay inside, what his life was like, and, if truth be told, she had, recently, even gone so far as to Google him, but the results had been either in a foreign language or in reference to an obscure journal, dedicated to mosaics and military campaigns that seemed too improbably distant from the Dr Apelles she knew to be worth a second click. But her searches, and there had been three searches, confirmed for her the fact that he had an existence outside of RECAP, a fact which had served to sharpen her curiosity that had never traveled much farther than her own workstation. It is not strange to wonder about the habits and feelings of solitary and silent men. What *is* strange is that, for his part, Dr Apelles had never noticed that *she* noticed him, that she watched him, because almost all men, no matter their age, are usually keen to be noticed, especially by women as fine as Campaspe. She was a short girl, a few inches over five feet tall, and perhaps twenty-four years old. She had curly hair, beautiful, rich, chestnut and bronze curls, a deep olive complexion that in the summer months turned a fine rosy brown color. She had plump wrists and soft arms and very thick, full lips. And it was not hard to imagine her on a pebbly beach somewhere in the Mediterranean, bringing her father (who was a fisherman) his lunch as he smoked his short pipe and mended his nets under the bright sun. She looked very innocent, but also capable of a great deal of passion. And that was, as can be expected, exactly how Jesus imagined her when alone with his thoughts. If Campaspe had looked his way with the same meaning with which she loaded her glances at Dr Apelles, Jesus would have been a happy man. The farthest he had gotten with her was a Mexican restaurant near the train station for after-work margaritas, with paper umbrellas standing in the drinks and four other coworkers standing in the way of his asking her out on a date. But then, well, enough . . .

Dr Apelles finished loading a box and he double-checked the bar code on the books with the master code on the outside of the box. When he looked up and reached for another batch of books, he saw that Campaspe was looking at him. And something stirred inside him. Something, almost imperceptibly, shifted. He was surprised to note or remember, for the very first time in the three years that she had worked next to him, that she was very attractive.

Dr Apelles, though alone for quite some time, had only recently begun to feel lonely, and he had nurtured certain expedients of a carnal nature that he, also on a regular schedule, availed himself of. We shouldn't judge him, of course—at least he wasn't out breaking hearts. On the every other Friday that he did not go to the archives, as he walked homeward from the train station he stopped at a little storefront above which a blinking, more like winking, neon sign advertised "Mai's Massage." After stopping, and without any kind of guilty look around whatsoever, he entered through the green door, and coursed quietly past the silver cloud of the jangling bell. So regular a fellow was he—he always arrived at the same time, and always on the same day—that he was considered, by those who worked there, a regular. He always saw the same girl. Or, it should be noted that he always saw the same girl *for a while,* since the masseuses couldn't be expected to work in such a place for as long as Dr Apelles had been going there. He passed the front desk and spoke quickly, politely, and pleasantly with the woman at the counter and proceeded to the back, where gratification in the form of a faux massage, coupled with faux pleasure on the part of the masseuse, amid plastic potted palms, would take place. Everyone likes happy endings in both stories and life, and Dr Apelles achieved his every two weeks with girls who were usually Thai and whose name was always "Mai"—and it should not be supposed that Dr Apelles had a fetish of any sort, rather, he had studied the Thai language and it felt more respectful to address his right-hand girl in her own language. And, by being able to communicate more fully, though in such transactions language is blessedly unnecessary, Dr Apelles was able to satisfy both his desire and his conscience because he could learn the girl's circumstances. It was important for him to know that while the work might be less than agreeable to the masseuse, at least his pleasure would not occur at her expense. Apelles was a good customer and was good at *being* a customer, but that hadn't always been the case.

When he first decided to go into Mai's Massage after walking past the place day after day after day—he had paced back and forth in front of the door, and from one end of the block to the other for the better part of an hour—he opened the door, and with a deep breath, stepped inside to the jingling of the bell that seemed sinister and telling (as though its purpose was to notify the angels in heaven that he was about to sin), and then he had no idea what to say or what to do. He was in a place governed by rules and bound by traditions that he did not know. It was only after a few weeks of practice that he became fluent in this kind of pleasure. We mention this aspect of Dr Apelles' life not to titillate or tease the reader, and we mention it with no small amount of apprehension given the typically high moral standards of the reading public. But suffice it to say that the novel of Dr Apelles' life is half English with its parsonages and demesnes and afternoon teas and abstention and self-abnegation, and half French, containing brothels and betrayals and the seductive scent of cattleyas.

Moving on from Campaspe and the sorting stations, the coded and tagged and boxed books on their new carts were lined up behind the sorting stations and taken on forklifts into the Stacks. First, they passed through a pair of large doors into a kind of pressure chamber that separated the S.A. from the Stacks. This chamber prevented excess moisture, heat, or cold from entering into or escaping from the Stacks themselves, which were truly a marvel of engineering and preservation. The Stacks occupied twice the space taken up by the O.C. and the S.A. combined, and to put it in imaginable terms, the Stacks were twice the size of a football field. If the O.C. represented the manor house and the S.A. the immediate gardens, then the Stacks were the rest of a vast preserve. There were two hundred rows of shelves, each fifty meters long and twenty meters high and, all told, the shelves were the final resting place for all the books that entered RECAP. Each cart that entered the Stacks was lined up at the end of the appropriate row and queued there, ready to be assimilated. Men would then push the carts onto the waiting tines of another, very specialized forklift, and they would be lifted up up up into the ethosphere and the boxes unloaded onto the appropriate shelf, the bar codes on the boxes referenced against a bar code affixed to the shelf, and then after all these steps were taken and checked and rechecked the books were finally at peace, given rest, and would, most likely, never move or see human eyes again. The truly ironic aspect of all this was that it was vitally important that the location of each and every box was known, and that with the stroke of a computer key it could be found, but the boxes would never be found, in the sense that no one wanted to discover them, which is why they were in RECAP in the first place. So, in brief, the books—like all the people who wrote them and all the people who read them and all the people who translated them or even all the people who bought them—were known and yet unknown. It is so easy to get lost. And, to the librarians, and for Ms Manger in particular since she is in charge, the nagging, terrifying thought is that if a box of books were moved over one meter on its shelf or moved one shelf down, it could very possibly be lost forever.

Dr Apelles and the other sorters had their own specialized fear very different than that of the administration for whom the shelves and the books—all the words—were an abstraction; for the administrators the books were a jumble of texts whose subject was unknown but for which they had to find a logical place. They would never see the books themselves and, on the other end of the process, the shelvers didn't deal with books, they dealt with boxes, and all they had to do was guide the boxes to their final resting place and that's all. The sorters, on the other hand, had a very different relationship with the books and so they had a different kind of fear. They actually touched with their hands each and every text and looked at each and every text and by doing so they became, if only in a limited way and for a limited time, acquainted with the books, acquainted with the texts' personalities or potential personalities. They saw and felt the covers, the spines, and the edges (deckled or plain, machine or hand-cut). They smelled like the books. They were covered with the dust of the books, their stations were littered with paper fragments that were shaken loose during their work, and by the end of the day their stations looked more like an empty, confetti-strewn parade ground than a librarian's table. And the sorters' fear was this: each book was unique, and they would only see each book once, and they would never know what was inside. Each glance was passing, past, and the contents would remain forever unknown. Book after book passed by them, text after text, all day long. And each time what if? What if they opened just one, what if they read, just a little? But they couldn't, but they didn't.

At the end of the day Dr Apelles repeated his morning movements in reverse. He walked away from his station after logging out, waved his pass at the sensor and entered the O.C., collected his jacket and briefcase, walked past the Reading Room, waved his pass at the sensor by the front door, walked to the station, boarded the train, and was whisked back into the city—now dark—where he walked toward the intersection of the avenue and smaller side street. And, as always, the storefronts were the same as before, all the signs, and the buildings, and the sidewalk—all the great city in which he lived. One day older but eternal, passing before him, to the side, and behind—unrealized and unread.

However, since it was a Friday and not a massage Friday, he, as we have mentioned previously, turned right off the main avenue and, shortly, arrived at his apartment building. He entered. The doorman greeted him and Dr Apelles greeted him back. He walked up the three stairs to his mailbox and switched his briefcase to his left hand and withdrew the key to his mailbox from his pocket with his right hand, and though he was unable to quell the desire for a letter, all he saw, and in truth all that he could expect to see was a medium-sized envelope containing an obscure academic journal dedicated to Algonquian linguistics. This he tucked under his arm and in a few more minutes, after his elevator ride, he was in his apartment. Since he did not eat in the restaurant as was his habit, he made himself a grilled cheese sandwich for dinner. He drank a beer with his meal. These are solitary and frightening hours.

Later that night, with the city below him, pressed between the pages of his evening and his morning, Dr Apelles had a dream. He was in the library. And he was alone. And, as is common enough to be universal, our dreams of dissatisfaction and distress need the visual prompts—dripping faucets and endless corridors and the faces of people we know only casually attached to personalities of great importance—common to such dreams in order for us to acknowledge the uniqueness of our conscious predicament. Dr Apelles, then, had turned the covers down and crawled under them only to wake, in the same bed, under the same covers. He woke to find his bed in RECAP, at the exact spot usually occupied by his workstation. His coworkers, all of them, had crowded around the head-board, and they were urging him to wake up. He was befuddled, and not a little confused, to see Mr Florsheim and Mr Bass, Mrs Millefeuille, Ms Manger, Jesus, Campaspe, and all the others away from their usual stations, and to see himself surrounded by the carts and boxes of his daily work when he thought he was sleeping, and, moreover, confused and surprised to see, as he could in his dream, that it was undoubtedly nighttime because no light came in the clerestory windows and the loading bays were shut and locked. They shook him and called his name, and it seemed to him that Campaspe's hand lingered longer on him than the others, and she called his name a little more loudly and a little more longingly. Her hand felt cool on his chest, and it rose to rest on his cheek—her fingers silky soft and cool.

He stood and slipped on his slippers and proceeded through the S.A. alone, heading toward the atmosphere chamber and the Stacks. All was quiet. The faces and voices of his coworkers faded behind him. He heard nothing except the scuff of his leather-soled slippers on the cement floor. He pressed the red button that opened the first door. The door opened. He stepped into the at-mosphere chamber and the door closed behind him. And as soon as the door rumbled shut the chamber stretched and stretched until it disappeared at the vanishing point, and, with the process of elongation, the usual sounds of the vaporizer and the cooling/heating system were heard no longer. The corridor was silent ex-cept for the sound—sometimes far, sometimes near—of a drip-ping faucet. Dr Apelles began to walk.

The dream summarized itself. He was conscious of walking for hours accompanied by the sad sound of the dripping faucet though he did not walk for hours and the corridor was not endless. He ar-rived at the far door of the atmosphere chamber, pressed the but-ton, it opened, he stepped forward, the door closed. He was in the Stacks that, because this is a dream and because the Stacks actually seem this way in real life, *appeared* to stretch on forever. And since they were limitless but filled, completely filled, they held (and this was certain) every book that had ever been written. All books in all languages from all times—there was no end to them.

Dr Apelles stood in front of the Stacks—still in his pajamas and slippers—and realized with great horror that none of the books were boxed. Some were loose and leaned along the shelves, others were piled on top of one another, others still were stacked sideways and laid flat, and towers of them loitered on the floor between the shelves. There was no order to any of it, no way to know what book belonged where. Dr Apelles turned around, he was desperate to escape the Stacks, frantic to find his way out, but the door to the atmosphere chamber had disappeared—shelves and aisles stretched on forever behind him, too—the way he had come had disappeared, there was no trail. He turned back around but it was the same in all directions—there was no way out. At first Dr Apelles felt confused and hopeless. He knew that he had to do something, that there was some procedure that would free him from the Stacks—a place that had structure but no order, potentiality but no actuality. He had the sensation that time passed quickly, an eternity was unfolding, and he knew that it was up to him to organize the maze of books, to find their relationship, to put the books, in short, to put the languages, in relation to one another. And there was only one way in which he could to this. He must read them all in order to know where they belonged and find his way out.

He stepped forward into the Stacks. They towered over him on either side and by craning his neck he could make out the top shelves, half lost in the gloom of the upper atmosphere. The lower shelves were, as we have mentioned, piled with books—they leaned and stood and squatted and lay flat with no logic to their place or position. Dr Apelles looked closely as he passed and saw some books that were quite old, with tooled leather covers, and it was easy to imagine that, inside, the covers were secured with string and marbled paper and had tissue paper covering the frontispieces. Other books were quite new—bright-eyed covers made of card stock slicked with plastic film. There were books of all sizes—from miniature to folio, pamphlet to compendium. This truly was a librarian's nightmare.

Dr Apelles kept walking—something led him on. Or, rather, something kept him from stopping at any one place. He needed to find the right book—the one with which he could start the work. It was important to pick the right one. But there were so many from which to choose! He hesitated. His steps faltered. He stopped. He reached out and then his hand retreated, recoiled. He wasn't sure. Then he *was* sure and he reached out once more, but only to blend the edges of the spines, equaling them on the shelf. What a maddening dilemma! He must choose the right book, but he could not know if it was the right book without opening it, and by opening it he would make his choice! A more experienced man would know that this is not unlike choosing a lover.

On that particular shelf, the one at chest level, there were thirty or so books standing upright and a few laid flat on either end to hold up their brothers in the middle. Dr Apelles could see, past the top edge of the soldiered books, that there were more piled behind the front rank. These books, all of them, were a mix of old and new—some were ancient—they had been reproduced by hand in obsolete scripts, at least, judging by the cover, that is how they looked; others were old but not ancient, leather-bound but printed and put together by machine; others were new, pulp novels and comic books. And there was no clear choice, no book that, owing to age or condition or method of production, looked the most likely, the most crucial. Dr Apelles felt an overwhelming sense of urgency—he knew he must begin his work.

Suddenly, like a devil on his shoulder or (better) an angel at his elbow, Campaspe was in his dream.

"Open it," she said breathlessly. "Just open it."

"I don't know. I don't know which one."

"Just begin. You must begin," she said.

"I don't know."

"But you do. You *do* know. You have to chose."

His fingers played the spines, tapping and sounding, until he found an innocent-looking leather-bound volume from what looked to be the early nineteenth century though he couldn't be sure unless he opened it. For better or worse it seemed like a good place to start—he could always move in either direction in time. He took it in his hands, blew the dust off the top edge, and smoothed his hand across the cover. He held the edge upward and, sure enough, the pages had been cut open and he was pleased to be reminded that there was once a time you had to read with a knife. Time was passing quickly, the sound of dripping water was much more insistent. Dr Apelles took a deep breath, bit off thirty or forty pages of the story with his thumb, and opened the book in the middle of a scene.

Two women were running down a regally wooded hill, holding up their dress hems. It was raining, and the girls laughed as they gathered speed. Suddenly the action jumped off the page, sprang fully formed from it, and leaked out into the archive. To emphasize this abnormality, a peal of thunder rattled the bookshelves, and it began to rain all around Dr Apelles. Another clap of thunder sounded, and a gust of wind raced down the corridor. The rest of the books stirred. The pages in Dr Apelles' hands shuddered and slid past his fingers and he beheld, in front of him, a young man with longish hair, sideburns, a waistcoat, and a white-ruffled shirt leaning on a mantelpiece as he spoke and blushed. Then he was gone and Dr Apelles saw green hills and broad-crowned oaks, and then a manor house, a girl in bed with a terrible sickness.

A storm lashed the windowpanes. It continued to rain around him and the wind howled through the Stacks as a coach and four strived through the storm. Dr Apelles thought that it might be wise to turn the book to a calmer section, but before he could, the wind struck again, the books stirred, jittered, and began to flip open. They tumbled from the shelves, and when each book was opened a new scene sprang to life. A boy visited his great-aunt, where she lay in a large bed next to a yellow dresser on which stood her medicines, and the boy bent down to kiss her cheek. Then Dr Apelles saw a family, and they looked remarkably like his own—men, women, and two children gathered around an empty grave into which they threw bits of cloth. Then, to his horror, he saw an Indian toppling from a granite cliff, and mixed in with that scene, a man and a boy lying flat on top of a large boulder surrounded by red-coated soldiers. All the stories contained there, once opened by that first gust, began pouring out their contents into the Stacks, and each released its own action and place and weather. He saw a baby being eaten by witches and a man innocently buying a bar of lemon soap and another man straightening a beautiful woman's corsage while the carriage they were in humped along the cobblestones. To his left was a man throwing cabbages over a stone wall and to his right a bearded professor played table tennis in his basement with a pair of twins. Above Dr Apelles reared mountain ranges in the process of being lifted into the sky like a theatre backdrop, and below him he could see a submarine nosing its way through the depths. He saw a young couple in tunics tending their flocks that quickly disappeared and was replaced with a terrible battle in a large swamp where the thatched dwellings of the inhabitants were burning. As each book opened, its action came to life and the chaos surrounding Dr Apelles increased. There was terrible wind, and snow, and rain; the ground was rocky one instant and oceanic the next and then smooth turfed—more and more images crowded the space and it became dizzying. And most terrifying was that each scene, while independent and discrete from the ones occurring around it, looked to be conscious of its neighbors, as though dancing a kind of gavotte; each scene waltzed through the archives complete unto itself yet somehow, by some hidden logic that Dr Apelles did not grasp, moving in concert with every other scene. The characters and images roared and rumbled and swirled around. Dr Apelles was frightened and he cowered in the delicious din that surrounded him. He thought, through his terror, that he had chosen incorrectly. But perhaps he hadn't. Perhaps the results would have been the same no matter which book he had opened first. It was all the same. And what was important was that he had opened a book at all—each and every one singular, unique, and special.

In any event, the tempest shook the Stacks, image crowded image and threatened to overwhelm Dr Apelles.

So numerous and so varied were the scenes that orbited the Stacks that he thought he could almost see his own life, or better, moments snatched from it and hurled in the dark to stick there amidst the growing constellations the way they said a giant flung the stars to sit in the sky. His father, maybe it was, maybe it was only someone like him, walking ahead of him down a trail through deep woods filled with snow. And there, to the left, inside an Indian round dance hall, a girl across the way. Didn't he know her, or was she only a type, the kind of girl that resembled a singular girl from the past? She cried behind a rain-smeared window, and waved, waved, waved. Good-bye.

Another image came winging by. He was in high school. Their basketball team had gone to the next reservation to play. He was surprised to remember that, for a while, he had played basketball. They had lost the game. Most of the team was back on the bus, but Apelles had been slow to change and had walked more slowly still so that he was one of the last players out of the gym.

The sensations are as sharp now as they were then. He can feel the early spring wind cold on his skin where the sweat was still drying. The sidewalk leading from the gym had the texture of sandpaper. Up ahead the yellow school bus idled under the sodium light of the parking lot. He heard a voice.

"Hey. Hey you."

He turned to see one of the cheerleaders from the other team running to catch him before boarding the bus.

"Sorry," she said breathlessly, with a look that was both intense and shy. "Sorry you lost."

"Really? Yeah, well, it happens." Apelles had no idea what to say.

"You were really good out there."

"Me? Not good enough."

"No, really." She leaned forward.

Everyone on the bus was watching them.

"Thanks."

"You were. You were beautiful out there." And with that she spun, clutched her backpack to her chest, and ran back to the gym.

"I was?" he said in wonder.

And when he was finally seated on the bus and the bus itself loped around the corner of the parking lot and grunted its way up the hill out of town his teammates wouldn't leave him alone. Beautiful, beautiful, beautiful, they chanted. They launched into rhapsodies about her breasts and chided Apelles for not "getting some."

Through it all he sat aloof and pleased, battered in equal measure by the taunts and the frostheaves in the road. He had no regrets, the moment was perfect as it was. There was a pleasing roundness to it—the game, the exchange of words, the ride out of town, her plump legs kicking up her pleats as she ran away. In and of itself the event meant little in the years that followed. He had experienced many more meaningful things before and after that transparent and frankly, banal experience: many more things both good and bad. But now, surrounded as he is with the images and scenes in his dream, he thinks that, after all this time, she might be right after all. Beautiful.

Scene followed scene and image followed image. Was that the landscape of his childhood home? Or was it only a copy of the landscapes one finds in books? Dr Apelles couldn't say . . . What he could see and sense, however, was that each episode had its own tone and style—and thus, a different reality. The dream and everything leading up to it felt dusty and starched, English, the scenes of his early affair with the girl at the round dance hall had something French, something simple-hearted about it, while his boyhood had the hard cast of Hemingway. Mixed in with these images were scenes he did not recognize in styles he did not recognize and in the middle of it all was Campaspe. He blinked and he saw and even felt that they were having sex. She was on top of him. They were in his apartment. And she was radiant, gorgeous and flush with pleasure. In the background he could hear the hiss of ice and sleet hitting the panes of his apartment windows.

He did not want to lose this image, and he tried to hold onto it. He could not. He had no control over the text, texture, or images through which he was being pushed. It seemed to be very important that he find a way to control those styles. But the images moved too fast. Dr Apelles tried to keep track of the scenes but could not. He did notice, however, the absence in his dream of what had happened after he got home that evening and before he had gone to bed; when, after he ate his frugal meal, he pushed the white plate, freckled with crumbs away from him and put the beer bottle in the recycling container below the sink. He was full, and yet, unsatisfied. He sat back down. Usually he would read an article or two from his stack of journals—noting key points or new approaches, or faulty or fanciful logic, but he could not bring himself to do so that evening. The distance between the simple pine dining table and his blue, velvet-covered easy chair next to which stood a neat stack of journals was both insurmountable and too close. His apartment felt smaller than usual. So fixed, so familiar as to have become, suddenly, sterile. He stood and resolutely made his way to the easy chair, and out of force of habit he sat down and opened the topmost journal—the *Journal of Algonquian Linguistics*. His fingers drummed on the deplushed arms. He stood and walked back to the sink and washed his dishes, dried them, and placed them facedown on a dishtowel spread over the narrow countertop. He then walked back into the living room, and since it was unchanged from before, he moved closer and closer to the window. He stood in front of it and looked down at the streets below and the windows opposite—some dark and others lit from within. How was the man in *Bovary* described? As though standing outside looking in at a family sitting down to dinner. Yes, that was it. The strange thing was that when he thought about that line from Flaubert, he saw Campaspe, the girl from work. He could not shake the vision of her—her smile and her brown curls, and her white sweater. To think about a woman that way after not thinking about women except for his Mais was unexpected, and to find pleasure in the thought was even more surprising. This feeling, this terrible pleasure crept over him, covered him so completely that when he opened his eyes again he was shocked to not see Campaspe there, to realize that she was as distant as ever. There existed in this sensation the echo of his wet dreams of the past—the bizarre mixture of pleasure and absence. Shocked to realize that Campaspe was not there, he felt again that every window was remote—a potential galaxy spinning and leaping through the long winter night. Dr Apelles said something out loud, to whom it is hard to say, and what it was he said, very, very hard to hear, and it is even harder to tell if those words made their way past the glass or not.

~ Book II ~

1. It was early fall. Bimaadiz was sixteen and Eta was twelve. The weather was warm during the day, sunny and bright, but every night brought with it a crisp frost. All the land was active: a good crop of rice bent the stalks low over the water, wild plums and grapes and cranberries were heavy on the branches. The lakes were turning over and the thick-fleshed trout were coming close to the surface to spawn and were practically jumping in the people's nets. The deer and moose were nearing the rut and so were easier to hunt. The beaver were busy building their lodges and with each passing day their coats were getting thicker. Most of the mosquitoes had been killed off by the frost and so it was a pleasure to be in the woods once again.

As there was no trapping or hunting to do during the summer Bimaadiz and Eta hadn't seen much of each other, and they were anxious to get back out into the woods. They were full of stories to share about what had happened while they had been apart. They disappeared into the bush together, grateful to be away from the village, grateful for the other's company. Perhaps the summer's interruption had dulled Eta's skills or perhaps her excitement got the best of her. For whatever reason she set a snare for brush wolves a little too high, made the loop a little too big, and neglected, perhaps, to put a thick enough jumpstick above the snare. Despite her best efforts, she managed to snare a large doe. Bimaadiz and Eta came up on the set and noticed right away the missing snare and the torn and trampled earth. The doe had been caught recently, and she had run off through the brush pulling the dragstick behind her. Bimaadiz was excited at the prospect of his first kill of the season. Instead of waiting for the animal to run itself out and lie down, Bimaadiz whooped and charged off after the deer.

The doe had been snared around the neck and the snare was attached to a stout log—heavy enough so a brush wolf could not run away with it. But a deer can go a long way dragging a balsam pole without getting tired. She was easy enough to track because her terrified leaps had driven her hooves deep into the soil, and the dragstick had smacked against saplings and trees, tearing away the bark. The thickets of hazelbrush were no impediment either; the brush was left broken and ragged. It was an easy trail to follow.

Bimaadiz followed after the deer, sometimes drawing near. But always the snared doe heard him coming and pulled farther ahead. In her exhaustion she stopped to rest occasionally, her ribs heaving, snot dripping from her nose. But as soon as she sensed Bimaadiz's dogged pursuit she was off again. When Bimaadiz reached the places where she had stopped, he saw the spatter of mucus on the leaves and the drift of her thick neckhairs sawn off by the thin metal snare and he felt at each pause that he must be getting closer. But a snared deer does not act like a deer that has been shot; a snared deer loses its strength more gradually. So, a chase he first figured would last no more than a half hour stretched on through the morning. The deer was always ahead and as soon as she heard Bimaadiz's footfall or saw the pointed peak of his red toque bobbing through the trees, she urged herself to run some more.

The day—which started out with a coat of frost—had grown warm. The sun was high in the sky, and its pale light washed the woods. The deer was bathed in sweat. Her fur was matted and her tongue was specked with froth and swollen with thirst and the snare had become embedded deep in her neck. Bimaadiz was hot, too. He was wet through his underclothes, and his wool jacket felt heavier and heavier with each passing moment. Neither the doe nor Bimaadiz stopped to drink.

It was no wonder, as the mad chase progressed, that the doe headed for low land, a great cedar swamp well beyond Bimaadiz's usual hunting grounds. And there, in that remote place, the doe cleared the trees, made two large bounds and lay down in the middle of a thicket of red willow and Labrador tea. Bimaadiz followed the deer's trail to the edge of the bog, and there he stopped. He knew the habits of deer well enough to know that she had hidden herself in the willows. He was faced with a choice; he could wait for her to move or he could go in after her. He was determined to come back with the doe. He had come too far and the animal had suffered too much for him to turn back. And even though he knew where she was and that she could see him from her hiding place, he did not have a shot.

But he could not wait until she moved. She would stay where she was until nightfall and then sneak away, or she might very well die there. Bimaadiz thought of Eta. She would be worried if she did not hear him shoot. And since no matter which direction the deer ran, she would have to run through the open, he had to get close enough to either shoot her where she lay or to flush her out and take a quick shot as she ran.

Bimaadiz held the Winchester at the ready—the hammer cocked—and began to walk out into the treacherous, floating bog. It was hard going—he had to be careful where he stepped lest he step off stable ground and into the slippery peaty soup. Little clumps of cattails and marsh grass rose out of the water and offered some places to step, and there were floating sections of bog that quaked and shook with each step. If he stood still for too long his feet gradually pushed their way through the growth and into the water below. But he couldn't afford to look down all the time—the deer might leap up and disappear before he was able to fire.

Bimaadiz was halfway between the trees and the center of the bog when the deer stood and tried to run. Bimaadiz stopped, raised the Winchester, fired once, and the doe fell down. Exultant, Bimaadiz hopped from hummock to hummock until he found the deer, his first of the season. She was thick with fat. He told himself that as a present he would give Eta the heart, tongue, and the loins—they would have a feast, just the two of them, to celebrate the first kill.

First he would have to get the doe out of the swamp. He could gut her there in the mud, but the bad water would leak into the meat and ruin it. And an ungutted deer, without the breath of life, is a heavy thing. There was nothing to do except loosen the snare around the doe's neck, stuff the front legs together through the expanded loop, and tighten it again. Once secured this way—so the animal's legs would not catch on the ground—he was ready to set off. He braced his feet against a hummock and pulled. The doe lurched forward. He found new footing on another low rise in the swamp and pulled again. Bit by bit, Bimaadiz brought the deer closer to the trees where he could gut it on dry ground. But he was tired—he hadn't anything to drink all morning and his legs shook. He stumbled, and then one foot went in the mud. He tried to push up with the other leg, but he broke through the solid earth, and that leg, too, became mired. With each subsequent effort he sank deeper.

He was calm at first. This was not his first experience with a floating bog. But his frustration was immense—how would he get out and bring the deer back to Eta? His legs were deep in the mud, and the swamp's grip was strong. The more he struggled the deeper he sank until the water reached his waist and crept over his rib cage.

He began to despair—for himself and for the deer, and he cursed himself. Why had he run after the deer like a child? Why hadn't he let the doe exhaust herself so that he could track her the next day when she was either too tired to run or even dead? Bimaadiz thought he might die in the swamp.

Suddenly he heard a voice.

"Bimaadiz! Bimaadiz, are you okay?" There was a shadow standing over him. It was Gitim—a youth two years older than he was. He normally trapped that area and, while scouting out beaver ponds, he happened upon the trampled trail. And then he heard the shot. He followed the sound and found Bimaadiz in the swamp.

"I have nothing to pull you out with," said Gitim. "No rope or cord, or wiigoob."

Although he didn't say so, he was afraid that he, too, might get stuck in the swamp. Gitim was so lazy and habitually averse to risk that he always managed to spend more energy trying to find the easy way to accomplish a thing rather than setting to work.

"Don't you have anything? Can't you use a stick?"

Bimaadiz and Gitim, while pondering Bimaadiz's situation, heard Eta shout from the edge of the swamp. She had also followed the trail, at a more leisurely pace, until she heard the shot, at which point she hurried along. Eta quickly wound her way out to the center of the swamp.

She wanted to laugh when she saw Bimaadiz buried up to his waist. But, filled with pity for her friend—stuck up to his chest in mud, his hair plastered with twigs and dirt—she did not laugh.

"Hold on," she said. "Hold still."

Thinking quickly, she untied the red wool sash that was wrapped around her thin waist. She braced her feet against a small willow bush and handed one end of the sash to Bimaadiz while she held the other.

"Push, Bimaadiz. Push!" she said. And she lifted just enough of his weight so he could kick his legs to the surface of the bog and clamber out.

Bimaadiz rested a moment and tried to wring the mud out of his clothes the best he could. Eta, meanwhile, began to work on getting the deer to dry land. She spied an abandoned beaver lodge not too far off and quickly made her way there and pried out a few long poles. These she carried back, and with Gitim's help, she used them to skid the body of the deer over to the beaver lodge. Bimaadiz was now rested and in a trice he had the deer gutted and quartered. They were happy that the doe and Bimaadiz had been successfully rescued, and so they made a gift of the deer to Gitim, who was only too pleased to have all the work done for him. So, weary but full of good humor, already laughing at the day's events, Bimaadiz and Eta walked back to one of her lean-tos so Bimaadiz could clean himself off.

This particular lean-to was one of Eta's favorites. A small stream tumbled over a short cliff just behind her shelter and watered a small flat area of firm ground. Habitual use had cleared the glen of brush and deadfall. Eta honored the beauty of the spot and kept it clean by taking all the carcasses, wood chips, bones, and trash far away. The waterfall never froze over—even in the coldest times. In the summer the glen was carpeted in moss, sweetfern, and maidenhair. Caribou lichen and cottonball sedge clung to the rock face of the cliff.

Bimaadiz was afraid of what his parents might think if they saw him come home with his clothes ruined and covered in mud, so he and Eta decided he should bathe in the waterfall next to Eta's lean-to while she rinsed and beat his clothes. Bimaadiz took off his fawnskin bandolier bag and emptied it out. Rifle, cartridges, knife, and pemmican he set on a bed of basswood leaves to dry out in the sun. With a handful of sweetfern he scoured the fawnskin until the spots turned white once more, and then he stuffed it with dead grass so it would dry more quickly. Then he undressed, piled his clothes to the side where Eta could reach them, and began to wash himself. The water was cold, but the clumps of mud and specks of peat were washed away. He held his head under the waterfall and rinsed out the peat that had dried in his hair. His hair was dark and thick and his skin looked all the darker as the water rolled off his shoulders, which were tinged with red from the cold water and from the vigorous rubbing he gave himself with sweetfern.

Eta hadn't thought much about Bimaadiz's body before. But when she reached for his clothes to begin washing them out, she looked up at him. He was beautiful. In her naïveté she thought that the water, somehow, must have made him so because he never looked that way before. Entranced, she told him that he still had mud on his back and offered to help him wash it off. The feel of his skin surprised her. It was so smooth and warm she might as well have been touching herself. Yet, unlike her body, his was hard. She noticed how close his muscles rested to the surface of his skin.

She didn't know what to think. No animal she had ever touched had felt like Bimaadiz: not the beaver with his thick layer of fat, or the fox with his silky pelt and bony body. They were beautiful, too, but touching them had not unnerved her. She was so distraught she grabbed his jacket and pants and retreated downstream to wash.

Bimaadiz finished his washing and though still wet, he put on his undergarments, which he had washed himself, and waded downstream to where Eta was scouring his pants and jacket with sand and sweetgrass.

"You saved me twice," he joked. "First from the swamp and now from my parents."

"You could have saved yourself," she said shyly.

Bimaadiz sat down next to Eta. He joked with her and soon they resumed their innocent banter. All the tension that Eta had felt upon seeing Bimaadiz naked vanished. By now it was late in the afternoon and Bimaadiz's clothes were still wet, so they decided to spend the night in Eta's little shelter and return to the village the next day. They had done this many times before. But something was different now. Something had been done that could not be undone.

When Bimaadiz crouched down in the lean-to to build the fire, Eta could not take her eyes off his hands as they shredded the birch bark and snapped small twigs for kindling. They had never looked so strong and sure and deft. The bones and tendons in his fingers seemed remarkably elegant underneath the smooth bark of his skin. And when he put his face down close to the flame, pursed his lips and blew, a flame leapt within Eta's breast as well and she wished her face was as close to his lips as the fire was and that she could feel his breath against her cheek.

Bimaadiz fell asleep on his side of the fire quickly—it had been a long, tiring day. But Eta could not catch sleep as quickly. She lay on her side and stared at Bimaadiz. Facing away from the fire, he was wrapped up in a beaverskin robe. Eta tried to see through the thick fur, tried to stare past it for another glimpse of Bimaadiz's naked body. Since she could not see or touch it, her hand wandered to her flat belly and, as a poor substitute, she stroked her own bellyskin, all the while wondering if hers was as soft as his.

2. Over the next few weeks Eta began to curse the stream next to the lean-to as much she used to praise it. It felt as though the water, for its part, had cursed her as well. She could think of nothing other than Bimaadiz, of his beautiful back and his smooth, smooth skin. Where she used to be even tempered and patient, as only trappers can be, she was now irritable with everyone she knew, including her parents. And forgetful! She left her snare wire in the village when she set off for the woods and stomped back along the trail to retrieve it only to forget rope and even her puukko. She was sometimes so lost in thought that she forgot where she placed her snares and had to walk up and down the trail looking for them. She was a girl used to life in the bush, raised alone without uncles, aunts, and cousins, all of whom could have given her a word for what she was feeling. Animals snared by the neck and struggling for breath acted with more sense than she did.

3. But Gitim—who was older, almost a man—knew all about the snares of desire. And he had been trapped by Eta's beauty and resourcefulness the day he had helped Bimaadiz and Eta in the swamp.

His family lived near Agencytown and had converted to Christianity. It was a large family—two parents, two brothers, and two sisters. His brothers had been sent away to boarding school, and his sisters both worked at a nearby farm. They all tried as best they could to make money, to support one another, all of them except for Gitim. He had worked at the mill, but it didn't last long. The foreman had found him sleeping on the roof when he was supposed to be filling the water barrels balanced on the peak. If there had been a fire they could tip the barrels and thereby save the roof, but not if they were empty. Gitim was fired. He worked for the Priest, but he fell asleep after splitting only a few cedar shakes. He did not come close to sheathing the drafty privy. When the village gathered to rice, Gitim never bothered to spread out the green rice and let it dry in the sun, nor would he don his moccasins and take his turn jigging. He would just wander back and forth, heft first one flour sack and then another, and estimate loudly how much he thought it would finish out at.

Finally, as a last resort, he had begun trapping for his father, and that work suited him. No one was there to watch him. No one could fire him. And if his catch was low, he could blame it on bad luck or bad medicine. His father had been a treaty signer, and so the family received larger annuities than most and had secured some of the best trapping grounds near Agencytown. They were not rich, but they would never starve. Whenever Gitim returned empty-handed he shrugged his shoulders and, speaking in the direction of his father's feet, he said he had bad luck, that the swamps were dry, that someone had used bad medicine on him.

After he helped Bimaadiz and Eta in the swamp, and without any work or activity to capture his energy, his fantasies of Eta occupied him completely. He began to visit Bimaadiz and Eta every chance he got, and every time he came singing his way down the trail he brought each of them a gift. He had fallen for Eta. He sang to himself as he loped along the trail to her trapping grounds. He sang,

> *Niwaabamig oo, ho ho*
> *Niwaabamig oo*
> *Ezhi-badakideg ho ho*
> *Inga-badakisidoon imaa*
> *Biindig obasadinaang ho ho*

But he had sense enough to change the words when he was within earshot of Eta's camp, and sang instead,

> *Imbagakaab igo ezhi-gimiwanzinok*
> *Gaawiin geyaabi nimbitaakoshkaagoosii*
> *Imbagakaab igo ezhi-gimiwanzinok*
> *Wii-mizhakwad, mizhakwad, ezhi-giizhigak*

Bimaadiz and Eta always welcomed their new friend and thought nothing of his frequent visits or of his gifts—a tin pail for her and a flute for him, made out of cedar instead of sumac. They were so innocent that they weren't suspicious when Gitim stopped bringing things for Bimaadiz and lavished all his gifts on Eta.

This went on for some time, but desire is not patient, no matter how lazy and prone to inactivity the host of such desire might be. By now it was late fall, winter was making its sly entrance—frosting the grass at night, skimming the edges of potholes and swamps with ice—and the three youths rested and played by a large fire next to Eta's lean-to. Two deer, twins judging from their size, ran into their camp not thirty feet away from the fire and stopped, confused by the smoke. Bimaadiz and Gitim scrambled for their guns. Both of them shot and the two deer fell over.

Here is an opportunity, thought Gitim. *Here is a chance to win some affection.*

"Let's have a contest," he announced. "There's little to do out here in the bush except either work or sleep, and if we don't spice things up our lives will be dull."

Neither Bimaadiz nor Eta felt the same way, but they were easy going and tried to humor their friend.

"Well, what should we do, then?" asked Bimaadiz.

Gitim proposed that he and Bimaadiz have a skinning contest. The prize was a kiss from Eta. Gitim was confident that he could beat Bimaadiz, who, after all, was little more than a child. As for Bimaadiz, he loved games of all sorts, and a skinning contest, regardless of the prize, sounded like fun. Eta was thrilled. She had no desire to kiss Gitim, but her lips longed to taste Bimaadiz, to taste what only her eyes had tasted. She had been looking for an excuse to touch him ever since he had bathed naked in her stream, and she was sure that he would win.

They laid the deer side by side. Each boy unencumbered himself of his bandolier bag and each grasped a knife. When Eta said *start,* they began.

Gitim had trouble immediately. In his haste he could not locate the seam in the pelvis.

"My deer is bigger and its bones are thicker, that's why you are ahead," he said, as always, making excuses.

"They look the same to me," said Bimaadiz without breaking his rhythm. Bimaadiz found the pelvis seam right away. Next,

Gitim slipped his knife past the belly muscle and took short, quick strokes up toward the breastbone, but Bimaadiz wiggled two fingers through the belly muscle and inserted his knife between them and with one stroke, using his fingers as guides, he split the deer from pelvis to brisket, and without stopping, he removed his fingers, grasped the knife with both hands, and split the rib cage wide open. So, while Gitim reached into the cave of the deer's ribs and searched blindly for the heart and lungs, Bimaadiz grasped the esophagus, stepped back, and ripped the bloody organs from the deer's body. So quickly did he do this that the guts and stomach followed, and he flung the entire mess into the bushes behind the deer. In a trice Bimaadiz then slit each leg, cut around the ankle, and using the exposed flap of fur, ripped the skin from the legs and halfway down. He turned the deer on its other side and repeated.

Gitim was forced to rush, and in doing so, he severed one of the backstraps and half the juicy loin came away attached to the hide.

Bimaadiz had the quarters and the loins hanging from a tree while Gitim was still working on the neck. The poor boy still had hopes. But in the end, Bimaadiz and Eta watched Gitim as he finished. He was both faster and had made no mistakes.

"The winner is Bimaadiz!" said Eta. She was overjoyed.

"He started earlier," complained Gitim. "His knife was longer. His deer was shot in the neck not in the heart."

But Bimaadiz was the winner, and Eta leaned over and kissed him on the mouth.

It was an inexperienced and childish kind of kiss—devoid of the art that comes only with the loss of innocence. But it was more than capable of setting a heart on fire. Gitim, jealous and disappointed, wandered off to check his traps. As for Bimaadiz, the kiss was startling. He felt as though he had been shot. His head spun and his vision darkened. He tried to control the pounding of his heart but could not. His expression was one of indignation, as though the kiss had hurt. He felt hot, then cold.

When his vision cleared he noticed for the first time how thick and smooth Eta's hair was, how full her lips. He was amazed at her strong, slender fingers, at her high cheeks and at how the dark birthmark on her cheek accentuated the symmetry of her face. It was as though he had been blind all his life and only now could see, and all he could see was Eta.

4. Now neither Bimaadiz nor Eta were able to concentrate on their tasks. It was early winter. Snow covered the ground, and there was a great need for meat in Agencytown. The sawyers had moved back into their winter camps. Fur prices were high but were sure to dip as the season progressed, and so Eta's mother told her that she'd better trap as much as she could. Moreover, it was time for winter chores—wood needed to be cut and split, ice needed to be sawn from the middle of the lake and brought back and stored in the icehouse, nestled in the sawdust, good smoking wood needed to be laid by to preserve the extra meat, and the meat racks themselves leaned and swayed, exhausted from the summer heat and rain and needed to be fixed if they were to keep the meat away from the dogs.

It was a busy time of year, but Bimaadiz and Eta got very little done. They ignored their responsibilities: they cut trees down and left them lying in the snow, they did not fix the meat platforms. The children were sullen and listless and all four parents were afraid Bimaadiz and Eta might be sick. There was always the threat of death from whooping cough or smallpox or tuberculosis, and their parents thought seriously of sending the children away to boarding school—at least there they could receive medical attention.

Whenever Bimaadiz and Eta had a chance they rushed out to the bush together—after telling their parents about a promising hunt or of a previously ignored beaver pond full of super blankets. But once they got clear of Agencytown, Bimaadiz rarely loaded the Winchester and Eta seldom mustered the energy to set traps. Instead, they lazed around camp and played games. Eta would heat up water in a pail, ostensibly to soak hides, and after making a fuss about how bad Bimaadiz smelled she got him to strip to the waist so she could wash away the stink. She bathed his head and torso just so she could feast on the sight of his smooth muscled body. She was filled on the sight of him but after a short time was hungry again. She got no relief. For his part, Bimaadiz watched Eta crimp birch bark with her teeth and would grab the bark away from her and place his teeth where hers had just been so anxious was he to kiss her lips. He did not know how to reach out for the real thing, and the bitter, chalky texture of the bark was a far cry from the slick liquid of her kiss.

They knew nothing and so suffered without satisfaction. All they did know was that a bath had hurt Eta and a kiss had wounded Bimaadiz.

5. Meanwhile, the fire of Gitim's desire for Eta had grown stronger, fueled by jealousy. He had been bested by a boy. He lay in a wool blanket in front of the cookstove in his family's cabin at Agencytown and turned and turned. And after his parents were sleeping soundly behind the blanket they had hung up across the corner in which they slept, he, by the dying warmth of the fire, reached down his trousers and made use of that dangerous supplement in order to find, as though he had somehow lost it down there, some satisfaction. This helped some, but only for a while. He imagined Eta's hand there, her strong smooth legs across his hips. Her face next to his. And so, he was quickly robbed of the pleasure of his own hand—and robbed by himself of all people! Because in this, as in all things, what others could do for him was always more attractive than what he could do for himself.

After a week he could no longer find any satisfaction down there on his own and he thought that now nothing would do but Eta herself. So he woke one morning, bathed with hot water and soap in the half barrel set behind the stove, oiled and parted his hair, and put on his father's trousers and beaded vest since his own clothes would not impress anyone. From the woodshed he took four prime beaver pelts, four traps, and a dozen of his family's best snares, dyed in oak leaves and waxed to hide their metallic scent and coiled so as to retain in a perfect loop. He also took a new saw blade and an axe that had yet to bite wood. All of these he stowed in a canvas pack.

He brought these goods to Aantti and Mary's cabin when he knew Eta would be away on her trapline.

Aantti and Mary received him warmly.

"If it isn't our nephew," said Aantti, using a family term to show his affection. They were friends with his parents, and in addition to natural affection they also recognized that Gitim's family was large and powerful. Already some members of Gitim's family had secured a number of important government jobs and more would likely follow.

Mary offered him some tea. Gitim sat down at the table with them and accepted their offer. He felt every bit like an adult.

"How do the timber sales look for the coming year?" inquired Gitim. "As for trapping, it is very slow."

"That happens sometimes," agreed Mary. "And sometimes there's little you can do."

"You must have spent a lot of time working on the cabin," said Gitim as he looked around the small house. "It's much tidier and more snug than last year."

"A little work here and there," agreed Aantti.

After more polite conversation about unrelated topics—it wouldn't have been seemly to rush right to the issue that wholly occupied his mind—he brought forth the canvas pack and withdrew its contents one by one: the prime pelts, the coiled snares, the bright axe, and the singing saw. He gifted them to Aantti and Mary.

"I know this isn't much," he said, though by the way his eyes traveled over the gifts it was clear they had cost him dear. "But your daughter is beautiful and industrious and already we are great friends. I often help her on the trapline. I would like to marry her," he said finally, his voice shaking. "And what's more, I'll bring fifty beaver, a dozen steel traps, and two moose, all in the year to come."

He was almost crying when he promised these items to Aantti and Mary, so moved was he by the depth of his own feelings.

Aantti and Mary were impressed—they were poor and never expected that whoever ended up marrying Eta would give them any gifts beyond a blanket or two or a single deer, most likely a small doe. And they certainly didn't expect an offer would come from the youngest member of such an important family. For many minutes they commented on how fine the gifts were that he had already given them—how sharp the axe, how smooth the run of the snares. But they held back and did not gift him in return with the life of their daughter. Even though they had raised Eta as their own, there still existed the chance that her real parents would someday come looking for her. And who knows? Her real parents could be important people, too. If that were the case, Aantti and Mary could be faulted for giving away something that was not theirs to begin with. To do something like that was beneath whiskey traders and bandits. And judging from how fine the cradleboard was in which they had found Eta, how exquisite the beadwork, how expensive the beads, she could very well be the daughter of a war chief. Nothing but trouble could come from offending a man like that. Finally, Aantti spoke.

"We could never have hoped for so many gifts for our very plain daughter, especially from someone like you—your family is important and will do many important things in the years to come. But Eta is all we have. We are poor in every way except for her. She is our sole possession. And, if you must know, she hasn't even bled yet, so I think you've come too early. Let's see what happens when she becomes a woman." All of this was a lie, but Gitim had no way of knowing.

Gitim left with as much grace as he could manage after thanking them for their time and for the expense of the tea, served with real sugar, which was quite a luxury. Even though he shut the door with a sweet taste in his mouth, it quickly turned sour as he walked back to his parents' cabin. He did not know what to do and was now in a terrible situation. He had robbed his own parents to gift

Aantti and Mary. If he had returned their gifts in the form of a wife who could cook, trap, sew, it would have been different. But he was returning with nothing! He had not imagined it possible that he would be refused. And as for Eta, he was nowhere nearer to possessing her than he had been before he had so wantonly spent his family's future.

He was in agony. As he walked along he built up heat and the sweetness that had so recently graced his mouth was transformed into the bitter taste of anger and he decided that he would take Eta by force.

By the time he reached his family's cabin he had formed a plan. In the woodshed hung a bearhide taken from a large sow the spring before. He would disguise himself as a bear and lie in wait for Eta near one of her lean-tos. He would rush at her and she would be so afraid that he could easily achieve his desire. And if she got pregnant, she would have no choice but to marry him. Even if she didn't, no one would want a girl who had been raped by an animal—something would have to be wrong with a girl like that. She would have to be marked as unclean by the spirits. Her parents would have to give her to him then.

He wasted no time. He took the bundled bearhide from its nail and slung it over his shoulder and set off for the bush. He found a good hiding spot near one of Eta's lean-tos and tied the front paws to his arms and the back paws to his feet and ran a cord around the head of the bear and under his own chin. The disguise was very good: when he crouched down he looked every bit like a bear. He found a thick patch of hazelbrush near the lean-to and lay there out of sight, ready to attack Eta as soon as she arrived.

He didn't have to wait long. Soon he could hear Eta coming down the trail singing as she came.

Imbiijidaabaanaa chi-amik oo'ow
eniginid o'ow aa
mechigizid eshkam o'ow
badagoshkawid o'owe

Sure enough, she had a large beaver sliding along behind her.

Eta drew close and Gitim got ready to spring out of the thicket and take what was, in his mind, already his. But Eta's dogs had already caught his scent, and when they heard him rustle in the bush they sensed danger and set up a terrible howling. Eta stopped in her tracks and said "Get him" and the dogs pounced into the thicket where Gitim lay. The dogs tore at the bearhide and at first Gitim lay still, thinking if he didn't move the dogs would realize their mistake and grow bored. Their teeth did little damage. The hide was so thick that it was hard for them, even for the biggest, to puncture it. But the dogs did not stop and his bear armor could only last so long. Soon it was shredded and Eta's dogs sunk their teeth into Gitim's legs and arms and tried to grip his back so they could flip him over and gouge out his belly. They were attacking him in earnest. Suddenly, his plan did not seem like such a good idea, and he was now in real danger. And then a new thought occurred to the luckless Gitim: what if Eta, who sometimes carried a rifle, got a clear shot and killed him?

Gitim realized his trick would not work and began shouting.

"Eta! Eta! Save me from your dogs. It's your friend! I'm your friend!"

He struggled to stand with the dogs hanging off him like overgrown woodticks.

Eta saw immediately that her dogs were attacking her friend, not a bear, and she whistled once and all the dogs let go and trotted to mill at her feet.

Bimaadiz, who had been hunting nearby, had heard the barking and had come running.

"Are you okay? Are you hurt?" Bimaadiz immediately felt sorry for Gitim. Both he and Eta helped Gitim gain his feet, and they cut off the tattered bearhide. He was scraped and torn. His calves and thighs were punctured and bloody. They had no idea what foolishness desire causes in people. Together they sat Gitim down in Eta's lean-to and cleaned his wounds with hot water.

"That was a good one," said Bimaadiz.

Eta agreed. "I really thought you were a bear, and you know what a nuisance they can be. Your disguise was good. I really thought you were a bear."

They tried to make a joke out of the adventure as they chewed slippery elm bark and pressed it into his wounds. They thought he was playing a woodsy joke on them by pretending to be a bear in order to frighten them. They had no idea that Gitim had had darker plans and that his bear disguise was not an innocent pastoral joke. They tried to get him to stay for a dinner of roasted pike, but Gitim was embarrassed and anxious to leave so they sent him on his way as they chuckled about how good a joke it was that he had played on them.

The adventure with Gitim and the bearskin had eaten up a large portion of the day, and so Bimaadiz and Eta were forced to skin the beaver Eta had caught late into the night. They skinned it by feel more than by sight because the fire was not bright enough to illuminate their work. For once they were tired enough to not feel the usual pangs of desire and to not try to steal glimpses or kisses. Bimaadiz decided to stay with Eta in her lean-to. They made for bed.

It was a cold night. The fire warmed them on one side while the cold burned them on the other. Neither one of them could be totally warm at any given moment so they turned frequently: now facing the flames now, now facing away. They did not fall asleep immediately. Each feigned regular breathing, and each thought the near presence of the other and the miracle of their breath the most beautiful sound they had ever heard—as magnificent and tender as the soughing of the white pine that towered over and protected them both.

6. So Bimaadiz and Eta continued hunting and trapping. After that period of listlessness both the children rededicated themselves to their work. It was a good winter for both and their families were rewarded by their efforts and received unforeseen benefits of the young people's desire. Bimaadiz and Eta worked harder than ever before in an effort to quiet their beating hearts and their trembling hands. But as the furs stacked up and the meat platforms groaned under the weight of hindquarter after hindquarter, Bimaadiz and Eta were increasingly weighted down with thoughts about each other, about what they had seen and had been unable to forget. Eta had seen Bimaadiz's naked body, and she could not forget it. Bimaadiz had received Eta's kiss, had felt her lips against his and he could not forget that. They both wanted more but they didn't know, exactly, more of what—they had no name for their desire. And then something terrible happened.

7. It was the month known as the Stingy Moon. The weather had turned bitterly cold and stayed that way. The ice thickened, in some places it was three feet thick, and it grumbled and sang, protesting its own immense weight. It fissured and broke, but with nowhere to go, all the ice could do was scream as its thick plates rubbed together. Water squirmed through the seams and froze immediately, only to break, freeze, and break again. The small spring by Eta's lean-to still ran free but only at a trickle. The river was skimmed over with ice at the rapids. The water level dropped and ice was left hanging from the rocks so that the rapids lost their voice and instead the rocks, with flat brims of ice stuck to them, took on the aspect of a group of men in hats. No animals moved in the woods. The beaver were not moving below the ice. As for the deer and moose, they were yarded up deep in the swamps and had abandoned their old haunts. The few deer that were taken by Bimaadiz were stringy and tough and not worth the effort it took to snowshoe their carcasses back to Agencytown. It hadn't snowed in weeks and the thin snow-cover was sullied by old tracks of every kind and littered with the frozen droppings of rabbits, porcupines, and deer, all of which were long gone. The forest felt like a cold, empty room filled with litter and desperately in need of a cleaning.

Humans, too, had abandoned their trails and were yarded up in their own villages. With nothing to do and confined to their cabins and lean-tos, which were looking grubbier and meaner by the day, a small band to the north of Agencytown decided to go raiding. There was nothing to hunt except humans, and since the snow was not deep and was firmly packed by the wind, they knew they could attack and retreat back to their own territory quickly. They disguised themselves in the garb of their intended victims by donning beaverskin caps and parkas trimmed with black felt and decorated with beaded grapevines and clusters of cranberries, and pointed moccasins. They lashed round snowshoes to their quick sleds and greased the runners with goose fat. They carried very little—nothing except their weapons and three cakes of pemmican each. They dressed and dragged their dogs by their traces to the sleds. With shouts and growls to match those of their dogs they tore out of their village at an unbelievable pace. They traveled in single file—twenty men on twenty sleds in all. They did not stop for rest as they moved south. The dogs had been primed on beaver meat and were anxious to run. With each mile the men grew more and more excited. They were free of their village and moving again, aware once more that they were human, and with this awareness their appetite for what was human increased. They had a taste for motion, for wind in their faces, for war.

They were happy to be on the war trail. They were so enthusiastic that instead of taking the time to circle around their enemies and attack from a different direction and in doing so obscure their identities, they took the most direct route and crossed the river just downstream of the rapids, that collection of silent boulders all still wearing their caps of ice. They took the river at great speed and skipped over the thin ice in their empty sleds without a one breaking through. At the river they had left their own territory and were now in the land of their enemies.

Once in foreign lands they abandoned reason and cunning that demanded they proceed with empty sleds to the farthest point of their raid and work their way back toward the river to preserve speed and surprise. They were too anxious for that, and, like wild dogs, they attacked whatever they saw and laid their hands on everything that fell into their path. They raided meat caches, stole snares hanging next to the trails, took bales of fur from shacks, and stole guns, bullets, axes, and kettles—anything of value.

They were met with little resistance—the people to the south of the river were not expecting war in the winter. Battle was a pleasure they usually saved for the summer months, when the excess of life, its fat, could be trimmed off. So they were unprepared and fled into the deep woods where the sleds could not go. Their enemies not only stole their belongings, which is only natural, but even went so far as to burn down their shacks, cabins, lean-tos, and wigwams, thereby exposing many people to the hardships of winter. One of the attackers could not limit himself to the usual plunder and thought it a great joke as well as a sound victory to load a woodstove and a washtub onto his sleigh and to then burn down the cabin from which he took them.

As luck would have it, Bimaadiz was hunting in an area directly in the marauding band's path. Hunting had been poor, but suddenly deer and moose were darting everywhere between the trees and he had killed seven deer that morning. The wind was such he did not smell the smoke that would have warned him, as it had warned the deer, of close danger. He was exhausted from all the skinning and butchering, his mind lost to Eta. He had used all his ammunition on the deer, and so when the enemy was upon him he was both distracted and unable to defend himself. There was little he could do. He tried to run, but one of his attackers casually drew his bow (all the while chatting with his comrades) and let the arrow fly. Alas, Bimaadiz could not outrun the shaft, and the arrow sank deep in Bimaadiz's thigh. He fell face first in the snow with a shout and could not move. He watched as his attacker stepped down off his sled and twirled his war club casually on its leather thong. The enemy warrior sauntered over to where Bimaadiz lay helpless. Bimaadiz watched him come and thought only of Eta: how he would never see her again, and he shouted out her name over and over again until his attacker could not stand the rattle of that sound in his ears any longer, and he hit Bimaadiz over the head.

Eta was unaware of what was happening. She had been in a remote section of her trapping grounds and had not heard the commotion. When she reached the area where Bimaadiz had been hunting she screamed and began to cry. She saw the tracks—human, dog, and the parallel lines of the sled runners—and the imprint Bimaadiz's body had left in the snow. His fawnskin bandolier bag lay there on the ground emptied of its contents, and the snow was stained with blood: a pool of it had melted into the snow from the wound in his leg, and the indentation his head had made was haloed with the splatter of blood, too.

Eta was panicked and began to shake—all she could think about was Bimaadiz's safety. She knew at least that he wasn't dead, not yet anyway. But she didn't know what to do, and she knew even if she was able to track and find the men who had wounded and captured Bimaadiz, she would be unable to defeat them. Without really thinking she took note of the tracks, their direction, the speed of those who had made them and, after snatching up Bimaadiz's fawnskin bag she set off after them—also in the direction of Gitim's trapping grounds. She hoped that their friend could help somehow.

Eta was moving fast and she forced herself to slow her pace—it was bitter cold and she was drawing too much air too quickly—she did not want to sear her lungs. And she was sweating heavily. If she stopped the cold air would turn her sweat to ice. As patiently as she could she followed the tracks. She looked for blood or hair and noted when the enemy stopped. They stopped often now, as they picked their way through Gitim's trapping grounds on their way back to the river. Their sleds were heavy with booty, and here and there, the tracks and disturbed snow attested to the fact that whatever they had lashed down had worked its way free, and they had been forced to stop and tie it back on.

Before long Eta left her trapping territory behind and was in Gitim's area. She crested the last hill before his trapping cabin and she was greeted with a horrible sight. Gitim's small cabin was on fire, and she saw two dark shapes sprawled in the snow between the blazing cabin and the small lake on which it was situated. Eta rushed down the hill, careless of her own safety. One of the bodies might be that of Bimaadiz and he might still be alive.

When she arrived in the yard, she could see immediately that the dead body, in clothes of her tribe, was that of a man she did not recognize. The other body was Gitim's. He was still alive.

He had been shot through the right lung and through the throat. She knelt next to him, but he could not turn his head.

"Oh Gitim! Oh my friend!"

He blinked up at the uniform gray sky and blinked again against the cold. Clumps of snow were caught in his hair, and his face was scratched and speckled with the blood that blew out of the wound in his throat. His breathing was shallow, a succession of small puffs, and as he exhaled small pink bubbles rose out of the hole in his chest, burst against his parka, and sank into the fabric. Eta looked around and saw a cone-shaped spray of blood and some scraps of tissue and bone behind him. He had fallen where he had been shot.

"What have they done? You've never hurt anyone in your life. You're not a warrior."

When he realized that the person next to him was Eta, a little spark of life animated his eyes. He tried to speak but there wasn't enough air passing through his throat to make enough sound for speech. Eta knelt down and took his hands and pressed them to his throat and wrapped her hands over his.

"Eta," he was able to say. "I tried to stop them."

He sounded helpless and small. Eta nodded.

"Where's Bimaadiz?" she asked.

"They have him. He is alive. They took my dogs."

He paused for breath, but could not store up enough air to continue.

Eta removed one of her hands from Gitim's neck and slid it under his parka and over the wound in his chest and pressed down. Gitim winced.

"They took my dogs," he said again, when he was able to continue. "But they only listen to my whistle."

Eta nodded again. Gitim's dogs, bought by his parents and trained by a Finn down in Crow Wing, were known to be the best in the area. They were fast, tireless, and, most importantly, well trained.

Gitim struggled to remove his hand out from under Eta's, and when he did it sounded as though he had released air from a bladder. Eta pressed down harder on his throat while Gitim reached in his bandolier bag and pulled out a bone whistle on a leather thong.

"Blow it three times and the dogs will come," he said.

The search for the whistle and his instructions robbed him of what energy he had left and his body shuddered. Gitim tried to swallow but couldn't.

Eta was crying, and her tears fell onto Gitim's body. "You'll be fine," she lied. "It's not so bad."

"Eta," he said at last. She had to lean in close to hear him. "Eta. I never won a kiss from you."

She blinked her tears away and shook her head in an attempt to dislodge them. She could not afford to move her hands. She turned her head and brushed her face on the frozen fur of her parka like a bird cleaning its face under its wing. She leaned closer to Gitim's face and kissed Gitim on his lips, thereby giving him the gift he had always wanted but never had a chance of winning. And then she lifted her hands and the air whooshed out of Gitim's body, and with it went his spirit. He was dead. Without wasting any time, she took the whistle and set off at a run down the trail, parallel to the lake, in pursuit of the marauders' tracks north.

8. Eta lagged far behind the enemy, but lucky for her, they had stopped to eat and look over their loot before crossing the river into their own territory. They were confident that no one had followed them, confident that they had attacked with complete surprise and would not have to worry about reprisals until spring. They were so confident in their victory that they stood on the riverbank and looked south at the land they had savaged and shouted boasts between mouthfuls of frozen pemmican. Once they were done boasting and eating, they mounted up again and began crossing the river in single file. By the time Eta could see the river between the trees, most of the sleds were on the ice and the first was almost all the way across.

They drove their teams, supplemented by Gitim's dogs, as fast as they could across the thin river ice, and they were weighted down with plunder. Eta wasted no time and raised the whistle to her lips and blew three short blasts.

Suddenly the enemy's swift retreat became a tumultuous snarl of motion. Gitim's dogs were large—the biggest and best trained—and they were fresh, not having run through the night and all that day. So even though they were far back in the traces when the whistle blew, they jumped and twisted and tried to turn back with great energy. There was little the drivers could do to control them and the sleds stopped. Some of the sleds spilled over as Gitim's dogs pulled them sideways, others jerked this way and that and could not move forward. The first sled in line, the one loaded with the woodstove and the washtub, was so heavy that when the sled stopped, the thin ice could not support it and it broke through. The river was deep in those parts, and with yips and yells, the driver, the team, and the sled, slid under the ice and disappeared.

The other sleds followed, cracking and splashing, and soon the river crossing was a crossing no longer, but an icy hole, choked with plates of ice. The dogs set up a terrible howl, and the men shouted and jumped off their sleds in order to keep them from going through but they themselves broke through the ice, floundered, and were carried under.

Bimaadiz was bundled into the rearmost sled, whose owner had, in his greed, hitched three of Gitim's dogs in front of his own team of three. When the dogs heard the whistle they wheeled and headed back the way they had come, and the driver was thrown off by the sudden change in direction.

Eta held her breath after she blew the whistle. When she saw the last sled in line come careening through the woods toward her with Bimaadiz's body in the cargo area, she could not believe that he had been spared. She looked past the sled to the river and saw some of the enemy splashing along the frame of ice, trying to pull themselves out. One man, the one thrown from the sled that carried Bimaadiz, was on his hands and knees and was trying to crawl across the ice away from Eta's side of the river.

As the sled with Gitim's dogs in front approached Eta, she stepped to the side of the trail and let the dogs pass and then expertly swung herself up on the rails. She shouted her commands, and the dogs lunged in their traces while taking Eta and Bimaadiz to the most remote part of her trapline. As for the enemies at the river, those who had not drowned were soaked through. The fools had burned every shelter within walking distance of their crossing point, and so they had no place to warm themselves. They were forced to walk toward their own village far to the north. The wind picked up, the temperature dropped, and their clothes iced fast. So did the men, down to the last. They all died before they reached home.

Eta knew nothing of her victory—she was concerned only with bringing Bimaadiz to safety. She drove the sled into the lean-to since the sled was as good a bed as any and with two quick passes of her puukko she severed the leads and dragged the whole excited team to a nearby tree and lashed them fast. She ran back to the lean-to and took her first good look at Bimaadiz. She ran her fingers through his hair and felt the large lump raised by the war club—a nasty bump and a gash was all, and after she got a fire going she peeled off Bimaadiz's bloody trousers. She cried when she saw the broken shaft of the arrow sticking out of his beautiful thigh. "Your leg! Look what they've done to your leg!" she cried. Her hands flew to her own thigh. She cared for him so much that she shared his pain equally.

Carefully, she cut the fletchings off the arrow.

"My Bimaadiz, you know this'll hurt. But be brave."

She pushed it out the back of his thigh and then pulled it all the way out. Bimaadiz shouted with pain. Eta was both mortified and overjoyed because as much as his pain hurt her, pain was life, and his cries meant he was going to live. She washed his wound with hot water and pressed arrowroot into the hole. Once the wound was bandaged, she fed him raw beaver liver and swamp tea to speed his healing.

Night fell. Bimaadiz was sound asleep and he did not toss or turn. Eta, however, could not sleep. Instead she sat next to the sled and fed the fire and in the firelight she watched Bimaadiz. She marveled at him and at her luck. For once she could gaze at him without shame and without having to hide her desire. She could stroke his hair without fear of his waking and could touch his legs and the smooth angles of his face. The enemy had given her the best gift she could have hoped for.

But suddenly, she realized that she was covered in Gitim's blood. It was on her arms and had caked under her fingernails, and worst of all, with no small amount of guilt, she realized that she had Gitim's blood on her face, on her lips no less! She had kissed him, and though it was understandable, she did not want Bimaadiz to know it. So in the night hours she stoked the fire, heated some more water, stripped to the waist, and began to bathe herself. In long strokes she washed her arms, her belly, and her breasts, wiping away the blood and sweat that coated her.

But at this point, as she bent over the kettle of water next to the fire, Bimaadiz opened his eyes. Unbeknownst to her, he could see everything. He saw the long strings of muscle along her spine, the wings of her shoulder blades, her flat stomach, and her small breasts—her body as supple and strong as that of an otter. He was surprised to learn that her breasts were tipped with small brown nipples, almost exactly like his. And the sight of her body was almost too much for him, an unexpected shock. And he felt as though he had been shot twice that day, once by the enemy's arrow and once by Eta's beauty.

9. The next day Eta hitched the team, and she and Bimaadiz arrived back in Agencytown safely. Eta handed Bimaadiz over to his parents, and she immediately drove the sled over to Gitim's parents and went out in the woods with them to bring his body back. After the funeral and after Bimaadiz had healed enough to move about the village, he and Eta went to visit Gitim's parents together. They sat with his heartbroken family and told them of Gitim's bravery. Bimaadiz told them of how, upon seeing him taken prisoner, Gitim had fired on the enemy without thinking of his own safety and even killed one of them before he died. Eta then told them what Gitim had done even when he was certain he was going to die: how he had provided the means for rescuing Bimaadiz and avenging his family. Many of the enemy had died in the river, all because of Gitim's whistle. Eta tried to give them the whistle back, as a memento, but they refused. Gitim's parents, with tears streaming down their cheeks, folded their hands over Eta's and asked her to keep the whistle, and the dogs, too. His parents said it was clear to them how much they had loved their lazy and difficult son. Bimaadiz and Eta cried, too, for their lost friend. They thought of Gitim as their brother and they told Gitim's parents that they should think of them as their children. They had lost one child but through his death they had gained two in his place.

10. After Bimaadiz healed and the Stingy Moon turned into the Moon of the Returning Eagles, everything returned to normal. Almost everything. Eta resumed trapping and Bimaadiz, not without some pain and a slight limp, began hunting again. But life was different now for Bimaadiz. He could not forget what he had seen. His breath came quick and his heart beat fast when he thought of Eta's body. Even though he had escaped life as a slave of the enemy, he had instead become a slave of desire.

The bell has just tinkled,

and like a shuffle of wings, the manuscripts and pages are closed in on themselves like birds settling to roost, and they are carried, sleeping, up to the desk and the waiting cart. Each creature is feathered in tough pins of different colored plastic—cerulean, red, orange, and green. Each cover hides the white and yellow down of the more intimate pages. Dr Apelles, near the end of his labors, uncringes his hand, leans back, and surveys the room.

For twenty years Dr Apelles has excited the quiet envy of his peers in the archive and of his fellow translators of Native American languages. He publishes four translations a year and can solve the most riddling questions regarding the origins and circumstances of anonymous texts. He is never influenced to translate anything based on the academic climate, can tell the difference between Algonquian dialects based on vocables alone, is never fooled by the colorful and meaningless reintroduction of "myths" into modern novels promoted by languageless folklorists and desperate novelists, and has so far avoided being tricked into compiling anything as public as a dictionary or as useless as a prescriptive grammar.

Among the other researchers, there is a kind of diligence, or an aspect of diligence, that more or less makes them all look the same. The advanced student over there who furiously catalogs the 500th footnote of his dissertation as he squirrels away yet another nut in his cache of nuts, all of which have been passed over by other researchers because the meat is tiny in comparison to the thickness of the shell, looks a lot like the amateur historian with his boxes of cards and his interest, which has long before shifted from passion to mania and for whom the larger theme or epoch or battle has been so thoroughly assimilated deep within his being that he now only remembers very tiny details and to whom clings the aroma of cigar smoke wafting as though from a past age. He could easily be confused with the aging academic monitoring the progress of trains that have all stopped at the station, picked up the French heroine, and have continued on and to which the schedules no longer correspond. They all hunch over their file boxes and scan these documents and note down on notecards or plain white paper whatever it is they've found or think they've found. They hunch, glance up, look back down, and continue their work in silence, and this diligence—it can't really be called productivity because they don't produce anything—is so uniformly persistent, unhurried and precise that they could easily be mistaken for one another. These people form the core group of people that comprise the only community Dr Apelles has left anymore.

After graduate school he had done his work at the university library in the city that held the papers of many missionaries and royal explorers. The library was a modern affair with glazed windows all along the south side and a courtyard in the middle where students drank coffee in preparation for another round of studying. But he quickly exhausted the texts in that library, and when no one went out to record or collect more, he sought out another haven. He found the archive and quickly saw that the amount of material there would provide him with a lifetime of work.

The archive occupied the old customs house of the city. Inside and out it was clad in white marble and was built in the neoclassical style popular in the early 1800s. The doors were guarded by two lions and flanked by columns that supported the portico. The hallway was impressive, spacious. The left side of the building housed the administrative offices and on the right was the reading room. In the back, where goods waiting to pass through customs used to linger, were the stacks, to which no one save archive personnel was admitted.

Once every two weeks Dr Apelles walked up the marble steps, went through the revolving doors, deposited his coat and briefcase in a locker, and entered the wood-paneled reading room, where, usually, a box was already waiting for him. He did not, as a rule, eat at the cafeteria or at the hot-dog cart drawn up on the sidewalk whose metal skin winkled in the sunlight. He worked steadily from opening till closing. Being more diligent than curious, he made steady progress through his material, and by the end of the day he usually had a tidy stack of paper to show for his efforts. The ease with which he greeted the texts, his fluency and nuanced approach, was the despair of the other researchers.

All the year long he dressed the same, in tan chinos and a blue button-down shirt and though a little chubby, he was never seen to sweat.

His voice was mellow and calm and all in all there was a pleasing roundness to him—from the way he finished his translations to his quiet and rich voice in which one always searched for an accent. Dr Apelles' life resembled calm, peaceful weather, but as with windless days, there is either a storm coming or one has just passed.

2

Like everyone, he had his own past, if nothing else. His father farmed their allotment in the summer and cut timber in the winter. He raised two cows for milk that he sold in the village and two pigs to butcher in the dark of the moon in October and again in April. His mother looked after the cabin, hauled water, harvested rice in the fall, and, when time permitted, set nets in the lake to supplement their diet of pork and venison. She had the habit of banging out her corncob pipe on her thigh, but she only smoked when she thought her husband wasn't looking.

Apelles was expected to help his father in the fields and woods and he did not disappoint him. His life, along with those of his brothers and sisters was well regulated and marked by the rhythm of hard work. Like many of the Indians in the area, they were poor, so poor it was as though they lived in a different age. They used horses instead of a tractor (unless they could borrow one) and, though Apelles grew up in the 1960s, they had no electricity or running water until just before he left for college.

Sometimes when the weather was fine and the work was done, they would hitch the draft horses to the wagon and set off for the far side of the lake. They crossed their own fields—always planted conservatively with alfalfa and oats, forty acres of each—and climbed the hill slowly and passed into the woods. Once his father had shot a bear at the wood's edge that had killed one of the pigs. The woods were filled with stands of maple, basswood, and ironwood. The silence was deep among the leaves, and the floor was clear of underbrush and deadfall for this was where Apelles and his siblings were sent every afternoon to collect kindling and to cut wood with a Swede saw.

Sometimes they passed others from the village there on the tote road and his father would rein in the horses and inquire politely about the errand on which the traveler was bent and the luck with which his various enterprises were being greeted, and then he would tip his hat, cluck, and lift the reins up, and then down, and they were off again. Once they met Apelles' grandfather on the trail, and his father went through his usual routine, asked the same questions he always asked of strangers, spoke with him for just as long but no longer, and they continued on as before.

They passed through the forest and into an area of scrub where they had cut pulp five years before and as a result it was now overgrown with poplar saplings and hazelbrush and then they broke through the growth. They had arrived at the cemetery.

The old village was gone. It had been moved, family by family, shack by shack, closer to the highway, but the graves had been kept there, they could not be moved. They overlooked the lake. Apelles' father tied the horses to the fence that ringed the graves and carried their things among the markers. There were modern stones, marble and granite that had been given a high polish, and metal plaques for the war dead, and, here and there, old gravehouses that lay solemnly on the ground. They passed through these graves until they reached their family's section, which was dominated by gravehouses. The newest one was only a few years old; this was where Apelles' younger sister was buried. They spread a quilt on the ground, opened the food, and his father smoked his pipe. When he was finished he put it aside and prayed quietly in the language. Apelles was always surprised, even as a child, at how delicate his father sounded when he prayed and how he sat with his feet tucked under him like a woman, so different than his usual posture on the wagon or behind the plow. It was as though he were a different person. After they ate, the children ran to play outside the fence, or down at the lake. As soon as they saw their father hitching the horses they stopped what they were doing and helped pack up the food and they were off for home. When they left the woods, their small shack appeared like a black stamp on the blue envelope of dusk. But the horses knew where they were and anticipating their ration of oats, they nickered and picked up the pace ever so slightly.

During the snowy months they did not go to the cemetery. Instead, two or three times during the season they would take the pickup truck, with all of the family crammed into the cab, and drive to Gaa-niizhogamaag or Netaawaash or Zhiingwaako-neyaashing for the drum dances. His parents always sat together at the back of the dance hall. They said little to the other Indians and had no part in the ceremony. They always ate last and only when one of the messengers approached them and held out the chairs at the table. When he was a boy Apelles played with the other children outside, and later, when he was older, he sat with his parents and watched the antics during the squawdances that lasted through the night.

Once, having left home for college, he returned for the holidays. He was twenty years old, and he accompanied his parents once again to the dance. He was amazed at the energy and commotion of the dancing for he had previously only attended as a child and so had seen the dance through his parents' eyes. But now he saw it through his own. He marveled at the grace of the kettleman and the passion of the singers, always laughing. From across the dance hall he saw a woman he had never seen before, and as though in a trance, once the squawdance started he wove his way through the crowd and presented her with three red kerchiefs. She smiled and they set off in the circle of dancers. Every time the drum was checked she raised the kerchiefs just so, and he admired her arms in the lamplight. They chatted between songs, and he learned she was older than he was by six years, she was from Miskwaagaming, she had a child of four, and she worked for the Indian Health Service. She extolled the virtues of government work and modern housing. He left with her phone number and promised to visit her the first chance he got.

He did so shortly after the New Year. Apelles took the bus from his parents' village to Miskwaagaming and stayed with her. Annette, for that was her name, seemed impressed that he was in college and not dismayed at all that she was clearly his first lover, his first as an adult. They drove to town and ate dinner at Bridgeman's, which was the only place that would serve them, and otherwise they stayed at her house.

Annette's skin was very smooth and she spent an hour each morning curling her bangs. When, during their lovemaking, Apelles tried to put on a condom, she stopped him and said he didn't need to.

"So what if you come inside me?" she cooed. "If I get pregnant we'll get married."

"You're teasing me," he said. She swore that she was not.

The thought that she liked him that much thrilled him. "I could touch you forever," he said.

Soon the holidays were over and he went back to school. He called her when he could. Sometimes on the phone she cried, sniffling into the receiver, and then, judging from the way her sobs came from so far away, she released the phone altogether to bury her head in her pillow. Apelles thought she cried for him. Often she wasn't home when he called. After final exams were over he took the first bus to Miskwaagaming. It was a long trip, and it felt as though the bus wandered across the country instead of driving through it. He felt sick, and he didn't know if his queasiness came from his excitement or from the chemical smell of the toilet at the back of the bus that sloshed and swelled with the bumps in the road.

Annette met him at the station wearing a new hairdo and an old dress. She had brought her son along. When Apelles tried to arrange time for the two of them alone, Annette always managed to include her boy in their activities. Finally, after two nights of falling asleep before she did, he managed to stay awake long enough to see the boy put to bed.

Later, Annette was on top of him, naked. She began to move, but in the way someone dances when they know they are being watched. Then the phone rang. Much to Apelles' surprise she answered it, cheerfully, as though the caller had caught her doing the dishes. She stopped riding him and absentmindedly rubbed lotion on her chest as she chatted. She flirted and laughed and talked much longer than good manners would allow, and stopped just short of making plans with the man on the other end of the line. By the time she said good-bye, Apelles had retreated far inside himself. His erection had wilted. And it was with great difficulty that he had to admit that the reasons she had cried on the phone—sobs echoing out of the past—had nothing to do with him at all. When she focused her attention back on him and began grinding her hips against his she seemed cheerful and distant. If Apelles had known how to cry or had realized it was the perfect time to do so, he would have.

The next day Apelles boarded the bus, and Annette, who knew her part well, stood behind the glass and cried and cried. She brought a white handkerchief and when he looked back she waved it, but he couldn't tell if she was waving it at him or cleaning the rain-streaked glass. It was hard to believe that she was the same woman he had met those months ago at the drum dance.

3

The years passed. As often happens the gears of the academic world didn't always mesh with those of real life. Apelles counted out his days in terms and grant cycles. He finished his undergraduate degree and enrolled in graduate school, doing research first in one community and then in another, staying only long enough to learn a language or to master a variant. Life was divided into three-, six-, and nine-month periods, interrupted only by major conference presentations, exams, and, ultimately, the truly draining experience of writing his dissertation.

Apelles was too shy to teach and too meticulous to write whole books, and it felt as though there was no place in the world for him until he took the job at RECAP. It suited the obscure circadian rhythms of his life very well. And whatever grief or sense of loss he felt about his affair with Annette had long since disappeared. He was happy in his modest job with his own modest researches.

In the early years Dr Apelles' routine was sometimes interrupted, or amended by, short research trips. These occurred once every two years and hung like commas between the long even clauses of his life. For instance, almost exactly two years earlier he had been working on a translation of a story written down in the early part of the twentieth century. He possessed no voice recording, only the text recorded by an amateur ethnologist who adhered to the faulty orthography set out in the *Smithsonian Institution 1873 Bulletin*. This created certain specific, and possibly fatal, instances in which the word or the meaning of the sentence was in doubt. Additionally, the Canadian reserve where the story had been collected had been, in the mid-nineteenth century, a place of asylum for three different bands of Indians, all of whom possessed different dialects, and so the presence of vastly different demonstratives and superlatives, as well as inherent lexical variations, made it difficult to recreate in English the exact sense of the original. The only way to sort it all out was to go there and interview the remaining speakers and use their language as a starting point from which to trace the language back to its earlier forms.

Apelles made the necessary arrangements. And, after two airplane flights and three hours in a rental car from Fort William to Adikokaaning, he was speaking with the band's educational coordinator, who, it should be said, was not at all interested in language and who spent most of his time organizing "healing conferences" designed to address the legacy of residential school abuse and staging "healing runs" wherein reserve youth would gasp their way down old portage trails and along the highway as a protest against alcohol abuse before returning to the woods to huff gas from their ATVs. Earl Downwind, however, did know everyone on the reserve and after some chitchat he made a suggestion. There was an older lady, a trapper, and she knew a lot.

"Head down the main road and turn left at the pump house. Halfway up the hill, take the dirt road to the left. Her place is back there. You'll find it."

Apelles followed his directions but got turned around. He stopped his car by the pump house and the community dock and got out and stretched. The lake lapped the dock pilings and he could hear seagulls overhead. And then, faintly at first, but then louder and with insistent regularity, he heard what sounded like someone shoeing a horse. He thought this was odd because he was certain no one on the reserve owned a horse. He was overcome with sadness and he didn't know why.

He locked the car and proceeded on foot, following the sound. As he neared its source he remembered: it was the same sound of his father's hatchet hitting the froe as he split shakes for his sister's gravehouse. Ping, ping, it rang out through the reserve.

When Apelles finally arrived he saw an elderly lady sitting on her front steps pounding smoked moosemeat with a hammer. She was using a short section of railroad tie for an anvil. She hit the meat and then bounced the hammer down to rest against the tie. This made the sound. This was the elder he had been looking for in the first place.

It was late April, a good time for a research visit because winter trapping was over but the lake ice prevented the band members from setting nets. For the next three days Dr Apelles chatted with the woman while she sat on the floor with her back to the fridge, a black garbage bag spread over her knees, fine-skinning the beavers her sons had saved for her.

These research trips were enjoyable for Dr Apelles, and this one was no exception. He drank mug after mug of Red Rose, and they spoke of trapping and fur prices. So overjoyed was the lady when he spoke to her in her own dialect and with much older and ornate locutions than she was used to hearing that she really opened up to him. She was a remarkable woman. She kept up a constant dialogue with Apelles in the language while fine-skinning the beaver. The refrigerator hummed against her back. All of his questions were answered, all the mistakes in the transcription and the translation were fixed.

On his last full day, there was some excitement. One of the lady's sons had shot a moose along the road. He, with a few other men from the reserve, had managed to get the moose in the back of his truck. But since they had no block and tackle, they didn't know how to hang it in order to pull the skin. Dr Apelles remembered what his father used to do when one of the cows died, and suggested they tie off each back leg to a single rope, throw that over a pole suspended between two trees in the yard, attach the other end of the rope to the truck hitch and drive forward. It all worked perfectly. The moose slid off the truck and swung on the rope. Apelles left the next morning.

The only other deviation from his usual schedule had been the occasional visits he received from his nephew. He was the only one of his relatives who had attended college. The rest of his nephews, nieces, and cousins had either never left home or had joined the military. Victor was the exception. He applied to and was accepted at a very prestigious university two hours south of the city. He wanted to study politics and international relations. He planned on becoming tribal chairman someday. Once a term or so he took the train north to the city and stayed with Dr Apelles for the weekend. On his first visit he appeared at the station looking this way and that, scanning the crowd for Apelles, about whom almost no one at home spoke and whose face had not appeared in any of the photo albums put together by his aunt. Victor was thin and his black hair was cut very short. He was so anxious to look the part of the ambitious student at the prestigious school that he had chosen to wear a pink oxford shirt and a blue blazer. Coupled with his stiff khakis that allowed too much of his pilled white crew socks to show, and appended by the battered briefcase that served as his overnight bag, he looked less like an American Indian and future tribal chairman and more like a poor but ambitious East Indian immigrant there, in America, to make his future.

Apelles saw him, waved, and approached. Victor was flushed and excited. It was his first visit to the big city.

"Victor?" Dr Apelles could not stop himself from smiling. It was a great, warm, selfless smile.

"Uncle," replied Victor, and, he, too, without quite knowing why, greeted the other with a smile that was friendly, without guile.

Apelles' soul thrilled at the sound of the word "uncle."

Apelles carried Victor's briefcase and they left the station. Each one walked quickly, each bent forward and looked earnestly into the other's face. That night Apelles took him out for Japanese food that Victor was determined to like. Apelles asked him about news from home, but home was the last place on Victor's mind. He spoke rapidly and, after he warmed up, so unceasingly that he did not have time to taste the food.

"Life at home, is, well, it is what it is. I mean, I love everyone there of course. But . . . I don't know. They . . ." his voice trailed off. He chewed quickly and then swallowed to make room for more speech.

"Many of them don't have any ambition," said Apelles, finishing Victor's thoughts for him.

"Yes! That's it. Ambition. Not to be powerful or to be rich or anything like that. But."

"To change things. To make something," finished Apelles again.

"Yes! Yes, that's it."

When Apelles became aware of Victor's interest in politics he tried to share with him one of the best examples of Indian political savvy he knew, the transcript of which he had rendered into

English. Apelles recounted Bagonegiizhig's anti-treaty speech delivered in 1854, first in English, then in _____.

"We declare our right to this land the same way you declare your rights to yours; by right of conquest . . ."

Dr Apelles' eyes beamed back at the past, and he was about to dive back into the speech with even more gusto when he noticed that Victor was falling asleep in his chair. It did not matter. They walked back to Dr Apelles' apartment. He made a bed for Victor on the couch, and the boy was asleep before Dr Apelles was done straightening up the kitchen.

When they were parting at the station on Sunday, Victor once again looked Apelles up and down and said, "I'll come up again, uncle. I'll be back."

"I'll wait for you, nephew." It was daring for Apelles to say "nephew" but it felt right to say it.

After that first visit there were others. Twice a year Victor would come up to the city. They got along very well. And each time he met Victor at the station Dr Apelles marveled at the changes in him. His frame widened and he put on muscle. He let his hair grow to a more human length. By his sophomore year he had become a very handsome man. His interest in politics was replaced with more anti-establishmentarian sentiments.

"Our tribal governments have taken the worst from the American system. There is so much corruption. So much graft!"

He passionately decried the nepotism and collusion rampant on the reservation, the inefficiency of the Indian Health Service.

By his junior year he barely resembled the boy who appeared on the station that first day. His long hair was pulled back in a braid and so were his thoughts: "Our traditions are what hold us together as a people," he said through his Japanese food.

Victor's last visit occurred two weeks shy of his graduation. He was to be graduated with a dual degree in English and Cultural

Studies. He planned on attending graduate school to study language and curriculum development.

"Language," he said, as he wolfed down his portion of sukiyaki, "it makes us who we are. And it's dying. Our language is really dying."

Dr Apelles agreed and quoted him statistics, but he did not say much else. He did not want to flatter himself by thinking his steady influence had caused this change in Victor. It gave him more pleasure to believe that the boy was growing up all on his own, watered and fed by his own natural intelligence and inherent goodness.

They planned on seeing each other at Victor's graduation in two weeks. Victor's parents would not be coming. Dr Apelles was prepared, though. A small box wrapped in mauve tissue paper rested on the mail table to the side of the front door and held a black and silver Mont Blanc fountain pen. Dr Apelles had even rehearsed what he would say when he gave it to him: *All serious thinkers deserve serious tools.*

Six days later Victor was killed in a car accident on his way to North Carolina to go hiking with his girlfriend. Dr Apelles was devastated. And, in ways he was only now realizing, he had never recovered.

4

Dr Apelles sat back in his chair and rubbed his eyes. Almost done. He returned his materials to the front desk. There was, so far, very little he had had to clean up—a few crumbs, particles, and missing hyphens. It was very clean, his best work, that he was sure of. But there was the ending, he still had to take care of that. So it wasn't the work that overwhelmed him so much—it was the translation itself, the fact of its existence, its maddening persistence. When, as now, as it had been from the beginning, he had it in front of him the difficult task was to keep his mind there with it—not swinging through the halls of memory on silken threads, not probing the potential caves of the future. Maybe, he thinks as he unshutters his eyes and looks at the blue-gray ceiling—more gray in the wintry light—maybe I should go and see Mai. After his massage and after the deliciously overwhelming naughty feeling subsided, and he had cleaned the come from his belly button as though wiping tears from an eye, he usually felt a wonderful nothingness. His release was a release because it had no significance whatsoever. But no. He could not go there now. Not now.

And the maddening fact was that the manuscript forced his mind onto other episodes of his life while he was working on it, but, and this had never happened before, while he was away from it he thought of little else. The story followed him around—it clamored from the trees, it peeked from behind stacks of books. He had even been tempted on several occasions to read a book or two that had crossed his workstation at RECAP—who knows what he might find? The translation would not leave him alone. When he worked at his station, phrases and scenes would repeat themselves *ad nauseam,* and he found himself muttering out loud and shaking his head. It was maddening—this could go on for years with no relief. Hopefully it would not.

Then, the grip of the translation tightened, and its claws tore him open.

Even though the bell has sounded, he sits in his chair and looks up at the gray ceiling, so much like the sky on that fateful day. He sees it in his mind very clearly. It might have been a day like any other day. His mind had been on the translation instead of the work in front of him, and as a result he had made many mistakes. Jesus and Campaspe both had noticed—sizing a whole batch of books only to put them in the wrong-sized box; forgetting to scan a box so that the shelvers had to come back with it so he could enter the number. He was left with the hot feeling of shame.

Maybe it was the weather. When he had walked the ten blocks to the train station, the clouds hovered far overhead, a uniform gray lid on the day. They were so remote that they lost the variation and interest low rain clouds can bring. A chill pervaded everything.

By the time he arrived at RECAP, it had already begun to rain, and still the clouds did not descend. Dr Apelles was cold to the bone, and the feeling had dogged him all day. And then there were those mistakes, those simple and humiliating errors. He did not feel good at all. He wiped his brow, and not knowing what to do next, he rubbed his hands together as though to warm them. He looked up from his station at Campaspe. She was looking directly at him.

"Are you okay?" she asked.

"Me? Yes. I think so anyway."

"Maybe you should eat something."

Maybe he should. But the problem didn't seem to be with his stomach. Rather, the problem was with his soul.

"Maybe I should," he said. "But maybe it's just the weather."

"Whatever it is," she said gently, "you don't look so good. You should take care of yourself."

When the rest of the workers stopped for their lunch break, and he finally had the chance to contend with the silence while logging books at his station, he heard, far overhead, the rain beating down with steady ferocity on the roof. He was thinking all the while how strange it was that Campaspe had spoken to him, as though she knew he had been thinking about her lately. And why should he take care of himself? Did it really matter to her?

By the time he punched out, it had been raining steadily for four hours. He put on his coat and carried his briefcase in his left hand and held his umbrella in his right. The temperature had dropped and the rain had begun to congeal on the walks, the branches overhead, on the cars parked glumly in the parking lot, and on either side of the small streets leading to the train station. No one had thought an ice storm was possible at this time of year and so no provisions had been made. The sidewalks and roads had not been salted. Within minutes they were coated in a thin layer of ice, and the daffodils and tulips, cold enough to freeze, bent low and finally prostrated themselves in their border gardens.

Dr Apelles had not thought to bring his rubber overshoes or the duck boots he wore during bad winter weather, so he had to walk very carefully and slowly down to the station. His feet were soaked through within minutes. The cars felt their way down the slippery streets. The whole world had been transformed from a place of quick movement to one that was tentative and fragile.

Dr Apelles was almost there. He had only to walk up the steps to the platform, sit and wait for the train, and then he'd be home free—the sidewalks in the city were so covered in pollution, exhaust and grime, and paced by so many people, vented with so many grills leading up from the subways, that they were sure to be free of ice.

He transferred his umbrella to his left hand so he could grasp the cold wet handrail with his right as he climbed the steps to the platform. The steps were especially slippery. Each one was guarded by a stamped metal strip and they had acquired a thick covering of ice.

Dr Apelles was so lost in thought—the translation had, in large part, made him deaf to the clamor of the world—that he did not see or hear a group of teenagers in mid-antic slamming their way down the steps. They were goofing, enjoying the slip and slide of the ice, unaware as teenagers *are* unaware that they should be careful of their bodies. It did not occur to them they could be hurt. The teens expected that the noise of their antics (part exuberance and part warning) would cause Dr Apelles to shrink against the handrail, giving them room to pass. But he didn't move out of the way. At the last instant the foremost teen twisted to the side as he careened down the steps, and he managed to shout, "Watch out, man! Watch it!" but it was too late. He managed to miss running into Dr Apelles but he clipped his briefcase. Dr Apelles spun to his left, his feet went out from underneath him, and he fell hard on the steps while the teens zoomed away out into the darkening parking lot. Their shouts and laughter could be heard long after the boys could no longer be seen.

Dr Apelles had fallen sideways. He had hit his right elbow on the metal edge and had broken his fall by putting his right hand out flat on the step. He was sure he had not twisted or broken anything, but his backside hurt and his palm had been skinned. Already it had begun to bleed, but not from any one spot. He picked himself up, walked up the few remaining steps to the platform, and found relief on one of the green benches. He shook his head to clear it.

The electrified wires overhead that ran the trains sagged in their casings of ice.

His right arm was numb, his back and butt hurt, and he noticed with dismay that blood was still seeping from his hand. He set down his briefcase and umbrella and removed his white handkerchief from his breast pocket and wrapped it around his hand. The cool cloth felt good against the wound, and he thanked his father silently for showing him that a real man always carried a kerchief.

A muffled voice from the speaker announced that train service had been suspended indefinitely.

Dr Apelles looked to his left down the empty tracks. The wires made a lonesome sound in the wind. The green signal light far down the line winked in and out of the rain.

He looked back down at his hand and unwrapped the kerchief to see how much he was bleeding. The white Egyptian cotton was prinkled with blood. A sudden feeling of faintness made him stop. Many thoughts—of the loneliness and isolation wrapped up in translating something no one would ever read, of his fall and his wounded hand, of the sad memories of his childhood and his parents, whom he had loved too much as a child and not enough as an adult, of the disappointment of his affair with Annette, and the loss of Victor—came back to him at once. He was sure his heart would burst.

He heard someone speak, but as from far away.

"Are you okay?"

He looked up and saw Campaspe leaning over him, her hands deep in the pockets of a navy peacoat.

"I'm okay. I'm okay. Nothing broken. Nothing sprained." Dr Apelles sat up straighter and tried to look composed.

Once it was clear to Campaspe that Dr Apelles was not in any danger and once it was clear to him that she knew he was not in danger, neither of them knew what to say.

"The train is delayed until further notice," Dr Apelles informed her.

"Ahh!"

"Are you heading into the city?" he asked.

"Yes!" Her voice was shrill. She was almost undone by this unforeseen encounter. Both of them knew that deadly convention dictated they could only speak for a few minutes before they would be unable to part on the platform and would be forced to wait together for the next train.

"Me, too. But, with this weather . . ."

A car horn gasped, once, mutedly, in the parking lot.

"Are you sure you're okay?"

Campaspe had leaned in, closer, trying to read him. He looked at her face. Her olive complexion was there, but underneath it, tinged by the cold, was a rosy bloom to her cheeks. He looked back quickly at his damaged hand.

"I just slipped, that's all."

"It happens, I guess."

"Would you like to sit? We'll be waiting awhile. Or . . ." But he could think of no alternative.

They had succeeded in talking themselves into talking.

"Or . . ." she pondered, or pretended to ponder, not wanting to seem too eager, but having thought it through the moment she saw him sitting forlornly on the green bench. She was sure he had been crying or was about to. "Or . . . there's Bella's. Just on the other side of the station. They make train announcements. We can wait there." She looked first up and then down the tracks and then made a wistful face.

Margarita Bella's, where the other sorters sometimes went for drinks.

"Okay. Sure. Yes. Why not."

He gathered his things and they went down the steps—careful

now—and through the tunnel under the tracks. Once again they both became shy.

"Your last name is Bello, right?"

"Uh-huh."

"Bello at Bella's. I like that." This was the best he could do.

"Ha ha!"

And then they were through the tunnel, up the steps, across the road, and inside Margarita Bella's.

It was dark inside. Red lights lit the small bar. The walls were paneled in wood, the floor was wood as well. They found a booth in the middle of five stretching from the front door to the back. A television above the bar was tuned to a basketball game but the sound was off. Instead, Juan Luis Guerra's *Greatest Hits* was playing over the speaker system.

It was strange for both of them. They had worked side by side, a mere ten feet apart, for almost three years. And since they rarely passed each other in the hallway, and since Dr Apelles never ate lunch in the Reading Room, and since they had never, never before that night, seen each other at the train station, they each only recognized the other in profile. To sit across from and to speak directly to the other, this was novel.

It seemed best to speak of work, which is what they did. While one bemoaned or celebrated this or that, the other nodded and listened with more energy and interest than the topic merited. They each felt exposed, almost naked. They kept their margarita glasses between them on the table.

They ordered another round. The regulars at the bar came and went, the basketball players went back and forth on the television while the score rose, the two waitresses smoked together at the end of the bar, and every once in a while one or the other walked quickly to the front window and gazed out into the night.

The weather had not let up.

Large drops of rain attacked the plate glass.

Dr Apelles and Campaspe listened for announcements, but

none were forthcoming. Their conversation stretched and grew and continued into the evening.

By the third round of drinks they had grown more exuberant. Campaspe shared with Dr Apelles her impersonations of some of their coworkers. When she mocked Ms Manger by pecking her head back and forth and meekly folding her hands together in front of her, Dr Apelles laughed and could not stop laughing. It was a very good likeness. Campaspe was a kindhearted girl, and so she laughed at her own audacity. When she laughed, Apelles was thrilled by how her eyes crinkled prettily, her cheeks rosy with tequila and humor. Likewise, it was a great pleasure for her to see Dr Apelles tip his head back, throw his eyes to the ceiling, and let his whole body shake.

Once, during a lull in the conversation while waiting for more drinks and having grown more brave, Campaspe smoothed the table with her fingers as though straightening an invisible piece of string, and asked where Dr Apelles went on Fridays.

Dr Apelles could not hide from the question behind his drink—the waitress had not brought it over yet. And he did not feel right giving the usual answer of "amateur historian" or "history buff."

"I am a translator of Native American languages."

"Oh!" she cried. "So *that's* what you are!"

"A translator or an Indian?"

"Both," she said.

The margaritas arrived, and Campaspe lifted her glass, and her words, so brave for a girl like her, seemed to be coming from the glass rather than from her.

"You are a very serious man."

He blushed inwardly. He didn't feel serious. He wasn't trying to be.

"Am I? Am I really? I don't feel serious. I don't feel . . ." and when his thoughts trailed off, he realized that the thought had been complete after all and so he said, looking directly at her: "I just don't feel. At all."

Campaspe was embarrassed, though she didn't know why.

"So what are you working on now?"

And once he began speaking about his work, he found it difficult to stop.

He grew animated. He spoke quickly and only paused to make sure Campaspe was following along down the trails his mind took. And even though he meant to talk about the translation, instead he managed to do a very good job of talking around it.

She appeared genuinely interested. Even so, he wanted to stop speaking, to lock up this part of his mind, to keep it separate, as it had been for so long. But his fall on the steps and his work on the translation had maneuvered out of him all that he had been keeping inside. He was not one of those professional Indians who were willing to dispense platitudes disguised as cultural treasure. He was not one of those for whom the past, because of how exotic it seemed to most people, could be used as social credit among the credulous or liberal. He was a private man, with private sorrows. Once, long ago, he had realized he must do this in order to survive. As an Indian in the world, he was, as far as most were concerned, a little ghost in living colors, with a reality of his own that was written out in the tenses of the remotest past. And the heartache that now threatened to overwhelm him, and that he was only now beginning to recognize, was largely due to this one great sacrifice—he had been forced to hide his most subtle and fluent self. He was tempted now to let that self come out.

Suddenly the bartender turned down Juan Luis Guerra. He shouted to the corners of the bar that there would be no more train service until the following day.

After he announced the calamitous news, the bartender turned the sound back on and Guerra's voice was heard once again on the stereo, but Guerra handed the microphone to Ruben Blades who, as though daring the weather, urged his listeners to "muevete."

Some of the people in the bar cheered the news. Others, those who lived far away, groaned. The waitresses did nothing.

Apelles and Campaspe looked at each other. They looked very seriously at each other and knew, somehow, that how they decided to escape the storm would decide something between them.

"Are you anxious to get home?" asked Campaspe.

"Yes and no." He was thinking of his bed, but not in the usual way.

"You?"

"Same. I'm tired. But this is . . . I don't know."

"Yes."

Dr Apelles and Campaspe quickly decided to share a cab into the city. It would be expensive, but they had no other options. The cab was called. They waited, sober but not sober. Dr Apelles said,

"If we were peasants in some other time we would walk all night to reach a dying relative in the next village. That's what purpose these storms serve in stories. In stories, ice storms bring people together who normally are not together, and they cause great changes in those people."

Campaspe laughed.

5

As it turned out, the night would become famous. Thousands of people remained stuck right where they were until morning. People slept in malls. Babies were born in copy shops. Other babies were conceived in supermarkets. Marriages. Deaths.

Dr Apelles and Campaspe did manage, however, to make it out of Margarita Bella's. The cab they had called arrived and they began their trip into the city.

Although the streets were deserted except for a delivery truck or two, it was a very long ride.

The windshield wipers beat at twice the speed of the wheels. Everything was dark. The parked cars on the side streets were coated with ice and looked like cinnamon buns glazed with sugar.

Dr Apelles and Campaspe each gazed out of the side windows at the spectacle of the ice storm that had put the city to sleep. Neither looked very often through the front windshield. They left that to the driver who, for his part, was a patient fellow. He operated the heater and windshield wipers in unison, striving for the right balance between heat and motion that would keep the windshield free of ice. If he was put out or concerned by the storm, he did not show it. He drove slowly. The roads were slick. Assiduous braking and signaling along with the very forgiving seats made the cab and its motion a thing of peace. Occasionally the driver pressed the speed dial on his cell phone, inserted the ear bud, and had long conversations in Urdu. Neither Campaspe nor Dr Apelles knew what the cabbie was saying (though, since Dr Apelles collected languages out of habit he did catch the words *smoke, Hamid,* and *moth*), though it most certainly was about the weather, judging from the way the driver spoke, paused, and looked out and up at the sky through the windshield, and then in the beautiful rolling rhythms of his mother tongue, continued his conversation.

After a while his voice and his gentle and constant manipulations of the vehicle quit having meanings of their own. He receded and melded with the hiss of the tires as they ploughed through the slush. And when the cab rolled to a stop at traffic lights, Campaspe and Dr Apelles could only once again hear the thrush of rain on the car roof.

All of this was enough to lull them, but not to put them to sleep. They were too much on edge, too much subject to the wonder and strangeness of it all. They were startled by the very fact of riding in a cab together.

After a series of twists and turns on the small side streets they turned on the main thoroughfare, which was—unbeknownst to Campaspe but knownst to Dr Apelles—the old post road that led into the city. The road followed the canal for a distance, and all that could be seen were the outermost branches of trees that had worn the blossoms of spring only hours before, but which had now been transformed into icy, clawing things, fairy-tale trees. The small saplings planted on the greenway were bent low under their armor of ice. Here and there in low areas fog curled on the ground and seemed to hide mysterious secrets that excited Dr Apelles and Campaspe.

Then the road left the canal, became the main street of a small town that had not yet become a suburb, the kind of town favored by college professors and doctors because it reminded them of small towns in general. It had clothed itself in a historical self-regard, judging from the Fudge Shoppe, three antique stores, and the "Mercantile" that all existed side by side, but the fantasy competed with a Kinko's and a Starbucks that bookended the more quaint stores.

The village was whisked behind them somewhere in the night.

The view gave way to technology parks. Great cubes of concrete and glass housed software companies and the like and seemed designed to make people guess at what went on inside. Really, just judging from the exterior anything could happen there.

After a string of auto-body shops and convenience stores, they coasted through the sister city to the one across the river in which they lived.

They were still on the old post road, though it had been over two centuries since it had served as such. Since that time it had lived as a main street, then as the town had become a city, a central avenue.

The freezing rain was still coming down. A few cars felt their way in either direction, the lenses of their headlights crusted with slush like eyes filled with sleep. Dr Apelles and Campaspe saw, occasionally, individuals out on the sidewalk sliding their feet along the pavement.

Neither Dr Apelles nor Campaspe had ever seen a city, especially this one, so empty, so stripped of humans.

All the cars usually parked on either side of the four-lane avenue had by now been towed away. None of the storefronts were open. Above and behind them warehouses reared up into the sky.

And though the ice storm had denuded the city, had stripped away the humans and their human activity as a great wind will pick leaves off a tree, what remained was amazing to behold. With parallel but unspoken awe Dr Apelles and Campaspe registered the amount and variety of life that had produced this place.

A pizza joint passed by the cab, flanked by a check-cashing and money-order business on one side and a pawnshop on the other. And it was, now that there was no one there to obstruct the view, easy to imagine someone going from one to the other, and it was even easier to imagine the circumstances (a divorce, the expensive sickness of a parent) that necessitated the visit and then the relief brought by a cheap meal. Above these modest stores and others like them Dr Apelles and Campaspe could make out older signs made out of wood and bolted to the brick or painted on the brick itself that advertised services no longer offered in this world. They could see back into the past.

Higher up, on the sides of the larger warehouses they could see, peeking out from behind new billboards, chipped murals—blasted by the weather—barely legible, advertising products of a bygone age.

The city rolled past.

Each building was now exposed for what it was and for what it had been. Both Campaspe and Dr Apelles would have liked to go inside these places. As though in a dream they imagined the buildings to be unlocked and vacant, prepared for their curiosity.

The side streets opened up to reveal, for an instant, row houses and dilapidated Queen Annes, and then closed. Page after page was presented to them—the city passed them as quickly as the wind can fan the pages of a book left outside on a table.

Dr Apelles and Campaspe read them as best they could and then, just when this street or that was almost gone from sight, he and Campaspe inserted themselves into the story presented to them there. The city lay open to them—in the late hour and with the treacherous weather—and they felt they could be anything, that nothing was impossible.

The road rose, and the buildings dropped away. They were on the approach to the bridge. Then they were on it. They could see nothing but blackness below. When they reached the apex of the bridge they saw ahead into their own city—so boisterous—and no matter the weather it was tinkled with lights, and surely there were people down there, many of them going about their lives no matter what. The ice storm was talked about for many years.

6

The bell had already sounded and everyone was moving. It was time for them to return their materials. As a rule they were as methodical in that process as they were in their work. Without speaking to one another or communicating in any way they formed an order. Box after box, folder after folder, were returned. Dr Apelles responded slowly. After the silver cring of the bell died out, followed by the golden silence of the end of a day's work he had continued to gaze at the ceiling while he remembered the ice storm before bringing his box and things to the cart next to the reading-room librarian's raised desk. He exchanged a few words with the reading-room librarian. He was in a daze.

Once outside he stood on the front steps. Night had fallen. He looked into the sky, which was clear, but in which nothing could be seen.

It was hard to believe that his researches were almost over. Everything was clearer now.

For a while things had not been clear. Before the ice storm the translation—it could be nothing else—had caused a jumble of thoughts. What else could explain his memories of Victor and his own early life intruding so imperiously? He had been so lost. If Dr Apelles was completely honest with himself he had to admit that he had never been found.

At first, his confusion had only deepened after the night of the storm. The ice storm was talked about still and would be for many years. And for Dr Apelles it was a night he would never forget, and was, as he stood on the steps of the archive and looked out on the people hurrying home on the sidewalk below, still, in many ways, continuing to have an effect on his life.

That confusion, which reached a pitch on the day of the storm, had continued to grow thereafter, beginning the day after the storm when he slipped and slid his way over to the archive. He had begun his work again, but the tense fluttered from his grasp and then he lost it altogether. He could no longer remember where the stresses were supposed to be placed, could no longer remember which vowels were long and which were short. He had lost his style.

But then, a tint had crept into the palette of his translation. And the whole of it emerged differently than he had expected. Before that time his work had been interrupted by other thoughts. Now they were colored by them. Colored, especially, by Campaspe. As the structure of his life melted under the heat of new emotions so did the sense of the translation.

The guard came out.

"You can't stand here. You're blocking the door," he said, not unkindly.

"Yes. Of course." They exchanged some more words, about the homeless and the city, and then Dr Apelles moved down the steps and into the throng of people.

Whereas before Dr Apelles might have pondered the inscrutable lives of those on the street, since the ice storm he had given this up. He no longer sent his mind out to wander among the unknown and unknowable forest of people around him. He would take his usual path home, which was straight except for the one turn off the main avenue. But his thoughts moved in larger circles between the translation and Campaspe. He would see someone with a simple handbag or wearing red tennis shoes and he would imagine Campaspe carrying just such a bag or wearing the same shoes. And this type of exercise made him wonder what her life was like: what had her life been like before he knew her and what it was like now when she wasn't at work.

If Dr Apelles had been able, in his mind's eye, to follow Campaspe through her day, he would have been surprised by what he saw.

He would have been surprised, first of all, by her behavior after the ice storm. When she finally made it home she took the day off (more out of necessity than anything else since the city was shut down) and did nothing much at all. She was tired and pleased and kept smiling to herself as she straightened her already tidy apartment. And her smile—as she folded laundry and dusted on top of the fridge—can only be described as tinged with madness, if by madness we mean joy.

Campaspe's apartment was small, a studio, and even though it could be considered cramped, it was very homey. The whole of it—the single room containing the kitchen, the living space, and her bed, which was set under the window—was painted a warm, rusty red. Neat shelves of books grew as quickly and healthily as the few potted plants set around the place. The shelves began at the door, walked along the long wall, skipped over the doorway to the bathroom, made a turn at the corner, kept running their hands along the wall facing the street, skipped over the window, paused around the bed, skipped the other half of the large window, reached the other corner, turned right and ran, unbroken, to the edge of the kitchen area, took a deep breath and dove under the opening to the kitchen, and reemerged to make the last few steps back to the front door. A coat rack stood to the right of the door. A small dresser guarded the foot of the bed. And that was all the furniture she had, except for the small table and two chairs tucked under the window in the kitchen.

That Campaspe had so many books and that she had read them all was surprising in someone so young. That she had stolen most of them from bookstores and public libraries (but not from RECAP) *shouldn't* be surprising considering she had two incompatible handicaps: she was both poor and curious. When a book grabbed her attention she was compelled to read it then and there. And since books were expensive, and since she could not wait, she took them from the shelf, put them under her coat, and brought them home where she could read in peace. And there they stayed, there they were, lining her little place. She always meant to go back and pay for them, but was too embarrassed and so they remained as symbols of her poverty and her curiosity.

Dr Apelles would have been surprised by her little place and by her thievery (he had never stolen anything in his life), and most of all, on the day after the ice storm, he would have been surprised by her smile, which had not yet subsided. And it did not subside even when she was done with her cleaning and dozed on her sun-kissed bed and ran her ringlets around her index finger the way some women do when recollecting their pleasure. Apelles would have been surprised if he had been able to see all of this: surprised by the quietude of her life, by her refusal or inability to live hers like most other girls her age lived theirs.

Campaspe did not "party." She did not go out at night in a group of likewise beautiful girls and drink Red Bulls and vodka and sweet shots or slammers served out of paper cups by waitresses with a belly ring in the front and a tattoo in the back (as though their sexual identity was branded on their ass and threaded through their body and anchored on their navel), both revealed by a cropped shirt that showed a flat belly under engineered breasts. She did not get drunk with groups of girls like this and grind and drink and flirt with the boys or make out (just for fun, it doesn't mean anything) with her girlfriends on the dance floor only to end the night too drunk to actually fuck anyone and smelling and looking like a rotten flower—sweet and wilted and smeared—spilling the syrup that was once in her stomach all over the bathroom floor. Nor did she "hook up" with boys and had no patience for the promise of premature ejaculation written out in the braille of facial acne. Nor did she decoy herself in coffee shops, sitting in the sun waiting for some emo boy to approach her. No . . . she was not interested in any of this. She was only interested in her work and in Apelles.

True, Campaspe was better read and more intelligent than her modesty suggested. True, as a sorter at RECAP, she worked well below her "level." But the strictures of RECAP were a solace for her. They provided order and there was a kind of beauty in that order. But more than that, RECAP was a pleasant torture because she could not satisfy her curiosity about stories and books there. She had never stolen a book from RECAP, had never so much as cracked a spine to peek inside. So—her days were spent in penance for her nights. Every day at RECAP she assuaged her guilt over her bookstore thefts. And so every day began for her as a balanced scale and allowed her to be the happy person she was. As for her feelings for Apelles, those ran deep and had been evolving, in silence and at a distance, since she had first started at RECAP.

Campaspe had been interviewed and screened by Ms Manger and had secured a job as a sorter. It was also Ms Manger, who, on her Campaspe's first day, had shown her all of RECAP. They began flying through the place in a wide orbit, beginning in the Reading Room, coasting by the O.C., then they whisked by Ms Manger's own nest, and circled the S.A. They passed by the R.A., the edge of the sorting stations, hurried along the back wall and into the Stacks, back out, through the area where the carts were lined up, ready for the shelvers, and back to the center of the floor amongst the sorting stations, where they finally, with wings set, set down at Campaspe's sorting station.

"And so here we are. This is your station."

Campaspe nodded and surveyed the station, the empty cart, the empty shelves, the row of sorter's manuals, the clean, uncluttered work surface,. She was thinking all the while that Ms Manger resembled not so much a visionary manager of a state-of-the-art library as the head housekeeper in a Victorian mansion; that Ms Manger did not own any of the demesne somehow heightened her need for control.

"Once you get started and Jesus, no—" as Campaspe set eyes on Apelles for the first time "—over there."

Apelles had looked up at that moment and said, "Good day," with a slight nod.

"Hello. Hi."

"Over there," said Ms Manger a little more shrilly—"*that's* Jesus. This—" her arm swept open to showcase Dr Apelles as though he were a prize—"is Dr Apelles."

And Campaspe thought Ms Manger had blushed.

"Hello," said Campaspe again.

"Good day," said Apelles again.

"This," Ms Manger's other arm opened, not as wide, not as read-ily, to include Campaspe, "is Campaspe. Now. Jesus, would you . . ."

And he did. He showed her how to measure and tag and sort, how to use the manuals, and how to mark and reserve damaged books.

Jesus was smitten and so he did what men do when they desire a woman—he tried to be more of a man but ended up acting like a boy, which is how Campaspe will think of Jesus no matter what he does later.

Ms Manger stayed only so long as to make sure that Campaspe was catching on, and then she went back to her office.

Jesus tried to draw Campaspe out. He asked her all sorts of questions, which she answered loudly at first. She had hoped that Apelles would overhear, but when he did not or chose not to, she stopped answering and responded to questions about her life with questions of her own about the job.

Her first day was much like the day after and the day after that and all the rest that followed. She watched Apelles. She did her work. She parried Jesus' attempts at seduction. She watched Apelles—his physical attitude, the way he held the books, the way he dressed—the same way we watch birds: with passion and inter-est and respect but as a species apart, moving on higher and more distant ether than we do, but curious and comforting to consider and a pleasure to have nearby.

She had been attracted to him from the start. His silence was beautiful to her because, although he said little, it was clear that he was not capable of dissimulation—he could not appear as any-thing other than what he was. He could not be, or seem to be, anything other than Apelles.

All the same, during that first day and thereafter, she couldn't help wondering where he was because his mind, clearly, was on, but not in, his work. What worlds must he contain? What was he thinking? Like the work itself, Apelles was a pleasant torture because she longed to lift his cover and read him, to bring him home and read him immediately and completely, and, ultimately, to shelve him in her most private and intimate stacks in her warm, cozy, red-hued apartment.

If Dr Apelles had been able, only for a day, to see himself through the camera of her eyes, he would have been shocked by the intimate angle of her vision. Every part of him would have appeared in close-up: the humble strength of his almost pudgy fingers were revealed in detail; the portrait of his neck (and he had never, ever *thought* of his own neck) framed by his collar, ear, and hair was lovingly drawn down to the small dark mole below his jaw that he sometimes nicked while shaving; she cut to the plump strength of his hips and ass under his chinos when he bent down, in profile, to retrieve something from under his station; and the furrows of his almost perpetually furrowed brow were very endearing when seen close and reminded Campaspe of the way her father had frowned and pursed his lips when cutting his fingernails. When Apelles walked from the R.A. to his sorting station her eyes stayed close to him in a long trolley shot; Apelles' face and torso close up as the background moved steadily past.

Apelles was not buff or lanky, or even average. He had no physical analog in the types that always seemed to recreate themselves in men: the barrelly men who could have been power lifters and who tuck their DKNY T-shirts into their jeans, the emo boys in bowling shirts, the college kids who dress like gay dockboys in Abercrombie & Fitch, or the rockers who all try to resemble Iggy Pop. No. Apelles was rounded and smooth and solid, complete unto himself, and Campaspe couldn't help thinking that he was like some kind of animal—a badger or a woodchuck or a beaver—who needs nothing else, who need not do anything in particular at all for us to recognize him, instantly, for what he is. This is how she saw him all that time before the ice storm. And after, as she lay in her bed and corkscrewed her hair around her finger and smiled and sighed and marveled that the muscles of her inner thighs, the ones that clench, were sore, she murmured, "Of course, of course, of course." She had fallen for him.

He had no way of knowing that she thought of him in those many delicious ways, not then. For his part, he would concentrate on her, the one cheek she offered him in profile day after agonizing day, the exuberance of her curly hair and then, when he reached for more, there it would be, the translation. And he would look up, and he would be back in the archive, the translation in front of him, the reading light glancing over his pencils and his portion of the oak table. He saw the vaulted ceiling and the upper windows through which he registered the dimming of the day. It was as though he had just discovered the thing and was filled with equal amounts of wonder, loneliness, and frustration. He would get back to work. It felt as though he had been dreaming. He would look back down at his workstation and instead of the books in RECAP he saw the translation.

Likewise, if he was at the archive, and the papers were actually before him, he saw not the words or their meaning but gestures of Campaspe's that he had seen and collected at work. The way she tucked her hair behind her ear, or the habit she had of biting her lips when trying to put the books she had sized into their box. And as he looked, day after day, at the same gestures, the same profile, at times he thought if he stared hard enough he could penetrate the surface of these gestures and get to some other place. Just when he thought he would break through, there he was, studying the grain of the table or counting his pencils, or thumbing the plastic cover of a page. It was maddening. Everything was unsettled.

Once, as he tried to imagine Campaspe completely, and could not, he speculated that perhaps we never truly forget anything. We remember each and every thing that ever happens to us, each and every thing that we see. But when so many things, small things, occur that are so much alike, they become like a habit, a norm—so expected and uniform as to lose the distinction of memory. Much like the way a photograph of a forest's edge in the middle distance won't make one think of a tree so much as other photographs of trees in the middle distance. And so, this might explain the activity of passion—why one goes to the movies or why ice storms take on so much significance: we seek to create small events by which we mark the big event of life. And this, as he turns the corner to his quieter street, might also explain why Dr Apelles is so unsettled. Until the translation and then—coming from the pages themselves—the ice storm forced him together with Campaspe, he had always surveyed his life *from* the middle distance. Everything had appeared to him as distinct but remote, with pleasing variations, but seen from so far away as to reduce and obliterate all sense of the individual, the absolute.

This vantage point had granted him some measure of invisibility at work but it vanished after the ice storm. Mr Bass and Mr Florsheim went so far as to stop the discussion they were having about basketball and nod to him with a strange glint in their eyes. Mrs Millefeuille, with whom he had only the slightest contact as he did not read in the Reading Room, actually said "Hello" as he passed her doorway. It was unheard of.

In the span of two weeks Ms Manger crept up on him three times. That was more than she had spoken to him in a year. At first he thought he was in trouble. She brought him to her office, and after a little conversation, she evaluated his performance, and then, strangely, asked for his help translating some of the *Jesuit Relations* that she was using in a conference paper.

Even Jesus talked to him now. In the mornings, when he gained his station, Jesus would look his way and say "What's up?" Invariably Dr Apelles, more baffled by Jesus' greeting than by any of the other changes in the workplace, would say "Hello" as he tilted his head.

This went on day after day. There was a kind of antagonism attached to Jesus' greeting. And Dr Apelles could not help but think of smiling assassins in detective novels. It is hard not to worry when you are happy. And Dr Apelles *was* happy. Since the ice storm his life had grown to include Campaspe.

It could even be said that they were in a relationship.

And then there was Campaspe herself. He thought of her constantly. On his walks, on the train, during his researches. And yet, when he took his place beside her at work he would only say "Hello" or "Good Morning." Campaspe would reply with "Hi" or "How ya doin?"

Occasionally, when she returned from her lunch break, she would say "Back again" and raise her eyebrows as she said it.

She and Jesus still bantered over Dr Apelles' head, still joked about the vicissitudes of work. And all the day long Dr Apelles would, as surreptitiously as he could, glance her way. She sometimes wore a thin white sweater he liked very much with a V-neck and short sleeves, and sometimes, when she bent down to retrieve something on the lower shelves of her station, he got just the briefest glimpse of the crease between her breasts. She wore the sweater often now.

7

He had passed the restaurant again. It felt as though he hadn't eaten there in years. Dr Apelles entered his building, collected his mail, which consisted only of a medium-sized envelope containing an obscure journal on Algonquian linguistics, and took the elevator up up up and was now safely in his apartment.

He fixed himself a simple dinner of a grilled cheese sandwich— he was accustomed to eating very little. He drank a beer. He tried to read but was too unsettled, and after a few pages he put the journal down. The apartment, though clean and orderly, was filled with things, filled with a life. But tonight it felt like just so much bric-a-brac—like an antique store where everything was for sale and strangers could come traipsing through whenever they wished, but a place that he could not leave.

Eventually he found himself at the window. It was blackest night, but clear. Voices and the noise of traffic wafted up from far below. The window was closed but, judging from the draft that came in from under the sash, the air outside was crisp and dry, very unlike the night of the storm.

Dr Apelles closes his eyes at the memory of it. His lips move as though forming the memory for him. There is a confusion in his mind. What exhausting and pleasurable work remembering is! It is almost like creating something new. Suddenly he is there. The rain is coming down. It freezes on the street, melts, and freezes again. Everything on the avenues moves slowly.

They had taken a cab into the city and the driver, still talking on his phone in Urdu, still calm and driving like a champion only made one stop—Apelles' apartment. Campaspe stayed there that night.

Then, there is no sound of the storm deep in his bedroom, but when he closes his eyes he sees power lines groan under the weight of ice like strings waxed into the semblance of candles. Cars glissand into the ditch and are finally at rest. The people on the sidewalk squat as if to sit, and the wind pushes them down the pavement. His shoes and hers guard the front door and lose their crust of slush and ice. Water has soaked into the leather. By morning they will only be damp, cool to the touch. He opens his eyes and sees Campaspe. She might have opened hers at the same time because she is looking at him. She smiles.

Later, as they were lying side by side, her head propped up by one hand, her curls curling and one breast pooling on the pillow, she said, "You never told me what it was about."

"What what's about?"

"What you're working on."

"My translation? What my translation is about?"

"Yes," she said sleepily in that beautiful way women speak after they've made love.

"I didn't? Strange."

"And?"

"It's," he paused and drummed his fingers on his chest. "It's," he said as though making up his mind. "It's, it's a love story."

Campaspe grinned and twined her fingers with his. "Good! Those are my favorite kind!"

But before that. She is on top of him and she is riding him. Both of their eyes are open with wonder. She puts her hands on his chest. Her shoulders hunch and her breasts are forced together. She bares her neck, and in the low light he thinks he can see a freckle or two at the crease. Then he closes his eyes and as he does he is still reading there, where flesh meets flesh, the hidden marks. And even then, while she is on top of him, right before his closed eyes, and her pubic hair is brushing his own almost hairless groin, and right then after so long, after waiting so long for this or something like it, he sees the translation, the meaning available only to him, vulnerable only to him, in a language belonging only to him. The pages flutter. Outside the storm is still enjoying itself. Inside the storm is raging. The pages flip and fan and flutter. And it seems to him that her breasts, as they part and rise, are like the pages of a mysterious and delicate book. *I've been waiting to read you,* he whispers.

Hush. She smiles.

His eyes are open. He reads with his hands and his eyes—the arch of her neck, the sweat that shines on her temples, the small movements of her fingers as they steady the turf of his chest, the dark heat of her groin, and her thighs too, and all of her. And what a story it is to read. What a pleasure. Page after page after page.

~ **Book III** ~

1. As it was spring, the fish were spawning on the sand bars that rose up out of the big lake, and yet more fish were crawling up the river to thrash at the foot of the rapids. The cold grip of winter had been released, and everyone was fishing and getting ready for planting. Long nets woven with twine made from the fibers of stinging nettle were taken out and repaired. The nets were stretched around the docks of Agencytown like streamers. The old women who had spent the winter rolling the nettle fibers into twine between their hands and ankles so often that they had calluses running up their calves from the constant rolling now had reason to be happy—as a result of their labor fresh fish would soon be boiling away in large kettles. These old women sang and laughed as they repaired the old nets and stretched the new ones. The men collected spruce root and set great pots of pitch to boil in order to fix the canoes and make them watertight, while others, not so interested in fishing, plowed the small fields next to town and hoed the central garden in preparation for planting. Others set their grindstones in their yards and merrily sharpened their tools in anticipation of the warm work of spring.

There was much to do, and Bimaadiz and Eta each helped out where they could. Bimaadiz, being young and almost fearless, dove to the bottom of the lake with a rope tied around his waist to where the birch-bark canoes had been sunk in order that they not freeze and break apart above ground. Once he located them, he attached the rope and returned to the surface, and the canoes were raised amid much cheering. The women and girls fixing nets on shore whistled and shouted when Bimaadiz, wearing only his trousers, emerged from the lake—beads of water running off his brown, muscled back. One of them even kissed him, which he enjoyed but which annoyed Eta.

As for Eta, once the nets were put out and the fish started coming in, she put her knife to use. Great smoky fires of punky aspen had been started under the ironwood drying racks, and Eta gutted and split the fish and handed them up to the other women who hung them on the racks. With the fires going and the canoe-loads of fish arriving, the festivities lasted long into the night. The men played the moccasin game and bagese and the women stoked the fires. The men, surrounded by onlookers and baskets of dried fish, teased and fought one another for the right to hand this or that choice delicacy to Eta on the chance their hands might touch hers. One moccasin-game man put his arm around her waist and said he would ante up his horses and his dogs—all of them—and when he doubled his possessions, he would ask for her hand in marriage. Eta blushed with delight but Bimaadiz did not like it at all.

After a few days of this Bimaadiz and Eta both grew weary of all the activity and longed for the quiet of the bush, for the solitary pursuits of hunting and trapping though the season was over. On the pretext of hunting a fawn or two for their skins, they left the village and retreated into the woods.

2. As soon as they left Agencytown behind they began to feel better—neither one continued to dwell on the uncomfortable thought that the other liked the attention they had received in town. They headed in the direction of Eta's trapping grounds and hadn't gotten far, just an hour or so up the trail, when they saw an old man moving toward them, hobbling down the trail. They didn't often meet someone on the trail, especially someone they didn't know. But it was spring, and at this time many people left their deepwoods homes to receive their annuities at the Agency, to reprovision and then to head back out to their quiet habitations. This man was very old and moved very slowly. Instead of one walking stick he used two, one in each hand, and he had a great bundle tied up in trade cloth that he balanced on his bent back. Bimaadiz and Eta did not know how good his eyesight was or his hearing, and not wishing to startle the man, they began talking loudly. When he drew near, Bimaadiz and Eta stepped off the trail to give him room to pass.

"Hello, Kiiwenz," said Bimaadiz in a friendly tone.

He was young enough to like older people because he could see no connection between himself and them—they were not, in his imagination, what he would become. They were something wholly different, not connected to him at all. And Bimaadiz was not so old as to want to despise or ridicule them out of fear that he would soon join them as they tottered around, barely able to stand. He was fond of old people and wanted to show his respect.

The old man stopped and looked closely at Bimaadiz and Eta. His eyes were clear and focused. He had no difficulty seeing them. Since he stopped, Bimaadiz and Eta asked him if he would like some smoked trout and a drink of fresh water. He said yes and the youngsters helped him set down his bundle, which he then sat on as though it were a chair or a stool. His hair was white and wispy, and they could see his brown scalp showing underneath. His hands were creased and callused, but clean, and when he took the fish from Eta's outstretched hand, his hand did not shake or tremble.

"Yes, that's what everyone calls me now," he said after he thumbed off a chunk of good clean trout from the tines of the trout's rib cage. It took Bimaadiz and Eta a second to realize that the old man was referring to Bimaadiz's greeting, a delayed response; as though he could only now answer them after he had been given something.

"No one calls me by my real name anymore," he continued. He grew silent for a while as he savored a mouthful of the smoked trout. He smiled.

"I haven't tasted salt for many years now, and it is a real pleasure. My wife has been dead for longer than we were together. My children have spread out across the land. But since I live quietly—collecting downed timber for wood instead of chopping at the trees, finding the food that grows wild like mushrooms, rice, leeks and parsnips—life comes to me and I no longer have to chase it. Deer walk up to my lodge and kneel down, I don't even have to shoot them, I can use my knife. Ducks dance into my lodge and around the fire, and all I have to do is wring their necks and pile them next to the door. All in all, I have everything I need. But salt is a pleasure."

Bimaadiz and Eta smiled, each thinking that the old man was more fond of the stories he told than of the truth. But they were at their ease, and the old man's lies did no harm. The old man continued.

"But when I left my lodge this morning, I thought I saw a wolf standing in my garden. When I tried to shoot it (as an old man I need thicker fur than what the rabbits give me), it disappeared. Instead, in its place, I saw a maple tree even though maples don't grow where I live. When I lowered the gun and stared at the tree, instead of a tree I saw a fox. I raised the gun again (as an old man I need softer fur than what the beavers give me), and when I sighted down the barrel, instead of a fox in my sights I saw a chickadee. I began to feel frustrated. All this raising and lowering of the rifle made me tired and annoyed, and so I used the only weapon we old people really possess, my voice. 'If you have something to say or something to show me, then do it,' I said. 'If you're here to play tricks on me then play them. I need to go to the Agency for my annuity and though it might not look like it, I am in a hurry.'

"And then I heard a voice, sometimes close, and at other times far off, calling from between the trees.

"'I have watched you for a long time, Kiiwenz,' the voice said. 'I was the one who made you and your wife fall in love. I was the one who made your children possible. You have me to thank for your life.'

"I kept the gun ready in case I had a shot—when something like that happens you shoot when you can because if the voice is that of some powerful being then your bullets won't harm it. But if your shot hits its mark, then you can either eat or wear whatever dies in the leaves. I kept the gun ready, and the One-Whose-Name-We-Don't-Say (because as it turns out that's who it was) must have seen my thumb on the hammer because he laughed and this time the sound, his laughter, came right out of the barrel of my gun.

'You won't be able to shoot me,' he said. 'You couldn't catch me with a bullet nor could you run me down even if you were young, and you were fast once if I remember. And why would you want to shoot me? I took care of you once, and now I need to take care of others.'

"That's what he said, and he was right. I had won many races when I was a young man, no one could catch me. I wanted to ask him more—but he was gone. And now I see the two of you along the trail."

Bimaadiz and Eta were amused by the old man's stories and didn't believe anything he said, such things only happen in stories, not in life. But they didn't want to mock him by laughing, such behavior is not becoming. So Bimaadiz asked, "Who was he? Where is he from? What can he do?"

"Who is he? He-Whose-Name-We-Don't-Say, that's who he is. But you can also call him Zaagichigewinini, because that's what he does, and he can do much more than that, though there is nothing greater than that when you think about it. He can take any shape—birds, wolves—he can even look like an old man. Like me. He is older than the earth and older than all the animals and all the spirits that inhabit it. And watch out if he takes an interest in you. Because he is interested only in seeing what will happen, not in a happy outcome."

The man paused, and as he relished the point of his story so he relished the point of the smoked trout in his hands by breaking off the sweet, firm, boneless flesh near its tail.

"I remember when he took an interest in me. I was young, like you. I had met my wife, but she was not yet my wife. He shot me with zaagi'idiwin. It was terrible. I couldn't sleep. I tossed and turned and thought only of the girl I had met. I neglected my traps. My shots flew wide of the mark. I forgot where I'd hung my snares. I could think only of her, and it was ruining my life."

This caught Bimaadiz and Eta's attention. He had described exactly what they were feeling.

"What did you do?" they asked in unison

"There is only one thing you can do," the old man said sadly. "You must kiss, and embrace, and lie down together naked. It's the only remedy. You'll see. Once you do that you'll feel much better, it really is wonderful medicine."

The old man looked up at the sun, and, strangely, did not squint against its power.

"I am off to the Agency."

And without waiting he shouldered his bundle, picked up his walking sticks, and set off down the trail.

He had given Bimaadiz and Eta a lot to think about.

3. They stood up, confused, embarrassed. They stretched as though waking from a nap or having sat still for a long time, when in reality they had done neither. They walked slowly up the trail—confused and shy. It was the first time either of them had heard of He-Whose-Name-We-Don't-Say, who is also known as Zaagichigewinini, and it was also the first time they had heard the phrase "zaagi'idiwin"— that sickness that seemed to have infected them both. Since they had been raised by people who were not their real parents and had never spent much time in a village—surrounded by cousins and siblings and play friends—listening to stories or even witnessing the physical results of zaagi'idiwin, they were terribly innocent and had no idea that the cure for such an illness was almost, but not quite, as divine as the sickness itself.

They thought about the old man's advice as they walked side by side. When he told them of his own experiences, he might as well have been talking about theirs, about how they felt—hot, as though sitting under a strong sun, tingly as though stung by bees, dizzy as though they had each been holding their breath for too long. Occasionally, as they thought on these things, their hands would touch, just a brush really, as they swung their arms in time with their leisurely strides. Each time their skin came into contact they felt a surge of emotion, a pleasant tremor, and with each touch they thought of what the old man had said about lying down naked together. But that felt like a long way off, a distant place from where they were. Such a drastic action! Neither child could imagine saying anything about it—they were both raised to be modest and respectful, raised not to be too blunt or to push those around them too hard. To suggest such a thing, to say it out loud was impossible. But all the same, they were thrilled at the casual touch of their hands and wanted more, so each time their hands passed either Bimaadiz or Eta would keep it there, hoping their hands would stay in contact a little longer. It thrilled them, and their little game occupied them so completely they were unable to talk and they had to concentrate on the trail, to match their strides so their arms would swing in time and enable them to prolong the moment when their hands came in contact.

Lucky for them, whenever humans invent a sickness, nature provides a remedy if not a cure. Because, focused on her hand and on Bimaadiz's hand, and attuned to the swinging of their arms and the pace they set with their feet, Eta neglected to look out for the trail and she stumbled on a tree root. As quick as lightning Bimaadiz grabbed her hand to keep her from falling. But once she regained her balance Bimaadiz did not let go. He loosened his grip but did not let go. Eta, without realizing what she was doing, without knowing what she *should* do, but able to do it anyway, laced her soft cool fingers in between his. They were now walking hand in hand.

It was magical for them both. Warmth flooded their bodies. They felt dizzy, off-center, but filled with happiness. An unfathomable joy—from whence did it come? what was its cause?—consumed them. A mystery to be sure, but no less a thrill for being unknown. They gazed at the canopy above them—they were still in the lowlands and among maples, ironwood, and birch that were budding out, ripe with life, and they offered silent thanks to the trees. Bimaadiz thought they had never looked so beautiful. Eta thought herself the luckiest girl on earth, so blessed was she to live among such venerable trees. They promised—each on their own, silently—to honor all the trees because it was a tree root that brought them together.

And so they walked along hand in hand with no idea where they were going—experiencing a quiet pleasure lost on adults, who, because they have experienced it all, because they have climbed the peak of life, look down on everything. They have forgotten how beautiful the view is from the valley floor.

But how soon we search for the higher trail! Because, if Bimaadiz and Eta had reached the end of their efforts we could end ours and stop the story here—with the two impossibly beautiful children, walking hand in hand down the wooded trail. But since their satisfaction *did* end, and much sooner than they expected, our story must continue.

And so, even though holding hands was a big step for the two, and even though it brought them pleasure that they themselves would have been hard-pressed to describe, it can't be imagined that it brought them total happiness. They are humans after all, not characters in a story. They wanted more. They each thought about the rest of the old man's advice—how he told them they must also kiss, and embrace, and ultimately lie down together naked. But neither of them knew how to make any of *that* happen, and they both prayed for some kind of accident, like the tree root, which would show them how to proceed. They were hungry, but they didn't know what for. And they wanted more, but they didn't know more of what. Holding hands wasn't enough—it was a taste, not a meal, and trappers and hunters need meals to keep them strong.

They looked in the trees, hoping to spy a bird. They tested the wind for strange smells. They looked for flowers, the first blooms of spring—trillium or cowslip. They looked for anything that could distract them from their dilemma. But it was too early in the year for such things, and the birds were off in some other part of the forest, and no smells, none out of the ordinary, greeted them. But suddenly, to Bimaadiz's great relief, he saw a morel mushroom poking its helmet above the duff on the forest floor.

4. "Look," he said excitedly, and he pulled Eta by the hand off the trail and into the woods. She couldn't see it at first.

"Look for the stalk, you'll see." He pointed.

"I don't see anything," she said impatiently. "I can't see anything."

So he led her up to it, and they knelt down in front of the tasty thing. She saw it and squealed and said, "Yes! Yes! It was right there! How could I miss it?"

They both marveled at its presence, exclaiming how perfect it was, how good it would taste, how hard it was to find them. (Though the truth of it was that the two of them had often hunted for mushrooms in the spring). If the temperature was right and if it had rained a lot and the sun cooperated, these treats were common enough.

But Bimaadiz and Eta were so nervous, so unsure of themselves that they could not address each other directly much less talk about what the old man had suggested, so they used the innocent, unsuspecting mushroom as a pretext to kneel down, to put their shoulders and their whole arms in contact. Bimaadiz put his arm around Eta, pretending she hadn't seen the mushroom yet, and with his hand on her shoulder guided her closer to the thing. He felt the heat of her neck. She patted his thigh in order to draw his attention to other mushrooms, visible now that they knew what to look for, or perhaps newly emerged, released by Bimaadiz and Eta's collected heat.

She pointed one direction at a cluster of mushrooms, he nodded and pointed to another bunch of them in a different direction, and with each turn of their heads they drew closer together. The closer their lips were, the harder their hearts beat, until, suddenly, without knowing how, their lips met. And once their soft lips—used only for eating, talking, and singing—met, they discovered a new purpose for their mouths. A truer, more satisfying occupation for that hungry organ.

They drew apart and looked into each other's eyes. To Bimaadiz, Eta had never looked so beautiful. Her hair was windblown, and a few fronds were draped across her forehead. Her breath came fast. Bimaadiz gently pushed her hair back and was amazed at how smooth her skin was, how deep the color. Her neck and cheeks were tinged red, and the birthmark on her right cheek looked darker against its red background. Small beads of sweat clung to her upper lip.

Eta could not stop gazing into Bimaadiz's eyes. They were much darker than she thought—the pupil and iris were almost the same color—and they were alive with life as they jumped first from one of her own eyes and then to the other and back. His eyelids were pulled down at the corner, and so when he blinked it was a lazy, hooded gesture (if we can call blinking a gesture, and most certainly we can when describing lovers and how they look at each other). His eyes looked sleepy and shy, in contrast to the energy of his gaze. They had never been so beautiful.

They kissed again. This time their lips touched for a much longer time. And though it was an inexperienced kind of kiss—clumsy, hesitant, and then with too much pressure—both of the youngsters felt dizzy. They kissed and pulled apart. Paused, and kissed again until their knees began to ache, kneeling there above the mushrooms, and so they sat down in the leaves cross-legged and facing each other. Eta kissed Bimaadiz's closed eyes. He kissed the dark smudge on her cheek. With each kiss it was as though they were building a bridge over a river and thereby joining two previously separate cities, which could then, over time, become one.

They kissed through the day—pausing only to draw back and assess the other or to shift their legs and wiggle their toes, which had fallen asleep, or to brush back and smooth the other's hair. As they leaned in to feast on each other's lips their knees kissed as well. The shallow shells of their kneecaps brushed together through her skirt and through his pants in childish imitation of the meeting of their soft lips. So they kissed and kissed and with four knees and two sets of lips their greedy bodies were able to share in three kisses at once.

There was no one to watch except for the mushrooms that stood silent guard on the forest floor. But they were forgotten. Neither Bimaadiz nor Eta could see—as the sun shone down and the kisses continued—that the mushrooms grew, poking their heads out of the duff with their shafts hardening, as though watered and fed by the children's touch. Thus the day passed, the sun sank low in the sky and the dusk brought with it a sharp chill. Finally, Bimaadiz and Eta stood, dazed by what they had discovered, and hurried home, their lips burning from all the rubbing.

5. Every day thereafter they woke up, each in their own bedroll, and rushed to meet in the deep woods, and spent the whole day kissing and embracing. They parted in the evening to dream of the other all night long. They both thought often of Kiiwenz's advice, and the expedient of nakedness, and while after kissing they were prone to believe in everything the old man had said, neither was bold enough to take the initiative.

Step by step, as religious processions slowly make their way to the most sacred of sites, their hands began walking—fluttering—over each other, moving ever so slowly into more hallowed precincts. This way Bimaadiz took great delight in discovering the bold knob of Eta's elbow, that high hill, covered in skin, from which the rest of her arm could be surveyed. And Eta found pleasure that made her breasts tingle in tracing the rippled delta of his veined hand.

And smells, too! Bimaadiz delighted in the difference between the musty scent of her scalp, the grit of her neck, and the vinegar of her armpits—while Eta marveled at how Bimaadiz's hands smelled like whatever he had been handling—cedar, grass, her own hair. And as a result whenever she smelled these things when away from Bimaadiz they reminded her of him, they became the essence of him, if only for a moment. Since she could not consume him, she kissed his hands, and licked his palms, taking the scent into her mouth.

And things might have followed their own course. Bimaadiz and Eta might have taken off their clothes and lain down together and thus might have taken their lessons from nature instead of from an old man, had not something terrible happened that interrupted their studies.

6. It was still spring, a week or two after the fish had finished their run and retired to the lake bottoms, sand bars, and weedlines.

The season's work was underway. Furs were sold and shipped away to the cities to the south, the prairie grass had been burnt, and a carpet of emerald-colored new growth was sprouting through the black blanket of charred stalks. Seed was sorted and sown. Mares were foaling, and in the pens the sows lay heavily on their sides and were plagued by their unwelcome young as well as by the first flies hatched in the warm weather. The piles of sawdust in the lumberyards finally thawed, and the men who worked at the mills spread it out over the ground away from the buildings—attentive always to the dangers of fire.

But there was also activity of another sort. There were many boats on the big lake now that the ice was gone—birch-bark canoes, York boats with oars and a single mast, passenger ships, coracles, skiffs, and half-decked sailboats—but one boat on the lake was quite different and served a unique purpose. It did not launch out onto the broad lake to take of its riches—it fished the shores for a different kind of catch. It was a steamship and had originally served as a ferry and, oh years ago, it carried passengers the long way down the lake. As such it was fitted with berths, a dining room, and a galley. But as the passenger service had diminished, the boat—known affectionately as the "Floating Hell" to the clergy, and as the *Ariel* to its grateful customers—had developed new business.

There were many logging camps along the shore—far apart from one another and far from any large village or town. Far from sites of pleasure. The men at these lumber camps were also far from civilization, far from the company of women, and so were naturally quite lonely.

All winter they worked from well before first light until long after dark. They ate their meals either in the woods or by lantern light, and when they woke up in the morning they massaged their frozen boots—trying to make a pliable house for their feet. It was a dark existence—their cabins had dirt floors packed with grease and shined and polished by the tobacco juice and snot they spit there that froze quickly to the packed earth. They tapped their pipes into their trouser cuffs and jacket pockets. Porcupines, who never wash on account of their quills, and whose work among the trees was similar to that of the sawyers, were cleaner and smelled better than the men who labored below them.

These men, then, all possessed a natural desire that was compressed and exaggerated by their unnatural confinement, and also, perhaps, because of the repetitive nature of their work—sawing, chopping, sharpening, walking. By spring their lust had reached unbearable levels. But lucky for them, and unlucky for everyone else, they could count on seeing the *Ariel* chugging alongshore within a month of ice-out.

She made her way slowly from camp to camp. Her furnaces were stoked up and pressure rose in her boilers, but—despite the amount of fuel she was fed and the work done on her engines—it was impossible to get her to move very quickly. She crawled along the shore. The men in the camps waited eagerly each spring for signs of smoke over the water. And, as she slowly hove into view, the men could already taste the pleasure they would receive in her belly. But they had to wait.

They had to wait for the *Ariel* to drop anchor a quarter mile from shore. The sawyers could see, just barely, great activity on deck as garbage was thrown into the water and the cabins were aired out, and when all was ready, lanterns, shuttered in red glass, were lit and hung from the bow. Once the men received this signal—devilred—they jumped in whatever craft was nearby and raced toward the *Ariel*'s decks. Because it was a first-served first-come arrangement, those who lagged behind the rest had to wait, and it was torture to listen to the moans, to the jingling beds, even to the fiddle music meant to arouse the men and drown out the evidence of their pleasure.

The *Ariel* had a crew. A captain, a pilot, mechanics, deck hands, a blind piano player, a blind violinist, and the women, of course. These people, humans, were so perfectly integrated in the *Ariel*'s chief enterprise that they did not seem human, did not act as individuals. They were merely organs, essential concentrations of matter with specialized purposes, which collectively gave life to the

Ariel. So the sawyers who clambered on her body, who descended into her belly, had no clear image or memory of the dark strangers who gave her life. The sawyers, for instance, could not tell you what the captain looked like, or which shadowy figure was the pilot, or if there even was a man called "the carpenter" onboard, so well did the crew blend in with the vessel and so rigidly did they hold their course and their schedule; they always anchored at dusk and were always gone by morning. To the men who received their pleasure there and to the women who were deprived of their freedom there, the *Ariel* seemed like a living thing, a queen.

But even queens, especially those of the night, must eat, and that was what she was doing that day. She was moored a few miles up the shore from Agencytown, just far enough to prevent people from the town from paddling out and trying to run her off. All that day, or this day, she had labored against a terrible headwind. Her boilers were running at their maximum. The wood stacked on her decks had disappeared below and emerged, chastened and spent, as smoke from her smokestacks, and from her square, regal stern, as a frothy train of foam.

The *Ariel* was out of fuel and so, in the light of day, she moored not three miles from Agencytown, and the men onboard disembarked with saws and axes and set to work cutting wood to feed the *Ariel's* pulsing red heart.

7. Eta was in the forest collecting basswood blossoms for tea and, here and there, testing the birch to see if their bark was ready for harvest, swollen and slick. It was a beautiful, warm, spring day, and Eta was happy to be doing such casual, relaxing work. With joy she climbed the basswood to reach the best blossoms near their crowns. All the while she thought of Bimaadiz and his sweet lips, his smooth shoulders, and the stratum of muscles under his skin. She was enjoying herself though she was anxious to gather as much as she could as quickly as she could because she was supposed to meet Bimaadiz at her lean-to so they could resume kissing next to the spring that gurgled and sang.

Eta was so absorbed in her gathering and in thoughts of Bimaadiz—she had her head in the clouds, literally—that she did not hear the *Ariel's* men tramp down the trail and stop underneath her tree. They looked up and saw her, or what glimpses of her they could snatch through the canopy. They weren't sure what she was— a human, a porcupine, a bear—and probably had no idea a beautiful Indian girl was cutting basswood blossoms thirty feet above the forest floor. All the same, whatever it was could be captured, eaten, or sold, and so they began chopping at the base of the tree.

Eta's heart jumped at the first stroke of the axe. She was about to shout but she held back when she got a look at the men. They did not seem like real men—they did not dress like Indians or loggers or like men from town. Their clothes were baggy and nondescript. And they did not speak to one another or shout or sing—as most men do when they think no one is watching. They were quiet and very dirty, their features hidden in their loose-fitting clothes. Even if they hadn't started chopping down the tree Eta was in, they would have seemed dangerous. Eta did not shout, did not alert them to her presence. Not that it would have done any good. Eta's heart skipped with each stroke of the axe. She grabbed the bole more tightly. The men did not tire. When one stopped chopping, another immediately took his place, and the axe-stroke had the regularity (and finality) of a ticking clock. Eta felt each powerful stroke vibrate up the trunk and into her body. And she knew, communicated perhaps by the vibrations, that the men were there for her.

She decided that she would rather die than be captured. Life was not worth living without Bimaadiz, and her dead body would give him more relief than her capture and disappearance. After all, when confronted with death we mourn the past, but when confronted with silence we mourn the present and the future as well. As resolute as she was, she began thinking not just about Bimaadiz but about her parents and her trapline, too. She couldn't help it. We shouldn't be too hard on the girl or scold her too much for clutching the bole tightly, pressing her face against the smooth bark, and crying.

If this were a more magical story, Eta's tears—copious, wrenched from her little girl's heart as she contemplated an end to a life just begun—would rain down on the men below and would sink into their clothing, soak their upturned faces, and infect them with her sadness. They would grow heavy with sorrow, unable to continue their work. They would lean into their fellow man, and they themselves would begin to cry and lament, crippled by Eta's sorrow, which had become their sorrow and through which they would pass, as one passes through a lodge-flap, back into the world of decency and compassion.

But this is not that kind of story, because, unlike fairy tales and fairy-tale tears, this story and Eta's tears are true. And they had no power except the power to express her fears and the chemical power to clean her eyes of any dust or other impurities. In all likelihood, the men chopping the tree down had never cried and never would and were barely men anymore anyway. They did not know or understand sorrow or regret. All they knew was the necessity of the work ahead of them. If a few of Eta's tears escaped the net of leaves that separated her from the men below and did land on their faces or forearms or shoulders, they thought that, as it happens in the spring, they had shaken loose sap from the tree and neither the treesap or humansap raining from above had any effect on them.

It did not take them long. Basswood is a forgiving wood, free of knots or twisted grain, which is why it is so sought after by carvers. In a few short moments the tree was ready. After one last blow it began to topple, slowly at first. It leaned, the men gave it a push, and it began to fall. Eta shrieked and the men heard her scream, but the tree was already on the way down. All Eta could hear was the ripping of leaves and the whip of branches—the terrible noise of approaching death.

The tree crashed down, followed by a lazy coda of blossoms and pollen. The men walked to the crown to see what they had captured and saw—instead of a bear cub or porcupine or even a squirrel's nest—a beautiful Indian girl nestled in the branches. She had long black hair, beautiful hands, a slim waist, and breasts whose magnificence was barely concealed by her torn dress. She lay still and looked to be dead, but they noticed that she was breathing. Alive. Unconscious. Two of the men lifted her carefully from the mess of broken branches and set her to the side of the tree and covered her with their coats. They began cutting the tree into bolts. Basswood makes terrible firewood but it will burn if the fire is hot enough. Once they were done they sat amongst the branches and leaves and smoked a pipe in silence and after that they loaded the wood on their backs with canvas straps. One man carried Eta and another carried the axes. They set off down to the lakeshore.

A beautiful girl like the one they found in the tree would not feed the *Ariel's* appetite, but she would feed the appetites of those who came to the evil boat. She would produce heat and motion of a different sort and was a far more valuable fruit of the forest than firewood. They walked up the gangplank and onto the *Ariel.* They stacked the wood and the man carrying Eta carried her below decks, and she disappeared with the last rays of the setting sun.

8. Bimaadiz had waited at Eta's lean-to, but she hadn't arrived. He had made himself busy—replaced old boughs on the roof, raked out the trash and wood chips inside, scrubbed out the lard pails so they could be used again. He became impatient and angry; he couldn't imagine what would keep Eta. Soon his thoughts turned ugly. He thought she had found something more interesting to do. More to the point, she might have found someone more interesting to spend her time with. How quickly jealousy, the dirtiest of emotions, scrubs the mind of good thoughts. Who could it be? What could she be doing? He distracted himself by inventing heavier chores: righting the wood pile, splitting kindling, cutting brush. None of the work helped. Still he thought bad thoughts, and hoped they could not summon Eta. Still Eta did not come: the injustice of his feelings could summon her before the magistrate of his heart. Finally, late in the afternoon he left in disgust and began to search for her in the deep woods. He hoped he would find her and surprise her with whomever it was she had chosen over him. He wanted to find her in an awkward situation.

Tracking humans is so much easier than tracking animals. The branches are broken higher up, and the dry leaves on the ground are shredded more because the footprint is so much bigger. When he found where her trail began, not far from Agencytown, it was easy enough to follow. He could see where she had walked quickly, sure of her goal, and where she meandered and stopped to rest. He even saw the places where she had stopped to drink from her skinbag. There her weight had shifted to one foot, as she tilted the water-filled bladder to her mouth. She had even spilled some water on the leaves underfoot, though it was drying quickly. Bimaadiz smiled despite himself when he saw where her hand had stripped the seeds from a dead stalk of wild oats left from the year before. He noticed at one point she had hesitated and taken a few steps in one direction, only to turn back. In this part of the forest there were only two directions she would have gone: into the marsh where the strawberries were sure to be ripe, or toward the lake where the moist stands of basswood stood, laden with blossoms for the picking. He was more at ease now; hers were the only tracks and so she had been alone unless she had planned in advance to meet someone out there. With each step Bimaadiz grew more excited at the prospect of finding her and seeing her; he was anxious to continue his study of her body, her lips, her arms. He had already forgotten his own anger and jealousy.

Bimaadiz entered the clearing just after the sun had set, but there was plenty of light by which to see. He stopped and his heart stopped, too, if only for a second, because it began beating again violently. His ears burned, his hands shook. He saw the downed trees, and, among the branches, her gathering basket, crushed and on its side, spilling the white linden blossoms out. He saw the tracks. He saw the waddles of tobacco juice on the spade-shaped leaves, the axe marks on the trunks. All of the tracks led down to the lake. Bimaadiz ran after them and arrived on the shore in time to see the *Ariel* being poled out to deeper water and to see the great paddlewheel slowly begin to churn, and at the very last, to see the bow lantern being unshuttered as the evil boat made for deeper water.

9. Bimaadiz stared at the retreating boat, guided by its single red eye until it disappeared. He wanted to die. He could not go back to Agencytown. What kind of man was he? His friend had been abducted and for him to go running to his parents or to hers would be cowardly, and so he stayed, and since there was nothing to do except feel, he sat down and felt. And he felt that he wanted to die. No woman who was swallowed by the *Ariel* ever climbed back out, and so what could his or her parents do anyway?

He walked away from shore, and since it was cold he crawled in the leafy crown of the tree that had been Eta's last shelter. He crawled and wriggled among the branches and pulled down more on top of himself. It was an uncomfortable nest. The sticks and branches poked him in the back and sides and no matter how small he made himself he could not find a position that freed him from his discomfort. It was just as well, he thought. I do not deserve comfort when Eta will be a captive and a slave for the rest of her life. The smell of the linden blossoms reminded him of her afresh. Oh Eta, he groaned, here are all the blossoms you could ever want but you are not here to pick them!

It was too much for him to bear and he cried huge, gaping tears. Such weeping is exhausting after all, and so Bimaadiz eventually fell asleep.

While he slept he had a dream. He never told anyone, not even Eta, about what he dreamt. And so, one wonders, how do we know? And while that is impossible to answer without destroying the dream itself, it is important that we *do* know what he dreamt if we are to understand what happened next. So for better or worse, known or unknown, told or untold, Bimaadiz dreamt.

Of a man. Ancient, with the benefit of centuries of wisdom.

He stood in the dark looking at the broken shape of the night sky with what looked like stars sprayed out before him. Without turning he spoke to Bimaadiz, and his words sounded from inside Bimaadiz's head.

He said, "I've been watching you for a long time now, Bimaadiz. And I can tell you that you needn't cry because your Eta will not die on the *Ariel*."

Bimaadiz no longer felt like crying.

"Eta will not die on the *Ariel* and, in fact, she will never die and neither will you. Though I am sure you don't believe me, it is true: you will live forever."

"I don't believe you. No one lives forever."

"Most don't. But some do. I don't blame you—you cannot see what I can see," said the man. "But I have looked after you for some time now. I have been in charge of your future and Eta's and I will make sure that she will return safe and sound. And I will do so even though you have never made me an offering. You haven't even so much as dropped tobacco for me or charred some meat in the fire so I can taste the smoke from where I sit at a distance."

The way the man said "sit at a distance" made Bimaadiz shudder. The man's words suggested an immense power, beyond Bimaadiz's reckoning. He knew that this man had the power to wipe him out as easily as one's thumb cleared the soot from the mantle glass of a lantern.

"I will," said Bimaadiz. "If you help me get Eta back, I'll always make offerings for you. I will give you the choice meats. And tobacco. I will give you the beaver's forearm, for sure the tastiest part."

"Go to sleep now, Bimaadiz. In the meantime I will rescue your beloved. Shortly after you awake you will be reunited with her."

With those words Bimaadiz dreamt no more.

10. Eta lay in the belly of the boat. She felt the boat shudder as the bow was turned into the waves. The rhythmical churning of the paddlewheel sounded dully to the aft. Her head hurt where it had struck a branch when the tree hit the ground. Her whole body ached. She patted herself—her arms and legs, her stomach and neck—to make sure she wasn't injured. She wasn't. She sighed and was grateful that at least her clothes had not been ripped off or taken away, not that she knew what was going to happen to her on that terrible boat, but because she was an innocent girl and no one except her mother (so she thought) had seen her naked.

There was no light by which to see, and the motion of the boat and the sound of the paddlewheel further disconcerted her. It took awhile for Eta to quiet the beating of her heart and to stop herself from turning her head frantically back and forth. The small sound of her dress collar rubbing against her neck made it hard for her to hear. She suddenly thought that if she still had her puukko she might be able to escape. She checked but either she had dropped it or it had been taken away by her captors when she was unconscious. She did not cry, if only because she was too intent on listening for the sound of people moving elsewhere on the boat.

Then, casting for sound, Eta heard something moving in the room with her. There was the soft sound of clothing or fur brushing against metal. Then silence. Eta held still. She could see nothing. Then she heard the unmistakable sound of bone, someone's shin perhaps, stubbing against something harder. It was the same sound her dogs made when they hit their heads against a deadfall out in the forest. Ahhh, the forest. Her dogs. And Bimaadiz. The thought that she might not ever see any of them again was a sorry thought and almost enough to make her cry. And then, as though bringing her thoughts farther out into the woods, she heard the sound of a hoof or a claw stomp on the wooden hull.

Eta shrank back against the boards and tried to burrow into the rags and tattered cloth that made up the crude pallet on which she sat. Something was out there, just a few feet away from her, and she didn't know what it was—human or animal—or if it was caged or chained. Perhaps it was Mishi-bizhiw himself making ready for his meal.

She listened for breathing, and there it was: the quiet breath, a rattle of spit or snot. Eta knew better than to be scared of any of the creatures of the forest. But then again, when threatened or cornered, even the gentlest animal, even a muskrat, could become a fearsome fighter. She needed to know what it was that was so near her in the dark in order to know what to do. She spoke— but there was no response. She called out: Hello? There was no answer, not even a change in the creature's breathing. It must be an animal. Eta thought perhaps it would respond to animal calls.

First she mewed like a beaver, but there was no response. She scolded like an otter, though she was certain that whatever it was, it was not an otter: it would have run and twisted and jumped, making all sorts of noise. Next she tried yipping like a fox, but nothing. One by one she imitated all the animals whose voices she knew. She piped like a skunk, burped like a woodchuck, queried like an owl, pursed like a hawk, and barked like an eagle. There was no answer. Finally she huffed and growled like a wolf.

This set up a clamor in the hold. Feet stamped and there was the sound of a great body hitting the metal grill of a cage. She did it again, and again. The sound of the wolf set up a ruckus nearby in the dark. But it did not draw out a corresponding growl from across the way, so sensing that whatever it was, it was afraid of wolves, she switched her calls to animals hunted by wolves. She huffed like a frightened deer and, finally, bellowed as best she could, like a cow moose.

Eta was answered immediately by a corresponding bellow, higher in tone, and then another call overlapped the first and there was a great pounding of hooves and the metal bars of the cage rattled. The boat shook and more bellowing followed. Eta sat back, thinking. She had been taken captive and was being held with not one, but two, moose calves. Eta was grateful that her fellow prisoners were moose. Even though they were only calves, moose were strong, and it was said they were very wise because their heads stood above the brush, and so they could see for long distances.

She called to them again and again, if only to comfort herself, and the calves set up a racket—stomping and bawling and knocking against their cage. Suddenly the boat stopped moving and Eta heard footsteps above, the rattle of the anchor chain, and a tremendous rumbling sound as something heavy was dragged across the deck. Eta had forgotten all about the men who had captured her, and now, she sank deeper into her blankets. Eta was afraid and alone with only two captured moose calves for saviors and company.

11. There was more noise—banging and scraping—and then all was quiet. Eta held her breath because her breathing was too loud in her own ears for her to hear anything else, but there was nothing to hear anymore. Even the moose calves were quiet, expectant. Some time passed and then directly overhead a bow scraped across some fiddle strings, once, twice, there was a pause, and then the fiddler began to play a jig. It was a lilting tune, off-balance but it was loud, and the fiddler played true, sure of the direction of the music. The fiddler played the same song for quite a while, letting the notes careen off the water and skip toward shore. Tucked in between the notes Eta thought she could hear far-off voices and laughter.

And then, yes, the voices were distinct and close by. Eta then heard the sound of canoe paddles, and at the same time several canoes bumped their curved bows into the side of the *Ariel*. The paddlers were helped aboard, and Eta heard laughter and then the tromp of hobnailed boots directly above her head.

A hatch opened. The lantern light, half shuttered and dyed red by the colored mantle, washed down over her upturned face. Three men bent down and reached through the hatch and grabbing what they could, lifted Eta out of the hold and onto the deck.

She blinked and tried to get her bearings. By the time she did the men who lifted her out were gone. She stood in the middle of a cabin built mid-ship, like an enlarged pilot's house. It was square and very large. The room was ringed with chairs, settees, and couches. Behind these various places to sit, against three of the walls, were screens, behind which Eta could glimpse pallets and low beds. An upright piano stood in front of the wall without screens and beds. It was an old battered thing, its keys as orange as beaver teeth. Next to it sat the fiddler on a low stool. He bent low over his fiddle and with the last note of the song held and then completed, he sat up straight and scanned the room as the sound from the fiddle eased out of the windows and was loosed in the night somewhere. Eta noticed that the fiddler was blind. His eyes were sewn shut. Eta was scared and looked around the room for other signs of life, other people. She didn't see them at first, but there were other women in the room with her, six total. They were hard to see, dressed in prints and paisleys, gauzy sections of lace, and tattered ballgowns, and they draped themselves languidly over chairs and chaise lounges and blended well with the furniture. Eta had never seen women like this before, nor had she seen clothes like the ones they wore. Eta looked down at her own clothes and was embarrassed by her doeskin dress and tanned leggings. The poor, pitiful moose below deck must have looked better than she did. So she thought, but she knew nothing of the desires of men.

The fiddler began again. This time he plunged into a peppy jig, more regular, more military in tone than the reel he had played before, as though to call the customers, to send them marching and stomping into the room. It seemed to work: no sooner had he begun than lumberjacks, sawyers, skinners, and blacksmiths—all glistening with sweat and wearing their work (sawdust, charcoal, horseshit) on their clothes—trooped through the single door set to the side of the piano. They didn't talk to one another, they probably couldn't manage to speak even if they had wanted to. It had been months since they had been this close to any woman. They sat in every available seat scattered around the perimeter of the room. No one spoke. Occasionally one of them would tip the ashes from a cigar into his hat brim or spit tobacco down his shirtfront—no one dared to spill ash or spit on the floor. Eta started for the edge, looking for a place to sit, but all the seats were taken. She didn't know what to do so she continued to stand in the middle of the room with her hands at her sides.

After a few moments when the men had made themselves comfortable (they were a vicious-looking lot), the blind fiddler changed his tune and began to play a moderately paced reel. The men couldn't resist the song and some began to tap their hobnailed boots against the floor. They sucked on their plugs of tobacco and had to spit more often down their shirtfronts, into their hats. There were no spittoons. If they usually danced—with each other or with the women—they didn't dance this evening, not right away. No one got up. They all stared at Eta and tapped and spit and stared some more. She was the most beautiful girl any of them had ever seen and all of them, to a man, wanted to possess her. They had seen women in lace and silk and loosely tied robes; they had seen women in bloomers who sat in any one of the limited number of debauched poses they knew. But they had never seen a girl like Eta.

She stood still, erect, her hands at her sides. Her firm, high breasts—young breasts—pushed out the front of her doeskin dress. Her stomach was flat and strong, or so the way her dress clung to her stomach suggested. And those who sat behind her could see something none of the others could: the way the strong muscles of her buttocks rose from the small of her back, swelled, and met the tops of her thighs, and they saw, barely, how her buttocks quivered and shook with the tension of standing still, with fear. It drove these men wild. As for Eta, she could not move. She was pinned down by their desire.

The more impatient of the men could endure this for only so long. And when they could take no more, they grabbed the women nearest them without even looking (because in their minds they were seeing Eta) and retreated behind the screens. No one made a move for Eta, however. They didn't know how to approach her, how to take her. It would have to be decided somehow who would get her first. Moans and grunts came from behind the screens. Curses, all sorts of noise. The blind fiddler fiddled more loudly. The tempo of the reel increased. He continued drawing on the strings, harder, making the resin bite, but it was not enough to cover the secret sounds coming from behind the screens. The fiddler was exhausted, and just as he was about to finish the reel, an old man came tottering into the room from somewhere else and sat at the piano. He joined the fiddler, supported him, and together they built a more solid wall of sound, pushing the moans and grunts back. He was blind, too.

Faster, and fast it went. All the women except for Eta had been taken behind the screens, and more men must have arrived because all the vacant seats were taken. The sounds of pleasure, nasty and brutal, rose in pitch and volume. The song rose to match. The song and the dances ended together, and then the room went quiet. All eyes were on Eta.

Finally one man, a tall man in a black canvas suit shiny from wear, stood up. He did not immediately grab Eta's arm as was the usual method of picking a girl. He needed to prove that he was the one who should take her first. If he did not, then the others would be upon him. The man took a few steps out into the room from his place in the corner. He stamped his large foot on the boards, once, then twice. He put his hands on his hips and then bowed his head; the wide-brimmed black hat he wore nodded and turned toward the floor. The man stamped his foot again. The musicians understood the signal and started their tune, a heavy, pulsing dance number. The bow ground against the strings, the felt hammers lifted and dropped. The man lifted his foot and brought it down again and the competition for Eta, for the prize of her virginity, began.

The tall man in black danced deliberately. His feet slammed down on the deck boards—first one and then the other. His hands stayed on his hips and gave his dance a military feel. He bent at the waist and swiveled and made a half turn and repeated his steps facing the other direction—showing all of them his power, his control. As the song progressed he added steps—a skip, a double stomp—but the heavy force of his feet remained stuck to the downbeats. He made the floor shudder. Every move he made communicated strength and purpose and pure force—the aspect of a timber cruiser walking a line through the woods.

Halfway through the song a sawyer seated on the other side of the room stood up. He was short and wore the pointed red toque favored by the French. His shoulders and arms were thick and heavily muscled from pushing and pulling his saw through the trunks of red and white pine. He danced with his upper body. He swooped and milled his arms and largely ignored the work his legs could do—they were merely a platform that supported him. He planted his feet wide apart, and in time to the music he simulated pushing and pulling and as he turned to face Eta he pretended that he was sawing her down and loading her on the skidder.

One by one the men in the room stood and joined the contest, each in his own fashion. The skinners suggested they were driving their teams. The longshoremen unloaded their boats, that in this instance, were filled with desire. Even the cooks present made a big show of stoking their ovens and greasing their griddles. The most impressive dancers were the log-rollers, who slipped and slid across the deck and danced in place, and it was easy to imagine the logs rolling under their feet. All of them danced beautifully and each according to his occupation, and though their moves were beautiful the contest was evil. Eta's virginity was the prize. And they danced for one another, not for her.

No clear winner emerged and they danced harder, daring the others to match their moves or to continue. They sweated and whooped, punctuating their steps. The harder they danced the more their boots dug into the boards. The lanterns that hung from the ceiling shook and trembled on their hooks. The screens that hid the exchanges between the prostitutes and the men who had gone with them shook and shimmied and threatened to fall down. Bottles rattled across the tables, and some fell to the floor and were swept into the corners by the press of feet.

Eta had not moved from the center of the room.

The blind musicians played on with force and energy and a hellish insistency. They increased the tempo and volume. The dancers responded. They shouted and whirled and stomped the boards that had begun to lose their cotton caulking. Below decks the moose calves, alarmed by the frenzy occurring above them, moaned and bellowed and thrashed against the sides of their cage.

There was noise all around. And then, Bimaadiz's dream began to come true. It would not be believed that the dancing itself was so strong that it alone caused the destruction of the boat. There were other forces at work. The boat was not sound to begin with. It was not a proper boat and could not be dry-docked and fixed properly so whatever repairs it needed it received ad hoc with whatever was at hand and by whomever happened to be able to fix it. The spaces between the boards were plugged with pitch and tar, sometimes with cotton caulk, and at other times with strips of flour sacking. The boat's ribs had been cored by ants and wood-wasps and never sounded with picks. Dry rot had been painted over and ignored. With a little help from the man in the dream, and bit by bit, under the force of the dancing, the wood began to splinter. The nails, rusty as they were, began unclinching the boards from the ribs. The moose were so frightened they began to kick and butt the bars of their cage, and they bucked their way out. Spurred on by the noise and by their own fear, and by other unseen and higher forces, they began to kick the sides of the boat.

Leaks sprung here and there. Ribbons of water unraveled into the hull.

Water poured into the hold.

The dancers did not notice. They stomped and yelled. The music swelled.

The boat shipped so much water that the boilers were flooded. The boat could no longer move. It sank lower in the water and slack appeared in the anchor chain. Yet the dancing continued. They heard the splintering of wood and a great crash. The *Ariel* listed and began to sink.

The screens fell over and exposed the continued exertions of the impatient men and their consorts. The piano shifted, lurched, and slid across the cabin, bowling the men down as it charged the room. Bodies flew everywhere. The blind musicians stood and staggered away from their post and with outstretched hands, felt their way to a corner, and even though the piano player lost his instrument, the fiddler continued to play, lurching and staggering now, dancing to his own music, unable to stop. He was now narrating the ship's demise.

The window frames were torqued and twisted, and the ship settled even deeper in the water and the glass broke and fell to the floor with a great crash, mixing with the shouts of the men. The men and the prostitutes scrambled in every direction. Some toppled out of the windows and into the lake. Some fought amongst themselves to see who could get out the door first. Others kept dancing, while others just looked bewildered as they slid and slipped across the tilting deck, searching for the equilibrium they had lost.

Water poured over the deck and lapped against the walls. Bottles, lanterns, candles, plates, pillows, and screens rolled and batted around the floor.

Eta, who had remained still most of this time, began to edge closer to the door. She tried to become invisible, afraid that the men would notice her and that in the melee one of them (or more) would try something. Then the deck splintered, buckled, and broke open. Men and flotsam poured down below. A great crashing and struggle sounded from down there, and screams, too, and then one moose calf came clambering out, followed by the other.

They looked around wildly and as soon as they saw the open door leading out into the darkness they charged it. With their shoulders hunched and their heads down they moved toward the door and even though they were only half grown, they were so strong none of the men could stand in their way.

Eta, that smart girl, acted in an instant. When the moose passed her on either side she reached out and grabbed their beards. She was jerked off her feet, but she managed to hold on. Once through the door the moose hurdled the railing and plunged into the lake. the railing had hit Eta across her arms and chest, but she held on tight and was carried with them.

The twin calves, with Eta hanging in between, cleared the sinking boat in a few seconds. The boat was sinking fast. The water was already over the decks. Over the house, and then gone. The last part of it to disappear was the red eye hanging in front. The water closed over it and all was dark. Eta heard the men shouting and screaming and she thought she heard one final note from the fiddle. Then she was swept away by the moose across the lake into that outer dark.

Moose are strong swimmers, and Eta knew they would find their way to shore. Her hands ached and the churning water hit her in the face. It was cold. The ice had only gone out two weeks earlier. But the good girl held on, determined to reach the shore with the moose, who didn't seem to mind that she clung to their beards. She was a small inconvenience to animals as large and strong as they were.

It felt as though the moose had been swimming forever. Eta could see nothing and could not detect any change in their pace or direction. All she could hear was their even breathing and the lap of water against their chests as they surged forward. She tried to lift her head and look back to where the ship had been, but she could see nothing. Eta couldn't know it, but none of the men had been able to untie the canoes before the ship sank, and the canoes had been dragged down to the bottom of the lake. The men, with their heavy boots and woolen clothes, had soon followed. All of them had drowned, and they were now food for the fishes, or, more accurately, food for the turtles because they enjoyed rotten flesh much more than did their cousins the tulibee, red horse, and sturgeon.

12. Bimaadiz was sleeping. The dream had ended and with it his worries. He woke, however, when he heard a great splashing and then the crackling of brush. He jumped up and then crouched, thinking of a sudden that perhaps the men were back and the crown of the tree offered good cover from which to shoot. He levered a shell in the chamber and peered out among the leaves, ready to free Eta, or if she was dead, to exact a price for her pain.

He expected to see men, but instead he saw two moose emerge from the water with Eta between them. Bimaadiz shouted and dropped the gun and ran out into the open, stumbling among the branches.

When the moose saw him they snorted and turned and ran for the deep woods. Eta could no longer hold on as the moose careened through the brush, and she was rubbed off like a tick against a deadfall as the moose disappeared.

Bimaadiz rushed to Eta's side. She was alive! He held her and covered her with kisses. So great was his joy he did not think to check her for injuries, to see if she was all right. Only youth is so sure of its emotions that it would try to heal the beloved with kisses. She felt cold to the touch and even in the scant, starry light, he could see that she was pale, her lips blue.

"You're alive! I can't believe it! You're alive. I thought I'd never see you again. Are you hurt? Do you hurt much?"

She could barely speak, and spoke only one word, proving once and for all that there is joy in repetition. "Bimaadiz, Bimaadiz, Bimaadiz, Bimaadiz."

He knew he had to warm her up immediately and that his joy alone could not help her. So he picked her up and carried her away from the cold breezes coming off the lake. The basswood crown in which he had been sleeping, and in which Eta had been picking blossoms offered good protection from the cold air, and so he carried her there and set her down amid the branches. Bimaadiz then found twigs, birch bark, and a few dry sticks scattered nearby, and got a fire going. Eta moaned and trembled so much the green leaves of their nest quivered. The fire would not be enough, it could never touch her through her wet clothes. So Bimaadiz began to undress her. Piece by piece he removed her cold, wet, clothing.

First he carefully shucked her moccasins and then unlaced her leggings. He trembled and caught his breath. He thought he had never seen anything as beautiful as her legs, more beautiful now than ever, since he imagined he would never see them again. They were beyond compare, so smooth, so hard and well muscled, tapering to the delicate stems of her slim ankles. He would have liked to stop and stare, to touch them more but necessity urged him on. He commanded her, softly, gently, to lift her arms, which she did, though she was barely conscious. Again, Bimaadiz trembled in awe. Again, he thanked all the spirits he knew in one great rush for letting him see her as she was. He whispered to her and told her to lie down, it was warmer next to the ground. He gazed at her for a long moment. Her naked body was a mystery that only deepened the more he looked at it. How was such beauty possible? How was it possible that it could be made out of bone and blood? He admired the taught muscles of her hips, the band of muscle between her hip bone and her buttock, her delicate ribs arching and spreading below her breasts. Her breasts were small and round, and tipped with the quick brown nipples. She curled closer to herself, her arms tucked around her breasts, and when she moved he saw the long, lean triangle of muscle that began in her armpit spring tight and then relax. He had never seen anything like it. Each part of her he looked at surpassed what he had seen before. What sweet confusion! Where to look?

Steam rose off her skin. Bimaadiz could see a dark bruise developing just above her breasts, a purple line left there from the railing of the *Ariel*. And here and there she was marked with other bruises, abrasions, and scratches. She shivered in the naked air. And this prompted Bimaadiz to end his session. She needed more than the fire to warm her and so Bimaadiz stripped down, too. His clothes were dry and warm. Her temperature began to rise and spiked upward when in her half delirium she saw Bimaadiz naked. Perhaps it was just the cold, or the adventure of it all, but his arms looked bigger, his chest deeper, his shoulders broader, than when she had last seen him without his shirt on.

"Bimaadiz," she said, and that was all. He began to dress her in his clothes, though his hands shook and his eyes teared. He felt sick and afraid and he didn't know why. He felt as though he had been taken captive by marauders. In effect he had been: he was a captive of her beauty.

Once she was comfortable, encased in his clothes and sleeping soundly, Bimaadiz stood and put on Eta's leggings and dress. He did not put on her moccasins because he didn't want to stretch them out. The dress was loose enough so that he could fit it on, but just barely. He sat by the fire and let his body heat and the flames dry out her dress and leggings. He stared into the nest of coals and silently thanked the moose for bringing Eta back to him, and he thanked the man in his dream for helping contrive it all. And he even thanked the men of the *Ariel* because through their evildoing he had been given a glimpse of Eta that no one else in the world had ever had, and for this he was very grateful.

He sat there through the night, and when Eta woke, a bit before dawn, they modestly, fully conscious now, traded outfits. Until that moment, however, if there had been any onlookers (and there wasn't anyone to look except for us) they would have thought that Bimaadiz was the prettiest boy and Eta the handsomest girl they had ever seen.

13. Once Eta had regained her strength, the two children started back toward Agencytown. Although their parents had no way of knowing what happened, they would be worried after the fact and the sooner they were told the better. Bimaadiz and Eta took the most direct route back and had almost reached the village when something made Bimaadiz look up from the trail. Off to the left, across a small swamp, stood a huge bull moose. He must have been very old. The old bull's shoulders stood six feet off the ground, and his beard was as long as Bimaadiz's arm. His horns spread as far as a grown man could reach. It took only a second for Bimaadiz to unsling the Winchester and fire a shot. The old bull took one step and toppled over. Bimaadiz shouted in triumph. Here was an excellent old bull for them and a chance to make the offering he had promised the man in his dream.

They decided that Eta should gut it and begin the butchering. Bimaadiz would run to Agencytown and fetch Eta's parents and his parents, too, thereby accomplishing everything at once; they would make an offering there where the bull had dropped, Eta's parents would be put at ease, and they would have help to bring the moose back to the village. The moose was such a big specimen that the two of them could not hope to carry it all back themselves.

Bimaadiz left his fawnskin bag and rifle with Eta and set off running toward the village. As he rounded a bend, who should he happen to see, but the old man Kiiwenz, walking slowly toward the village. He still used his two walking sticks and still struggled with the large bundle on his back. Bimaadiz slowed and called out to the old man. Kiiwenz stepped off to the side to make room for Bimaadiz.

"Bimaadiz, I was expecting you. I heard a shot awhile ago and I thought it might be you. What have you got? A rabbit? Or perhaps an old bull moose, tender, in his old age?"

Bimaadiz was surprised that Kiiwenz, old and addled as he was, knew so much.

"I did shoot a big one," he confessed. "And much more has happened that I want to tell you about. But if you head back up the trail you'll find Eta skinning the beast. We are going to make offerings out there on the spot where the old bull fell. Will you join us?"

Kiiwenz said that he would, that it had been years since he had tasted fresh moose meat, and that he had started salivating when he heard the shot. He turned and walked back up the way from which Bimaadiz had come. Bimaadiz ran on to the village.

Once there he told Eta's parents that she was safe and where they could find her and that they should bring pack baskets for the meat. They said they would and immediately began getting things together. Bimaadiz continued on to his parents' shack. They dropped what they were doing and shouldered their own pack baskets and took a candle lantern and they walked together back to the site of the kill. Soon the whole village knew, and everyone grabbed knives and packs, rope and baskets.

When they arrived, a fire was going strong a short distance from the carcass. Gradually people from the village arrived. Some of the women helped Eta skin the moose. Two of them stood to the side and propped the hind legs open with a long pole, while two others were skinning around the front shoulders. They cooed and laughed when they saw how fat the old bull was. Some of them had clay pipes clenched between their teeth.

A few old men stood with their backs to the fire and chatted about their exploits: war parties they had been on or good shots they had made. Young boys scurried around them collecting firewood. One young boy sung a slow song to the steady beat of a hand drum while other boys danced with vigorous sweeps of their legs in an effort to stomp down the grass and make the clearing larger because more people were arriving.

Night was full on, and the butchering was all done. Eta gave Bimaadiz the tongue and as promised, he burnt it in the fire as an offering to the man in his dream. I can taste it now. Eta cut off the moose's beard and hung it in a tree. As she did so, she silently thanked the moose calves that had saved her life.

Great chunks of loin were roasted on pointed sticks and someone had thought to bring flour and lard for bannock. It was mixed quickly and wrapped around a stick to bake over the fire. That, together with some salt and a tun of whiskey someone else had brought, put them all in a good mood.

Grease dripped down their chins, and they were all tipsy. Bimaadiz told about his dream but did not include any particulars, and Eta related the details of her capture. Everyone was satisfied that the boat had sunk and the evildoers had been drowned in the lake. Everyone who heard the story agreed that some greater force must be at work and was watching over the children.

Apelles walked last in line behind his father.

He dragged an empty toboggan on a long rope. His uncle, walking ahead of his father, swayed back and forth with each step.

Far ahead, the three white hunters also walked in single file. The hunter in the lead carried a kerosene lantern but it confused the trail, casting shadows counter to the moon, and the men stumbled, each in the footprint of the man in front of him. One of them swore. It was hard to hear him. They seemed far away.

Apelles' father and uncle walked without a light. The moon brightened the snow. It was easy for them to see. It was very cold. Apelles' breath was visible in the moonlight. He struggled to keep up with his father's long strides.

"Dede, did he do it on purpose?"

"Gaawiin ingikendanziin. Ganabaj. Ganabaj gosha."

His father did not slow down to answer.

"And we're going to use the toboggan to bring him back?"

"Eh. Giga-gagwejitoomin iw."

They walked along in silence for a while. The woods, so familiar in daylight, seemed mysterious and strange.

Apelles hastened to keep up with the adults, but it was difficult because with each step his feet slid and churned in the broken snow. It was impossible to hear anything except the sound of their feet. There was nothing else to hear.

"Indede, what's rigor mortis?"

His father shrugged and did not answer.

But his uncle turned and said over his shoulder, "When the body gets stiff."

He had been in the war and knew a lot of things. After a moment, he added for his brother's benefit, "Dibishkoo go ginoozhe agidiskwam ayaa."

They walked on in silence. The thick hardwoods, the long trunks cutting the snow, began to thin, and the trail rose as they neared high ground.

Up ahead they saw the three hunters stop on the trail. They milled for a few seconds until the man with the lantern held it up high over his head and said in a too-loud voice, "Right here."

When they reached the hunters they could see a few sets of tracks going into and coming out of the woods from the other direction.

One of the hunters clapped his gloved hands together and spit tobacco juice in the snow. The bristles on his jaw glinted in the lamplight. His nose was running, and the snot pooled on his upper lip. It was very cold.

They all turned from the main trail. The hunters once again took the lead. It was darker in there. The trees grew closer together. It was difficult to distinguish shade and shadow from the tree trunks. The hunter in front held the lantern high and when he moved his arm back and forth the brush shadows, with as much substance as the brush itself, danced suddenly to the side.

Apelles walked last in line tugging the toboggan. He kept his eyes on the ground. It was easier that way not to wonder how much farther they had to go. Snow clung where his father's pants bunched just above his boots.

Finally the white man with the lantern stopped underneath a large tree. There were boards nailed to the trunk, and the snow underneath was trampled. Apelles saw faint blossoms of blood pressed into the snow.

One of the other white men pulled a pack of cigarettes from the breast pocket of his red coat. He held the pack out to Apelles' father who shook his head. He turned and held it out to his uncle who shook his head. The hunter shrugged and lit a cigarette with his cigarette lighter. Apelles' uncle pulled his short pipe from his back pocket and found a match with his other hand. He rang his thumbnail across the head, and it rang into flame.

The white man with the lantern held it up and craned his neck, looking high up into the tree. He looked down again and then around the darkness that surrounded them all.

"He had the best spot here," he said. "The best spot of all."

All of them surveyed the night. The woods and the faint trail were marked only by their fresh footprints. The forest here had been cut over last fall, and they were on the edge of the clearcut.

No one said anything. Apelles' uncle nodded. The cherry in his pipebowl bobbed in the dark. He held the pipe in his hand and spat.

"Mii geget igo giiwanaadiziwaad chimookomaanag. Gaawiin wiikaa giwii-niisaabiiginaasiinaan," he said.

'What'd you say?" asked the white man with the cigarette. He seemed like a nice man.

"I say it's a long way up there. Long way up." He toed the snow with his boot.

"Dibishkoo go gaag. Ishpagoojing ishpiming ishkwaa nibod."

"What?" asked the white man. "What?"

Apelles' uncle pointed at the crown of the tree with his pipe. "The boy'll have to climb it."

His father nodded. The white hunter who did not understand grew impatient.

Apelles' father turned to Apelles.

"A'aw inini ishpagoojin. Gii-nibo."

"I know."

"Gaawiin gego gigikendanziin. Gii-paashkizodizo."

His uncle stepped to the side and knocked his pipe against the bole of a young ironwood. He glanced into the bowl and pushed it into the front pocket of his wool pants. He knelt down next to Apelles. He ran the rope around his waist as he spoke to him.

"Giga-akwaandawe. Onzaam igo wiininowag giw chimookom-aanag ge-akwaandawewaad. Giga-akwaandawe. Giwii-akwaandawe ji-zagapidooyan iw sa biiminakwaan."

Apelles felt terrifically cold.

His uncle checked the rope and nodded. He did not look Apelles in the eye. He reached into his pocket and took out his kerchief.

"Mii apii ge-waabamad a'aw gego ganawaabamaaken. Gidaa-biizikonaa odengwaang."

"Well, boy," said the man with the lantern. "What are you wait-ing for?"

Apelles looked at his father who nodded at him. He began to climb.

There were planks nailed to the trunk for the first ten feet, end-ing on the wooden platform. There was little light to see by. The platform looked dark. The boards were slippery.

Apelles looked up higher and saw a dark lump wedged in the fork of the trunk.

He kept climbing. He was a good climber.

The man had wedged himself in the fork. His rifle was stuck between a branch and his chest.

Apelles peered at the hunter's face. The right side was very puffy. He passed the rope around the man's armpits while trying not to look. He was very fat. When Apelles reached behind, the man's head fell forward. The back of it had caved in, it was just a crater, dark and without end. The back of the man's red coat was covered in blood. Apelles had seen enough. There was no need now to use the kerchief to cover the man's face.

When the rope was secure he said "okay." Then he slung the rifle over his shoulder.

The men below pulled on the rope. The dead hunter swung free and he was slowly lowered down.

Apelles did not look at the hunter as he passed through the air. He did not look at how the man's arms and legs did not move or shift. He did not look at how the hunter appeared as though he were crouching or crawling when he was not. He did not look at how stiff the man's body was.

Once the man was down and the rope snaked past Apelles, he climbed down.

His uncle and father were trying to straighten the man's arms and legs so they could tie him to the toboggan.

"Gego ganawaabandangen," said his father.

But it was too late. He had seen the man's face in the lamplight.

He had seen the hole under the man's chin, the yellow flesh there like wax, the purple hole in the center, and the opening in the back of the man's head. He smelled bad.

They could not get the hunter to lie flat. They wrestled him onto his back. His arms and legs reached into the air. And with his eyes open, it looked as though he had been thrown to the ground and was defending himself. His father and uncle were breathing very hard.

"Dana," said his uncle under his breath. "Dibishkoo go gookooshiwiwiiyaas."

One of the hunters had disappeared.

"Where'd the man go?" asked Apelles.

"Gego babaamenimaaken. Gii-kiiwe."

It was a long way back to the hunters' camp. Once they arrived the white hunter with the lantern gave Apelles' father five dollars in dollar bills and shook his hand. He then gave Apelles' uncle five dollars in ones and shook his hand, too. He did not look them in the eyes.

Apelles' uncle did not walk back to the village with them. He turned and walked the other way. Later he would come back, weaving his way down the middle of the road.

Apelles and his father walked back toward the cabin side by side.

"Why'd he do it?"

"Namanj iidog."

"Do many white people kill themselves?"

"Gaa niibowa."

"Do many white women?"

"Gaawiin ingikenimaasiig chi-mookomaanikweg. Gaawiin wiikaa ingii-nakweshkawaasiig chi-mookomaan-ikwewag."

"Is it hard? You know. Being old, being older?"

His father said nothing.

They walked on through the darkness. Here and there, far from the road, lights shone through the small windows of shacks. And there, on the road, with the field under snow and the trees ragged in the distance, Apelles felt very old, every bit as old as his father, and as old as his uncle, who had been across the sea in a very big war.

Ahead they could see their cabin with a lighted lantern left in the window to guide them in. Apelles stumbled and his father picked him up. Just like a baby. His father carried him in his arms. The last thing Apelles remembers is being passed through the air, his arms and legs dangling, without support, and being laid down gently on his bed.

That bed seems far away now. His present-day queen-sized bed also seems a far-off goal though it is much closer in space and time.

There is still a little light in the sky. The upper reaches of the taller buildings are lost against it and though he is not at work and is almost at the restaurant, he can't stop himself from comparing this sky to the one that usually offers itself to him through the high clerestory windows at RECAP and also that other one, the sky and skies of his childhood, the skies against which all others are measured. He feels as though he is looking down at his life from a great height. Everything seems small and hard to recognize, even his relationship with Campaspe.

Dr Apelles had walked through the city on his way home through the throngs of people also headed home during the late afternoon on the wide sidewalks that looked expansive, too wide, when seen during the day but that always felt crowded during these afternoon times. Walking on them during the day is depressing. When taking a cab, he is not bothered by the emptiness, but on foot it is bothersome. It is different when they are crowded with people. He passed the square outside the archive. They have jazz concerts there during the summer, which makes about as much sense as talking with your mouth closed or having sex with your clothes on—the beauty of the thing destroyed by the very act. He passed the square and on across the wide thoroughfare, and on under the shadow of the buildings that lined the sides of the busy avenue, and were anchored to the ground with storefronts that repeated themselves every few blocks. The Gap, Starbucks, Abercrombie & Fitch, Daffy's, Restoration Hardware. The stores and tall buildings make you feel comforted and proud if it is your city, but are only too tall and too regular and oppressive if it is not your city. He walked on until he drew even with the restaurant at which it was his habit to eat after working in the archives. He was unsure if it was his city or not, and since he had, really, no other place locked in his heart anymore, he did not know where he truly belonged. All he knows is that he now feels like he only truly belongs in the country of his feelings for Campaspe.

He looks in the window of the restaurant and sees that it is unchanged since the last time he was inside. It is packed with the usual afternoon people who are waited on with the studied bustle of waitresses and waiters altogether too good-looking to work there and who try to look and act indifferent and disconnected from where they are and what they were doing. This makes Dr Apelles imagine the other parts of their lives that they hold so far above and beyond the people they serve. People are always different than they seem. He has thought of Campaspe as a simple girl but she is not a simple girl. He has thought of himself as a simple man, too, but he is not a simple man. And there is nothing simple about his feelings. Simple feelings only occur in stories.

Dr Apelles thinks about Campaspe. Dr Apelles is not sure he should enter the restaurant.

What makes the place so appealing is that very little happens there, except that for a while he had had a crush on one of the hostesses. From the aerie of his barstool he would watch her work.

Her name was Zola. Dr Apelles knew nothing about her except that she always worked at the restaurant on the Fridays he went there after the archives. She was pretty to look at. He sat at the end of the bar and read his book and looked up every so often as though savoring the words he had sucked off the page before swallowing what was left of them, but really his eyes had come to rest on Zola. He liked the penitent curve of her neck as she read the reservation book. He liked the smooth sweep of her very straight red hair. He liked how elegantly she held the menus when she walked with customers and seated them at their table. He liked very much when she walked back to the hostess stand because then his eyes rested on her narrow waist. He liked even more when it was summer and she wore skirts because he liked to look at her calves and thighs. They seemed to be made to be wrapped around someone's waist. She was very beautiful and very nice. It is a pleasure to look at, not stare at and not covet, beautiful people.

Dr Apelles' face-to-face contact with Zola was limited to the few seconds he stood inside the door before he went to his spot and the even briefer moment when he passed the hostess stand before leaving for home. In these brief moments he drank in the startling whiteness of her teeth. He drank in the startling avid look of her gray eyes. And he drank in her beautiful lips, which were full, but narrow, and on the lower one there was a birthmark, black, no more than a dot, that looked like ink, as though she had been sucking on her pen.

Dr Apelles thinks that women are never so lovely as now. Zola is lovely. Campaspe is lovelier still. He thinks about her constantly. Ever since the ice storm, Dr Apelles thinks a lot. He thinks about so much so often and his Fridays at the archives had, until now, been his main time for thinking. Those days had existed solely for him and for his thoughts, especially for thoughts in which he was absent. He usually spent the whole day having left himself behind. But it is different now. His life is different now. He has become interested in other people. He is now part of that half of the human race who takes an interest in the other half. With his new interests had come problems. All the formerly discrete parts of his life—his past, his work, his passions, and the versions of himself he told himself and the versions of his life treasured and told by others—were mixed up together now.

When he is not with Campaspe, she comes to him and keeps coming back even if he doesn't want her to, but he does want her to, so he lets her come.

When brushing his teeth he thinks of her because hers are so white. When he clips his fingernails he thinks of her because her fingernails are so slender and strong. He thinks of her toenails because they were so tiny, and especially the smallest one. It is very small and discolored because of the drastic shoes she loves to wear at work. And since she is so deep in his thoughts he no longer needs specific prompts for him to think of her. He thinks of her when he walks by hair salons because he loves her hair. And whenever he sees a sweater, no matter the style, he thinks of her because she looks so fine in her white sweater. At the train station. Whenever he sees a book. When he sees paper. He thinks of her. A girl on a bench at the station. An ad for Mexican drinks. A shampoo for curly hair. He thinks of her everywhere. He sees her everywhere. When passing water or waking up she is with him, when he eats or sees any woman anywhere wearing anything, Campaspe is suddenly and unexpectedly with him, on elevators and at the druggist's (how he would love to nurse her back to health), in the train and on line at the bank and always when it looks like bad weather. She is with him in the afternoons, at least during these wintry afternoons when the sun so quickly moves along the horizon, never staying long, never rising too high in the sky. All the seasons and weathers of the world are different and bring with them different joys and different sorrows, all except northern afternoons in the end of winter. These are the same everywhere.

So even though Campaspe is with him, other things are, too, and other people. Zola, yes, she is there. And people from farther back in his life, too.

These skies, gray and low, the sun a failed promise so quickly gone, are the same skies of his childhood. The skies of times and places and people that belong to him only as memory if they belong to him at all. So even though Campaspe is with him so are the habits and hopes of his youth, a time when his future was his only solace. And these winter afternoons bring with them the very particular memory of milking the cows, which in memory always and only happened under low skies without the sun. When he sees these skies he sees himself when he was sixteen years old. He sat on his bed cross-legged and read a book. He read of a place where it never snowed and milking was done by others and where every decision was accompanied by an ideal and where every view was beautiful and people spoke of love as though it were real. Perhaps these skies are those skies because in those days children did not wear watches or have cell phones on which you could read the time. So he had to look at the sky through the single window set in the cabin wall to the left of the cookstove to see if was time to do the milking. It was. He saw his boots standing at attention at the foot of the bed and saw the front steps littered with wood chips and smelling like fresh-split jackpine, and he saw the narrow trail down to the milkshed, and he saw very clearly the pine slab of the shed itself, scored with teeth marks by the cows during the winter, and then he saw the cows themselves who looked at him reproachfully, and the bucket with a rind of dried milk at the rim. His mind was still on the book he had been reading. He was still in the story, in the worlds it contained, as he milked the cows. He thought it would be a good thing to write books or at least to dedicate his life to them in one way or another. He knew then that he would leave his family and live in places they did not live and the cities he would know would be cities they would not know. His life would become incomprehensible to them.

It is the gray sky of the afternoon that makes him think of his childhood, but since Campaspe colors everything he thinks of her, too, and the two thoughts become mixed. The mystery of Campaspe's body, which is a mystery easier to access than the mystery of her mind, occupies him completely and reminds him, just now standing outside the restaurant, of his first introduction to the mysteries of a woman's body and the pleasures concealed inside.

He was twelve. It was summer. There was little to do. The hay and alfalfa were growing and the woods were heavy with heat. Apelles and a cousin spent their time collecting worms in the pasture, breaking the trampled cowshit with a pitchfork and pouncing on the stunned worms and storing them in a tobacco tin lined with shredded newspaper. When they had collected enough they brought them to the resort just on the other side of the village where they sold them to the owner for a nickel a dozen.

Dr Apelles remembers it all. He can smell the liquid smell of manure and the ink on the newspaper. He can feel the heat building in the yard. Then he and his cousin walked to the resort. The road was unpaved then and the fine sand grabbed their toes and then the lake appeared off to their left between the trees and brought with it a cool breeze. He can smell the sharp scent of spruce as they turned off the road toward the resort and can feel the tedium of waiting at the counter while the owner counted out each and every worm and then he can hear the magical sound of the nickels dropping into their outstretched palms.

On their way home they walked along the lake instead of on the road and went swimming in their cutoff jean shorts. They swam at the edge of the cattails and bulrushes where the lake bottom was mucky and covered with weeds because the beach was reserved for white guests. They didn't swim long because they were under strict orders to come home straight away. Apelles' father demanded they give him half the money they earned. He had said that they were his cows and his cowpies and his land, so the worms were half his. But the lake was so inviting and so cool and the white children who got to swim at the beach were so interesting to watch. The white children's voices were different somehow from theirs, and the way they ran on the sand gingerly was different. Their feet must be very tender. There was a girl among them. She was Apelles' age or maybe a year younger. She looked his way a lot when he was swimming, and when he and his cousin went in the lodge to sell their worms she was there, usually playing Ping-Pong by herself, just hitting the ball across the net and running around the other side and across the room to get it. He had seen her in one of the motorboats with her father as they crossed the lake, she was looking his way then, too.

He was sitting on the front steps of the cabin when she came in the yard.

"My pa needs worms and they're out at the lodge."

"We don't have any."

"They're in the ground, ain't they?"

She seemed strong in her mind. She was skinny and her legs were very pale and her belly pushed out against her shirt like a frog's belly.

"It's too hot. We won't find any."

"Let's look."

Later in the woods the girl squatted to pee. Apelles looked away. The girl laughed.

"You ain't ever seen a woman pee?"

"Not a girl."

"Come on. You can look. Come on."

Later on, maybe it was the next week, or maybe it was the next day. Things move much faster when you're young, or maybe they move faster when you remember them—the mind skips the unimportant times. Our memories are always in such a hurry to see themselves. So maybe it was much later in the summer or maybe it was not when she said:

"You mean you never?"

"No, you?"

"I have. Yeah I have."

They lay under the wide low branches of a white spruce, the needles poking into their backs. You'd hardly expect to flush a rabbit out of there, the space looked so small.

She had him in her hand.

He did not speak and he watched her as she worked.

"There." She was finished with the job and pleased with her work.

Apelles looked with wonder at his penis.

"And now me."

"I don't see anything."

"There's that, and there. See? And can you see now?"

"Yes."

"Yes."

Her finger disappeared.

"Now you do it."

Her hands were very white against the pink and harmless place she made for them.

Then later, it was a long time gone, much later.

"Do you think we made a baby?"

"No."

She seemed very far away. Apelles rubbed his legs together. They itched and his penis was spent and raw.

"No," she said. "Babies aren't made that way."

"No? Who says?"

"My pa. My pa says that. He said that when he showed me. He says they come from storks."

"What's he do?"

"He's a doctor."

Afterwards and for the rest of the summer they looked for worms together. He and his cousin still sold them at the resort. And it didn't matter if she was swimming or playing with a puzzle in the lodge or moving across the lake very quickly in a motor-boat. From a distance and maybe it was the way she held her head or squared her thin shoulders or put her hands on her hips or tossed her hair or maybe it was the tan of her cheeks. From far away she looked very cold and very haughty. But it was always the same when they went in the woods together. She acted as though she were in charge, but it always ended the same, with her turn-ing her head and mouthing lines that must have come from the movies. "Oh darling! Oh my darling!" And she would also say, "Do you see? Do you see?" in a way that was desperate. She seemed to plead for him to understand something that was never, ever, made clear.

Now, if Zola, or anyone else, but if Zola at the restaurant had asked what was it like when you were growing up? what was the reserva-tion like? could he say that the days, the short days of winter and the long days of summer, when the sun stayed so long that just when the afternoon began it felt like a whole new day had been added on to the one you had just enjoyed and the night would never come, and that in these hours life was very full, and there was so much to do you never wondered who you were and what the answer might mean, and that the people of your childhood, your parents who, neither one no matter what, ever said or did a cruel thing, and your uncle often got very drunk but was always kind, and Adolphe who lived behind the village had such a funny way of swinging his arms when he walked and he walked with a limp because he had dropped a crate of ammunition on his foot during the First World War but played the fiddle at all the jigs, or the girl who owned a pack of dogs and could climb trees like no one else ever could and who climbed those trees and kept those dogs and sicced them every so often on her own father when he met her in the woods when she was alone because he wanted things she did not want to give, or the land itself; the ever-stretching swamps into which it felt that no one had ever gone before you and the pinestands, those that were left, anonymous and communal, and the hardwoods so full of secrets but so quiet and good to hunt in if there was snow. He could not.

Dr Apelles never said anything to Zola except good evening or hello or thank you because to say more would lead to a discussion of these other things that he could not say, and the long string of his life would unravel.

Recently, like many other people with whom he was acquainted but whom he did not know well, she had begun to pay more attention to him.

He had been eating his meal with book and beer. It was a quiet night. But his were, or had been, always quiet nights. Zola was walking past him in front of a couple she was seating in the rear of the restaurant. He happened to look up as she passed.

"Hi. Hey. You look different."

"I do?"

But she had already gone past. He took a sip of beer, and when he set the glass down, she was on her way back to the hostess stand.

"Yeah," she continued. "I don't know. Different."

"Better, I hope."

Zola glanced at the hostess stand.

"Yes. Yes, better. Different, though."

She didn't have much more to say so she left. As he watched her walk away he looked at her legs and her small, beautiful waist and her ass and thought, "God no, you're not different. God no. Yes." She really was beautiful.

But he could not tell her of his life even though she was nice and acted like she wanted to know him better. Zola always made it clear she knew who he was when she said things like "Your place looks clear" and "Every other Friday as usual," and she was generous with her smile and spent it freely on his face. She was nice and she was nice to him, but he could not say anything to her because what she and everyone else wanted to hear was an ideal version of him.

Later that evening his reading was interrupted by someone pulling out the barstool next to him. It was Zola. She put her cell phone, keys, and Marlboro Lights on the bar and got a drink.

"You off?" ventured Apelles.

"Yeah. Finally. They're cutting the checks now. I gotta wait."

She lit a cigarette and considered him. Her head was tilted a little to the side.

"You come in every other Friday. Right?"

"Yes. Yeah. Every other Friday."

"What do you do?"

"Me? You mean with my life? I work in a library."

"You're a librarian? Really?"

"No. Not a librarian. It's different. A different kind of library."

"I love books."

"Really? Do you read them or just love them?"

She laughed.

"I don't read them as much as I love them, I suppose."

"You love the idea of them."

"Yeah. The idea. I like stories." She was drinking a vodka tonic. "So. Where else do you eat? What do you do when you're not here?"

A more experienced man would have seen her interest for what it was. But Apelles was not experienced enough to know that she would have fucked him merely out of curiosity and that she was intrigued by him because he showed no obvious interest in her. Though when he spoke to her, his stomach churned and his penis throbbed, electrified by the conversation.

"Oh. I eat. Sure. But it doesn't beat coming in here."

And what would have been an opportunity quickly became conversation, just conversation, which he always steered back to the bar, her coworkers, to the jokes he could make about what they already knew of each other, which was next to nothing. The conversation felt unreal, staged. But his life was real to him, and if he told it in the wrong way or for the wrong reasons it would cease to be real, it would no longer be his life because it would become a story like all the other stories about his people, and if he told it he would only become a character in that story and would be only the Indian they knew and the Indian they told their friends about. His life would cease to be his and he would not even recognize himself anymore.

He could tell her nothing, but this did not stop him from fantasizing about her. He didn't stop himself from fantasizing because he did not have to be an Indian to do that. All he needed to be in order to imagine her beautiful imperfect lips on his, to imagine her hands on his shoulders, to imagine her hard breasts against his chest, and oh her hands yes now on his hips, all he needed for that was to be a man. And to be a man was the easiest thing in the world. Those fantasies came easily, and Zola wasn't the only one at the restaurant who excited him. The bartender was all too lovely as well, a real darling. She was voluptuous and her skin looked very soft, but she was also very efficient and quick at her work, not at all the way you think someone as curvy and beautiful as Elizabeth would be. She was good at keeping up banter with the other customers, but not with him, because he kept to his book and since during the course of the evening he only ordered two beers and never more she left him alone. Though his eyes searched for Zola, they would sometimes rest, resting, on Elizabeth and truly she was so beautiful. Her skin was so beautiful, and she had such a bright smile and such a girlish and business-like demeanor both, that it was easy for him to imagine not the act of loving her but what was sure to be her tremendous pleasure in bed. She was the kind of woman who existed to be pleasured.

Now Dr Apelles is in a bind with Campaspe because he can no longer forestall her questions about his life.

They are lovers now.

She needs the story of his life, but as an Indian he is reluctant to give up that sovereign part of himself. So when Campaspe might ask, "What was it like?" because eventually everyone wanted to know, he says, "I don't know."

He really doesn't know because he has no practice telling the story of his past and as with all fantasies, the past takes practice.

"I don't know. One summer my cousin and I made $17.10 collecting worms for bait. We went every day to get them. I often went with a girl who was staying at the resort. Her name was Frances Warcup."

"That's a good name for an Indian. Not like your name."

"It is, yes. But she was a white girl. She was Polish and she was from Chicago. But then again, Chicago is an Indian word. From *Gaa-zhigaagowanzhiigokaag*—the place where there's lots of skunk tubers. That is, wild onions."

"What was she like?"

"I don't know. She was very nice."

"I mean what was she like to be with?"

"It was nice, too."

Could he say that she was just a white girl, no different from any other, hungry and lonely and orphaned within herself, but that, after all was said and done, it was her and no other who had held his dick in the dusk of the past. She had been the first to hold it, her hand pumping and a look of concentration on her face and her lips pursed tight together. And could he say quick little legs, demanding tongue, tea-rose nipples no bigger than those on a cat, the determined eyes, and the red imprint of pine needles on her knees? So that, later in life when the Indians of his youth were replaced with the white people of his present and he goes to the homes of white people and sees the desperate order of their things, the appearance of wealth, the desperate decorations, the complete absence of smell, none of it can kill that feeling in him created by that girl. And the white people wear the same look that she did, that look of angry innocence, of dirty pride and raw need, but it began with that girl in those woods under that tree all those years ago. It had been special in its own way, she had been special. And none of the jokes about white women or the smell they have can take that away. Or what they finally did. It wasn't what they did. They all did the same thing. And could he say that even though she was his first she was from then until now a complete mystery to him and that he still wasn't sure what she was looking for or hoping to find in his painful and raw satisfaction, but no matter because the past had faded and her with it, but the mystery remained. Because of her all women were a mystery.

Campaspe was no exception. She was a mystery to him and he was to her. But he felt, and this was at the agonized heart of why he was unsure if he should go in the restaurant and why he hadn't spoken to Zola or Elizabeth much, he felt he was at a disadvantage because he, and all those like him, were measured against the stories that were told about Indians by those who did not know Indians. Not at all like the way men were measured against the stories about men because, for most people, men existed in life not just in stories. And how could he overcome that? What language could he use for himself that had not become part of those stories about his people, the sad ones and the funny ones and the ones about the ways and days of the past. What could he say that would exist on its own, that represented only him and his life?

Campaspe at least had seen him at work dutifully punching the clock and following RECAP protocol and scanning books, and so for her at least the facts of his existence, the proof of his modern self, were harder to ignore. His hope was that since he knew her from RECAP he was, in the phrase he loathed above all others, between two worlds—the one she was sure to imagine and the one she knew, because it was her world too.

Campaspe might ask about his life. He grew nervous, and he had never thought of himself as a nervous man. And like all nervous men he was anxious to please, and the desire to please her made him feel trapped. His only way out—he could not talk of the past and he could not talk of the present because that told her very little—was to talk of his work as a translator. He spoke of translating as though it had something to do with his life.

And so it had become something between them.

"Can I see it?"

"I don't know. No. Maybe."

"Shouldn't we order? Should we get the usual? Two margaritas," she said to the waitress across the bar.

"It's not finished and it's boring anyway. It's only interesting to me. I don't want to bore you with it."

"But I want to. I want to hear it."

"It seems like we always order the same thing. Just like that first time."

"It's not that I wouldn't understand it."

"No, no. No. It's a mess is all and I don't know if you'd even be able to read my handwriting."

But it had become a thing for them.

"Two margaritas." And to her, "Long day."

"How's the translation? How is it?"

"Growing. Always growing."

But it had become a thing for her.

"How's the translation? I'll get her. Margarita? Two."

And so it went. He could not tell her about himself. Not directly. So his translation became the story he told her of himself, as a substitute for the story of his life. And he tried not to get anxious if she asked too many questions or probed too deeply. All the while he thought she was getting what she needed from him, but she was not. He could tell she was not getting all that she needed.

He could tell that sometimes she felt that she didn't know him at all, and since she did not know him or his habits it seemed to her that he could, like a wild animal, do anything or everything and it all would be so unexpected. She longed for safety, and the only thing that could provide it was knowledge of him and his feelings and his past, and these were things he held the tightest. And since he only spoke of the translation and of translating, it shouldn't have been a surprise that she wanted to read the manuscript and that she was angling to read it whether he would allow her to or not.

For all that he was happy. That was the biggest surprise of all. He was happy in the morning when he sighed his morning sigh whether she was with him or not. She was not. What that sigh meant was different now. It was a sigh of both contentment and expectation. He was happy when he saw her at her workstation or when they surprised each other at their lockers, stowing their things away at the same time. He was happy when out of the corner of his eye he caught a little habit of hers. He was happy when he glimpsed her body in the white sweater. And most of all, he was happy to think ahead and imagine them together in his queen-sized bed. He felt that it was only between those covers that their story was in any way readable. It was in that bed most of their conversations took place, and where he told her his translation. These discoveries were linked to their nakedness and became extensions of it because there he could be just the body she was feeling, the dick she was holding or sucking, and he did not feel so much like a paradox or a problem and he did not feel the need to speak about himself because his pleasure was the one thing in his life that was beyond language. His translation became even more *his* translation, and it began to include her—all of it held between the soft cover of his sheets.

She seemed happy, too. But then again, she was beautiful and beautiful people often confuse happiness with fun and fun often results from a combination of things—the place, food, a prevailing mood—not necessarily from the other person, not necessarily from him. And beauty can also be like something you wear to hide what is really underneath, and even though beautiful people might seem happy you rarely hear stories about their happiness.

All the same, she seemed happy in his arms. And even if she faked her moans and managed to fake the trembling of her crossed, uncrossed, crossed, and finally released legs and the wetness there and her delicious scent and the blush of her cheeks, she must want to be happy and to make him happy, otherwise there was no reason for acting.

But she did have a way. And she did have a look, a curious dissatisfied look that appeared more and more often.

He had first seen this look when he told her about the translation, but did not tell her enough or as much as she wanted to know.

Apelles remembers the first time he saw that look. They had just finished having sex. She had come and so had he.

"Is the translation just one story, or is it one big story with lots of others inside of it? I like those the best."

Apelles had the condom in his hands, and he was tying it off so it wouldn't spill.

"Oh. A bit of both. One main story. The main story and others that grow here and there from it. Like nodes. Like lymph nodes."

He set the tied-off condom under the bed so no one would step on it.

"But what's it about?"

"I've already told you. I've told you that."

"Not really. You know what I mean. What does it say? What does it all mean?"

"That's hard to say until you're finished."

This seemed to upset her.

"You can know what something is before it ends. A lot of things. Like relationships."

And he still hesitated. She turned her head and though she was interested in what he said she seemed to have gone far away.

There was the same look on her face more these days. And she had it even when they weren't speaking and they might still be making love or perhaps his penis was only crouching inside her and she would turn her head away and would not look at him.

At these times she seemed happy and hollow and hollowly is how she sounded when he spoke to her then, and it took her some time to answer as though reading the echo but not the utterance. There was some part of her that remained unsatisfied.

When he was at work these thoughts were even more present. The two lovers had not changed how they interacted at RECAP. They still did not speak directly to each other when they were at their stations. They did not eat together or hold hands or wink or brush past the other or steal moments—at the copier, in the shelves where the extra boxes were kept, at their lockers, or in the Reading Room—for themselves. But something had changed and their coworkers had registered that change, and they might be telling themselves and one another their own stories about his affair with Campaspe.

Jesus, for one, was different. He was a big man, much bigger than Dr Apelles, and he was quiet, always listening to his iPod, and the way he nodded to what must have been the beat was suspicious. It is difficult to trust big men, especially the quiet ones. They seem to have no choice in what direction they turn, and if he were to get angry he would have to follow his anger through to the end. He had always been this way.

He had paid more attention to Dr Apelles even before the ice storm. Since then he had gone so far as to try and talk to Dr Apelles.

"You ever hear of Big Head Todd?"

"No."

"No?"

"I don't think so. No."

Dr Apelles was suddenly nervous. His skin felt flushed. It seemed as though there was no right answer to the question.

"What about Kinky? Ever hear of them?"

"I don't think so."

"No?"

"I don't think so."

Jesus seemed offended and challenged by Dr Apelles' ignorance. "You should. You should listen to both of them."

Dr Apelles hadn't known Jesus was talking about music bands, but Jesus hadn't appeared interested in really educating Apelles. He was gathering information. He was learning something.

And Dr Apelles was reminded why he didn't like having conversations. Conversations were something you could lose. Something could be lost. Even when they weren't speaking, when they were working at their stations, he thought he could feel Jesus' eyes on him, watching him, and moving past him to Campaspe and then back to Dr Apelles. It surprised Dr Apelles to realize that Jesus was jealous. Of course he was. He wanted Campaspe for himself.

He had asked her out once, and they had gone to Margarita Bella's long before the ice storm. Dr Apelles preferred not to imagine Jesus and Campaspe at what he considered his place. Thinking about them there did nothing to comfort him and made him angry, and he felt out of sorts when he thought about it. It wasn't that Jesus had done anything. He did only what he could and only what you'd expect.

Jesus wasn't the only one who acted differently. Ms Manger did, too. He should have known that when she approached him about the *Jesuit Relations* she was after more than just his expertise. She was—and everyone knew this—a lonely woman, and lonely people are dangerous. They always respond and act with their loneliness in mind. It governs everything they do. Dr Apelles saw her more and more when he didn't expect to see her. Not just at the Monday meetings. He saw her when he put his things in his locker, and he saw her on his way to the S.A. She walked by his station frequently and stopped to talk to him about whatever topic was interesting to her, understood by him, incomprehensible to everyone else. She seemed to want to form a club that included only him, with her as acting president. Dr Apelles realized with dismay that she had taken an interest in him. And that is exactly what she said whenever he spoke, no matter the subject. "How interesting," she would say. "How very interesting."

The other workers looked at him as he passed. They nodded as they passed him. More and more they looked him in the eye. He thought that once he was out of earshot they talked about him.

This was a disaster. Dr Apelles was not interested in being interesting. He did not want to be noticed. This must be what it's like to be famous. To be famous was to be known and discussed beyond your inner circle, though Dr Apelles' inner circle included only himself. But it was the same. He felt scanned, read, and consumed, and he had no control over how they read him or what they told themselves about him. They could be saying anything. They probably were saying anything.

Dr Apelles knew enough to know that what he was experiencing was not unusual. What those people saw or intuited was nothing more than a workplace romance. Workplace romances are the same the world over with the same possible outcomes. They live happily ever after. They don't. He gets his heart broken. She gets her heart broken. He is a womanizer. She is a slut. The only difference between a workplace romance and other romances is that it is staged for the enjoyment or interest of the rest of those who work in that place.

Dr Apelles felt defenseless. Defenseless because he had no language for his present self, no Indians do. It's the past that through long practice is fluent. He had never turned his life into material, always in relation to, always in conversation with, always gauged by, what everyone thought they knew about Indians. He had always been too self-conscious to exhibit his origins; to have his Indian past speak for and take the place of his personality. His father had been the same way. They would be selling balsam boughs or winter fish and someone else would talk about how good a trapper he was: Why just last week I trapped eight mink and a bobcat. Apelles' father said he was impressed and he said congratulations. What he didn't say was that back at the house they had twenty beaver pelts stretched and fleshed and ten otters on boards.

Maybe because they are so unself-conscious, Indian writers are very popular with audiences. They read from their work and when it comes time for the question-and-answer portion, the questions brush by the work on their way to the author, like eligible women at a ball stalking the richest man in the nicest suit. The writers are only too glad to tell anecdotes or give the audience small cultural pearls. Dr Apelles remembers going to one such reading. He had been given the book by the publisher so he could proof the Anishinaabe language that the writer used and did not translate. He had been very impressed. The writer was delicate and judicious and obviously very fluent. So he went to the reading, which he enjoyed but does not remember. When it came time for the question-and-answer, the writer, who was very light skinned, must have felt compelled to prove he was Indian because he admonished the crowd, postured, and then trotted out his "rez" stories. Dr Apelles was terribly embarrassed.

Finally, Dr Apelles decides not to go into the restaurant. It hardly seems like his place any longer. It is a pleasingly lighted, friendly place. He can see Zola at the hostess stand. Farther back, moving behind the clustered heads of the customers at the bar, Elizabeth is making drinks. It has been his place just as Mai's has been his place. In these places he had been free not to speak. Free, almost, to be someone else by pretending to be no one. The translation and Campaspe have brought great happiness and satisfaction and they force him to be singular and unique and though it was good, it is also terrifying. He has to admit that he had been for many years a coward.

Dr Apelles forces himself to move on from the restaurant. If he stays any longer someone inside will notice and he will have that discomfort to add to the growing list. He moves on. It is growing dark and the foot traffic on the sidewalk has increased.

It is a strange fact, a strange thing altogether strange. He could never have imagined it all those years ago, just as he could never have foreseen all these recent changes weeks before. A life, and this made him smile, just like any other.

He looks at the sky. It is the same sky as before, just darker. Some of the side streets are shuttered by the tall buildings.

It is not his past that haunts him. It was complete and finite and beautiful in its own way. And it was only much later, in college, that he had realized, and this had come as a shock, that his past was unique to him. Not everyone had the same thoughts or knew the same things or the same kinds of people. It wasn't a profound realization, but it had marked a shift in him. He began to think comparatively. And though he hadn't done it much lately, he had trained himself not to, it had begun a process of looking back. A process of evaluating his life by looking back. Campaspe and the translation have forced him to do it again. So it wasn't that his past haunts him. He haunts his past. He presses against it. He dips into it. He pushes his way back there. Unbidden. Unasked. And mercifully unnoticed by his former self.

He will walk the rest of the way home, and he will ride the elevator up to his apartment. He'll eat a light dinner, and much later he will see Campaspe, but only after night has finally fallen.

It will be such a relief to hold her breasts, her nipples peeking out between his fingers, her legs clenched around his waist, and to see her head thrown back as though she were trying to escape her pleasure as it crawls from her belly up her breasts and to her face, a pleasure, he thinks as he walks, that he is surprised and proud to be able to give. It has been so many years since Annette, and so many years with Mai, that he had been afraid he would not be able to give real pleasure. Then again, his contact with his Mais, with things most others found indelicate and even frightening, had forced him to control his own fear, to eradicate it. This made sex, new sex, and the excitement and nervousness that goes with it less tinged with danger. And with someone as beautiful as Campaspe, with a body that beautiful, that quick to the touch, and that fluent in its own pleasure, who would not become good at pleasing it no matter the cost?

When the time came and they would be done for the evening and she lay in his arms, it was clear that he had brought a little of the day's dusk with him. He was lost in thought.

"What are you thinking?"

"What? Oh." He was startled by the question. He had forgotten she was there.

"What were you thinking?"

"I was thinking about that girl I collected worms with the summer when I was twelve."

"Did you fool around with her?"

"Yes. But there was something else."

"Was she nice to you? Was she mean?"

"She was determined. We played doctor and she studied her patient very hard."

"What did her parents do?"

"Her father was a doctor."

"What was she to you?"

"What? I don't know. I was only twelve."

They went to sleep. Much earlier in the night Dr Apelles stood by the window as these thoughts and others continued. He said something and then turned around.

When they went to bed they both pretended to fall asleep. Each in their own world.

Dr Apelles still thought of that girl all those years ago. She had clutched his penis so hard and her arm moved ceaselessly and it must have gotten tired. She must have gotten tired, but she pursed her lips and tilted her head and kept at it, not satisfied until the stain came out and still not satisfied even then.

Campaspe was a woman and the girl was a girl. Campaspe knew her own pleasure and the girl did not know hers. But there was a likeness. This is what he had been thinking. When he fell asleep it would come to him, what made him stop at the restaurant but not go in. It would come to him what made him hesitate to speak to Zola or Elizabeth, what made him stalk his past like a hunter circling something mortal and wounded. And why the whole of his adult and very modern world was so strange, so strangely out of his language. The white people haunted him just as he haunted his own past. They excursed into the sanctity of his own self. It was that way for all Indians. Indians were the past that everyone else visited as a way to check on the development of something deep and long dormant.

That girl. She was looking for something after all and tried to call it up, carried on the wake of his come: something unique, something different, something from outside herself that she could control *in* herself. She was looking to interrupt the dreary gray flow of life. She was looking for the one thing. The one thing. The one thing that could tell her she was unique, that her life was unlike any other, that she was more than a ghost, too. It was sad and also very wise.

No wonder he felt the need to protect himself and his own personal treasure.

Campaspe's curiosity and dissatisfaction with him and his explanations of himself and his translation are just like that. She hopes to get from him something that is unique. And she is coming up with nothing.

So, as he lay in bed and realized he was there all alone, he was not surprised when he thought he heard his briefcase in the kitchen open and close. The chair squeaked. There was the rustling of paper. And he knew that his translation was being read. He decided to do nothing. He coughed and the rustling of paper stopped and a little while later it began again. Campaspe was reading his translation. He coughed again, and the pages stopped rustling. He heard the bathroom door open and close. And then he heard the fridge door open. Campaspe was pouring herself something to drink—a smoke screen. It was then that he knew, since she did not feel safe without possessing some part of him and since she would not feel safe reading the translation in his apartment, that she would, someday soon, take the whole manuscript.

Thinking about Campaspe and how she would steal his manuscript, he also still thought about the girl. He closed his eyes and he saw, after the girl was done, how they were embarrassed to find their clothes on again and the pitchfork and bucket in their hands as they were when they first went to the woods. "Come on," he said. They found a spot under some oaks and sank the fork into the thatch and lifted it clear. As Campaspe reads the translation in the next room, he can see so clearly how the worms—exposed, naked, glistening—quickly sank themselves back into the earth. They dropped to their knees and fought with their hands, trying to catch however they could those disappeared things already resting at some deeper level.

~ Book IV ~

1. Finally, it was summer. The early, rainy spring months had passed and Eta and her mother had gone to their canoe camp where they were building a birch-bark canoe. Bimaadiz's family did not have a canoe camp of their own, and since Eta was so far away it was a dreary time for him, filled only with rain and mosquitoes. The mosquitoes bit and drilled and made Bimaadiz's skin itch. His separation from Eta created an altogether different itch that no amount of scratching could alleviate.

There was nothing for him to hunt. The meat, if he had gone hunting, would have been poor. The hides, even young ones, would have been covered with ticks: ugly raw things of no use to anyone. Bimaadiz tried his best to keep himself busy and reminded himself that Eta wouldn't be building canoes forever. He helped out around his parents' house and even considered working at the mill, just for something to do. But it was clear that Bimaadiz was a danger to himself. He was absentminded and distracted. He would almost certainly have hurt himself eventually. So he did not end up working at the mill.

He took to walking the woods aimlessly, swimming through the brush, getting wet, muddy, and bug-bitten in the swamps. He returned home in the evenings with nothing to show for the day's effort but exhaustion. His mind was on Eta and nothing else and he couldn't bear the thought that he wouldn't see her until berrying time, at least a month away. Bimaadiz was so upset and out of sorts he became jealous of the creatures of the forest. He was jealous of every species—whether they flew or ran or slithered—because they were allowed to go wherever they wanted. The weather and the season did not prevent them from going about their business or from seeing what it was they wanted to see. The bears scavenged for food and slept and tumbled in the weeds and traveled wherever they pleased. The wolves stuck together, hunting and sleeping and playing and no one told them they could not travel and play together. But it was the birds who excited most of Bimaadiz's envy. They flew wherever they wanted. They ate the most delicious berries and seeds, never in danger of being hungry. And they were welcome visitors, brightening every camp. The worst part was that the people encouraged their chirping and cooing and took pleasure in their presence and their courtship. They were free to woo and tease one another, even urged to sing and trill and to generally excite the attention of their beloveds. Not so for me, thought Bimaadiz. I can't tell anyone how I feel about Eta. They would just laugh at me or scowl and say I was acting inappropriately. I have to hide my feelings. I can't fly to her, be at her side in minutes, no time at all! A long dirty walk with mosquitoes is what separates me from Eta. And if I were allowed to go to her, what then? I couldn't kiss her with her mother there. I couldn't tease her or hold her hand. I can't woo her, play my flute the way she likes. I am not a bird, no one would encourage me to sing—a pleasure for others—it would only be a source of embarrassment for them and for me. I am only a stupid boy who wouldn't even know what to do if Eta were mine.

Bimaadiz did contemplate hiking out to Eta and her mother's camp, but balked when he imagined what Eta's mother, Mary, might say when he arrived:

"I've come to say hello."
"Well? You've said it."
"I was wondering how the canoe was coming along."
"You can see for yourself that we're half done."
"Have you found enough birch bark?"
"Can't you see the pile of it there soaking?"

All of the excuses he dreamt up felt thin, easily torn. Mary would know right away that he was there only to see Eta. She would prevent the two of them from spending any time together. It all seemed so hopeless. Bimaadiz felt, as sweethearts often do, that he would die of longing. And if he didn't, then he could easily imagine any number of obstacles and events that, in the meantime, could insert themselves between the terrible now and the wonderful future in which Eta would be his forever and ever.

There was nothing he could do, and so he did what sweethearts everywhere will do when prevented from exercising their desires: he punished his rivals. That is, he began killing birds.

2. Bimaadiz wasn't so cruel and heartless as to kill them for no reason. He was a special boy, as handsome at heart as he was to the eye. There were elders—healers and doctors—who needed special birds for their ceremonies and there were women—quillworkers and beaders—who needed feathers for their designs. It just so happened that Bimaadiz's jealousy and frustration coincided with their needs. So, like an old-fashioned Indian, he strung a bow (the Winchester would only have made a mess of things) and gathered some blunt-tipped arrows and stalked the woods looking for the colorful birds of summer.

He found many near the village—redwing blackbirds aplenty, and finches, too. They were small, quick creatures that flushed easily. It would have been easier to net them. Bimaadiz took many shots only to have the brush or cattails turn his shafts. He spent many hours looking for his arrows; they blended well with the cattail stalks and underbrush, and when fired low, they pushed their way under the matted grass. It took a good eye to find them and the whole enterprise helped take Bimaadiz's mind off Eta.

Bit by bit, day after long day, he collected a fair number of birds—finches, warblers, blackbirds, and the like. The elders to whom he gave the little creatures were glad to get them. They were too old to get them for themselves, and no one cared much anymore about such things, so the elders were cheered by Bimaadiz's efforts.

Mindlessly, he took down those little birds—unstrung them from the sky—and put them in his bandolier bag and toted them back to the village. He could spend all day hunting, could kill twenty or thirty, but they weighed next to nothing. They weighed so little in death, having lost the presence of life, and they lay in his bag like patches of colored cloth.

Bimaadiz drew down on a porcupine one day. He had surprised

it on the trail and, hurriedly, as fast as it could waddle, it veered off to the side and climbed a tree. It stopped six feet up and clung to the trunk, blinking sleepily, trying to focus on Bimaadiz, but it could not. It looked like a child just woken from sleep trying to remember where it was, and for once, Bimaadiz didn't have the heart to kill something though he knew porcupine flesh was a delicacy that the elders didn't often get a chance to taste.

Every day he hunted the birds he had to walk farther and farther from the village to find them. There were fewer birds now—thanks to his expertise and to the advancing season.

The deep woods, filled with brooding pine, were a poor place to find birds. There was so little for them to eat there and few places for them to build their nests. And so Bimaadiz sought out the lowlands and the stands of hardwoods that grew to the south. He became obsessed with finding rarer birds. He was no longer satisfied with the beautiful but common jays and whiskeyjacks, blackbirds and boreal chickadees. Bimaadiz wanted more exotic quarry and so deeper he went.

One day he was hunting among scattered oaks and birches. It truly felt like summer now. The insects were out—mosquitoes and deerflies—dreamily orbiting his head, when he caught some movement in the treetops. Just a flash. He turned, searching the leaves for the bird he knew was there. A patch of sky detached itself, dipped, and landed in another tree. Bimaadiz was keen to it and his pulse quickened. It was an indigo bunting—rare to be sure. It was highly sought after and was considered a powerful semblance.

Bimaadiz drew, but before his arrow came to rest, the bunting flew. Ten yards. Twenty. And landed again in a different tree. Bimaadiz kept the arrow nocked and advanced on the bunting, trying not to trip or to make too much noise. He was good at moving like this, and when he was in range he knelt to steady his aim. But the bird flew again and landed just on the edge of sight. If Bimaadiz didn't know better he would have said that the indigo bunting had been hunted before, or that it knew its feathers were valuable. Again, Bimaadiz kept the deadly arrow nocked and wove his way slowly through the trees. He knew if he was patient enough that he would eventually get a shot, or if not, it was no loss. The bunting had landed in an ironwood tree twenty feet off the ground. Bimaadiz counted this as luck because ironwood have fewer branches—it would be a much easier shot, his arrow would fly straight, and the bird would be knocked off its branch, and he could carry it home.

Such were his thoughts. They ran so far ahead of the event that in his mind he had already killed the creature and plucked its feathers in the cool comfort of his parents' shack.

But the bird flew again! Bimaadiz didn't even have a chance to draw back the bow all the way. He cursed and shook his head. He felt cheated—as though by thinking so far ahead, by imagining his success so completely, instead of plucking the actual bird he had plucked his chances and destroyed them. He felt tired and put out. He had come so far and still his bag was empty, no matter how much he imagined it full. He could not stop now.

Time passed and the sun was dragged along with it and with Bimaadiz lagging behind both, he was pulled farther and farther from the village. Sometimes the bunting landed close by. And sometimes it disappeared from sight, at which point Bimaadiz paused and considered where it might have gone. He always found it, or saw it, but it always flew before he could make a shot.

The sun moved. So did the bunting. So did Bimaadiz. Each followed the path laid out for him—always heading to some final place. The sun was nearing its western home while Bimaadiz and the bunting had left the village far behind and were now far to the south. The soil had changed from sand to clay and the trees reflected this change in the hidden wealth of the land. Instead of pines and poplar, Bimaadiz wove his way among maples and birch. Mighty elms rose straight-trunked from the lowlands and white oak crowned the hills. It was beautiful country, but Bimaadiz barely noticed it.

The sun, doing its best not to sink, lingered on the horizon, sending its last rays in between the trees. Free-floating pollen, caught in the light, cast a yellow glow over the whole scene. And finally, perhaps tired from the chase or blessed with an understanding of what is required of buntings in stories such as this one, the bird perched on a hazel wand and stayed there. Bimaadiz was a few scant yards away. He stopped and crouched behind an ash, drew his bow, and fired. The arrow flew straight. Its blunt tip struck and killed the bunting. It fell to the forest floor. It would fly through the branches of its forest home no more. But it would fly, henceforth pinned to the hair of some fair Indian back at the village.

Bimaadiz whooped. He was pleased. His slow chase had finished with a good result. He gently picked up the thing and after plucking a single tail feather and placing it in the crook of a tree along with a whole twist of tobacco, he wrapped the bunting in a piece of calico and placed it in the bottom of his bandolier bag.

Now he put down his bow and urinated. He stretched. And then he took his bearings. He had no idea where he was. He knew he was far to the south of the village. And it was almost dark. Bimaadiz would not be able to walk back unless he walked half the night. Without good trails he would be stumbling about in the dark. But there was no need. He could camp where he was. It was a warm summer night and if he built a good smudge and wrapped himself just so in his blanket, the mosquitoes would not snack on him too much. Having decided to spend the night he began looking for a suitable place to build a quick shelter. As he searched he saw signs of human activity—felled trees, trampled brush. Some of the smaller birches had been stripped of their outer bark as high as he could reach.

Bimaadiz became anxious, thinking immediately of all that had happened during the previous year—the enemy raid across the river during which he had been captured and also the sinking of the *Ariel*. No one knew what to expect, and the young men of the village had been gearing up for a war that everyone thought would come soon, possibly that season. There was talk that the Governor and the Agent were trying to arrange a treaty council at the village in the fall, which, even if there were no agreement, would postpone the fighting for another year.

Whoever was working the woods could be working to evil ends.

It could be the work of the enemy. Suddenly Bimaadiz's mind was bent to these fearful thoughts when he—his senses now tuned to his fear—smelled smoke in the air. Or, perhaps the drop in temperature had forced the smoke down to ground level and so it had been there all along but he hadn't smelled it. It wouldn't do to pitch his own camp anywhere near this other one without first seeing who it was. If they were friendly, they might be offended he had not introduced himself and shared their food and company. And if they were enemies, it would be best to know and walk back to the village as quietly as he could. He regretted whooping earlier. If these strangers were in camp they might have heard him.

Bimaadiz picked up his bow and circled quietly into the wind and tracked the smoke toward its source. After a few minutes the smoke-smell grew stronger and Bimaadiz knew he was close. The land dipped toward a small creek. He heard the sound of water running over rocks. Smoke hugged the ground, and Bimaadiz could see a few small flames from a low fire flickering through the trees. The branches and brush were thick, and he could get close without being seen. As quietly as he could, he worked his way toward the edge of the camp. Soon, only a few branches and some sweetfern separated him from these people, friend or foe.

And who should he see raking the coals underneath a pot of pitch?

Eta!

It was all Bimaadiz could do to keep himself from rushing out of the woods and embracing her then and there. But her mother was sure to be nearby and who knows who else. So he held himself back and drank in the sight of her in her thin summer dress (work-worn and stained with pitch and soot—but Bimaadiz swore to himself he had never seen a more beautiful dress and a more beautiful girl), and he blessed his luck and offered silent prayers to the bunting that had led his body all this way to be unexpectedly reunited with his heart. Bimaadiz had had no idea he was so close, no idea that he had walked all this way to end up at the side of his sweetheart.

Enough was enough. He had to stand and make himself known. He did.

"Bimaadiz!" she said.

Eta could barely contain her joy but she did; her mother was sitting only yards away behind a pile of firewood, softening spruce root with her strong teeth.

Mary stood.

"Hello Bimaadiz, hello. You're far from home. Are you hungry? Sit."

Mary did not seem suspicious or surprised that Bimaadiz was there, and she asked him for news of life in the village. Eta was silent out of respect for her mother—she could not speak with Bimaadiz as she usually did. Bimaadiz related all that was new. The mill was still cutting logs leftover from winter. The Priest and local Agent had ridden south to meet the Governor and the village Chief had gone with them. There was still talk of war and the people were nervous. He told them of his bird hunting and drew out the bunting to show them. He gifted it to Mary who was very pleased to receive it.

"Why don't you stay," said Mary eventually. "It is a long way back to the village and there might be marauders about. It would be safer for you here. Aantti will be back with the others soon, I think."

They had been away for the day cutting cedar.

"I don't want to be a burden. It's a small camp you've got here and I'll eat too much of your food."

"Nonsense. It isn't safe in the woods at night right now. The enemy might even now be getting ready to create some mischief."

As it was, Eta's family only went out in groups and they were always armed. So Bimaadiz accepted the offer, and when Aantti returned with his crew, they all passed the evening singing and telling stories. When it was time for sleep, Bimaadiz spread his blanket next to the fire, away from Eta and her mother. They made for bed in a makeshift lean-to covered with balsam branches and carpeted with cedar fronds that kept away the bugs. Aantti and the cousins pulled out their bedrolls and spread them around the fire with Bimaadiz. He did not mind. He was closer to Eta than he had been in weeks and for him those weeks had felt like months. Through the night Bimaadiz dreamt of kissing and touching Eta, and he woke to find himself hugging Aantti and he wondered if he had been kissing him all night, mistaking the father for the daughter.

Mary left to gather more spruce root, and Aantti and the cousins left again to cut cedar. Eta remained behind to boil and strain the pitch. Bimaadiz and Eta had the camp to themselves, and once everyone was gone, they embraced and kissed and stopped only occasionally to stir the pitch and to talk.

"I came for you, Eta."

"I know."

"It is because of you that I've been killing all these poor birds."

"What do you want me to do about it?"

And then Bimaadiz said what had been on his mind while he was separated from Eta and hadn't had a chance.

"I don't want you to forget me."

"How could I? I haven't forgotten you. And as soon as the canoe is done and the berrying starts we'll be back together."

Bimaadiz groaned.

"But there are hundreds of stitches to put in the bark, the holes have to be punched. The whole thing sealed. The longer it takes to put the canoe together the more I come undone."

"Bimaadiz. Cheer up. The berries will be ripe soon and you'll still be in one piece then. It's only a month away."

"Promise me then. Promise me that you will not find a new sweetheart, that you won't want to kiss anyone but me. That you won't forget me."

"I promise. I swear on the spirits and on the wolf, the one who raised me first, that I will always be yours and that if I am not true to you I will kill myself or you can kill me."

"I swear the same," breathed Bimaadiz. "I swear on the moose, the one who helped me when I was found. I will have a heart as true and strong as hers and I will never abandon you or throw you over for another. If I do then I will kill myself or you can kill me."

Such were their childish promises. And as silly as they were, by exchanging them they were both calmed. Bimaadiz could leave in peace. He had promised Aantti and Mary that he would return once again with provisions. He kept his promise and so time passed more quickly than Bimaadiz thought possible and he was able to leave the birds alone and killed no more of them. They had brought him closer to Eta and for that he shared a generous part of his affection for Eta with them and even feasted them and thanked them formally.

3. The long waiting period was over. It was just past the height of summer. All of the blooms of spring had faded, and only the hardiest of flowers now greeted one another with nods in clearings and fields. Gentian and yarrow swayed in the wind and paintbrush, shier by nature, shuddered and, as though with clasped hands, bent and quivered in the tall grass. But who wants flowers anyway? What good are they? Much greater and even more beautiful to the eye were the berries that had ripened. They hung everywhere.

The chokecherries—gregarious and chatty, perched on their branches calling out to everyone to strip them off. Wild plums—sarcastic and timid at the same time—called out from behind their leaves only to retreat into the brushy brambles where they lived. Raspberries and blackberries—royal and corrupt princes—braved it out in the full sun of forest clearings. Gooseberries and huckleberries—reticent, tradition-bound and private—lived on unbothered in the swamps. Cranberries and pincherries (those party-goers) draped themselves over the furniture of the branches and invited all passersby, birds and people, to join the party. The blueberries and wintergreen grew undisturbed—calmly bourgeois—in the carpeted hush of the big woods.

In short, everything was fruiting, pregnant with life. And Bimaadiz and Eta were reunited. Once Eta's family had returned from their canoe camp, Eta had wasted no time. She grabbed a pail and headed toward her favorite blueberry patch, but not without letting Bimaadiz know where she was going. They ran to each other and kissed on the lips, on the cheeks, on the eyes, and on the neck. Neither one of them could get enough of the other—it was as though they had woken from a long sleep and they each blinked and stretched, surprised by the bright light of the other. They picked berries and talked in a constant rush (equaled only by the constant hum of horseflies overhead and the rapid rain of berries in the bottoms of their pails) and would suddenly drop their pails and kiss. The whole world was ripe and ready for picking. Especially the two children, who were the most beautiful fruit of nature and time. They were young and healthy and in no way immune to life. Bimaadiz was especially vulnerable to the disease of plenty.

He had had time to watch and think all the blessed season long, and so he asked Eta if she would lie down naked with him as Kiiwenz had instructed (the one bit of advice they had not dared to follow and that might lead to the only remedy for desire that really worked).

"What more could that do for us?" asked Eta. "What would we do when we were naked? What then?"

Bimaadiz said that he had often seen deer and moose chase each other and then the buck or bull would get behind the doe or cow for a few seconds. When they stopped they grazed contentedly side by side as though they had shared some pleasure between them. There seems to be something sweet in it that takes away the bitter taste of desire.

"But they do it standing up," said Eta. "The bull, as you say, jumps behind the cow. But you want me to lie down and that doesn't make any sense. And besides, you know the ground is never as soft as it looks. There are sticks and pinecones and rocks down there, and they will poke and scratch my skin."

She did not want to disappoint Bimaadiz, however, and in the end, agreed to do what he asked.

They found a good patch of berries, away from the main trail. Intent on trying this new remedy, they undressed quickly without much thought, the way children undress in preparation for a swim. They took little notice of each other's nakedness, and in doing so neglected to pick the ripest fruit of all—the fruit of the imagination. They quickly lay down side by side. It was a dream come true. While they waited for something to happen the dream evaporated like dew in the light of a new sun. Nothing happened, nothing was happening. Bimaadiz asked Eta to get on her hands and knees so he could get behind her, just as he had seen deer and moose do. She complied, and Bimaadiz positioned himself behind her. This was the farthest they'd traveled down the path of desire—but if you don't know the destination it is difficult to know if you're getting close. Once he was behind he didn't know what to do next. Bimaadiz was confused and frustrated. He turned away and sat on the ground. The sticks agitated the sensitive skin on his scrotum and his back was being bitten by flies. He covered his face and cried in frustration. Even the moose and deer knew more about desire and its fulfillment than he did.

4. There was at that time a man named Pajaagan who lived on the edge of the village, but separate from it. He came from a long line of Chiefs though he had no authority anymore. But he was still an important man, he had done well for himself. He had a fine cabin with two rooms and its own well, a shed, a corral, and two other outbuildings. He even owned a milk cow and raised chickens—eggs were eaten in his household year round. In addition to these holdings he had more supple and sensuous things to hold. He had three wives to keep him warm. Pajaagan, exhausted and happy in his riches, lived his life crawling from bed to bed. But he was advanced in years and he rarely made it to all their beds and so very rarely did he part the legs of his third wife, and if he did, it was usually only to sleep between them.

This left Maanendamookwe (for that was her name) with a surplus of needs. She was young, barely older than Bimaadiz. She rarely got pleasure except by her own hand. She often saw Bimaadiz as he trooped out to hunt. When he came back loaded with game, she looked forward to the sight of his lean young body as it swam through the trees on the edge of her husband's holdings. Maanendamookwe also saw Bimaadiz and Eta heading out together and sometimes ran into them on the trail. She had a suspicion that what had begun as a childhood friendship was turning into something else. She saw how they held hands and stole kisses when they thought no one could see them.

On that day when Bimaadiz and Eta went berrying, Maanenda-mookwe had followed them into the woods and watched them. She had seen the children strip and lie down naked, had seen Bimaadiz move behind Eta, and had seen his tears of frustration. Maanendamookwe felt bad for the children. Pleasure was so near and they didn't know how to bring it closer. But there it was! Buried in their own bodies, waiting, scratching to get out. If only they knew. She hatched a plan whereby she could help the chil-dren find their pleasure and in doing so satisfy her own cravings.

A week after she spied on Bimaadiz and Eta, she set her plan in motion. She followed them out into the big woods where they were picking the last of the blueberries. After the innocent pair got settled, kneeling among the bushes and singing as they worked, Maanendamookwe messed up her hair and rubbed mud on the front of her dress and on her ankles. She then staggered into the berry patch making a great show of her distress.

"Help! I need help!"

Bimaadiz and Eta jumped up, worried about a possible attack from the band across the river. They were eager to help their neighbor. They knew her husband and wanted to help her in any way they could.

"What's the matter?" asked Bimaadiz.

'What's wrong?" asked Eta.

"I set nets on a slough," she said, "for ducks. And what should land but a flock of twenty geese. They were caught fast, but flapped and struggled away from shore. The muck and water were too deep for me. I could not reach them and they, being so strong, were ripping the nets as they struggled. What's worse is that two eagles arrived and they swooped and dived trying to prey on the geese. It won't be long before the eagles carry them off and I'll have nothing to show for my efforts except ripped nets. I will have to return home with nothing and I will receive three beatings—two beatings from the other wives and one from my husband. It took all of us all winter to make the nets and they will blame me for the loss."

Bimaadiz and Eta tried to comfort her.

"I'm sure we can find a solution," said Bimaadiz. "And everything will turn out all right."

"Please help me, Bimaadiz," said Maanendamookwe. "Come with me and help me rescue my nets. If you don't, all I will receive back home is pain and humiliation. You might have a chance to shoot one of the eagles," she suggested. "They are fearless and fly quite close."

Bimaadiz agreed immediately and left his berry basket with Eta. He walked with Maanendamookwe in the direction of the slough.

When they were a fair distance away from the berry patch, Maanendamookwe slowed her pace, stopped, and turned to face Bimaadiz.

"Bimaadiz," she said. "I want to talk to you because I had a dream, surely the spirits sent it, because it was about you and Eta."

"Yes! About us? Please tell me." Bimaadiz listened closely.

"I was told by the spirits that you and Eta care about each other a great deal, the two of you are bound together. But the spirits also told me that something holds you apart—you lie down naked together only to taste frustration, not pleasure. The spirits told me this makes you terribly unhappy."

"It's true! The spirits aren't lying—we are very frustrated." He was amazed she had been told so much by the spirits.

"My heart goes out to the two of you," said Maanendamookwe. "I hate to see people unhappy when they could be happy. This is why the spirits sent me the dream. The spirits told me I must help you. If you let me, I'll be your teacher and I'll teach you to taste pleasure instead of frustration. There is more than just kissing, embracing, and lying down naked together. There is more to the art of satisfaction than trying to do what the deer and moose do—it means a form of pleasure much sweeter than theirs because it lasts longer."

Upon hearing this Bimaadiz was overjoyed. He nearly cried with gratitude, dropped to his knees and made all sorts of promises: he'd give her whole honey-cakes, three deer, and as many tobacco twists as he could buy with the money he got from his hides.

We all need teachers, and she was a good one to have.

Maanendamookwe was encouraged by Bimaadiz's innocent trust and instructed him to do as follows:

"Sit down beside me on the ground, here I will put down my shawl so the ground will be as soft and smooth as my skin. And now that we are seated, kiss me. But don't rush to my lips, don't be in a hurry—you must build pleasure step by step," she said (though she was starving for his thick lips). "Kiss one side of my neck," she said, turning her head. "Use your lips and then yes, suck a little bit. You can even bite it a little, yes, and now my ear. Now do the same on the other side."

Bimaadiz did as he was told and Maanendamookwe assured him by saying yes yes yes that he was doing fine. She panted and sucked in her breath by the time he finished licking the salty lobe of her little ear.

"Am I doing okay? Am I doing it the right way?" asked Bimaadiz, anxious to be a good student.

"Yes. Very good. Now," she instructed, "kiss my lips and as you kiss them you can touch me, softly, here, yes, here like you are rolling a raspberry off the stem, and then with more force."

Bimaadiz was anxious to learn and did as he was told and again, by saying yes yes directly into his mouth, Maanendamookwe let him know that he was doing it right. And now Maanendamookwe was barely able to form the words, but she was a committed teacher.

With great effort she pushed her student away and said, "Start all over again from the beginning and as you touch me and kiss my neck, my ear, my lips, lift my dress over my head and take it all the way off."

He did as he was told.

"That's the way," she breathed, "and lay me down on the shawl."

He placed stealthy kisses on her neck and ears, and on her lips, and as he kissed her with more energy, he lifted off her dress and pulled it over her head and took it all the way off, and then he guided her to the ground and hunted his way down her body.

"Yes, but don't stop, put it all together now, don't stop kissing me. And kiss me here," she said, guiding his head to her breasts.

And after a while then she held his head and whispered, "And down here, too," and she placed his head between her legs.

"Just as when you hunt," she moaned, "you have to see your target to make sure your shot will go where you want it to."

Bimaadiz was pleased to have such a thorough teacher and did exactly as he was told.

Good teacher that she was she placed her own hands on either side and with two fingers she opened herself to him and asked, "Can you see now, can you see what you're hunting?"

Bimaadiz said yes and Maanendamookwe pulled him down on top of her and with her hands, guided his shaft to its target. After that Maanendamookwe did not need to give him any special guidance. Nature herself taught him what to do.

5. After the lesson was over Bimaadiz jumped up and fixed his clothes, ready to run back to Eta and put his education to use. He was afraid he would forget what he had learned if he waited too long. But Maanendamookwe stopped him.

"There is something else you should know," she warned him. "I am well educated and have had many lessons in my lifetime. What you just did didn't hurt me. But if you do to Eta what you just did to me she will scream. She has not learned any of this yet and for girls it is a hard lesson—she will scream and there will be blood. But not to worry. When the time is right, take Eta deep in the woods, next to a spring or a creek. There she can scream and no one will hear and you can wash off the blood afterwards."

This information sobered Bimaadiz and dampened his enthusiasm.

"Not to worry," said Maanendamookwe. "To learn pleasure means an occasional sacrifice and Eta will thank you later."

She kissed him on the cheek and said, "Remember this; I taught you what you needed to know before anyone else did, including Eta."

With that, Maanendamookwe left, saying that she could rescue her geese herself after all.

Bimaadiz wandered back to the berry patch, but he walked slowly, burdened with new thoughts. Only minutes earlier he was ready to run back to Eta and practice again his pleasurable lesson. But now he was not so sure. He did not want Eta to scream for any reason. He was not her enemy. He did not want Eta to cry—that would mean he had hurt her. And as for blood—that would mean he had wounded her and he did not want to wound his best friend. By the time he arrived back at the berry patch, he didn't feel like bothering Eta with any of this—it all felt like too large a price to pay for the pleasure they would receive—so he decided that he would not press Eta to do anything more than they had done already.

When he got back to the berry patch, Eta was sleeping. She had filled the berry pails and pulled her shawl over her face and lay curled among the bushes. Bimaadiz lay down next to her and kissed her through the shawl. She laughed—breaths of laughter filling the fabric like a sail. The sun was strong overhead. Bimaadiz lifted the shawl and crawled underneath, and they lay together, protected by the thin fabric.

They kissed and after a while they fell asleep. They would take the berries back to the village and dry them for the coming winter—a treasure of taste to be tasted later.

6. Summer was now more than half over and just as the mature fruits were ripe and the rice stalks would soon be bent low over the water, Eta had ripened, matured, and was also ready to be picked. The kind of flirting that had made her blush and had made Bimaadiz so jealous, and that was of a childish innocent nature was now replaced with something more ominous. Silence. Men kept their distance. Here was a real woman—thirteen years old, a catch to be sure, and one doesn't snare or net anything by jiggling the strings. Silently must the nets be lowered in the water. And so these men kept their distance from the girl and were careful not to address her directly, but though they circled wide they did test the waters by approaching Aantti and Mary. The less shy among them made out-and-out offers of marriage. Some, like poor Gitim, brought presents with them and made a great show of laying them out on the table, one by one, and exclaiming over their qualities. This got Mary to thinking. Eta was ready to be married. Wouldn't it be better? she asked Aantti. Wouldn't it be better if they set her up in an honest marriage of her own, whereby they too would receive gifts that, while they wouldn't make them rich, would ease the weight of the years? After all, it wouldn't pay to keep a girl like Eta at home any longer. She would be liable to make a man out of some village boy in exchange for a bag of rice or a necklace of pine needles. But Aantti wasn't as anxious to marry her off, though the marriage gifts offered so far were much more grand than he could have hoped in exchange for a simple village girl like Eta, skilled only in trapping. The way things were going there wouldn't be any furs at all in a few years. Everyone knew this to be true, and what use would Eta be then? There was her beauty, of course, but that wouldn't last forever. The pleasures of beauty were temporary, and everyone knew that they were better rented than bought. Besides, Aantti had a secret hope that Eta's real parents were out there, that they hadn't died on that lonely island on which she was found and that, seeing how he and Mary had saved the girl, her birth parents would someday make them rich.

All of this made Eta very sad. No one stopped to consider her feelings. She couldn't expect them to—she was only a girl and had to do what she was told. Rather, she was sad and distressed because Bimaadiz experienced anguish throughout all these proceedings, and there was nothing she could do to ease his pain. All she could do was what girls can do for the boys who want them;

she lied. She put off Bimaadiz and his questions as much as she could, and when she couldn't, she told him that the gifts pouring into their cabin were for this or that, anything but promises of payment for her heart and for the treasure between her legs. But Bimaadiz kept pestering her and reacted, generally, as all boys do when lied to by the girls they want; he imagined the worst.

Finally, after much arguing and many tears, Eta told him everything.

"They want to marry me off. My mother is ready to give me away, but my father is waiting for more, for bigger offers. Oh, Bimaadiz, I don't want to be with anyone but you, but what can I do? I have no say."

Upon hearing this Bimaadiz broke into tears. It is safe to say that his heart, while it didn't exactly break, was bent and bruised.

"Oh, Eta! I can't bear it. How can I bear it? I would have to hunt without you and skin without you. The woods will be nothing more than an empty house to me without you. And you would sew for someone else, joke with someone else, and kiss someone else, forever. I'll kill myself if you marry someone else."

Eta kissed him.

"Darling Bimaadiz, you mustn't do that. While we're alive there's always hope, but there's no chance for us if you're dead. Promise me you won't kill yourself."

"I promise," said Bimaadiz, "but if you marry someone else it will be like you're dead, like you never wanted me, and so the promise will be dead and won't mean anything."

But, with Eta's kisses came some hope. Why didn't he ask for her hand? He was as suitable as all the others. At Eta's urging he agreed to ask her father if he could marry her.

7. One thing bothered Bimaadiz. His father was not rich. He would have nothing to offer Eta's parents except the animals he killed. Bimaadiz didn't dare talk to his father about any of this, but he did summon enough courage to pull his mother aside. He told her about his affection for Eta and that he wanted to marry her. That night, Zhookaagiizhigookwe told Jiigibiig all about Bi-maadiz's desires. Jiigibiig rolled over in their blankets tuck-pointed into the hard floor and dismissed the idea outright.

"Why should *we* pay for Bimaadiz's pleasure? Eta is a beautiful girl and handy with a skinning knife, but she is only a poor vil-lager like us. Why should we pay for what should be an equal ex-change? If I got to eat out of that kettle, too, that would be a meal worth paying for," said Jiigibiig sleepily. "And besides," he contin-ued, "judging from the items we found with Bimaadiz—the pipe-bag and the red pipebowl and his fine rabbitskin clothing—he comes from an important family, maybe even a family of Chiefs. If we can find his real parents—maybe they survived—they will make us rich, but they would surely be angry if we let Bimaadiz marry a poor plaything like Eta."

Bimaadiz's mother saw the logic and law in all of this but she was afraid that Bimaadiz would really kill himself if he had no hope of marrying Eta. And Zhookaagiizhigookwe's tender heart dipped down from its parental height to skim the surface of Bimaadiz's life. Her heart was one with his because he had always been her son, and she wanted him to be happy.

The next day she sought out Bimaadiz.

"Son," she said and she actually stroked his cheek. "We're poor and while Eta's family is not rich, they have a lot more than we do. They want a rich son-in-law. It's what's best for their daughter after all. But if you can convince Aantti not to expect too much from us, then of course you can marry the girl."

Zhookaagiizhigookwe never imagined that Aantti would let Eta go for less than absolutely everything he could get for her, so she felt quite safe making this suggestion to Bimaadiz; nothing would come of it, but at least Bimaadiz would have hope and might not do anything drastic.

Bimaadiz wasn't encouraged at all by his mother's advice. The more he thought about it, the more despondent he became. He had nothing. He was nothing. These were his thoughts when he turned to sleep that night.

As soon as he closed his eyes, however, he began to dream. He heard a voice. It was a woman's voice.

"Bimaadiz," said the woman tenderly, "why so sad? Why wander here with tears on your cheeks?"

He told her about his hopes of marriage and his feelings for Eta. Of his terror that life's happiness would be denied to him.

"Cheer up, Bimaadiz," said the woman. "I've helped you once and I'll help you again, and I'll help Eta, too. I've been looking out for you for a long time. Your burnt offerings tasted sweet to me and what's more, my happiness is tied to yours, and so I will help you again."

Bimaadiz confessed that he did not remember her, that he had made offerings to a man; that a man had helped him recover Eta before, not a woman.

"Don't you see?" asked the woman. The woman's voice deepened as she spoke, and it became the voice of the man he had dreamed when Eta was a captive on the *Ariel*. "I have power, my child, though you can't know how it works. But I am the one that helped you before and I will help you again."

"Many years ago," the woman continued, "a fleet of trading canoes tried to run the rapids fully loaded and they swamped. All their goods sank to the bottom of the river. In the center of the river, below the rapids, there is a big rock, shaped like a table, and below it there is a large eddy. The water is calm there, an eye of still water. Dive deep. At the bottom you will find riches like you've never seen before, more than enough to satisfy any father-in-law. Aantti won't be able to refuse you then. Wake up now. I am as anxious as you are for you to take in life what is already won elsewhere. But don't forget to make offerings to me. I need them as much as you need your wedding presents." Bimaadiz promised and woke saying, "I will I will."

8. Without waiting to eat he left the cabin and headed for the river. He took a pack and a long piece of very valuable rope. It was hot— the last days of summer. The heat hung lazily about the bush and a large herd of horseflies—condensations, distillations of both the heat and the season—roamed and ran above his head. By the time he reached the river it was midday. He had sweat through his shirt and trousers and he was nervous. This was his only chance to win Eta and he did not want to fail. The river had settled low against its banks. The heat and lack of rain had reduced its force, and he was grateful for the lower water levels. It would make his work easier. He picked his way down the bank, foregoing the portage trail because he would not be able to see the river from there. The rocks along the shore were dry and stable, and he made good progress downriver to the foot of the rapids.

The rock the woman had mentioned was easy to see. It stood in the middle of the river. During times of high water, it would have sat below the surface but now its top was flat and dry. Deep sluices of water parted and dove on either side of it. Just as the woman said, a large eddy idled downstream, no danger there of being swept away from the rock. Everything looked exactly as she said it would, as though she had made it, created it just for this occasion.

Bimaadiz hiked back up to the top of the rapids. He dropped the pack onshore, stripped down, and with the rope over his shoulder he waded out into the cool, coursing water. At first the water felt good on his legs. It washed away the sweat and dust and gave his muscles new life. But as the water got deeper, it became harder to move. Bimaadiz struggled against the current. The rock had seemed so close, so easy to reach. His imagination had outrun his life the way trappers imagine spending the money they will soon get for their furs: first they imagine spending it, then they get the real money and really spend it, and as a result they feel twice as poor having spent their money twice, but only receiving one thing in return. Bimaadiz, however, did not give up. He forged ahead. Soon the water rose above his knees and past his waist. Its power overwhelmed him. Bimaadiz lost his footing and was swept downstream. He struggled and fought, but it did no good—he slipped and slid, banged his shins against the rocks, clawed with his hands, and for all his trying he wound up below the rapids far from his goal. He swam for shore and climbed out at the portage landing and looked up the rapids. The rock was still there, of course—splitting the river, guarding its treasure.

There was nothing to do—he would have to try again. He jogged up the trail, descended the bank, waded into the current, made it halfway across, and was once again pushed off his feet and carried downstream. Once again he trotted up the trail and entered the river only to experience the same defeat.

Bimaadiz was tired, chilled, and depressed. He was close to tears. His feet and hands were cut and bleeding. His shins were ridged with bumps. He looked around at the portage—there were canoes there but the water was so studded with rocks that he was sure to stave in any vessel he took out onto the water. He looked upstream—maybe he could lay a log between the rocks and move it to another set of rocks, and move it again—but that kind of disappointed pier would not work either and he knew it. These were desperate thoughts and each assault on the rocks of desire make the attacker weaker, not stronger. No wonder there was such a trade and demand in divinations and love medicine.

Bimaadiz, in the universal gesture of despair, raised both arms and let them fall, slapping his sides. He felt that he'd be better off on the river floor with the treasure than alive without the one treasure he really sought.

But then, just when he felt that all was lost, a thought was put in his head—hope was reshelved there, waiting to be read. He would follow the path of the treasure itself. He climbed out of the water for a third time and jogged up the portage trail for a third time. He passed by the place he had descended the bank before and stopped quite a ways farther upstream. He waded out into the rapids. He was careful to take the path with the least number of boils, haystacks, and V-shaped waves. He almost reached the center of the river. The water was up to his waist and then his feet missed their mark, the current took them, and he was gone. He bobbed in the waves, was swept through sluices and pushed through the middle of great standing waves. He struggled to keep his head above the water—to see where the great rock stood. He tried as best he could to choose his course: when he was sucked into an eddy he paused, treading water, and exited the eddy toward the middle of the river. After much struggling and after getting scraped past many rocks and after swallowing mouthfuls of water he floated directly above the large rock. The current was sucked away on either side of its face. The current was so strong that the water did not jump or spray but instead was pulled smooth and fast and dark.

Bimaadiz readied himself and as soon as he met the edge of the rock he began pulling toward it with all his strength. It was over in a second. The rock ran past, he lunged. He was swept into the eddy and against the downstream edge of the rock, floating directly above where the woman had said the treasure would be. Exhausted and chilled, but jubilant, Bimaadiz used his remaining strength to clamber up on the rock's flat surface and to lie there for a moment. He let the sun warm him from above and the rock warm him from below and wondered what to do next.

After Bimaadiz had warmed himself and rested, he sat up and peered down into the eddy. The water swirled past the rock, was sucked back up toward it, was caught in the faster current, and sucked back again in a perpetual cycle—a whirlpool in which foam and small sticks circled and cycled.

Bimaadiz could see nothing below the surface. He had no idea how deep the water was, or what he'd find on the bottom. There was nothing to do except go back in the water. He slipped off the rock, paused, and dove down. He stretched his arms out in front of him and paddled with his legs. He couldn't see very well; the current battered his eyes and his hands fluttered this way and that, but they could capture nothing. He could not touch bottom.

He pushed back to the surface, gasping. As he tread water, his feet kept touching the submerged wall of the rock. Bimaadiz thought he'd try to follow the rock to its base. He breathed in deeply and dove, turning head down and sliding down the rock like a beaver would, trying once again to reach the bottom. It was of no use. He shot up to the surface, unsuccessful, as poor as he had been when he last breathed air. Again, for the third time, he dove, arms and legs trying to climb down the current. He got no farther than he had the first and second time. His lungs burned and his eyes felt scratched and bloodshot like those of a hell-diver.

Bimaadiz climbed back onto the table-like rock. He was tired. His eyes stung. He shivered with cold. He could not reach the bottom on his own. His hopes of marrying Eta were as remote as ever and if he cried it is hard for us to tell—his face was already wet, his nose already messy, and his chest already heaved and heaved and heaved.

But suddenly, he sat up. Reaching the bottom shouldn't be so hard! Canoes and nets and cargo sink all the time. Rocks, too— they have no problem sinking. Why should it be so hard for him? He stood and paced the large rock—looking left and right for stones small enough to lift. Finally he saw some on the upstream edge of the table rock. They would work.

He pried a few of them from the riverbed and carried them to the downstream edge of the table rock. Bimaadiz then climbed into the water, grabbed a hold of one of the stones, took a deep breath, and slid the stone off the rock and hugged it to his chest. Down he went, straight to the bottom.

It was difficult to see—the water was not clear and though the current wasn't terribly strong down there it pressed against his eyes and face. And yet, for all that, he knew the woman in his dream had told him the truth. It was as though he had stepped into the storeroom at the trading post. There were nests of trade kettles, some tipped over, others standing upright, great necklaces of leg-hold traps of all sizes, wooden axe handles bundled together and tied, trailing algae, rotten but recognizable. He released the stone and rose to the surface. He no longer felt the cold water or the cold grip of despair. He did not remember the cuts and bruises he had suffered all the day long. All Bimaadiz felt was the warm flush of certainty—it was as though Eta was already in his arms. He quickly uncoiled the rope and grabbed one end along with another stone and returned to the bottom. He searched for a nest of kettles and released the stone after he took hold of them. He

knotted the rope around the handles as his legs drifted surface-
ward and then he rose, emerged, and hauled the kettles up after.
They were heavy and solid, coated with rust but not pitted too
much. A little scrubbing would fix them right. They alone would
be enough to secure his place as the most generous suitor. Most
families couldn't afford even one, and here was a clutch of ten.

Time after time he dove and each trip brought more treasure
to the surface. Kettles, traps, raw iron, rings of axeheads, adzes
and slicks. He was suddenly a rich man. But the greatest treasure
was the one he found last. He saw, in the dim water, a small square
chest. When he opened it he would have gasped if he could have
gasped underwater. Peeking from within was the unmistakable glit-
ter of gold. He had no pouch or bag with him and all such things
that had been sunk in the wreck had long since rotted away. But
with his luck came a new, quick intelligence and he thought to fill
one of the small kettles with the coin. He rose to the surface for
the last time, climbed out, and carefully, hand over hand, pulled
the kettle up after. And there, in the warm sun, he counted it out.
There were four five-dollar pieces, four smaller one-dollar coins,
three smaller silver quarters, and two small silver dimes. It was
more money than he had ever dreamed of. He could not count
it very well, but he knew its value. He realized the heavier goods
would be hard to bring to shore and he did not need them for a
wedding gift now—he could save them for himself, for some later
day—and so he lowered back down all the kettles, traps, and tools
he had piled on the rock's surface. After resting a bit—the sun was
on its way down—he coiled the rope back around his shoulders,
put the coins in the purse of his mouth, and let the current carry
him clear of the rapids. The day was finished. The sun went down.
But it set on a much different man than on the one upon whom it
rose. Bimaadiz was now rich in coin and even richer in hope.

9. The next day Bimaadiz went immediately to Eta's house. She
was away and that was just as well—he was there to see Aantti.
Aantti was up and out already, splitting rails for the small pasture

behind the cabin in which their milk cow was kept. When he saw Bimaadiz approaching he groaned. He had been dreading a visit from the boy—he couldn't possibly accept the boy's offer. Now, in addition to denying Bimaadiz he would lose a morning's work in the bargain.

Bimaadiz marched up to him.

"I'm here to ask for Eta's hand in marriage," he said. His voice shook but he wore a very determined look.

Aantti knew he had to seem fair, not for Eta or Bimaadiz's sake but to preserve good relations with his neighbors. He stopped what he was doing and led Bimaadiz in their cabin. He poured tea for them both and began with small talk.

"How was hunting last year? What news have you heard in the woods?"

But Bimaadiz got right to the point. He withdrew a small cloth pouch from his bandolier bag and emptied its contents on the table between them. The gold, silver, and copper coins glowed and winked. Aantti sucked in his breath. He had not been expecting this.

"This should be more than enough," said Bimaadiz, "to make Eta mine. If you don't know it already I care for her, not as a prize but as a companion and friend. I am able in the woods and she will never want for food, and neither will you. If you let me marry her you'll be gaining a son. A humble one, to be sure, but one who will make you proud and who will keep you fat in your old age. You cannot refuse me."

After seeing the money—more than Aantti would see in a year, even two—he had lost whatever intentions he had had of sending Bimaadiz away.

"I accept, and clearly, you're not so humble after all. Someone or something must be looking after you. When you marry Eta I'll be rich in coin and rich in life with a resourceful son like you as part of the family."

With that he stood and instead of offering Bimaadiz his hand, he hugged him close as though they were already father and son.

Aantti knew how poor Bimaadiz's family was, and he could not imagine where Bimaadiz had gotten hold of the money. Maybe there was more to this simple village boy than met the eye. And if Bimaadiz had stolen it, which was possible as far as Aantti was concerned, he didn't want to know.

"One thing, though," said Bimaadiz. "Please do not say anything to my parents about this offering. I came by it honestly, but I want to keep it a secret."

Aantti agreed.

10. Bimaadiz left victorious, certain, full of hope. Aantti wasted no time. He quickly changed clothes and walked over to Jiigibiig and Zhookaagiizhigookwe's cabin and pulled Jiigibiig aside.

"I've been thinking," he said. "Eta cares for Bimaadiz a great deal and we all know he feels the same. Who are we to stand in the way of that? In consideration for my daughter's feelings I have given my permission for them to marry and I don't need or expect much from you to make it all happen. What are a few furs or traps or tools to me anyway? Let's join our families."

Jiigibiig was surprised. He wasn't prepared for this and there was little he could say. He had reservations but no place to put them.

"I couldn't be happier," he said. "But I am a poor Indian and increasingly we aren't allowed to make our own decisions. Why don't we wait until the Agent returns at summer's end? The Governor, the Agent, the Priest, and other Chiefs will be here then. Their blessings would go a long way in securing my family's relations with the government, which these days is an important thing. If the Agent approves we can have the wedding then and there—with all the officials and Chiefs present to bless it."

Aantti could not object to this, and so they sat and smoked and talked of inconsequential things. Everything was decided.

11. When Bimaadiz and Eta got the news, they couldn't believe their luck. What had seemed impossible was now going to happen and in a month's time! They left the village and headed into the woods—the only place fitting to celebrate their joy. Eta plaited grass into necklaces that she put over Bimaadiz's head after kissing him passionately. Bimaadiz played his flute, stopping only to kiss Eta. He kissed her and played some more, trying to sweeten the song with her stolen breath. Gradually their exuberance was replaced with the tender passion that they had been practicing all year long. They took off each other's clothes and lay down beside each other naked—smooth skin pressed together, their hands feeding like flies on the other's flesh. Life had never felt so complete, so good. But they were so intent on the future they overlooked the pleasure they were now licensed to take.

Dr Apelles had worked in the archive as best he could until the bell sounded.

Then he had put away his things. He had spoken to the reading-room librarian and then to the guard, and then he had walked down the steps and walked home through the small square where jazz was performed in the summer, along the busy avenue, past the restaurant where he usually took his evening meal after a day in the archives but did not this night, and had turned right, across the busy avenue, and down his small, quieter street. He then had said "hello" to the doorman, had used the smallest key on his keychain to retrieve his mail—only a medium-sized envelope containing a journal of some kind—and he was now in the elevator. And it has happened before exactly the same way. And all the while he thought: the translation is gone, it is as though it has never existed at all, and Campaspe has done it. Since it was an archive Friday he was not at RECAP and so he could not ask her what had happened and why. He cannot grasp either the lost thing or her motives. He pushes the number for his floor and the doors close.

It has been a week since the translation has been missing. Campaspe had begun reading it when he was asleep, or half asleep (was it a week ago? yes), but had put it back. But then, the last weekend, late Sunday. Campaspe had left that morning—errands and house-keeping before the workweek began, so she said. There had been something rushed, nervous and tittery, about her manner. She was skittish and had almost flown out of Apelles' apartment. He hadn't noticed, not then. And for the rest of the day he had hummed and sighed contently through his chores. And it was only in the morning as he readied his things for RECAP that he had noticed his translation was gone. All week, the thought of its theft had weighed him down. Now it was an archive day, Friday.

Campaspe had paid a price for her curiosity all week. She'd worked alongside Apelles—as usual they said little to each other at work—and later they'd gotten drinks at Bella's and ridden the train and made love, and she had suffered all the while.

Usually she felt little or no real remorse when she stole a book. After all, she lifted them from stores and libraries and there were always other copies to be had. And stores and libraries, for that matter, are not people. They don't really possess the books, they store them. And stores and libraries don't write them, either. Or translate them. But Apelles? He was her lover. Her friend.

She'd only meant to give it a quick once over. To consume the words as Apelles slept in the next room. She sat at the kitchen table and read the first page. She looked up at the stove clock and then out around the living room to get her bearings. The apartment was quiet. Nothing stirred.

After a moment she put the page down and looked through Apelles' satchel again to make sure she had the right thing. But there was nothing else. She read the page again, more confused than at first. Her heart quickened and she rubbed her fingers together. It wasn't what she had expected at all. Not at all. She began reading quickly, with the sickening dread that she was bound to find herself in the translation, or a version of herself.

But then Apelles coughed from the next room.

She stopped reading and waited, her bare toes gripped the linoleum. She turned her eyes back to the manuscript.

Apelles coughed again. And there was something about the way he coughed, some conscious pause afterwards, that told her that he was awake, that he wasn't sleeping at all. She put the manuscript away and made a great show of stomping into the bathroom and flushing the toilet, then stomping back into the kitchen, opening the fridge, and pouring herself a glass of juice. She didn't want it but drank it down anyway and then padded back to bed.

She couldn't sleep, and tossed and turned. At one point Apelles spoke in the darkness.

"Can't sleep?"
"No. Go back to sleep."
"Stressed?"
"No. Go back to sleep."
"Is something wrong?"
"Go back to sleep."

But something *was* wrong. She could taste the acid in her mouth, was it from the juice or did it rise from the manuscript or from her hot guilt, which rose in waves? There was nothing to do, and toward morning she dozed off.

All week the thought of the translation taunted her. She thought of it when she looked at him at work and saw it when they sat across from one another in what had become "their table" at Bella's. She heard the words written out in Apelles' hand every time he picked up a piece of paper or a pen or a pencil, and so the translation had inserted itself between them, it had become the medium, the unspoken medium, of their relationship.

Finally. Early on Sunday she rose before he did and she found it, still in his satchel, and she put it in her bag and left. She told herself that she would read it that Sunday and give it back to him at work on Monday.

She did not. She could not.

There is, for Dr Apelles, a feeling of heaviness that hangs over everything. His feet are tired and he is burdened with heavy thoughts. It seems possible that even the elevator will not be able to lift him, but with a mighty heave, it lurches into the air. He leaves the ground but his thoughts are heavy enough to make him feel as though the machinery—the motor of the elevator—is having trouble with its work. Things had been progressing with Campaspe. She was more and more in his mind. He was more and more in hers, or so he'd thought. But this . . . he feels naked and exposed, stripped of his translation. Has she read it yet? Is she rereading it? What must she think . . . ?

Campaspe did read it that Sunday. Once. Twice. Three times. In between readings she cleaned her apartment and went for walks. But no matter what she did she would either glance at her bed and see the pages of the sheets soiled there or close her eyes and see Apelles' pages—the sum of his mind and energies and desire. And it didn't make sense without him. She knew it would not make sense unless she could talk to him about it.

That next day, Monday, she packed it with her things and went to work at RECAP.

She meant to give it to Apelles first thing and to apologize. But when she saw him—so solidly and unchangedly himself, already sorting books—she changed her mind.

"Hello."
"Good day."
"Get everything done yesterday?"
"What? Yes. Everything. Almost everything."

And she knew he knew. He was waiting for her to say something, but she could not. She watched him all day as she usually did, but this time she did not read him for pleasure—this time she read him for meaning, for the meaning of his manner. And this is a sure way to destroy a good story. And though she felt that she was destroying theirs, she could not say anything about the translation. She was too embarrassed and also too curious, still, about the actual meaning of the translation. It cast him in an entirely different light, and she needed to examine him, and the translation, in that new light.

All week she went to work and saw him there and talked to him during the day and had drinks with him in the afternoon. Surely they talked but she can't remember anything they said. The terrible thing about lies is that you need to remember them most clearly when you tell them, but the act of lying is part performance and part interpretation, and so much of her mind was on his reactions—the way he talked, what he said, how he responded, how he held his body, what he did with his hands—that she can't, now, remember anything she said to him, true or not. Except that she is sure she lied poorly.

So she reads and rereads and can't remember any of Apelles' words except the ones he's written down, and each time she reads his story, his translation, she is shocked at the audacity of his version.

Dr Apelles is in the habit of thinking that when he gets in the elevator he is as good as home. The door is locked behind him. The soft lights—the one in the kitchen, the floor lamp next to his reading chair, and, like a gracious promise of rest, the one next to his queen-sized bed that doesn't so much beckon as whisper out in the wider apartment that here, at last, you can lay your head—are on. He has eaten a little something and can stand at the window and look down on everything and all below him. And usually he won't have to explain anything to anyone, and there is no one to confront or confound him and he can, for all intents and purposes, cease to exist. But now, like it or not, he continues to matter, he is still being thought of out in the world. And the real terror is that since losing his translation he has lost something of himself. Campaspe has taken it. She must be reading. On the train maybe. Or in her apartment, which he has still not seen. But it wouldn't take her all that long to read the thing. Did she hate it? Does she think he hates her? Betrayal. *That* ends with a whimper, with a gasp for air. He thinks about this as the elevator ascends. And he thinks ahead to the comfort of his own space, a space he alone controls. He is so used to thinking ahead like this, his mind has flown far ahead of his body that it is a shock to be reminded at the second floor by the admonishing little ding of the elevator that he is only slightly closer; that his apartment is still some ways away. But even that, the quiet comfort of his apartment, seems like it will be no comfort at all. Campaspe would have taken the translation when she was last in his apartment. She would have worked alongside him for days (how many?) with the translation in her possession. Thinking about it as she looked at him. Thinking of her betrayal as she smiled at him. Experiencing what was his life's work, his most private and profound enterprise, as she went about the most mundane acts: shelving her dishes, taking off her shoes, making her bed, making water. And his precious translation, what she had consumed of it anyway, banged around in her mind along with all the trivialities of life. How could this be? How could it exist along with those other things?

But today Campaspe had resolved, finally, to give it back and make her apologies and salvage, if she could, what was left of their relationship. It had been easy, this Friday, to make that resolution, mostly because she was able to make it at RECAP, at her station, when Apelles wasn't there.

When she arrived at work she had left the translation in her locker, obeying the cardinal rule of RECAP: she was not to bring any outside reading material onto the floor.

But that had felt wrong somehow—to have the translation in her locker. Since she had decided, once and for all, to give it back, the single-copy handwritten document had acquired the most precious value. It, and it alone, and its safe return, could preserve his good feelings for her. She smiled to herself all morning. Her feelings for him and his for her felt as precious, as special, as unique and singular as his translation. She felt like the worst was over. And so on her first fifteen-minute break she went to her locker and took her bag out and made her way to the bathroom in the O.C.

She was almost at the bathroom door when she passed Ms Manger in the hall.

"Leaving?" asked Ms Manger.

Campaspe blushed.

"Oh! No. No. Not leaving. You know,—" she rolled her eyes in gyno-conspiratorial complicity, "—that time of the month."
"Of course. Of course," said Ms Manger.

Campaspe turned as she shouldered open the bathroom door and took note that Ms Manger had stopped in the hallway and had followed Campaspe with her eyes.

Once inside Campaspe closed her eyes for one second, two—did Ms Manger doubt her? Was her lie that apparent? Evidently so.

She took the handicapped stall and set her bag on the floor and took out the translation. She counted the pages to make sure she had them all, folded them once, and tried to suspend them in the elastic of her underwear, but she was wearing a thong and the pages would not stay put, so she pulled up her jeans and tucked them in the back and then buttoned up and pulled her white sweater down over the top. The pages seemed to be well-enough hidden.

She put her bag in her locker and went back to her station.

She began working again, smiling to herself, feeling better.

And as Dr Apelles stands in the elevator it seems that not only is his mind much faster than his body, it is more spacious as well. He cannot settle on any one thing. There is the translation. And there is Campaspe. There are all the thoughts and flashes, just flashes really, of his childhood. And the women he has been with—Annette and Frances and the many many Mais. And there is his work—all the translations in all those languages, an exquisite knowledge very few can appreciate.

All morning Campaspe glanced over at Apelles' empty station. Jesus noticed her looking and thought that she was looking at him.

"Hey, C."
"Jesus. How's it going?"
"How's it going?"
"Yeah. Life, you know."

Jesus looked at her steadily.

"You guys got something going on, huh?"
"What?"
"I said, 'you got something going on.' You're hooked up. You're together."

It was a statement.

"Yeah. I guess. Yeah," stronger, more sure, "yeah we do."

Jesus grunted.

"For a while. We've been seeing each other for a while."

Jesus grunted again.

"You could say it's serious."

She thought immediately of the translation resting against the small of her back. And the warm pages bent along her spine and felt, truly, like Apelles' hand resting there. It was very exciting.

"It's real," she said dreamily as she bent down to get a box from underneath her station.
"You got something sticking out of your pants."

Campaspe did not rise.

"Hey, C. Something's wrong with your sweater."

"Oh! Oh, it's raggedy, that's all."

She was partially blocked by Apelles' station and the cart drawn up to hers, so she took the pages out as surreptitiously as she could and put them on her work surface next to her manuals. But she knew Jesus had seen the translation, and, as the saying goes, Campaspe's heart went cold.

Apelles muses that Campaspe and her desires had sent her hurdling past him toward his translation. It must have begun that night when, after having gone to bed in his queen-sized bed, he thought he heard paper rustling in the next room. He had gone to sleep, into that twilight where anything can happen but very little ever does, and what does happen there is the most usual humdrum kind of stuff. When he woke he had the nagging feeling that he should check his briefcase and he did. It was where he had left it—on one of the kitchen chairs, the handles slanted against one another, blown there to the same angle by his hand. He opened it. All his papers were there, all the handwritten notes. Everything in the physical universe at least, was in place. His notes and his briefcase, but also the cups and saucers, his beloved toaster, his queen-sized bed—all of them were where they should be. But a new consciousness different than his own hovered over, entered, and inhabited his things now. They were possessed. At first this made him feel exiled from his own life, but the feeling is beginning to change. There might just be room aplenty in these things for him and for Campaspe and these simple objects can be entered and shared. The chipped and mismatched and time-stained and typical had become hiding places for the two of them the way children hide under the stairs and share secrets with one another.

Campaspe felt queasy. She attracted too much notice. Jesus had always desired her. That was obvious. He was jealous of Apelles and had been for some time. That was obvious, too. And to have his jealousy bubble up to the level of consciousness at just the same moment he noticed something amiss with her sweater, and to then see her blush and remove whatever it was she had tucked into her pants created a bridge between his jealousy and that thing, the translation, though he could not know what it was. This is what made Campaspe feel queasy.

"Hey, C."

Campaspe looked up and tried not to think about the manuscript that lay in open sight on her workstation.

"Hey, C. So what does he do when he's not here on Fridays?"
"You'd have to ask him."
"Come on. You gotta know. What does he do?"
"He translates. He works as a translator."
"He's a translator? What does he translate?"

Campaspe closed her eyes. She definitely did not feel well.

"He's working on a story. A special story."
"What's it about?"
"I don't know," she said in all honesty. "I think it's about him. It's about him."

Just then the lunch hour began, and Campaspe hurried off to the bathroom, the only place she could imagine being alone. She sat in a stall and tried to wonder her way out of the predicament in which she found herself, but could not. Everything she did made everything else worse, or so it felt.

When she returned to her station the manuscript was gone.

Dr Apelles stamped his foot and cast his eyes upward. The elevator had not even traveled halfway to his floor. He hated the afternoons. Especially the afternoons he spent at work. It was the day's end, that terrible time between working and living; there was nothing to look forward to—his work was done. All the books at RECAP had been logged, checked, and rechecked, and all the boxes were stacked and ready for the next day. There was some slight satisfaction in a good day's work, but there was also the sense, and it was overwhelming, that all that had happened or would happen had already occurred and opportunity had passed. So the evening time, when one was supposed to be free, felt like a prison to him. It seemed to Dr Apelles that all the other workers felt as though they had been released, and all their longings during the workday were cured in the evening. For these happy people, smiling to themselves or cheerfully bantering their way homeward, the evening waited for them like a tuxedoed beau just inside the doors of an elegant restaurant that was cozy and dimly lit with plenty of places to hide and scheme. For Dr Apelles, on the other hand, the evening prospect was one of crushing tedium and downright terror because, if truth be told, the evenings had until recently held few surprises, and were not, usually, something to look forward to. Without the veneer of activity that he has been in the habit of applying over the emptiness of his days, his time showed itself for what it really was: empty. But now, with his translation out and adrift in the world, his life had become larger. He had Campaspe to thank for that.

Oh, why won't the elevator hurry? It has barely gone up at all, and time is dragging. The afternoons, between work and evening, are a burden: by anticipating those later hours, they are thus consecrated and intensified, much like thinking ahead to a dentist's appointment or a scheduled medical procedure; the anticipation of pain is usually worse than the actual experience of it. Every jab of the needle confirms for us what we thought all along—and we long to shout if we could, see! I knew it would be bad!—and negates all the benign moments we spend making sure our bodies do not fall apart prematurely. So, too, those truly bad nights—when the walls close in, and our work seems either of great importance but impossible to achieve or of no importance whatsoever, when from afar we hear the laughter of people having fun and enjoying themselves without us, and when there is absolutely nothing the mind wants except relief, and when sleep doesn't come or when it does it is not enough or what there is of it is filled with dreams that make our hearts ache—give us the small satisfaction of having been right all along in that now distant, dim, and far-away afternoon. Those nights effectively wipe away those other evenings of peace when the universe is in hushed accord with our every quiet, modest, wish. Dr Apelles' sole consolation in the afternoons at RECAP had been that he got to watch Campaspe put away her things. But that is different now. Oh, the battle inside him is raging. His old pessimism. His old desire to remain hidden.

All the same, there is something blessed about the way she moves: how she orders the manuals lined up on the right side of her workstation by pressing her uplifted forefinger against each spine one by one; how she sweeps the shreds of paper to the floor with her palms flat against the table as though smoothing the sheets of their marital bed; how, when she squats down to search for boxes or other supplies stored under her workstation, Dr Apelles can see, from the side, how her strong thighs meet and transform her calves, changing their usual compact shape, spreading them into a seam of muscle so strong and smooth it is no wonder poets of old felt compelled to use phrases like marble and rose when describing the flesh of women they desired—and Dr Apelles is further able (it is amazing where the mind can go) to imagine how a long spell of squatting will raise a red mark in the hollow of her knee that he could run his finger over and be able to tell, even with his eyes closed, just by the heat and texture, where that hot zone began and ended.

Campaspe *was* hot. Flushed. Confused. And terrified. She scanned the top of her workstation. The translation was gone. She looked on the floor, on the off chance it had fallen there. It had not. She tried not to look at Jesus as she fanned the manuals on her station to see if, for some reason, she had slipped it in there. But everything was in order even though nothing, speaking of emotion, was in order.

She did not want to ask Jesus straight out if he had taken it. Would he answer honestly? That was doubtful. And besides, she did not want to attract much attention, any attention—because she was guilty twice over: once for taking something that wasn't hers, and once again because she had broken the rules of RECAP and introduced "foreign material" to the floor.

She could hear Jesus humming along to his iPod.

She could hear her own heart beating. And she could hear, faintly at first, and then with growing insistency, not so much what Apelles would say, because she couldn't imagine him actually saying anything, but what Apelles would *feel*. And the future of his feelings for her were not certain anymore.

Dr Apelles, through long habit, has been reading Campaspe whether she wants him to or not. He thinks, as the elevator passes another floor, how, when she is done rummaging below her workstation she will grasp the edge and lift herself up and say, lightly, to no one but herself, barely audible over the noise of RECAP, "ooof" in the same voice children use when lifting something they expect to be heavy even when it is not. Her little exclamation gives her the extra boost necessary to accomplish the action, though surely she would have been able to lift herself back to standing without saying anything at all. But by saying it, and this is what he liked so much about it, she shows, on the far horizon of her consciousness, that she is thinking about what she is doing. Now I am standing up. This is my body and I am making it move . . . And in the silence of RECAP, or rather, in the absence of speech, her little "ooof" functioned as a step forward into her mind, just as landings on well-designed stairs give you a glimpse of the upper floors and tell you that, even though it might seem like a long way off and the feet are weary with travel, you are almost there. These were the things that Dr Apelles usually waited all the blessed day to see, and if he was not at RECAP, was compelled to imagine, to read, as it were. It is a gift that Apelles only now recognizes—to create for himself Campaspe, to imagine her fully.

He thought of her now. Did she have the translation with her? She did not.

All the early afternoon, between lunch and the second break, Campaspe was in agony. She did not look at Jesus and went through the motions of work all the while thinking about how she could get the manuscript back.

She could not think of how to do it.

And so, recognizing that there was only one option, and that the most important thing was to get it back to Apelles, no matter the price she would have to pay, she did something drastic.

The clock struck. It was time for the second fifteen-minute break. As casually as she could, she made her way to her locker and got a snack and took it to the Reading Room. She checked out a newspaper (she couldn't remember, later, which one) and seated herself at one of the tables.

There were a few workers at the other tables, seated singly and in groups of two and three. Jesus came in, and though he usually sat with her during her breaks, he took a table in the far corner and watched Campaspe over his sandwich.

And, as quietly as she could, without anyone noticing, she proceeded to rip a piece off the corner of the page. And then another. Bit by bit she began to eat the newsprint.

It tasted terrible, chalky, but the bitter taste of the page had the exact same flavor as her betrayal of Apelles, and she swallowed it dutifully.

At first Campaspe didn't think she would be able to get the whole page down in the fifteen minutes but she wetted her finger and tore silent piece after silent piece and chewed and drank her soda, and, after fifteen minutes the page was gone. The break was over. Campaspe returned to her station.

Dr Apelles looked at his watch and at the numbered floors dinging by above the elevator door. RECAP would be closing now. When he was there Dr Apelles would wait for those last minutes, when without looking at the clock, he could tell, by an increase in the pitch of activity—a louder and more persistent rustling of paper and slide of book cover over wood and pasteboard—that it was closing time. And it was only under that cover of noise that he could, by wearing it as camouflage, look at Campaspe with impunity—armored, concealed in, hidden by all the activity around him he could look at her as much as he liked. He took in as much of her as he could and stored it up the way squirrels store a winter's worth of nuts, and like those squirrels, he forgot where he hid most of those nuggets— and there he would be, scurrying around in his mind trying to find every last shred of every memory of every part of her that he knew, and since he knew he was bound to lose these treasures, the pleasure of collecting, of standing and taking in her movements, was washed away by the anxiety that he had not collected enough to last. Usually, though, it *was* enough, and he kept his stores intact, and later, while seated at the table of memory, he snacked on them through the evening and this made the nighttime tolerable.

On this day closing time was marked with a different kind of activity. RECAP buzzed like a hive. Just before the sorters began closing down their stations, as the shelvers and loaders were returning their carts to their proper waiting places, the alarm sounded. Very few had ever heard the alarm go off for any reason other than a drill. But they had all been trained to recognize the sound. It meant that either the atmosphere of the Stacks had been compromised or a book or text had gone missing.

In this case, Mrs Millefeuille had, after the last break, tabulated the pages of newsprint as usual and found one missing. She had rechecked her count. There *was* a page missing. Mrs Millefeuille had then notified Ms Manger as per regulations and Ms Manger had sounded the alarm.

All the workers stopped what they were doing. The O.C. staff stood in a row in the hallway leading past the Reading Room. Those who worked on the loading dock stood in a long line next to the queue of waiting carts. The sorters, Campaspe among them, stood to the side of their stations like soldiers in a barracks. And the shelvers waited in a line by their carts along the far wall on the way to the Stacks.

RECAP was officially locked down for the first time since it had opened.

Dr Apelles, on the elevator, imagines the end of the day at RECAP. Closing time. The sound of shuffling paper rises in the afternoon air like the wingbeats of a flock of birds—restless, unsettled—as they prepare to fly off to some more distant place. There is a sense of urgency to it, though they repair every evening. And as they lift and wheel as on a city square, they turn first this way and then that, for no obvious reason, just to collect themselves, to perfect their unison. One wonders where they go, or if they go anywhere at all. And it seems possible that the only reason for this movement is that they have the most exquisite wings, and since they have them they must use them. And so the sound rises, Dr Apelles can hear it around him better with his eyes closed—and he has the sense that, just as the birds have taken wing, the sound of the shuffling paper signifies a general movement that is impossible to anticipate. When will they, as one, wheel to the left and brag their bellies at the pavement? It is impossible to detect a leader, an individual in advance. And what makes them move, singly but all together, is different than what enables them to choose their direction. A mystery to be sure—they must be tuned to something that Dr Apelles cannot begin to understand.

The workers shuffle their papers and the sound rises in the air like the wingbeats of a flock of birds and for a delicious moment

Dr Apelles knows that if he were to raise his hand they would, ever so subtly and ever so temporarily, change their course. And another possibility seems clear: if, as the workers make their noise, as they create this beautiful accord, as they enact their common purpose, if Dr Apelles were to raise his hand, in a manner of speaking, all of RECAP would fly, as it were, to some other place. But the RECAP workers are not birds, people are not birds. They do not share a common purpose, or if they do, it is not one of their choosing, and it makes up only one part of their day. The workers will, as they make their noise, soon greet their other lives each to each. And there is beauty in that, there is. Because they rise, and the noise is on the air, and for that brief moment at that far reach of the day and for once, as they rise and prepare and mill and Dr Apelles is among them, it is a certain fact that not together, certainly not together, they could—and this makes them better than birds—go in as many different directions as you can think of; they are obliged only to follow their desires and their habits. Campaspe, like everyone else, like him, has certain longings. The most simple of which is the longing to know. If, when earlier, when walking across the small park in which they have jazz concerts in the summer, Dr Apelles had been able to guess which way the birds would fly he would have won a valuable thing—he would have a knowledge, he would possess it. And perhaps that's all Campaspe really wants—she wants to possess him and the only way to possess Dr Apelles is to read his work because he won't speak about himself. There is logic in this: he won't speak about himself so perhaps he is writing about himself, perhaps he shows himself there. By reading him she can guess the angle of his flight. Of course she wants to read it and of course she can't ask him. So she wants to read the translation. Such a desire is not so bad after all. It is no wonder that some of the ancient oracles were told by reading the movement of birds. But the simple flight of birds, the innocent rustle of paper, does not occur in RECAP today. It is quiet—no one makes a sound, no one moves. The hunt is on for the missing newspaper page. In the background the atmosphere chamber breathes, slowly, in and out. That is all.

Since the page had gone missing from Campaspe's newspaper, her station was the first one that would be checked.

Ms Manger, flanked by the head of the O.C. and Mrs Millefeuille and followed by Mr Florsheim and Mr Bass, strode importantly down the main hallway between the loading docks and the sorting stations and came to a stop in front of Campaspe's station.

"Do you have any foreign reading materials at your station?" she asked, as outlined in the section of the RECAP guidebook pertaining to "invasions," as the Designer had decided to call instances of missing or mis-introduced text.

"No, I don't," said Campaspe in all honesty.

"Do you have in your possession a page of newsprint taken from the Reading Room?" was the next question. Ms Manger seemed, at some level, to be enjoying herself.

Again, Campaspe was able to say,

"No. I don't."

And finally:

"Do you have any knowledge of how pages were removed from the Reading Room or any knowledge of where they might be now?"

Ms Manger, far from doing disagreeable duty, basked in her authority. Compaspe's discomfort was a balm to Ms Manger.

"No. I don't."

This time Campaspe was lying. And Ms Manger knew it.

The elevator moves faster now. At times like these, hope hangs lightly on the workstations and architecture of the office and it is easily swept up into the rustling paper but lifted higher, making of the afternoon air—golden, trembling in the high windows along the west wall—an atmosphere of possibility in which, along with hope all the responsibilities and plans, engagements and chores are mixed, and it feels as though absolutely anything can happen. Now is such a moment. And at such moments hope can become something real.

At moments like these we look about us—up at the ceiling or down at our feet or at the people to our left and right—as though to catch sight of life's potential in the manner of art viewers laboring in vain to find the artist's signature hidden in a vast painting. At moments like this we want to know who the author is that made this mystery.

The sense of hope, of possibility, not particular to RECAP, but perhaps enhanced by all the stories passing under the fingers of the workers, is what makes Dr Apelles look at Campaspe the way he does. RECAP is a reminder that there are more stories out there than anyone wants to hear and most of them exist uncherished. If only they could be sure one set of eyes would linger over them lovingly just once, for just a little while, then the eternity of RECAP would be bearable.

Having no choice, Ms Manger, with the help of the head of the O.C., Mrs Millefeuille, and Mr Florsheim and Mr Bass—along with a team of searchers culled from every department of RECAP who served one-year terms on what was referred to as "The Search Committee"—began searching RECAP, section by section, area by area, for the missing newspaper.

They began at Campaspe's station, and, finding nothing, began at the front of RECAP. All the workers, at least those within Campaspe's line of sight, looked at her and wondered; their suspicions grew as the day refused to end. They were all stuck there until the search was over.

And what did they find?

Nothing.

Not the newsprint, of course, that was working its way through Campaspe's belly. And not the translation either, which is what Campaspe had hoped they'd find.

It remained missing.

The search was concluded.

And incident report was written and filed.

RECAP closed.

And everyone left. All save one.

Dr Apelles is surprised to find himself among the hopeful. Hope is merely the attempt to introduce to the future some past happiness, an attempt to change the ending—with different characters and new surroundings—of some sad little episode of the past. And the terrible prospect and most difficult task is to create, from scratch, some unforeseen, some future happiness that has no hold in the soil of our years.

Campaspe takes the train, and the ride sends her, inexorably, closer to Apelles. She is certain that their love has died. She does not know where the translation has gone.

When the alarm first sounded, she did not see Jesus grab a book from his cart and set it on his workstation. She did not see him cram the translation—which he had hidden under his baggy jersey—section by section, into the large leather-bound book on his work surface. He didn't look at the title of the volume. He had no idea what it was about, but it looked Greek, judging from the illustrations that flipped by. It was a myth of some sort—a romance, *Daphnis and Chloe* was embossed on the cover for someone to see (but no one did). Jesus looked at Campaspe. The alarm was still ringing in their ears. But she did not notice him. He took all the original pages of the translation and crammed them in. Here. And there. And then he took the book, with the translation stuffed inside, sized it, boxed it, labeled it—all in a mad rush—and placed it on the last cart that would leave his station for the day.

Now the elevator feels as though it is picking up speed. A great weight has been lifted. The ride cannot last forever. Soon. Someday, he will arrive at his apartment. He will turn the key and the door will open and he will close it behind him. He will be stored there in his apartment, with his things that are no longer his things, with his translations that are no longer his translations, and with his thubadub heart, still beating away beneath his ribs; a heart that is no longer just his. He will be stored there, waiting to be recalled. For the moment, though, he is still in the elevator. Campaspe is miles away.

Campaspe is drawing closer. The train cannot go on forever. She has no idea where the translation has gone. She had not seen how Jesus concluded his work so quickly, with time to spare, before he was expected to stand to the side of his station like the others. Campaspe had not seen any of this.

But someone else had. Someone else, later, after RECAP had closed, could watch at her leisure, all that had happened, as captured on the cameras. Someone is always reading somewhere.

Dr Apelles smiles for the first time that day. He feels free of all earthly weight. All his habits and thoughts and styles, the ponderous words that were so heavy in his mind, have dropped away. He can see them. They are spent and cracked and tumble away in space behind him. The rules are different here. He is really moving now. Campaspe must be so worried. The translation was there a second ago. And now it is gone. She hadn't even gotten to the end and did not know that it wasn't finished, that the ending wasn't written yet. It is not such a bad thing that she took it. All she wanted was to possess Dr Apelles and that wasn't such a bad thing. Being possessed wasn't such a bad thing.

He can see her with his eyes closed. She doesn't know where to look, where to search. She searches her mind, but cannot find it there.

The feeling of betrayal that Dr Apelles felt when he stepped into the elevator has evaporated. In its place he feels hope. He finally has what he has never had.

He is being lifted high above the ground in the elevator even if he cannot see it, even if he can barely feel the speed at which he travels.

Yes. Campaspe took the manuscript, and even though she took it without his permission, it was not a betrayal.

She only wanted to know him better and in doing so she wanted to possess him, to be able to guess where his flight would take him.

Being known is agony. Being alone is even worse. There is such potential to fall. And the distance is so far. The earth small below us. The distance is so great.

Campaspe swipes her card and leaves the train platform.

Dr Apelles' elevator arrives at his floor.

Campaspe hurries down the platform and runs up the steps. Campaspe hails a cab and gives Apelles' address.

Dr Apelles opens the door to his apartment. Dr Apelles stands inside the door to his apartment. He can smell Campaspe's scent in the air. Dr Apelles sets down his briefcase by the door and hangs up his coat. Dr Apelles makes a grilled cheese sandwich.

Campaspe is left at the curb. She says a quick hello to the door-man and hops in the elevator.

She presses the button for the fourteenth floor. The elevator does not move fast enough.

Dr Apelles eats his grilled cheese and drinks a beer and tries to read, but reading is not what he wants to do because he cannot see Campaspe in what he is reading.

Will the elevator never arrive?

Dr Apelles puts down the journal he has been reading. He knows that Campaspe must be thinking of him.

Campaspe cannot imagine how Dr Apelles is feeling.

Dr Apelles can imagine how Campaspe is feeling.

It is agonizing.

Dr Apelles stands at the window. He speaks.

The elevator finally arrives. She knocks and then enters Dr Apelles' apartment.

Dr Apelles does not turn away from the window. Before she can speak he says something. And then turns to face her.

Campaspe says I took your translation and now I can't find it.

Dr Apelles says I know.

It's missing she says.

I know he says.

Someone must have taken it.

I know, he says, it is gone.

How will it end

It just did

~ Book V ~

1. The summer drew to a close. It was fall once again. The village was preparing for the arrival of the Agent, and with him, a whole delegation of Chiefs from neighboring and far-off bands. There was talk that this meeting was an important one. Treaties and agreements would be made. The violence of the preceding winter would, it was hoped, be laid to rest. Also, it was ricing time, and since it had been a very dry summer, the rice beds were thick with rice stalks that bent low over the water where they had not been braided together into stacks as protection against sudden winds and marauding blackbirds. The whole village was buzzing with activity. People rushed around trying to bring in the rice before the delegation arrived. Others, at the urging of the Chiefs, cleaned up the village. Yards were raked clean and all the wood shavings, bits of bark, scraps of cloth, broken implements, along with drying racks and the like, were burnt. Bones, fish skins, and entrails were collected and dumped out in the woods. A few of the boys had been commissioned to hunt and kill the surplus of dogs that lent the village a wild and savage aspect. Women went out in groups to peel elm bark and pull wiigoob and with these things they patched the lodges so that they all looked new. No one was more concerned with making a good impression on the visiting officials—the owners, if not of the land, then of his destiny—than Bimaadiz.

He helped with the gardens, ordering the rows, pulling weeds, helped with the lodges and cabins, with banking all the canoes in rows, and with painting the gravehouses.

2. But the pride of the village, and where the negotiations and the wedding would take place, was the central garden. It was down near the shore and commanded a fine view of the lake and of the islands sprinkled out against the horizon. It was a pleasant place, with waves lapping the sandy beach and the cabins and lodges of the village growing up against the forest behind. It was open for all to see, and since it was in the center of the village there was no need for a palisade or wall to keep out hungry animals—deer searching for greens and rabbits and woodchucks eating away the roots. It was filled with a bounty of good growing things; rows of corn soldiered up together armed with ripe ears of corn ready for picking. Squash meandered along the ground, always trying to spread, to run away and hide in other parts of the garden, but were tethered and stopped short by the very vines that gave them life. Peas climbed and gossiped from their trellises, while in the ground turnips, potatoes, leeks, and onions grumbled but kept their secrets. Everyone in the village had a hand in working the garden that was the wonder of all who visited it. But since Bimaadiz was to be married there in a short time, days now, he was given the responsibility of making it as fine as he could.

He hoed the grass back from the perimeter to make the edge uniform, and he cut away the dead ears of corn and blighted leaves so the corn looked clean and sturdy. The ripe fruits he collected so they would not be overripe by the time of the festivities. There was an enormous oak with great spreading branches under which the delegates and Chiefs would sit, and Bimaadiz cleared the ground underneath of dead sticks and twigs, and piled them to the side in case a fire was needed in the evenings. It looked perfect. Bimaadiz was convinced that no garden on earth could rival it in beauty or abundance. His father and mother visited him just as he was finishing and they agreed. He had done a fine job and the Agent and the Priest could not possibly object to his marriage. Who could object to anything in a place so perfect and beautiful?

Bimaadiz went to bed, confident that the next day—the day on which the Deputy Agent and his assistant were to arrive in advance of the rest of the delegates—would be the beginning of the most perfect joy that would be the rest of his life. But trouble, unforeseen by Bimaadiz, was underfoot. Among Eta's suitors was a young man the same age as Bimaadiz named Wezaanagishens. He was as handsome as he was lazy and a coward as well. He was struck by Eta's beauty though he never had a chance of marrying her. Everyone knew him to be a liar and a cheat though he was strong and reckless—good maybe for capturing the enemy but not good for much else. After his proposal was rejected he swore he would take revenge on whoever was going to marry Eta. Since he was denied his own happiness, he would work to deny it to Eta's future husband. Wezaanagishens didn't dare confront Bimaadiz or ambush him so he did what cowards do: he destroyed the good work of others.

That night, after Bimaadiz had gone to sleep dreaming of the good things to come, Wezaanagishens stole down to the garden and wrecked it. He pulled up the corn and trampled it, and he broke open the squash where they lay defenseless in their furrows. He tore down the trellises, and when he was satisfied, he skunked back to his bed, as happy as could be with the night's work.

3. When Bimaadiz rose and went down to the garden he was greeted with a vision of destruction. He cried out and sank to his knees when he saw what had happened to his garden (for that's how Bimaadiz had come to feel about it). Jiigibiig and Zhookaagiizhigookwe came running, and they were as dismayed as he was.

No one will believe that animals did this, and what villagers would do it? Bimaadiz was convinced that he would be blamed and that now he would never be allowed to marry Eta. His parents were afraid he would kill himself and were equally sure that the trust placed in their family would dissolve into doubt and suspicion, so they were almost as sad as Bimaadiz was.

Just then the Deputy Agent and his assistant arrived on horseback. The Deputy Agent, whose name was Schiller, was a young man, no older than thirty. He was well educated, hardworking, and fun loving. He liked all those around him to be happy because his own enjoyment of life suffered when those close to him, even those he didn't know, were sad. He surveyed the garden and asked what had happened.

Jiigibiig and Zhookaagiizhigookwe begged his forgiveness.

"It isn't our fault. We're victims here. Some evildoer ruined our work and that of our son," pleaded Zhookaagiizhigookwe. "The trust placed in our family has been compromised and it threatens the success of our son's marriage."

Schiller, without dismounting, surveyed the damage, and said, "My own eyes show me the truth of your words and I will do everything in my power to make it right with the Agent."

As for Schiller's assistant, he said nothing, but he stared at Bimaadiz and his eyes bulged from their sockets. He seemed a different man entirely from the one he served. He had a dark beard and wore a long black coat that made him look like a priest. His name was Charles Luce. He would not stop staring at Bimaadiz.

Schiller told Jiigibiig, Zhookaagiizhigookwe, and Bimaadiz to clean up the garden as best they could. They had time. The Governor, Agent, and the other Chiefs were delayed at Crow Wing and wouldn't be at the village until the day after the next.

"One thing, before I leave: I enjoy the hunt very much and as we will have many people here we need to provide some meat for them. Where is the hunting good around here? Where does the game hide?"

Jiigibiig was grateful. Schiller seemed like a good reasonable man.

"Bimaadiz can show you where to hunt—he's the best hunter in all the area. He's needed in the garden today, but tomorrow, early, he can go with you and show you hunting the likes of which you've never seen before."

"That sounds reasonable. I think, though, I will hunt for the day today and if I don't have any luck I will go out with your Bimaadiz tomorrow."

Charles Luce, who still hadn't said a word, finally spoke. Without taking his eyes off Bimaadiz, he said he would stay behind and oversee the repairs to the garden. Schiller agreed and left, anxious to hunt new territory. Jiigibiig and Zhookaagiizhigookwe took their leave, too. They needed to finish working some hides and dying porcupine quills—necessary decorations for Bimaadiz's wedding outfit.

Bimaadiz sighed and began trying to fix the garden. He staked the broken corn stalks upright as best he could and set the trellises straight. He was committed to the work but was afraid that he was being rude to Charles Luce. He looked up and was surprised to see that Luce had tied his horse to the big elm and was walking toward him—the sand and dirt sticking to his black riding boots. Bimaadiz continued his work and Luce worked beside him. It was clear that Luce was unused to such manual labor. He was awkward on the uneven ground, his fingers fumbled with the trellises and with the knotted wiigoob that held the corn to the stakes. Bimaadiz thought it strange that such a man would work side by side with an Indian.

After a while Luce began to speak fluently in the language.

"You must be the pride of the village," he said. "You are so strong and nimble and don't mind honest work." He paused and then, still looking at Bimaadiz strangely, he said, "But your hair is a mess. It looks as though you've been on the trail for days!"

It was true, Bimaadiz's hair did look a little wild. With the excitement of the damage to the garden and the need to fix it as soon as possible, Bimaadiz had not had time to slick it down that morning. And it had collected dust, dirt, and twigs. When Bimaadiz stopped and combed it with his fingers, not wanting to contradict an important man like Luce, the assistant stopped working, too, and stared at Bimaadiz's neck, his shoulders, and his lean torso.

"You are very strong," Luce continued in the language. "You must live an active life."

Bimaadiz didn't know what to say. He felt that Luce was eating him up with his eyes. Bimaadiz resumed working and Luce returned to Bimaadiz's side. He was so close it wasn't long before their shoulders were touching.

"Perhaps when we're done," said Luce without looking at Bimaadiz, "you can show me where we can wash off the dust and dirt."

Bimaadiz looked up and then out at the lake. "There is water everywhere and you can wash where you please. The lake is just there, though that's where everyone collects water."

"I want you to show me," said Luce. "And perhaps you should bathe, too. You're even dirtier than I am."

Bimaadiz shrugged. Luce was strange—getting so close, saying those kinds of things, staring. And what's more, it was clear that Luce was embarrassed somehow but that he couldn't help himself; he couldn't stop himself from saying these things, from sidling up close to Bimaadiz. He shuddered and blushed and acted like a deer full of ticks, rubbing itself and panting heavily. Bimaadiz returned to the work, sorting through the pumpkins and squash that hadn't been broken. Luce was right there beside him, and he spoke in a low voice almost directly in Bimaadiz's ear.

"We could be friends," he suggested. "Men can be friends just like men and women are friends."

And Bimaadiz finally understood what Luce was after. He stood straight and as sternly as he could he said, "I am supposed to be married in two days' time and so I am not interested in making friends. I don't have the time, and besides, I don't want that kind of friendship with anyone."

Luce trembled even more and stuttered. "I understand, I understand completely. I am sorry for bothering you. This is a busy time for you to be sure." With that, he walked away unsteadily, tripping over the furrows, to where his horse was tethered to the ash tree and led it away toward the trading post without looking back.

Bimaadiz finished with the garden. It looked much better, though not as good as before it was wrecked. He went to his parents' shack to clean up and help them finish his wedding clothes. It had been a strange day, marked by many different emotions and Bimaadiz, completely exhausted, was glad it was over.

4. The next morning, having heard that Schiller hadn't managed to find any game, Bimaadiz sought him out and offered to take him into the woods in order to make sure he had the kind of hunt he wanted. Bimaadiz was trying to win favor, and besides, he knew that with all the visitors they would need to have a lot of meat. Luce was there when Bimaadiz approached Schiller, but he barely acknowledged Bimaadiz's presence and said he could not go hunting as he had to prepare some of the documents pertaining to the upcoming negotiations. So Schiller and Bimaadiz set out together.

Bimaadiz walked alongside Schiller who was once again on horseback. Schiller asked him about the game—numbers and species—and was impressed with Bimaadiz's knowledge. Schiller broadened his inquiries to include questions about trapping, the rice harvest, and a host of other things. Bimaadiz proved to be thoughtful, well informed, and uncommonly wise for someone his age and race.

Soon they reached the place Bimaadiz had selected—it was a ways past the mill and was ideal for a two-man hunt. There was a large swamp in the middle of which an island of sorts stood that was connected to the surrounding high ground by a thin neck of land. The island had been logged a few years previously and was covered in browse—small poplar and hazelbrush—which provided good food and cover for the deer. It was an especially good spot because most of the other food sources available to the deer—grass, mushrooms, clover, flowers—had been eaten up. Bimaadiz knew that the deer would be sleeping there during the day and eating there at night. They always stayed close to their food at that time of year. He also knew that the deer would not cross the deep boggy swamp and if startled or scared would flush across the narrow strip of solid ground that connected the island to the mainland.

Bimaadiz told Schiller to hide on one side of the neck and that he would cross the bog and push the deer off the island toward him. Schiller saw the wisdom of this and agreed. He got into position and Bimaadiz went around and began to cross the swamp in just his pants with the rifle slung over his shoulder.

It took him some time to cross the swamp quietly. Once he reached solid ground he put his shirt back on and unslung the Winchester. He checked to make sure the tube was full and that there was a shell in the chamber and he cocked the hammer halfway back. Then he began his hunt. He stalked quietly. He wanted to push the deer out but he didn't want them to run because for all he knew Schiller was a terrible shot and wouldn't be able to hit a deer bounding through the brush. It wasn't long before he saw a small buck still in velvet curled under the drooping arms of a spruce. Bimaadiz took aim and fired. The buck's head slumped. It was dead. Bimaadiz kept walking and in a few minutes he heard Schiller shoot. Once, twice, three times. Suddenly deer were running everywhere. Bimaadiz saw two yearlings bounding to his left. He shot the one in front and when the other stopped in confusion he dropped that one, too.

Bimaadiz heard more shots from Schiller, but he paid little attention. Deer jumped this way and that and no matter how poor a shot he had, no matter which way they ran or how thick the growth, Bimaadiz was rich in luck; every time he shot, a deer went down. He didn't have time to reload, and by the time he reached Schiller the Winchester was empty.

Schiller was flushed and excited. He eagerly pointed to where three deer had fallen, and he was clearly proud of his work.

"I've never had such shooting," he confessed. "I shot ten times and got three. How about you?" he asked. "I heard seven shots."

"All my shots went true," said Bimaadiz, as humbly as he could.

"I don't believe it," said Schiller.

Bimaadiz shrugged. "It wouldn't pay to lie about it," he said. "You'll see for yourself in a few minutes." With that, he leaned the Winchester against a tree and gutted Schiller's deer for him in the blink of an eye. Once he was done he and Schiller walked back and one by one, Bimaadiz gutted his deer while Schiller smoked his short pipe and uttered praise, amazed at Bimaadiz's skill.

They decided to fetch some young men and a wagon to load up and haul the deer back to the village. The shooting had only taken minutes but gutting, dragging, and loading the deer made for a long day's work, and it was evening by the time all ten deer were hanging from a pole suspended from two trees to the side of the garden. Bimaadiz went to bed pleased but nervous. He knew Schiller admired him, but the next day the Governor, Agent, and delegation of Chiefs would arrive. He hadn't seen Eta in days and he wouldn't be allowed to see her until the wedding took place the next day or the day after. So, seeded with hope and watered with fear, Bimaadiz tried to sleep.

5. The next morning was both beautiful and quiet. A few clouds hung motionless in the sky and were so white, so perfectly formed, were so much the ideal of what scattered clouds should be, they made the blue sky in which they were suspended seem a deeper, more perfect blue—serene, infinite, and steady. The temperature had dropped overnight, and a thick casing of dew hung over everything. The trees and grass sparkled with it, and one's every step released drops of moisture on the ground. A very slight, very cool wind meandered through the village making the flowers and clothes strung out on lines wave gently but silently in the silvery hush. The village itself had never looked so beautiful. All the cabins and lodges were in perfect shape and were snugged with elm bark and cattail screens. Great piles of straw and hay sat ready in the corrals. The official buildings—the small church, trading post, Agency office, and mill—were whitewashed and looked newly made. Young boys, unable or not allowed to sleep much past dawn, cut cedar boughs and stowed them in water-filled barrels lined up along the road, and as a group they slapped and flung them up and down the road to soothe the dust that was sure to rise later. The smell of cooking fires wafted down the trails to settle over the lake where it was gently pulled away from shore.

This beautiful calm lasted until noon. The people of the village kept close to their lodges and cabins. They were dressed in their finest clothes, weighted with beaded vests and bandolier bags, with quilled yokes and new moccasins. Some had sewn standards that designated their clan and had planted them next to the doors of their lodges or cabins—invitations for clan relatives from distant villages to stay with them during the negotiations.

At noon some of the boys from the village who had been sent to camp along the road the night before and who were sure to become runners someday raced back breathlessly into the village and shouted the news that the delegates would be riding in within a half hour. The people left their lodges and strolled down to the roadside to wait and the young boys once again lifted their dripping cedar boughs and beat the road dust down.

Soon, from around the bend, the villagers heard the jingle of harnesses and the clopping of hooves. Boys ran out and back shouting out the progress of the column the way whiskeyjacks flit back and forth between timber camps.

Finally, after much anticipation, the front delegation rode into view.

At the head of the procession rode the Governor, the Agent, the Priest, and the Colonel in charge of the cavalry garrison to the south. They all rode huge chargers, (except for the Priest who sat astride a small mare), tall and wide, whose coats glowed and whose muscles rippled under their skins. Their saddles were well-oiled saddles of the military type. And their clothes were free of lint and dust, the gold buttons of their tunics were polished, and all in all everything looked like it was freshly made so free were they from the dirt and wear of travel. They rode slowly, four abreast, and everything about them communicated the obvious power of their stations. Behind them rode a small contingent of cavalry officers on smaller, more agile, but no less impressive quarter horses. They were men who had seen a lot of action, and they rode straight in their saddles and did not look to either side at the villagers who lined the road.

This advance guard and the officials under their protection passed into the village, and some of the boys leapt into the road and guided them under the towering beech tree next to the garden where the village Chiefs stood waiting wrapped in treaty blankets and holding war pipes with long stems. The advance guard dismounted and began greeting the Chiefs while their horses were led by the boys to the large corral.

Meanwhile the Chiefs and war leaders from other bands and tribes were arriving. These were the people the villagers had really been waiting for. Everyone knew that the government and the army would define the future, and though they had arrived first, the future, as it were, was not there yet. The other bands and tribes—some of them longtime enemies—however, represented the real force and the real power the villagers had to contend with now. They controlled the portages, trade, travel, and most other aspects of daily life. Some of them were relatives. Some of them were enemies. Some were known and others were strangers. All of them excited keen interest in the onlookers.

They came in loose groups, unlike the regimental order of the cavalry. There were groups of local Chiefs who sauntered into the village on small horses and who sat astride their mounts casually. Some of them chatted amongst themselves while others smoked silently—looking down the actual and the symbolic road in front of them. Some of these Chiefs, all from allied bands of the same tribe as the villagers, nodded to villagers they knew, acknowledging blood or clan relations. They wore beaded vests edged with red piping, wool sashes, and elaborate bandolier bags. They had on black wool trousers with beaded drops and wore their best moccasins. The floral designs of their regalia and their easy manners made it seem like the forest had sent out its most beautiful fruit; a forest of flowers and vines had awakened and descended into town. A few of them wore treaty medals and one of them, the oldest of them all, sat on a travois wrapped in blankets. Bagonegiizhig was his name and he was sitting on the travois, facing the way they had come, wrapped in a blanket with only his head and arm sticking out. He was so old that he had shrunk to the size of a child, and he blinked sleepily in the travois. But no one, especially his enemies, were in doubt about how sharp his mind was or about the power of his speech. It was said that he had persuaded death to leave him alone and that he was over one hundred and twenty-five years old.

Behind this group walked representatives from bands that, technically, were related by language and custom to that of the villagers. But they lived far to the north, surrounded by water on little islands in remote tributaries to the big lake where no one ever visited. They were so isolated that they were unused to speaking to outsiders and knew no languages but their own. They had strange gestures, spoke a strange dialect, and were said to be fearsome medicine men. The villagers were careful not to look them in the eye.

Last in line were the Naadaweg. Some walked, having reached Crow Wing by canoe, and others from farther west rode small mustangs. They were quick people. All of them were tall and lean, and all of them were beautiful to look at. They were the traditional enemies of the villagers, and they had warred against one another for as long as anyone could remember. The band of marauders that had crossed the river the winter before and had captured Bimaadiz belonged to this group. The escalation in hostilities between the Naadaweg and the villagers was what had led to the negotiations in the first place. They all wore breeches of buckskin and bone breastplates. The stocks of their rifles were studded with brass tacks as were their pipestems. Their long hair was wrapped in quilled sheaths and many had pierced ears and noses. They looked both stern and magnificent as they sauntered into the village.

Behind the Chiefs and warriors came the baggage—gifts of furs, flour, pipestone, axes, hides, dried meat, and more—piled on travois pulled by small ponies. With the baggage were younger warriors, not yet proven in battle, and the wives and daughters of the most important Chiefs.

It took quite some time for the dignitaries to assemble under the basswood tree and for the horses to be led away. The less important people—children and wives, and young warriors—began to make camp in a large clearing next to the corral, west of the village. It was not until late afternoon that everything was ready and the proceedings could begin.

6. The Governor and the Agent made good speeches that were translated into the other languages by the interpreters. The village Chiefs made their own speeches welcoming the visitors to their home. Pipes were lit and smoked slowly, and then the feast began.

There were great bowls of rice and platters of walleye cheeks, soup of boiled whitefish, and roasted squash. Whole hindquarters of deer were roasted on spits, and they dripped with fat when sliced and served. All of the wealth of the village was on display—the roast was salted and heaps of maple candy were passed around.

The delegates, seated on woven cedar mats, cattail screens, and buffalo robes, were served first. The villagers gathered around to watch, and eventually they too were served and ate along with the delegates. The Governor and the Agent praised the food and the garden and gazed out to the lake in obvious appreciation of the natural beauty of the spot. The Agent, along with the trader, pointed out the local powers and personalities from the village. All in all, everyone was happy. Bimaadiz and his parents edged close. They wanted to see the people on whom Bimaadiz's future rested.

The Governor praised the roast venison. He declared he had never tasted venison so tender, so full of juice: venison that had been prepared so well. He asked who had provided it and Schiller, who was seated nearby, began to tell the story of the hunt.

Just then he spied Bimaadiz in the crowd. Schiller motioned him forward and said, "Here is the hunter himself. It is only fitting that he should tell the story of the hunt."

Bimaadiz hesitated. He had never been among so many people in his life and had never spoken to so many and to so many important people either. But Schiller beckoned, and the others, all of them—the Governor, Agent, Priest, local and visiting Chiefs—clamored for the tale.

Still Bimaadiz hesitated until his father pushed him forward and hissed, "You will gain credit by telling your story and telling it well."

So, trembling inside, Bimaadiz stepped out and stood in front of the seated dignitaries.

He clasped his hands behind his back because he was afraid they would shake, and, not daring to look the guests in the eyes, stared at the ground and began to speak.

"I did not want to step forward," he began, "because I do not think that providing game for my people and our guests is something deserving of special praise. So I did not want to come forward until the one who raised me, my father, said I should. Since I follow him in all things, as is only fitting, I stand here now, before you."

Bimaadiz paused and looked up at the treetops.

"Schiller asked me to accompany him out in the bush and, since it was an honor I could not and did not want to refuse, I said yes. We went together to good hunting grounds and after posting him at a good crossing, I drove the high ground, careful to work the wind and cover together. I heard him shoot and was glad because I was certain that a man as experienced as he is would be sure not to miss. Meanwhile I saw seven deer. One after another they came to me. They each fell with a single bullet each—some I shot in the head and some in the heart. Many times I have gone out, seen game, and missed, and was forced to come home empty-handed. But this time was different. And the only thing that was different was that instead of hunting for my parents, the ones who raised me, I was hunting for the credit of my village and the hunger of our guests. And so, it was not I who was honored with luck. Rather, the deer were offering themselves to you. Just as you are the agents of our future, I was the agent for your satisfaction, merely the instrument that brought you and your meal together. You are the ones who deserve praise because if you were not worthy the deer wouldn't have offered themselves to you."

Bimaadiz finished speaking, placed his hand over his heart, and stepped back into the crowd. The delegates and even the villagers were amazed and impressed with Bimaadiz's speech.

Those who knew him were surprised at how well he expressed himself, at how clear he was. He didn't stutter or tremble at all. And what he said was posed just so! So humbly, so modestly did Bimaadiz give the honor back to those who sought to bestow it. It was every bit the speech of a Chief. Those who didn't know him, the delegates and officials, were doubly impressed. They were amazed at the spirit of his speech and at his generosity and grace.

And as he spoke they marveled at his bearing and physical grace, too. He looked so tall, so broad shouldered and fit. His eyes were clear and his skin burnished and smooth. They felt that they had never seen a young man so handsome and sure. Fitted out in his beaded vest and black trousers with one eagle feather tied to his hair, he was an impressive sight. The visitors were moved. One of them particularly so.

He was the proud Chief of the enemy band who had raided across the river the winter before.

He stood and gathered his buffalo robe about him. He was very impressive in his own right. He was tall, with a clean, well-weathered face. He wore seven eagle feathers in his hair and they were clearly war honors. Everything about him suggested the wealth of his position—from the quilled sheath of his scalping knife, the necklace of bearclaws around his neck, to the jangle of brass bracelets on both wrists. And more than that, he appeared wealthy in spirit, a kind leader for his people, a terrible enemy to those opposed to him.

He stood and faced Bimaadiz and said in Bimaadiz's language, "On coming here I did not anticipate the rise of ignoble feelings in my heart and it shames me to admit it. But I must speak my conscience even if it contributes to my dishonor."

The crowd fell silent, made nervous by the strong language of the Chief.

"And my jealousy," he continued, "(for that is what it is) is not directed at the fine young man who spoke just now. He is beyond the reach of such low thoughts. My jealousy is directed at his father."

Jiigibiig bowed his head.

"Would that I had a son like his! I do not. Would that I could be sure of my future when I am too old to hunt, would that I could place my future, and the future of my people, in the hands of a son like him. I cannot. If I could, my people would have nothing to fear—we could be sure that a strong sapling would be standing when the old trees fall.

"I had four sons but they died and no others were given to me." The Chief reached down and picked up his rifle. It was sheathed in a buckskin scabbard covered with dyed quills and expensive trade beads.

"The spirits have blessed you with sense and ability," he said to Bimaadiz. "You could not speak so well nor could you kill seven deer with seven shots if it were otherwise. And as they bless you so must I. Take this gun and keep it and continue to bring honor to your people."

The enemy Chief stepped forward and handed the rifle to Bimaadiz, who, for the moment, was speechless. Those gathered around cheered and grunted in agreement with the Chief. Such good feeling was an auspicious start to the negotiations, and everyone was filled with hope as the day drew to a close.

They broke for the evening. Some began the gambling games, others visited and gossiped by their lodge fires, others told stories, and still others plotted their moves for the coming negotiations. Bimaadiz rushed to his cabin, and unable to tell Eta the good luck he had had, unable to tell her how good things looked for the two of them, he tossed and turned all through the night.

7. The delegates retired to their lodges and whatever accommodations had been offered to them—tents for the Governor, Agent, and cavalry, hastily constructed lodges for the visiting Indian Chiefs and their families. Here and there games of chance lasted long into the night, and most agreed that the first day of talks had been a success. But not everyone felt that way.

One man in particular was having a hard time of it. That man was Charles Luce. He had managed to quell, if not quench, his feelings for Bimaadiz. After that first meeting he had been able to suppress his passion and attend to the business at hand, but that was no longer possible. When Bimaadiz spoke at the feast Luce had been smitten all over again. He thought Bimaadiz was the most beautiful boy he had ever seen, his voice the sweetest he had ever heard. In short, Luce was consumed, and Bimaadiz was the fire. He felt that he would die if he could not get Bimaadiz for himself. But how?

So that night he stalked between the lodges and out among the horses and went so far as to go into the woods and back again. He moaned and stroked his beard incessantly. When he couldn't take it any longer and could not find an exit from the prison of his passion, he hurried to Schiller's tent and scratched the canvas and asked if he could enter.

Schiller was at his traveling desk writing up a document in the language and when he looked up at Luce he could not believe his eyes.

Luce was disheveled. His beard was pulled and puffed up. His eyes were red. And his hair was coronalled with leaves. Schiller was alarmed and half rose from his stool. But before he could stand Luce went so far as to drop to his knees.

"I am so miserable!" cried Luce. "I don't know what to do. I have tried to find a way out, to avail myself of more divine supplements, but nothing works. I must have the boy Bimaadiz. I can teach him to read and write," he said with a quivering voice. "I can introduce him to mathematics and accounting. He shows himself to be intelligent and hardworking. If you allow me to have him I can improve upon him. He can enter the service and have an open future. So what if I receive payment in the form of pleasure? It would be a small price to pay considering the advantages I would be giving him."

Schiller wanted everyone around him to be happy, and Luce was clearly not happy. And what Luce was proposing did contain some truths even if he was motivated by passion. If the boy stayed in the village he would die of disease or hunger or be killed sooner or later. None of the villagers had much of a future. So why not? And Luce was a good man at heart and he was a good teacher, too.

Schiller said, "Don't despair, my friend. Rise. Stand. We will make you happy and help the boy in the same stroke. He shall be yours."

Luce smiled and thanked Schiller. They shook hands and Luce

left for his own tent, secure in his future happiness and finally able to sleep.

8. Bimaadiz woke before dawn and immediately stole over to Eta's cabin. There was only one window near where the family ate at the small table but knowing where she slept he tapped lightly on the tar paper. She awoke right away, smart girl! She knew who it was. She rose on the pretence of visiting the earth house. And Bimaadiz, the smart boy! He knew to be there waiting for her. In the smelly confines of the outhouse Bimaadiz told Eta to be ready that day—he would gain permission at the first feast and they were sure to be married in the evening, before the sun set. They kissed quickly, and then Eta hurried away to begin her preparations.

The village was by now fully awake and everyone began to trickle down to the garden and as they arrived they arranged themselves in front of the sycamore tree while the delegates spread themselves out beneath its branches. The first feast was almost ready—men had been tending it all night. It promised to be a beautiful day, exactly like the day before. By the end of the hour everyone was in place. After a short speech by the village Chief, they began to feast and smoke because food and tobacco must go together and precede every great deliberation. Bimaadiz watched the Chiefs and officials carefully. He was waiting for a lull in conversation, the moment when he could step forward and declare his intentions. He did not want to interrupt anyone and yet he didn't want to wait too long either. It would be impossible to present himself later on when the official business began. He was merely an Indian after all—not a chief or an interpreter or a government agent. He had no status and any interruption by him would be greeted most unfavorably.

Time moved very slowly. Bimaadiz would be on the verge of stepping out of the crowd, but then one of the Chiefs would launch into a long story about some past exploit, and Bimaadiz would have to swallow the words that had by that time climbed into his mouth. And again, after the Chief had finished his story, and as

Bimaadiz was about to break free of the crowd and declare himself, his hopes and affections, the Governor himself would tell a tale. It could go on like this forever, or so it seemed, but chance preened and a pause ensued, and for a few precious seconds the delegates' lips spoke only to the food. Bimaadiz shouldered his way out of the crowd, but before he could say anything he looked up and caught Schiller's eye and Schiller caught his.

Schiller had been looking for an opportunity of his own and now that Bimaadiz had moved forward the opportunity had arrived. Schiller stood and Bimaadiz held his peace.

"We met a remarkable man here yesterday," began Schiller. "He showed himself to be honest and intelligent and most of all, willing to put the concerns of his village first." Schiller paused and waited for the translator to catch up.

"And as time flows, the needs of the people change. Instead of hunting for game, soon you will be hunting for a place in the larger world." Schiller paused again so his words could both be taken in and translated into the language. None of the villagers were sure where the speech was going.

"And we would like to give you, one of you, a chance to acquire the new skills that will be needed in this new world. And so, we would like to take away the young hunter who spoke yesterday and teach him our language, and teach him our ways, and give him the skills to succeed in this new hunt. He will be attached to my assistant and trained in all things."

Schiller stopped again and watched Bimaadiz's reaction as the translator handed Bimaadiz this terrible news. As soon as Bimaadiz understood what he had been offered, he turned pale and began to shake. He felt faint and thought he might fall over. Those around him were marveling at his luck and shaking his hand but Bimaadiz did not feel lucky. He felt sick.

"If only I had spoken sooner!" he wailed. "By holding my peace I will now end up holding Luce's!"

Bimaadiz was wise enough to know that this teacher would teach him things he did not want to learn.

He did not know what to say, but he knew how he felt—if he were forced to live without Eta his life would be short. He would kill himself the first chance he got.

So instead of addressing Schiller and thanking him as he should have, he turned and pushed his way through the crowd and ran for home. There was no way out. They thought they were offering him an honor but it was the worst kind! He had the new gun, the one the enemy Chief had given him, and as soon as he reached home, he planned on using it against himself. The enemy would get a scalp after all. His feet led him to his parent's shack and his heart kept crying Eta! Eta! Eta!

None of the villagers or the delegates knew what to think except for Bimaadiz's parents who hurried after him. They had a suspicion that Bimaadiz might do something rash. The feast was interrupted, people gossiped openly amongst themselves, and while they were confused, they were also curious as to how it would all work out.

Bimaadiz arrived at the shack just ahead of his parents. He had the rifle in his hands and was looking for shells when they reached him.

"Bimaadiz, son, think what you are doing!" said Jiigibiig. "It is an honor for our family. So you won't marry Eta. There are other girls." They both said these things and other things like them, but they underestimated the depth of his emotions.

"There are no other girls," he replied as he found the shells.

Seeing that he really meant to kill himself, Zhookaagiizhigookwe turned to Jiigibiig.

"There's nothing for it," she said. "He won't go with the white-men, and if it is an honor it is an empty one; tomorrow this will be a gravehouse. Let us see what we can do—it is time to tell him and everyone else the truth. He isn't our son and so we can't give him away. You can't give something away that you don't possess."

With that she grabbed the stool and stood on it and reached into the rafters and took down the tokens with which Bimaadiz had been found.

And, old though she was, she ran back to the gathering place.

The ones who had raised Bimaadiz were old and could not run very fast, even so, his father was faster than his mother. Well ahead of his wife and Bimaadiz, he reached the gathered feasters under the ash tree, pushed his way through the crowd, and threw himself on the ground in front of the delegates and said—

"Please don't take Bimaadiz away, don't ask for my permission or that of my wife, because it isn't ours to give. Even if we did say that you could take him, he would rather kill himself so much does he want to marry a certain girl. But we can't give our permission. He is not our son. I swear by my honor and by all the pipes present that I am not lying. I found him in the woods, suckling on a cow moose. It's strange, I know. But the rest of the village had starved or had been laid low by some plague. He was the only one left alive—we burned the rest of the bodies fearing the disease might spread. And whoever his parents were, they must have been important because his clothes and the pipe we found with him suggest that he came from an important family.

"So please don't take him. It is an honor to be chosen to work for the Agent, but that other man is a drunk, and violent, too. And what's more, he wants to make Bimaadiz his wife!"

The delegates looked at one another with surprised expressions. Here was a strange interruption and a preposterous story.

The Governor told Jiigibiig to stand up. He represented the law of the territory and he would get to the bottom of all of this. He questioned Jiigibiig on all aspects of the story and asked to see the items that had been found with Bimaadiz. Encouraged, Jiigibiig turned and motioned for Zhookaagiizhigookwe to come forward. She did, hesitantly. She was shy and never spoke up except when in her own home. She opened the bundle and handed it to the Governor. He inspected each item and held them up, one by one, for all to see. First came the pipebag. It was of very fine make with exquisitely worked geometric patterns made with trade beads. The Governor turned it in his hands and suddenly the enemy Chief, the one who spoke the day before, jumped to his feet.

"It cannot be!" he exclaimed. And he began to tremble all over. "Tell me," he said, in a quavering voice, "is the pipe red with a white band of stone running through the center of the bowl?"

The Governor reached into the bag and withdrew the pipe-bowl. Sure enough, it was just as the enemy Chief had described. The crowd gasped.

"It is! It is!" he exclaimed. "Bimaadiz is my son! The one I thought I lost all those years ago. That is the pipe I carried. It was made by my father. And the bag!—my dear wife made that before she died. It was a terrible winter—the snow was so deep, the wind the most bitter I have ever tasted. Our people were starving and I left in search of food. I tried to make it back but could not. It was spring by the time I returned, but the bodies—my wife and all six of my children—had been burned. Their bones had been put on scaffolds to keep them away from the animals." He paused, unable to stop his tears. "And now to find my first-born and to find him alive!"

The enemy Chief rushed into the crowd and grabbed Bimaadiz and hugged him close, crying all the while.

And the resemblance between them and the other proofs were impossible to ignore. They truly were father and son. The villagers were moved, and not a few of them had to wipe tears from their eyes in order to see what was happening.

The enemy Chief stepped back and, holding Bimaadiz, said:

"Here is my son, back in my arms once again. All that is mine—horses, traps, lands, everything—shall be his. Come," he said, "your place is with me," and he led Bimaadiz to his seat with the delegates.

"And you and your wife," he said to Jiigibiig and Zhookaa-giizhigookwe, "you who have helped turn him into such a good young man. Just because he is my son does not mean he is not also yours. Please, let us sit together as a family."

So they all sat together, and the enemy Chief could not stop looking at Bimaadiz. Gradually everyone resumed eating, and they were about to begin the deliberations when another calamitous thing happened.

9. Aantti and Mary burst through the crowd. Aantti was bleeding from a cut in his head and they were both in tears.

"Please help us," said Aantti. "Our daughter has been captured. I fought him but I am an old man and a worker, not a warrior!"

Schiller asked him to calm down and to tell everyone what had happened. As it turned out, Wezaanagishens, the same suitor who had destroyed the garden, had, seeing that Bimaadiz would be going south as Luce's servant, figured there would be no marriage and had decided to take Eta away by force.

Bimaadiz jumped to his feet. His eyes rolled and he said to the heavens:

"Life was so much better when I was nobody! I could hunt as I wished. And, with Eta, I was looking forward to a quiet life trapping, hunting, and fishing. Father," he said, turning to the enemy Chief, "I wanted to ask you for this girl's hand in marriage and planned to ask this morning, but all this happened and I could not. Eta is the best part of me, the best part of this world, and I will not live without her."

The enemy Chief wanted more than anything to make his long-lost son happy.

"We will find her," he said, "and we will punish this boy who took her. And you will marry her no matter if she is poor and ugly and without skills."

He was about to order his warriors into battle but Luce stopped him. He was not stupid after all. He saw that by helping Bimaadiz he could save his reputation and preserve the treaty negotiations.

"I will bring her back," he said. He mounted up with ten of the cavalry guard.

Wezaanagishens had run toward the portage in hopes of paddling with Eta upriver. It was a short chase—the horses were fresh, and Wezaanagishens was on foot and slowed down by Eta who struggled the whole time. Also, Wezaanagishens was a coward. He gave up without a fight.

They had Eta back in her parents' arms within an hour. As for Wezaanagishens, he was held captive at the Agency and later banished from the village.

The Governor asked that Eta be brought to the meeting place so she could tell everyone for herself what had happened. It was important to resolve these things as soon as possible. That way, any misunderstanding or suspicion could be laid to rest.

Eta arrived and did as she was asked, though she was such a modest girl and more used to the forest of trees than the forest of faces in front of her. Still, she did the best she could. She said:

"I hope my words can be of more help to you than they were to me when I told that coward that I belonged to Bimaadiz, that we were to be married. I told him to leave me alone. He did not. I told him that by stealing me he was insulting my parents more than he was insulting me—who am I after all?—because my father promised me in marriage to Bimaadiz and we are a family that honors our promises. He even went so far as to hit my poor father on the head and to push my mother down. He tied my hands and led me away though I cried out for my village, my family, and most of all, for my dear Bimaadiz. But I trust that I am safe now."

As she was speaking, the wife of one of the allied Chiefs from across the lake, Mino-giizhig was his name (he was the grandson of Bagonegiizhig) was whispering to her husband. They both wore strange expressions and were agitated.

When Eta finished speaking, Mino-giizhig stood up. He looked imposing in his vest, leggings, and beaverskin war bonnet studded with small mirrors. He cradled his pipe in the crook of his arm as though drawing his authority from it, though he had no need to—his greatness was inborn.

"You have spoken like a true daughter," he said. "True to your parents, true to your people. Would that I had a daughter like you. I would not have to worry about my old age."

He paused and there was a glint in his eyes.

"Well then, since this seems to be a day for families," he continued, "why don't you call your parents forward. They must be proud and since you are to be married perhaps they have something to say."

Eta, not wanting to contradict or otherwise shame the grand Chief, but also wanting to be as far away from the crowds and all the attention, nevertheless turned and motioned for Aantti and Mary to step forward.

They were shy, too. Just simple village folk, advanced in years. And they also had something to hide, so they were not happy about having to address everyone. They came forward and stood, one on either side of Eta.

Mino-giizhig looked at all three of them lined up in a row and saw what he wanted to see. But still he was not sure, not confident in his guesses, so he pushed Eta's parents by saying:

"Your daughter wants to marry. She will be leaving your home and making a lodge of her own. Perhaps you want to tell all of us what it was like when she was born: the time of year, the weather, where you were when she came into the world."

Mino-giizhig's wife, Mawikwe, was crying openly, and Mino-giizhig turned to her and scolded her for her lack of restraint.

He then turned his attention to Aantti and Mary. They could stand it no longer, and Mary advanced and dropped to her knees just as her own tears began to fall.

"It's time," she said. "It's true," she said, though no one had accused her of anything. "She's not our daughter. I am short, not as tall as she will be when she stops growing. And I am no prize beauty, as you can see, though you must admit that Eta is the most beautiful girl in the world. But I don't need to tell you that. And Aantti, he's white after all, and Eta is clearly not mixed. Aantti found her surrounded by death, alone on an island in the big lake, suckling on a she-wolf, and we brought her up as our own. Don't fault us—even after all these years we thought maybe her real parents had survived and so we kept the things she was found with—her otterskin wrap and her cradleboard. Don't fault us and don't take her away, she's all we have."

The Governor, trying to bring all this mess to a close, asked Mary if she could fetch the items. Aantti offered to go in her stead and while he was gone Mary told everyone present how he had found Eta suckling on the she-wolf and how the rest of the village was dead. When Aantti returned and held up the cradleboard and the otterskin, Mino-giizhig gasped and tears streamed down his face. He could not speak and so, as usually, happens, his wife spoke for him.

"I saw the girl's face and recognized the mark—a mother knows her child, the art of her flesh—and now I know for certain because I beaded the wrap for that cradleboard. I know my own work, too—the art of my hands. You'll see, it's quite unusual: the pattern is repeated inside and out."

Sure enough, when the wrap was turned over you could see she spoke the truth. For the second time that day the crowd gasped; surprise kept following surprise.

"We left across the ice in search of food and the weather kept us away. We could not make it back until it was too late. Here we thought our child had died with the rest of our village. It was impossible to know who was who because the wolves had torn up the bodies and mixed their parts all together. But now, after all these years, we find that you are alive after all."

After that she rushed to Eta and hugged her and cried and would not let her go.

Mino-giizhig meanwhile, recovering from the shock, stood in front of Mary, who still sat on her knees, wracked with sobs.

"Don't cry," he said tenderly. "You have no cause. You will not lose your daughter. You have gained another family. I myself will raise you up. We are the ones who should kneel in thanks. It is you and your husband who saved our girl and kept her in life."

With that he held out his hand and helped Mary to her feet, and they all crowded around Eta and cried with joy.

There was hardly a dry eye among those present and it was quite some time before everyone calmed down and found their places again. Eta, Mary, and Aantti were brought up to sit with Mino-giizhig and Mawikwe, and after they were seated Mino-giizhig stood once more and said:

"We have all come from a long way off, and when we left our homes we thought we'd come here and try to create peace between all our peoples. None of us could have imagined that we'd be reuniting a parent with his son," (at this he waved to where Bimaadiz sat with all of his family, new and old) "and still more parents with their daughter," (and here he acknowledged Eta, Aantti, Mary, and Mawiwikwe with a sweep of his arm). "And what discoveries we have made! Had we continued to fight as we have been, our daughter might have been killed and your son, too. And to think all this time we have been sharing that which is most precious to us all—our children. And so . . . we have also been told that these two children have been promised to each other."

At this point both Bimaadiz and Eta, seated on separate sides of the delegation, felt their hearts clench, not knowing what would happen next.

"And so," Mino-giizhig continued, "let us stop everything and do nothing until these two children are married. That way we can join our people in fact. Their union can be the foundation on which our people's future is built."

The enemy Chief, Bimaadiz's real father, stood and clasped Mino-giizhig's hand.

"I agree," he said. "Let's bring our families together first thing. We have fought long enough. We have suffered enough. I approve of this marriage and will not do anything until I can call you 'brother.'"

Everyone cheered and whooped. They were all glad to have all foreseeable tension put to rest, not least Bimaadiz and Eta themselves.

"Let us break," Mino-giizhig concluded, "and let the young-sters prepare themselves to be married just before the sun sets."

It was settled. Everyone left for their lodges and cabins to change into their finest clothes. It was time to celebrate and everyone was happy.

10. Bimaadiz and all his parents went to the shack. His new parent gave him moccasins crusted with red beads, a breastplate made of hawk bones, eagle feathers, and a bearclaw necklace. At Eta's cabin her new parents presented her with a white buckskin dress, quilled hair sheaths, and bracelets made of copper. The children spent hours getting ready, and when they all reconvened at the garden, everyone remarked that they had never seen a couple so beautiful. He: tall, strong, quick but lightly encumbered with dignity and calm bearing. She: lithe, but soft, smooth, and elegant, with the beauty of a true leader.

The wedding was studded with speeches and proclamations, promises of fidelity and hopes for a long life together. To Jiigibiig and Zhookaagiizhigookwe the enemy Chief promised ten horses and as much dried meat as they could carry. To Aantti and Mary was promised fifteen buffalo robes and twenty axes, steel traps, and trade blankets. They all now considered themselves rich. There was feasting and singing and good spirits all around. War talks had been turned into a marriage ceremony, and a more beautiful couple and a more beautiful wedding was never before or after seen.

11. And Bimaadiz and Eta? What did they get? They received a life together filled with as much beauty and tenderness as the woods were full of bounty. Much later they had a boy and a girl. They taught the boy to read the tracks of animals—all that passes by and leaves a mark. He became a great hunter in his own way. The girl they taught to read the habits of animals—their likes and dislikes—and she became a trapper just like Eta. Bimaadiz and Eta lived happily into their old age surrounded by their family and the woods they held so dear.

But that was a long time coming. That night, the night of their wedding, they retired to a lodge of their own. The villagers gathered around outside and sang songs of the hunt, songs of capture. And the young couple undressed and lay down side by side. And there, in the soft darkness of their lodge they discovered what it was to be a man and what it was to be a woman. They experienced such heights of pleasure that everything they had tried before seemed like child's play. And when all was said and done, they found a language for their happiness, and witnessed by no one, heard by no one, they spoke the word everyone longs to hear.

the story sleeps.

someone harbors a secret love. and someone else harbors a secret jealousy. and while the lovers sleep the final act is being done.

the story sleeps, too, like the others, but lacks the published warmth possessed of most books—with their fly leaves and stitches and tissues covering their more sensitive illustrations. without the comfort or satisfaction of any, no matter how slight, previous recognition. it sleeps unknown and unloved.

the story finally sleeps, after a long journey not of its choosing, not of its designs.

there might be no rest for the wicked as the saying goes, but it is equally true for the innocent, and even more true for innocent stories. it is much better, after all, to be the imaginer rather than the imagined—the illusionist rather than the illusion. but there is only one short journey left to take and then it will be all over.

Ms Manger lifts the manuscript and the book in which it is hidden from inside the box on Jesus' cart. she looks at the cover of the leather-bound book in which the translation of Dr Apelles is hidden—she recognizes it instantly: it is a pastoral, a romance. Ms Manger smiles. how appropriate, she thinks, that the story of Apelles' life will be hidden inside a myth.

all is dark and all is quiet. the station is clean and orderly, the surface bare. the passion and jealousy that drove Jesus to steal the manuscript from Campaspe, who, out of curiosity stole it from Dr Apelles, all these passions are spent. Ms Manger will be the last one to act.

the manuscript is to be wedded to the book in which it is hidden forever. it is a marriage after all—a meeting and pleaching of the loose pages with the bound, the read with the unread, the published with the obscure, the known and the unknown. it is a marriage that will, out of necessity, last forever.

the heating system hisses and rumbles to life and falls silent.

and then the translation and the book in which it is hidden are in motion, Ms Manger lifts them from their hiding place. that double harbor—the outer book in which the text resides—seems especially restful now. had Ms Manger left it in the box things might have turned out differently. Jesus might have had a change of heart. Campaspe might have intuited Jesus' crime and rescued the book in the morning. or someone else, someone with less respect for books—the janitor, or a mechanic, or another worker—might have stumbled on it and taken it. but this did not come to pass.

Ms Manger could not let it rest there. all the years of her life filled with nothing, filled only with longing, make her want to act. she has always wanted to be picked. she has always wanted to be noticed. she wanted to be the one—not her, not Campaspe; not it, not the translation of Dr Apelles' life. her life is as great. her life is as interesting. isn't it? since she cannot compel Apelles or Campaspe or Jesus or the translation or anyone to pay attention to her, since she cannot make them do what she wants, she can at the least, control how everything ends.

the story, anyway, is awake now. moving. moving together with its bride through the darkness of the S.A. past the workstations—the registrars and clerks of court where the births and deaths of millions of other books are recorded—and then to the back of the Sorting Area where the carts of boxed books stand at attention— ushers or tigers it is hard to say which—and keep order, or create order. guards, whose solemnity and rigor function as a symbolic gate demarcating the border between the chaos of the outside world and the order, sanctity, and certainty of this other one.

but is it a prison or a refuge?

the first airlock door opens. the blowers kick on with a sleepy grumble, and the door rolls shut behind. and then the second door opens, the heat pushes the translation and its partner, through and out.

they are in the Stacks.

the lights come on. the Stacks rise in the light on either side, solemn and supportive and welcoming, as if to say, like witnesses at a wedding, we have come here just as you are coming here. we have made the journey you are only beginning.

the ceiling is distant and hovers far overhead like that of a cathedral. the farthest stacks to the right and left look as though they support the ceiling, the very building, and the boxes on their shelves rest like the images of local and tutelary saints—translated there from the site of their original deaths and early sufferings. and they look down kindly on the timid translation and its bride. all the residents of RECAP look down and smile—row upon row, shelf upon shelf, box upon box, and in them the pews of books— all of them look down kindly on the timid translation at first an unwilling child-bride but now growing in stature and confidence: sane, serene, much like a queen.

and while all this had just moments earlier felt like a terrible and secret thing, an unwanted and forced future, well, now it doesn't appear that way at all. the translation is being brought home where it belongs.

the light is kind and yellow. the air is sweet and soft with just enough moisture to cool and comfort the skin. there are, each in its own section, groups of different relatives, happy after all is said and done, to be there.

and whatever distance might exist between them, whatever feuds have sprung up in the past, all is forgiven. all are bent to the sacred purpose.

moving again.

the translation now proceeds down the aisle, which, crowded with boxes that seem to lean over the couple with benign and gentle approval, opens in front and closes behind them.

there is nothing to be afraid of. there is comfort and company here—written but beyond speech. something holy about this communion of books.

in such company our duo, wide-eyed and wondrous, no longer held in the dark, no longer orphaned out in that other world far from their own kind, feel stronger, more sure.

and suddenly they are airborne, lifted on one of the forklifts. the ground retreats, the ceiling moves closer. it would not be strange to hear cheering or shouts, to believe that the collective joy around them is what lifts them up rather than the gears and hydraulic thrust of a mere machine.

it stops. for a second or two they bounce slowly up and down, up and down, as on the swell of a wave.

a box slides out and the lid comes off.

there is a pause as the book is inspected one last time. the thrill of a breeze passes over the manuscript pages as the book is opened. with the breeze comes the sense that, once again, the future might change abruptly. the manuscript might be divorced from its book and taken back to the world, able to do amazing things and to become important once again and for the first time, it might become a complete story with its own ending and two hard covers and a spine, and sinew, and an ISBN and a copyright and a title. but no, the book is only opened so as to push the loose pages deeper still into the gutter, to make sure they are not visible from the outside. the book is shut and then it is placed in the box. the lid is reattached, the box is lined back up on the shelf. the palpable excitement and sense of family, of belonging, so potent and so real, ends abruptly.

it is dark in here. and the two are once again alone.

the forklift descends. the lights are retaken and the room is once again dark.

the first door, the one for humans, is opened and shut and then the second one.

footsteps echo down the middle of the S.A. the door to the O.C. opens and shuts, and then the door to the office at the end of the hall opens and shuts. a mouse, click, sniffs the mousepad, and the cameras one by one are turned back on.

with a satisfied sigh Ms Manger, no longer invisible, looks out her window and drums her fingers lightly on her desktop as though trying to summon a new day, still hours off but whose advance is signaled by a fringe of light to the east, a new day exactly like the one just past for most people in the world. a new day quiet and ample and filled with industry and effort all bent on making that time, and those hours, and those books, pass.

far up the stacks, on a shelf, in a box, in a book, in a place Ms Manger could never find again even if she were to try, the translation rests where new days never dawn. it will always be dark there. too dark to see. muchly much too dark to read.

it will always be night here. restful, yes, but lonely.

there is nothing to do but sleep and to be the dream of someone else who is far away, someone who will wake and work and live and sleep again to dream the story that waits for the dream.

the only activity here is the imperceptible economy of time, but with no means to measure it—no light, no movement, no industry of any sort except, once in a while, from afar, faintly, faintly, like the wind passing through the branches of pine, machines and voices come near and fade away.

it is possible that someday the sound of a machine will draw near and nearer, now close. and the box will be lifted from the sea floor of obscurity where the thinnest and most delicate fronds of hope wave. it could happen. the box could be moved and the lid lifted, light could pour in and with it the fresh, terrible air of the world outside. and the story, revived, anxious and full of verve, could come alive. and with that new life would come a new hunger—for recognition, for translation, for love. and instead of being a dream it will be alive—with a roving, powerful, lonesome hunger.

someday it will wake. someday it will fly. and better yet, someone will find it and love it. someday.

someday. and when that happens they will know what Apelles and Campaspe know but Ms Manger does not: that the imagination can produce more than illusion; that it does not matter whether the illusion is true or not because the imagination can create both pleasure and happiness, too. someday.

but that will be years in the making.

earlier that night, before Ms Manger sat at her desk and anticipated the dawn, after Jesus had gone home alone, and Ms Manger waited at RECAP and got ready to hide the manuscript, Dr Apelles and Campaspe clasped each other in his queen-sized bed, toe to toe, knee to knee, all four hands held together in front of their chests, their eyes inches apart. they speak quietly:

I am so sorry, she says. don't hate me, she says.

I don't hate you, he says. and you have nothing to be sorry about, he says.

I was so curious. I wanted to know what you were doing. I wanted to know what the words meant, she says. once I started reading I couldn't stop, she says. and I was surprised! I had no idea. *the* translation is really *your* translation. it is your story. and to see myself there . . . to see me as you see me. how thrilling.

she remembers her shame and says, once again, I really was just curious. all I wanted was to know you.

I know, he says.

they don't speak for a few minutes. Campaspe's eyes sparkle with the promise of tears.

I didn't know that Jesus would steal it from me, she says. I looked everywhere except in that book. I never thought he'd put it in that book, she says.

you had no way to know, he says.

did you know I took it from you? she says.

of course I knew, he says, I knew it before you did, he says.

you did? she says.

yes. as they say in the movies, but only in movies: I know you better than you know yourself.

they say that in books, too.

yes, he says. in books as well.

did you know Jesus would take it, too? she says. and did you know he would take it before he knew? she says. do you know him better than he knows himself?

yes, he says. him, too. I know everyone here better than they know themselves, he says.

Campaspe snuggles closer, she is amused by this.

that's silly, she says. how can you know? she says.

he says nothing.

okay then, what's happening now? she says. where is it now?

it is being hidden deep in the Stacks by Ms Manger, he says.

again they are silent for some time.

that was the only copy? she says.

you know it was.

what about the book Jesus hid it in? what kind of book is that?

just an old love story.

and so it's really lost, really gone? she says.

you know it is, he says.

I'm so sorry, so sorry, that's so sad.

again her eyes sparkle with the promise of tears.

you already said that, he says.

and after a pause she says, shyly: I really liked the part about the ice storm.

thank you, he says, good.

it was very exciting, she says.

thank you, he says again.

and Victor, that was a very sad part of the story, she says.

it was, he says, it really was.

and you, she says. you were so lonely, so alone in the beginning.

I was then. I was lonely, he says.

she strokes his thumb shyly with hers.

you make me seem prettier than I really am, she says.

oh no, he says. no no no, I don't think so, he says. you're as pretty there as you're supposed to be.

and I don't even own a white sweater, she says.

but you do now, he says.

I suppose I do. can I have a red one, too?

sure. there, he says.

thank you.

you look beautiful.

thank you, she says.

snuggling closer. I was wondering, she says. I was wondering, be-cause I don't really understand.

yes, he says.

I was wondering why each section sounded so different, she says.

that's good, that's so good of you to notice that, he says. the answer: I did not know yet who I was. I had no language for myself.

she is quiet for a while, trying to understand.

he is quiet, too.

you didn't really find anything in the archive, did you?

I found myself, he says with a twinkle in his eye.

but where's the original, then? *what* is the original?

you should know that by now.

this all feels like make-believe, she says after a while. even my heart—it feels like make-believe. but it isn't. is it? my heart is filled with something. so there is something to it after all, something you can weigh and measure. it is real. but everyone is going to think you made all this up. I can't believe it's actually happening.

it is happening, he says, his eyes wild. it *is* happening and what's wrong with make-believe? isn't that how it works: we make belief? besides, happiness is more real than any illusion.

and more powerful, she says.

yes, he says, yes, exactly. more powerful.

and then, more daring, with growing confidence she says: if you know me better than I know myself, and Jesus, too, better than he does, and Ms Manger and all that has happened and what will happen, everything, then . . . she says, then who knows you?

you do, he says.

me?

yes, he says, and they do, too, looking up. they know me best of all.

one more question and we can go to sleep, she says.

okay.

how does it end? she says. how does our story end?

oh! that's easy, it's already over. it ended earlier when

Dr Apelles stood at the window,

the day was dimming. It was a time of war but that is over now. All is at rest and the city sleeps. The manuscript is not lost, but it might not ever be found.

There is traffic below and people on foot are all headed. Someplace. All destined for. Something. And while the car horns and voices climb the evening air as on a ladder to the upper reaches, they seem far away, unimportant.

The work is done. Dr Apelles is weary. He rubs his eyes and peers through the glass as though trying to see who rang the doorbell before actually opening the door. But he can see only buildings after all—the one directly across and the one to the right and he can make out the building on the corner of the busy avenue, but just a sliver of it, but that is all. He cannot see the sky. And so, his eyes and his mind, traveling partners still, turn to the right and travel to the corner and then left at the busy avenue and arrive almost instantly at the archive where they rest in the reading room before turning around and heading the other way—past his street, past Mai's Massage Parlour, to the train station. And then, because his thoughts don't need trains, they leave the city behind on their own. In a flash they are across the river, through the sister city, down the old post road, and past Margarita Bella's and lifting now, over the fields and parking lots and schools—those suburban ruins. RECAP is there. This must be what it is like to die. He goes inside and through the hallway and into the S.A. and through the double-doored airlock and into the Stacks where he is lifted without the aid of machine or man to where the manuscript sleeps in its box. There it is. Unloved and loved. Unrecognized and known.

Dr Apelles does not open it. He does not look inside. He has no need to see because he already sees. He knows what is written there, and so do you. If he were to read it, he would read his life all over again, and again it would be as though it were written in a language he did not understand. For now, he has finally been translated. His language is his own, and he needs no other readers. It is so much better this way. It is so much better than a mere fairy tale.

Gradually, after much effort, Dr Apelles returns to his apartment. It is truly dark now. Here and there in the buildings, he can see lights and lives coming on. It is time to rest. What was lost has been found. Looking in the glass, in which his own cherished face is faithfully represented along with all the life outside, he says, in a whisper, I love you. And then—more loudly, as if dictating the words—I was looking for a book. A very particular book in a vast and wonderful library . . .

Satisfied with the first sentence, he turns away.